A RELUCTANT DRUID

BOOK ONE OF THE MILESIAN ACCORDS

Jon R. Osborne

New Mythology Press
Coinjock, NC

Chris Kennedy/New Mythology Press
1097 Waterlily Rd.
Coinjock, NC 27923
http://chriskennedypublishing.com/

Publisher's Note: This is a work of fiction. Names, characters, places, and incidents are a product of the author's imagination. Locales and public names are sometimes used for atmospheric purposes. Any resemblance to actual people, living or dead, or to businesses, companies, events, institutions, or locales is completely coincidental.

Ordering Information:
Quantity sales. Special discounts are available on quantity purchases by corporations, associations, and others. For details, contact the "Special Sales Department" at the address above.

A Reluctant Druid/Jon R. Osborne
ISBN: 978-1942936879

Two people really made this book possible.

Chris Kennedy, a publisher willing to take a chance on a rookie author based on one story, who has also been my mentor through this process.

Mark Wandrey, my long-time friend and fellow gamer, who gave me a foot in the door and a kick in the ass when I most needed it.

Thanks guys!

This book is dedicated to my mother, Glenda Marcussen. She was an avid reader, and she shared her love of books with me. Many of the classics I read by authors like Asimov, Niven, and King were from her collection. She let me follow my own path, even when it didn't seem practical, and she encouraged my creative endeavors. I wished she had lived long enough to hold this book; I'd like to think she'd be proud.

Chapter One

"Excuse me, Liam?"

One of the joys of working retail, Liam Knox thought, was complete strangers thought they were on a first name basis with you just because you wore a nametag. Some acted like they were old friends, using your name in a chummy manner, while others seemed to hit you over the head with it, as if knowing your name gave them some sort of authority.

Liam looked up from the books he had been sorting, pushing back the reflexive reaction. The young woman standing on the opposite side of the library cart was probably a college student, not surprising since the store dealt in used textbooks. Students came from the handful of small colleges scattered around Peoria, hoping to save a few bucks on the money earmarked for books so they could afford something more fun than Fundamentals of Geology.

Her voice bubbled with perkiness and had a slightly musical lilt that spoke of somewhere in the British Isles. Her hair was a riot of purple and pink, some of it barely contained in her ponytail, and her loose lilac blouse was open over black yoga pants and a pink sports top. Barely standing five feet tall and bouncing in hot pink sneakers, she was the personification of a modern pixie hopped up on Mountain Dew. She even smelled like flowers.

"Can I help you?" Liam tried not to take note of her pierced navel or the swirling tattoos winding up her right hip above the waistband of the yoga pants. He thanked the gods for yoga pants, then felt guilty, chiding himself that she was probably half his age. He made a conscious effort to focus on her violet eyes, which for a split second seemed to glow. He was so distracted, he almost missed her request.

"I'm looking for books about druids," she said earnestly. Liam couldn't put his finger on it, but something seemed wrong, as if the girl was out of place among the narrow rows of worn shelves and fluorescent lighting. She regarded him steadily with those bright eyes, the corner of her mouth turned up in a half-smile.

"Do you mean druids in fantasy books, or in games such as Realms of Quest?" Liam tried to put his mind on the job. He normally didn't pay much attention to the coeds who often came in to Word Nerds looking for cheap books, not even the cute ones. He usually let one of the younger employees deal with them. "Or are you looking for historical references regarding druids, or perhaps something from the New Age section?"

She wrinkled her button nose at the last suggestion. "I mean real druids, Liam."

Liam arched an eyebrow, wondering if she had been sent to him as some sort of joke. Liam referred to himself as a 'self-proclaimed druid,' practicing what some referred to as reconstructed Celtic paganism. It was no secret in the local pagan scene, but he wasn't heavily involved in the community, at least not anymore. Some of his fellow pagans certainly didn't consider him a 'real' druid, a claim he never asserted. "Depending on who you talk to, 'real druids' could cover a lot."

"I know what it covers." The purple-haired girl held her gaze on him. As Liam met her eyes, there was buzzing in the back of his brain, and he was struck with double vision. One image of the girl remained normal, except for her eyes, which lit up with a violet glow. The other image gave her skin a greenish-cast, her ears ending in points, and her hair moved in a silent breeze. In the double image, her eyes also glowed with an inner light. He thought he could hear a whisper in his mind, the same musical accent.

"Knox, aren't you done shelving those books yet?" Clark Hayes, Liam's boss, emerged from the back room, frowning. Liam's awareness snapped into focus, the double vision gone, and the murmuring voice silenced. Blinking away a wave of dizziness, Liam fought the urge to shake his head. Clark didn't add the unspoken 'I don't pay you to chat with coeds' as he tried to straighten the perpetually-crooked tie he wore like a badge of office.

The young woman turned to the manager, cocking her head to one side, still smirking. "Liam is busy helping a customer. Surely that's more important."

Again, Liam could have sworn her eyes had a light of their own, beyond anything which could be attributed to weird contacts or naturally bright irises.

"Of course that's more important." Clark looked confused for a moment, as if he had forgotten what he was going to say, then turned and stomped toward the front of the store. Liam assumed Clark's next stop would be to hassle Kenna, the employee manning the coffee bar. Clark didn't seem to think he was doing his job unless he gave his employees grief. They put up with him because it was still better than working in fast food or a big box store.

"Did you just 'these aren't the droids you're looking for' my boss?" Liam had never seen Clark agree with anyone, even a customer, so readily. Even though the manager was a couple of years younger than Liam, there were times Clark treated him like one of the college kids they had on staff.

"Hi, I'm Pixel." She extended her hand, and Liam took it by reflex. Her small hand felt warm, warmer than cute-young-girl warranted, as though she had a fever. "So, does he always boss you around like an angry ogre?"

"He's brusque with pretty much the whole staff." Liam looked toward the front of the store where Clark had gone, mainly to break eye contact and collect his thoughts. He considered finding another employee to help the young woman. In the back of his mind, he considered whispering a quick protective verse. Something wasn't quite right.

Pixel placed her hand on Liam's arm, banishing the cautious voice. "So you're going to help me with druids."

"Right." Surely she wasn't any sort of threat, but her interest in druids couldn't be a coincidence. Someone sent her to look for him and ask him about druids, he was almost certain. If it was someone's idea of a joke, Liam couldn't figure out what was supposed to be funny. Maybe the prankster hoped Liam would ask her out or do something that would make him look like a fool. If he didn't have grey creeping into his sandy beard, maybe it would have been tempting, but he was keenly aware he was closing on 40. His days of chasing college girls were long behind him, even colorful ones smelling of flowers.

"Since you said real druids, let's go to the history section," Liam said, trying to get the conversation back on business. He nodded toward the aisle in question and led the way through the mismatched bookshelves. Having her walk in front of him would have been too distracting. Liam mentally ran through the rosters of pagan groups he had mingled with, looking for someone who would have a grudge and would think this was funny. While feuds were far too common in the pagan community, they were mostly conducted online, and he had stayed out of them. "Some of the neo-pagan druids might argue they are 'real' druids, but they have no historical connection to the Celtic priesthood."

"Druids didn't gather in pseudo-covens." Pixel responded from behind him, her tone turning from chipper to serious. "Being a druid was a job, not a party game."

"There's not much here, a handful really." Liam gestured to the books in question, which prompted her to brush past him for a better look. The scent of blossoms tickled his nose. Liam tried not to let his thoughts get derailed by her proximity and casually backed up a couple of steps, continuing to turn the puzzle over in his mind. Perhaps she had gone to someone in the pagan community asking about druids, and they had told her about Liam. Given her last remark, the local neo-pagan druid grove would have turned her away. He knew the leader of the group, Don Potts, who went by the craft name Taliesin. Don wasn't going to have the time of day for someone who didn't buy into his grove's idea about druidism. The party game comment would have definitely rocked the boat. Liam found himself wishing he could see Don's face as she said that line.

He waited as Pixel absently flipped through Word Nerds' meager selection, trying to resist the magnetic pull she seemed to exert on his eyes. Most of the books Liam had chosen personally, as Clark hadn't wanted to deal with it, and the home office didn't have any direction on the matter other than not to tie up too much money in slow moving titles. Liam tried to balance the few books he could stock between what he felt were the best source material, and what seemed to be the most recommended by other pagans. Gone were the days of shelves upon shelves stocked with a deep selection of titles; now it was mostly top sellers, used textbooks, and a café in an attempt to keep from getting buried by online sellers.

"Do you have any copies of the Mabinogion?" Pixel asked without looking up from the book she was leafing through. Despite her flighty, energetic demeanor, she seemed to be assessing the books seriously.

"Next aisle in the classical literature, top shelf on the left all the way at the end." Even though the most recent addition to the shelf was six months old, Liam could have rattled off the contents of the shelf in order. He had a knack for memorizing anything he read, a talent Liam's father had frequently reminded him was squandered.

Pixel closed the book in her hands and carried it to the next aisle, following Liam's directions. "Right where you said." She had to stand on her tiptoes to reach the books and Liam caught himself watching her stretch. "You have a good memory."

Liam scanned the store for other customers in need of help, in part to force himself to look away, and in part because it was what he should be doing. The tall shelves and claustrophobic aisles made it difficult to see everywhere, but from what he could see by looking down the aisles, it was quiet, typical for the middle of a weekday. A few regulars were in the café, and a handful of other customers perused the magazine and best-seller racks. He shrugged. "It doesn't hurt that the books are supposed to be in a certain order, but yeah, I'm pretty good at remembering things."

"So you must have done pretty well in school."

"For all the good it did me," Liam replied. His grades had actually been excellent, despite his lack of focus. Rote memory had been a useful talent in school, but he had changed majors three times. Now, years later, he was an assistant manager in a small Midwest bookstore.

"What did you go to school for?" Pixel paged through one of the copies of the Mabinogion, rocking on the balls of her feet as she read.

"History with a minor in theology, which doesn't do you much good unless you want to be a teacher." Liam still remembered his father's disappointment over finally settling on a liberal arts degree. His father died before Liam could find out if graduating with a degree would have assuaged any of his disappointment. "I actually thought about it, but I didn't want to deal with parents."

Pixel looked up from the book, the smirk had returned. "I bet you would be good with kids."

"Yeah, I did an after-school Spanish class when I was in college. That's when I figured out parents could be a pain in the ass." Liam tried to find an excuse not to look at her without seeming awkward or rude. If he didn't know better, he would have thought she had an honest-to-goodness spell on her, which even with his beliefs was a stretch. Magic and spells were an analogy for prayer and requesting divine intervention, not something out of one of the fantasy books on the other side of the store.

"How many languages do you speak?"

Despite her friendly tone, Liam felt as if he was in an interview. "English, passable Spanish and Latin, a smattering of a few other languages." Being able to memorize words was one thing, but it didn't make up for a lack of practice or his tendency to get distracted by something else a few weeks later. "I can read better than speak."

"Do you know who Cathbad was?" Pixel closed the book, turning it over and reading the back of the jacket.

"He'd be in the Ulster Cycle, not the Mabinogion. Assuming you mean the mythological druid and not one of the neo-pagans who have taken on the name as a handle." Liam knew some pagans got their nose bent out of shape when he referred to their adopted 'craft' moniker as a handle, which did nothing to deter him. He always found the notion of using a mythological figure's name a bit gauche, and using a god's name pretentious and asking for trouble, but there were those in the pagan community who went around calling themselves Loki or Morrigan.

Pixel looked up, and for a second Liam thought her eyes had the strange glow again, then she smiled and wrinkled her nose in amusement. "I know that." She added the copy of the Mabinogion to the other book in her hand, a fairly serious treatise on historical references to druids and the Celtic cultures associated with those references. "I'll take these."

"Great, Kyle can ring you out up front." Liam nodded toward the cash register. Even now Kyle was trying to catch a glimpse of Pixel from the counter. A tattooed and pierced twenty-something who stuck around after college, Kyle relished the chance to talk to women from the nearby colleges, trying to get a phone number or app handle, whatever it was kids these days used to track each other down. Liam was sure Kyle had already noticed Pixel's tattoos and would use them to start a conversation.

Pixel glanced toward the front of the store, prompting Kyle to suddenly feign disinterest. She turned back, the corner of her mouth crooked up.

"The tatted kid who's been checking me out?" she asked, obviously referring to Kyle's tribal sleeve covering his left arm. Liam thought it was amusing that she called Kyle a kid, considering he was probably a couple of years older. Pixel's eyes went to Liam's bicep. "What's your tattoo?"

Liam glanced down to where the edge of blue Celtic knotwork was peeking out from under his shirtsleeve on his right arm. Normally it wasn't visible unless he reached for something. "Just some Celtic stuff."

Pixel reached out and pushed up the sleeve, exposing a knotwork band with a string of Ogham above it. Liam tried to ignore how warm her hand felt on his bicep as her finger traced the line of Ogham. "Gods, Spirits, Ancestors."

"You know Ogham and Irish." Liam was mildly impressed. The words of his tattoo were not only in the ancient Celtic alphabet, the words themselves were in Irish, albeit modern Irish. While it was possible someone had told her in advance about his tattoo, hardly anyone knew about it. Maybe she was a serious seeker, especially if she could read Ogham. "Are you Irish?"

"Technically I'm Welsh, but I've studied the other Celtic cultures." She seemed intent on the ivy that formed the upper border of the tattoo. "How about you? Are you Irish?"

"There's probably some in the Euromix of my family's background. They came to the states before the First World War." Liam tried to think of how to gracefully end the conversation, mentally shoving aside the part of his mind looking for excuses to keep talking to her. He'd already directed her to the check out, and he hadn't meant to start another topic by bringing up family history, but it seemed a safer topic than asking about her tattoo. From Kyle it might have sounded like a casual pick up line, but from someone as old as Liam, it would have probably sounded a bit creepy.

Pixel finally withdrew her hand from his arm. "Well, I suppose I should let you get back to work before your boss comes back around."

"Probably a good idea." Liam gave her a polite smile.

"If I want to talk about druids some more, can I get a hold of you?" She pulled a cell phone from behind her back.

"Why don't I give you my e-mail address?" If this was some sort of prank, he wasn't going to do the whole 'can I get your number' routine, and if it wasn't, e-mail would work just as well. Granted, he would have to remember to check it, something he only did sporadically. He rattled off his e-mail address, making a mental note to check it in a few days. If Pixel was disappointed when he didn't offer his phone number, she didn't show it.

"I'll see you around, Liam." She turned and bounced toward the front, her floral perfume taking a few moments to fade.

Liam caught himself watching and turned away, returning to the cart of books he had abandoned. Without looking, he picked up the book he had set down and went to its location on the shelves. After several minutes Kyle rounded the corner.

"Dude, the girl with the purple hair was *hot!*" Kyle may have thought he was whispering, but his excitement countered any discretion in his volume. Fortunately no customers were nearby.

"She was cute," Liam conceded, continuing to stock the books. Now that she was gone, the buzzing in his mind faded, and he could think more rationally, though the memory of her scent lingered.

"Cute? Dude, when she was checking out your ink, you should have asked to see hers!" Kyle was grinning like a kid who had opened a Christmas present. "Did you see it? I wonder how far down it went?"

"If I was your age, not 20 pounds overweight, and not in the place I worked, sure. But I'm not, I am, and I was." Youth was wasted on the young, Liam thought.

Kyle mock punched Liam's shoulder. "But you got her number."

Liam shook his head. "I'm too old for that kind of nonsense, I'll leave that to you kids."

Kyle looked confused. "I was going to, but I kind of forgot. I was going to ask her about her tattoo, then next thing I knew she was asking about your schedule, and when you'd be here next."

Liam paused, books still in his hand. The suspicious voice flared in the back of his mind. "What did you tell her?"

Kyle shrugged. "I think I said you were off the next couple of days. Dude, she's totally into you."

Liam snorted, shelving the books. "She came here to pick my brains, not get picked up. Someone probably referred her to me."

"That sucks." Kyle sounded disappointed. "I thought she was more interested in you than the books."

"Knox, aren't you done with those books yet?" Clark stomped down the aisle leading from the coffee bar down the middle of the store. "And Kyle, finish that display up front between helping customers, don't hang out back here gossiping." The manager disappeared into his office.

Liam sighed. "Thank the gods I have the next couple of days off."

* * * * *

Chapter Two

Liam

"**D**on't crank on it; you'll strip it."

Liam paused from trying to loosen the stubborn bolt holding the oil filter housing on his Yamaha motorcycle, looking for the source of the unsolicited advice. The voice was gruff, with an accent and cadence that made Liam think of the Swedish Chef from the Muppets. The garage door was open for air circulation, and two figures were standing in the driveway, illuminated by the setting sun. As they approached and stepped into the shadows of the house, Liam could see they were Pixel and a short, stout man with a greying beard that would do ZZ Top proud. The breeze blowing into the garage carried a hint of flowers.

Liam experienced a moment of double vision as he looked at the pair. Pixel's eyes took on the violet glow he thought he had seen before, while her companion lost six inches in height, until he was only as tall as Pixel. What the short man lacked in height, he made up for in physique; he was built like a fireplug. He was packed into blue jeans and a biker's leather jacket, and goggles were perched over the bandana covering his salt and pepper hair. Leather biker boots crunched the gravel as he walked toward the garage. Pixel followed him, having traded her workout clothes for black jeans and a pink t-shirt that left her midriff exposed. A pair of sunglasses dangled from the neckline of her t-shirt.

"He's seeing through the glamour," the short, bearded man grumbled to Pixel, his bushy eyebrows furrowing.

"Well duh. We're on his home turf, and this is his place of power," Pixel replied nonchalantly. "He was pushing back against my glamour yesterday, and I'm not adding two hands to my height."

Liam set down the socket wrench and ran through the mental inventory of items in the garage that were weapons or could be used as them. The back half of the garage was a workshop, which included the results of his dabbling with blacksmithing and sword-crafting, so the list was considerable. But the most suitable were also the farthest away.

"Can I help you?" Liam stood and brushed off his jeans; a crowbar was three steps away. Where had they come from? Liam hadn't heard a car or motorcycle outside, and the house was a mile and a half outside of town.

"Ja, you can." The stout man stopped at the threshold of the garage. His steel-grey eyes flicked from Liam to the workbench and back. He held his hands out, palms down. The hands were larger than his and weren't strangers to hard work and possibly violence. "And there's no need to be unhospitable; we come as friends. My name is Einar, and you've already met Pixel."

"Hi, Liam." Pixel was as bubbly as yesterday. While she didn't seem to be making the same connection as Einar regarding the workbench, her eyes darted about the cluttered garage and the dim workshop behind it. "Wow, you have a lot of junk."

"What's this about?" Liam sidled a half step toward the workbench, regretting he hadn't kept up on his martial arts. He had three brown belts, a year of kendo, and some miscellaneous weapons training scattered over two decades but not much experience in the way of real fighting. He could probably hold his own in a brawl as long as his opponent didn't have serious skills. He suspected Einar was more than a Friday night brawler in the local watering hole. "Is she your daughter?"

Einar turned to the purple-haired girl, his caterpillar-like eyebrows gathering. "What did you do?"

"What? I only asked him a few questions and checked him out," Pixel protested, her hands going to her hips as she squared off with Einar. "It's not as if I tried to jump his bones right there in the store or something."

"Look mister, if you think something untoward happened between me and your daughter—" Liam began.

"She's not my pocking daughter, and I don't give a troll's ass if you diddled her," Einar interrupted, his accent thickening with his agitation. He took a deep breath, his barrel chest heaving. "Now, will you hear me out without you trying to brain me with that tire iron you've been eyeing?"

"You said diddle." Pixel giggled.

"Can you be serious for five minutes, you pocking faerie?" Einar glowered, his leather jacket creaking as he crossed his arms.

"Remember 'dwarf,' you're here as an 'advisor.'" Pixel included air quotes with the last word, her eyes turning magenta. "The Nine Realms are only involved out of politeness."

"Politeness! If you pocking Tuatha and Tylwyth Teg hadn't folded up when the Milesians came at you, maybe we wouldn't be here to begin with!" Spittle accompanied Einar's protest. "Tylwyth? More like Toothless!"

"Like your jarls didn't roll over and show their bellies when the Avramites showed up with their One God and their gold!" Pixel rose up on her toes. "Your people took their god and took their gold and then attacked our ancestral lands!"

"Guys!" Liam had stepped over to the workbench but hadn't picked up the crowbar. "Are you playing one of those live-action role playing games or something? Because if you are, I'm calling my garage out of bounds. Take your LARP somewhere else."

"We've come a long way to speak to you," Einar replied, looking away from Pixel. "I'm from Asgard."

"Asgard? You mean like Thor and Odin? What kind of game are you playing?" Liam hadn't moved from the workbench, but he had mapped in his mind the steps he would need to take to reach a stout pole which would serve as a staff while he back-pedaled to his workshop, where a half-dozen half-finished sword prototypes rested. From where he stood, though, he didn't feel as threatened. He knew a bit about gamers because there were a fair number of them among the pagan community, and he had absorbed bits and pieces of it. Maybe someone had pointed Liam out to Pixel as research about druids for one of these games—an over-enthusiastic player who wanted to more convincingly roleplay one.

"Gods I hate those pocking things," Einar grumbled, rubbing his forehead while Pixel stifled another giggle. "Look, can we sit down and talk to you? This is much more serious than some pocking games you folk play with your costumes and your toy weapons."

"This isn't a game, and we aren't hippies with New Age books and a need for self-validation." Pixel added. Her eyes had faded to a lavender color. "Liam, we need your help."

"Fine." Liam grabbed a couple lawn chairs from the wall and unfolded them near the stool by the workbench. "Let's hear what you have to say. And, for the record, I don't play those games; I've just heard enough about them."

"So can we come in?" Pixel bounced in her boots in the gravel at the threshold. Neither she nor Einar had set as much as a toe on the concrete floor of the garage.

Liam stopped. "Do you need an invitation? What, are you vampires?"

Pixel and Einar exchanged a glance. "It's your wards." Pixel said. "No, we're not vampires. Since we're not from the mortal world, we can't cross through them without your permission."

"Though if you let her, I bet she'd suck something," Einar mumbled, earning a cross look and a flash of violet from Pixel.

"My wards are keeping you out? You mean my home blessing verses? I cast those to keep out spirits and negative influences, and, to be honest, I never knew if they worked." Liam tried to reconcile the idea of a protective blessing on a house keeping out flesh and blood people, even ones claiming to be supernatural.

"Oh, they pocking work. Here, watch." Einar rolled up his leather jacket's sleeve, revealing a hirsute forearm as big as Liam's leg. Balling his hand into a fist, Einar thrust it across the threshold of the garage door. His boots slid back on the gravel as an unseen force pushed him away from the threshold. Smoke rose from the burning hairs on his hand and arm. The dwarf clenched his teeth as the skin began to turn red.

"Okay, you can come in." Einar almost pitched forward as resistance disappeared with Liam's words. Liam dismissed the whole role-playing gamer notion, his mind boggling at what he had seen.

He thought again about potential weapons, then finally decided to settle for sitting in one of the lawn chairs. Whoever these two people were, if they had really wanted to hurt him they could have waited until he went outside; he had been in and out of the garage all day. Besides, his curiosity was piqued. He'd just witnessed magic having an actual, physical effect. While part of his mind protested what he had seen was impossible, the rest of it wanted to know more.

Behind him the door going from the garage to the house creaked open and slammed shut. He turned at the noise, but there was nothing to be seen through the screen door. He turned back to the two visitors. "What was that?"

"It's only Scooter," Pixel said, perching on the stool while Einar gingerly lowered himself into the remaining lawn chair. "Don't worry, he won't break anything."

"If my blessings or wards were keeping you out, how did he get in?"

"You need to be more specific with your invitations." Einar finally seemed to decide that the aluminum and nylon chair would support him and let his weight settle into it. It creaked a bit, but held. "Lucky for you he's a brownie and not something nasty."

"You mean as in folklore?" Liam looked over his shoulder again. There was no movement in the hall leading from the door to the kitchen and no more noise from the house. "Assuming I'm not really out of my head from the fumes of something, as this keeps getting weirder, why is there a brownie in my house?"

"Only two of the Seemly Holts got to send representatives. Scooter is representing the Lochar Holt from Scotland." Pixel made it sound as though she was explaining someone was from St. Louis. "He's actually pretty excited about it, since your wards have kept any house-fae from taking up residence. But he's shy, like all brownies, so you shouldn't call out to him, or even really try to look at him."

"A brownie? There's a Scottish brownie named Scooter loose in my house?" The old farmhouse Liam had inherited from his uncle had plenty of places to hide, especially if this 'Scooter' really was as Pixel claimed. Liam ran a hand through his sandy hair and then stood up. This was getting weirder by the minute, and his brain needed time to catch up. "I need a beer."

He walked over to an old refrigerator in the corner. Like any good garage fridge, it was well stocked with beer. "Anyone else want a beer?"

"What the Dunwold calls beer, especially here in the Americas, is fizzy piss," Einar replied. "Now if you have something you're afraid to drink near an open flame, that's booze."

"So that's a no?" Liam opened the fridge, rummaging through a shelf of mismatched bottles.

"I didn't say that," Einar protested. "I would be a poor guest to turn down a drink."

"Guinness, Smithwicks, Magners Ciders, and Anvil Stout from Harter Brewery." Liam fished a bottle out and set it on the fridge. "And right now, I feel the need to kill a couple of brain cells, so I'm going with the Anvil."

"When you put it that way, the stout sounds promising," Einar said. "I'll have the same."

"I'll take a cider," Pixel chimed in. Liam considered questioning her age then dismissed it.

Opening the bottles, Liam returned to his guests and handed out the drinks before sinking back in his chair. "So, let's skip the whole am I dreaming or going crazy routine; if I am either of those, then this conversation isn't real. Why is there a faerie delegation at my house?"

"I'm not a pocking faerie, I'm a dwarf," Einar said defensively over his beer before taking a swig. "Not bad for a soft drink."

Liam ignored the jibe at the beer, despite it being one of his favorites, and took a draw of his own. "Right, a dwarf from Asgard, along with a faerie and a brownie. First she shows up at my work yesterday, and then you guys come here. What's up?"

"Wow, straight to the point." Pixel shifted on the stool. "He's not freaking out or getting all googly-eyed. I told you I wouldn't have to whammy him."

"Most pocking dunnies get worked into a lather over the stupidest things." Einar regarded Liam over his beer. "Maybe his blood's not so thinned out after all."

Liam added a couple of more items to his growing list of things he wanted explained. He turned to Pixel. "Were you doing this 'whammy' at my store yesterday? That's how you got my boss to go away and Kyle to give you my schedule?"

"It's called glamouring. It can be used to change someone's perception of you or to influence them." Pixel looked embarrassed as she nodded. "I wanted to keep your attention, and your boss is a huge tool. As it was, you kept fighting it, which is more than most dunnies can do. I should have expected you to shake it off, but I figured it wouldn't hurt to try. The kid at the front desk didn't even need any encouragement."

Liam looked over Pixel again. Despite the glowing eyes, greenish under-tone to her tanned skin and slightly wilder look, she was still cute, really cute even, but he no longer found her distracting. Well, not too distracting, as his eyes caught the tattoo winding to the waist of her jeans. "Okay, back to my question, why are you here?"

"We need a druid," Pixel replied. "Specifically, we need you."

"You must have gone pretty far through your list of druids before you got to me. I don't even know if you can call me a druid; I don't have a congregation or a grove anymore." Liam thought back to the last time he'd performed a ritual for a group, almost two years ago. "There are people out there a lot more knowledgeable."

"Just because they are well read doesn't mean they know the right things." Pixel drank from her bottle before continuing. "Knowing a lot, or even being really smart, isn't what's important here, especially if a lot of what they know is drivel."

"What about needing 20 years of study to be a druid?" Liam was lucky to focus on something more than a handful of months, let alone dedicate two decades to one course of study.

"How many years of schooling have you had?" Pixel took another drink from her cider.

"Seventeen." Liam didn't count various online or short-term classes he had taken over the years since graduating college. In one way or another, he'd been studying something almost all his adult life.

"Druids didn't spend 20 years learning only about theology and how to conduct rites." Pixel held up her free hand, ticking off subjects as she named them. "History, Law, Science, Poetry, Magic, and they weren't nearly as efficient about it as your dunnies' modern education system. Especially back when you went to school, before you could Google everything."

"Pocking Google," Einar grumbled.

"Plus you actually got the structure of druidic magic, draoicht, right," Pixel added.

"Structure?" Liam took a swig of stout to mollify the implication he had gone to school a long time ago, even if it was true. Maybe especially because it was true. He had learned from books and libraries, not a little glowing screen.

"Gods, Spirits, and Ancestors, the Three Kindreds." Pixel drew three circles in the air as she spoke. "And the Three Realms, Land, Sky, and Sea. Too many neo-druids cross-pollinate their practices with Wicca and the suggestions of questionable authors passing off their musings as history."

Liam had pretty much taken a 'whatever works for them' attitude regarding various pagan practices of others, druid or otherwise. He'd certainly met people with 'my way or the highway' stances, as well as those whose ideology give credence to the herding cats analogy in paganism. "I can't be the only one. I've read other folks' work that follows the same structure."

"They lack a certain qualification," Einar remarked, taking a deep draw from his stout. "Your bloodline."

Liam mentally ran through his family tree, working on his beer as he thought. He knew it three generations out, and tried to remember anything significant. It was the typical immigrant Euro-mutt mix of mostly German, English, and Irish. "I didn't stick with genealogy long when I messed with it, so you're going to have to fill me in. Most of my family was in the States by the beginning of the 20th century."

"Remember when I asked you about Cathbad?" Pixel smiled as though she was about to give someone a birthday present. "You are descended from him."

"Neat. Probably not something that would turn up on one of those ancestry websites, but I don't see what the big deal is." Liam did some quick mental math as he took another drink. "There has to be something like 60 generations between us."

"More like 91." Pixel drained her cider, then slid down from the barstool. "Blood is a really potent source of magic. Especially your blood."

As she walked past Liam, his eyes were drawn for a split second. Glamour or no, those black jeans were tight. He turned back to Einar, who politely pretended not to notice where Liam's gaze had gone. Liam heard Pixel open the refrigerator and rummage through the bottles.

"So you guys looked me up because Cathbad is my great-times-a-lot-granddad." He finished his beer and set the bottle on the floor. "What do you think I can do?"

"Magic," Pixel called from the refrigerator. "Almost no dunnies, I mean mortals, can draw on the Gwuedd, the weave of magic, at all. As your wards show, you can." She approached behind him, reaching over his shoulder to hand him another beer. There was a faint whiff of flowers.

"Gwuedd, that sounds Welsh," Liam pointed out. He knew that draoicht was Irish and had experience with pagans that pulled a few words out of dictionaries and mashed them together to sound impressive. One Celtic Wiccan group he knew called on an Arabic spirit for one of their quarters because they'd seen it in a book and didn't research any farther.

"You'll find we use words from multiple sources," Pixel replied. "Welsh, Irish, what you would call an evolved form of proto-Celtic, Norse, and a smattering of others."

Liam filed linguistics for future questioning. "So, you need me to ward someplace?" If Liam could ward his home, he could repeat the process for other locations. Despite the outlandishness of him drinking beer with supernatural creatures in his garage, the task itself seemed rather reasonable in the grand scope of things. He would merely need to alter the verse a bit.

"We need you to make a sword—a magic sword—and you'll need to issue our challenge on behalf the Exiled Folk." Einar accepted another beer from Pixel as she returned to the stool with a cider. "Then we need a hero to battle the Champion of the Milesian Accords."

Liam's list grew significantly, but he kept it compartmentalized. "Aren't I a little old for the whole hero's journey thing?"

Einar's roar of laughter startled Liam, almost causing him to spill his beer. Pixel giggled on her stool, and Liam could almost swear he heard a snicker coming from the direction of the door to the house.

"What's so damned funny?" Liam felt slightly insulted at their mirth. While he couldn't really see himself as a hero, they didn't have to find the notion so humorous. Sure, he was nearly 40 and out of practice, but he could probably get back up to speed. He might not be athletic, but a variety of physical hobbies had kept him strong over the years.

"You're not the pocking hero," Einar managed as his laughter subsided. Once he could breathe again he set to work on his beer. "We've got someone else lined up to take on that task."

"But you're crucial to making this work," Pixel added, trying to mollify Liam. "We need a druid to issue the challenge, then the hero has to actually do the fighting."

"So I'm the equivalent of a lawyer who moonlights as a sword-smith?" Liam worked on his beer until his flush of embarrassment subsided. Whatever this supernatural scheme was, he wasn't Arthur; he was more like Merlin.

"That's pretty much the way of it." Einar nodded, draining his beer in a long chug. "And before you waste five minutes protesting that there are better people to make swords, it needs to be a magic sword, so it needs to be you."

Liam looked toward the corner housing his neglected sword-smithing workshop. "I'm out of practice, and I was only mediocre at best to begin with. Maybe better than the Pakistani crap people would sell at the renaissance faire, but only because I started with decent steel. I was nowhere near as good as the guys who did this for a living; I've only made a handful of blades."

"That's why we have someone coming to mentor you," Pixel said.

"What, you lined up a real smith to tutor me?" It actually wasn't a bad idea, Liam mused. He had enjoyed making swords, but as with almost all things, it hadn't kept his attention long enough for him to get good at it. But if they brought in a pro to work with him, to coach him through the process and make sure he didn't make any major mistakes, he could probably turn out a serviceable blade. He wasn't ready to wrap his head around the magic part yet; that went into another compartment of his mind.

"Something like that." This time it was Einar who went to the fridge and began to pick through the bottles within. Despite his criticisms, the dwarf had downed the stouts quickly. "We could always drink something stronger."

"Yeah, all I've got for hard liquor is some tequila and maybe half a bottle of Drambuie." Liam thought of tequila as Spanish for 'I did what?' And Drambuie was too thick and sweet for serious drinking. Besides, despite some encouragement from the edges of his sanity, he wasn't ready to get hammered. "So have I heard of this guy? I know of a few swordsmiths who do the ren faire circuit."

"Oh, you've heard of him." Clinking bottles heralded Einar's return. He handed one to Liam despite the fact he was still working on the second beer. Einar set another cider on the workbench behind Pixel, then settled back in his chair.

"Then who is it?" Despite his better judgement, Liam polished off the half full beer to free up a hand because he felt silly holding two beers. As he set the empty bottle down to join the other dead soldier, he noticed that he still hadn't gotten an answer.

"Might as well tell him." Pixel looked fit to burst, rocking on her stool.

"Why not? He hasn't freaked out yet," Einar agreed.

"Really, how much weirder can this get?" Liam started on the third beer without even thinking about it.

Pixel shrugged. "Gofannon. Gofannon is going to guide you."

Liam thought for a moment, still working on the beer. "Is he local?"

Einar sputtered his beer. "Local? Are you pocking daft?"

"Sorry, but a lot of pagans adopt the names of gods as their handles, so I could totally see a pagan smith taking Gofannon as a craft name." Liam didn't really think it was much of a stretch, although Goibhnu, the Irish smith god, was more popular than his Welsh counter-part. Granted, both gods were pretty obscure, and Liam placed even odds that anyone taking on the name of Gofannon would forget that the Welsh 'f' sounded similar to an English 'v.'

"No, we're talking about Gofannon himself." Pixel sounded the most serious Liam had heard, bordering on religious.

"You mean Gofannon, the smith-god?" Liam needed a moment to process the idea, taking another drink while he did. He had managed to come to grips with these otherworldly people being here, raiding his beer fridge and talking about him participating in some sort of supernatural plot as though they were asking him to help roof a garage, but it was another to grasp the concept of being face-to-face with a god. Until now he had been dubious whether gods actually had faces or physical forms at all, let alone that one would come to rural Illinois. "Gofannon is coming here?"

Pixel nodded. "He is obscure enough we can slip him across without anyone noticing. Hopefully."

"Pocking hope so or this will all be for naught," Einar agreed.

"Why does he need to sneak here? He's a god, right?" Liam could have tabled the question for later, his head already aching from the info dump, but his curiosity had not abated.

"Despite what some may think, being a god does not make one omnipotent," Pixel said. "While they are certainly more powerful than even one of the Court Lords, they still have limits, especially given how few mortal worshippers they have nowadays.

"Even so, the more powerful an entity that crosses over, the more likely it is for someone to notice," Pixel continued. "That would draw attention and maybe tip our hand."

"It boils down to the pocking Milesian Accords. Because of the treaty, the Avramic Gods—their followers really—control the Dunwold, while the old gods and the Exiled Folk were consigned to the

Glaswold." Einar regarded Liam. "I know you're busting with questions, so you might as well start asking them."

Liam took another gulp as he organized his thoughts, questions continuing to emerge even as he decided what to ask first. While he could put a few beers away, putting away one potent stout after another this quickly was bringing on a buzz. "Let's start with Avram and Avramic Gods. You referred earlier to One God. What's the difference?"

"Go ahead, you're the one who likes to go on about this stuff," Pixel said. "Makes me wish we could have our own wiki site."

"Alright, you know who Abraham was, ja?"

"If you mean the Biblical Abraham, sure." Theology minor for the win, Liam thought. "So let me guess, Avram is Abraham, who started out as Abram in the Old Testament. But Abram, Abraham, Avram, whatever you want to call him, was a monotheist. How can there be plural Avramic Gods?"

"If enough people put enough belief in something, it can be made manifest." Einar leaned forward with the creaking of leather. "So, the followers of Avram started off with one god, and they preached the One God through the ages, but their faith became a lot more complicated, as did their prayers. You have Jesus and Mary added to the mix, both being prayed to alongside 'God,' and then there's Satan. From the Inquisition to the modern fire-and-brimstone preachers, so much stock has been put in Satan that he is manifest."

"Shit, you're saying Satan is real?" Liam needed a good drink while he pondered the notion. One of the pagan counters to accusations of Satanism was that Satan was a bogey-man constructed by Christians to keep people in line. Now it looked as though they had literally built him. What else had mass-belief conjured?

"There are even some saints who have manifested because of the devotion to them," Einar continued. "Though they are more like collective spirits rather than gods. And all of this just covers the various flavors of Christians."

"So on one side you have the Exiled Gods, which I presume to be the various pagan gods." Liam waited for a confirming nod. "And on the other side, you have these Avramic gods, grown from the various Abrahamic religions. That puts you at odds with roughly half the world when you lump together Christianity, Judaism and Islam. The pagan side has what, maybe one percent if we're being generous?"

"It's not like we'd be picking a fight with the rank and file believers," Einar countered. "Most people follow their faith unaware of anything beyond the mundane world and the powers that move through it. The vast majority of Christians have no clue about the various Avramite powers. They just want to go through their lives knowing they'll be rewarded in the afterlife."

Liam thought the assessment was a bit generous; in his experience many people paid lip service to their religion, but only a few held to the tenets when it became inconvenient. "So your plan is to throw down with the clergy?"

Einar stifled a sigh. "No, when we talk about the Avramite powers, we're not talking about the pocking clergy, at least not in general. Only a handful know more than the general public. The Elohim, what you might call angels, generally don't let mortals in on the secret and pocking wouldn't want them to know about the Milesian Accords."

"So what are these Milesian Accords you've mentioned?" Liam filed the fact that angels were real in another box. Made sense if he accepted that faeries and dwarves were real and sitting in his garage.

"I'm familiar with the Milesians from the invasion tales of Ireland."

Einar looked over to Pixel and picked up his beer. "You want to take this? I'm parched."

"A lot of what you—what the Dunwold—call myths and legends started somewhere." Pixel brushed back a stray purple lock, tucking it behind a pointed ear. "Over time, a lot of embellishments creep in, things get jumbled, places and characters get renamed or merged, but there is often a basis for the legend. As for the Milesian Accords, when the mortals invaded the lands of the Fair Folk, there was a great war.

"At first, the Fair Folk had the advantage, mostly through magic. When it looked as though the Milesians might swamp the Fair Folk and their mortal followers through sheer numbers, the greatest of the magicians among the Fair Folk created what was called the Fiwer Pact. They extracted a promise from the Earth that certain metals would not harm the Fair Folk and other supernatural creatures that were fighting off the Milesian invasion.

"Copper, tin, lead, zinc and gold." Pixel ticked off on her fingers. "These metals couldn't hurt those protected by the Fiwer Pact, which, when added to the magic of the Fair Folk and their druids, turned the tide of the battle."

"So the Iron Age came along and messed things up." Liam met Pixel's glowing eyes. "Is that why iron is so dangerous to fairies and such?"

Pixel picked up the crowbar from the workbench. "Unlike what a lot of legends say, iron isn't toxic to creatures from the Glaswold. We can handle it just fine, although it will cut through most magic protections. Between that, and the superiority of iron weapons and armor over their bronze counterparts, there gave rise to the stories claiming iron was an anathema to supernatural creatures." She set the crowbar back down and returned her gaze to Liam. "By the way, Cathbad supposedly had heterochromia."

"What's that?" Einar turned back to the conversation, having spent most of Pixel's part of the history lesson studying Liam's motorcycle.

"My eyes are different colors; one is blue and one is green," Liam explained. He was struggling to keep all of the questions popping into his head from derailing the conversation. "So was that another of my qualifications? You needed a druid with heterochromia like Cathbad?"

"No, just a fun bit of trivia." Pixel set her empty bottle on the workbench behind her. "So where was I? Right, the Milesian Accords. So when iron was introduced, the tide of battle switched again. When it became apparent they were going to lose, the Tuatha De Danann, the Tylwyth Teg, and the other assorted Fair Folk decided to sue for peace. They managed to convince the Milesians to settle things with a battle of champions. To that end, the leaders of the Milesians and the Fair Folk drew up the Milesian Accords."

"Should have read the pocking fine print," Einar grumbled.

Liam turned to Einar. "What do you mean?"

Pixel sighed. "What he means is that the Fair Folk assumed the Milesians were a bunch of barbarians who happened to get lucky and figure out iron-working. They didn't know there were Nephilim in the ranks of the Milesians."

"Nephilim, as in the offspring of angels and men?" Liam was getting more use out of his theology minor today than he had since he earned it. "Weren't they giants, as in Goliath?"

"Not necessarily, in fact many of them could pass for human, especially if they used magic. So there was a handful of them coaching the Milesians. They probably gave them the secret to working iron and helped them set up the Milesian Accords, guessing the lords of the Fair Folk would think themselves too clever to be outwitted by mortals.

"So the challenge was made, and the Milesians agreed if the Fair Folk won they would return to Iberia, but in turn, if the Milesians won, the Fair Folk vowed to leave the mortal world. The Milesian champion won, so the Fair Folk and their gods were exiled to the Glaswold, the Green World, which is the world that exists below the Veil."

"So the Glaswold is what some refer to as the Otherworld?" Liam had conjectured as much through context. "And the sidhe, faeries, and so forth went there after losing the fight with the Milesians?" Liam realized he had already finished another beer. He considered another, especially in the light of this huge paradigm shift, but didn't think it would be smart. "But weren't the Milesians Celts, with druids and so forth? Didn't they worship the Celtic gods?"

Pixel rolled her eyes. "The Celts weren't a homogenous people. They swept across Europe in waves of tribes, and there were differences between the various tribes. They also had a tendency to absorb parts of the cultures they swept across. The ones who came with the Milesian invasion were already being influenced by followers of the Avramic religions.

"The Nephilim were playing the long game. With the Fair Folk and the pagan gods in exile, and the pathways between the worlds closing, the druids lost most of their mystic power. They continued for a while as priests and arbiters, but they could no longer draw on the draoicht of the Kindreds or the Realms. A few centuries later, the Romans broke the back of the druidic faith across the continent and much of the Isles. Then the more fervent adherents of the One God came, and the rest is history." Pixel stood up again, pausing to stretch before making another trip to the refrigerator. Liam pretended not to notice, appearing intent on his emptied bottle.

"Of course, the exodus wasn't 100 percent." Einar glanced in Pixel's direction and nodded. "There's always some pocking rebels who will take the risks of staying behind. The pocking Avramites killed a bunch of their own people trying to root out a few of the Folk and followers of the old ways."

"So how are the Norse and Asgard mixed up in this?" Liam found a cold beer being pressed into his hand as he noticed Pixel's floral scent. He tried to ignore how her hand lingered on his shoulder and focus on his question to Einar. "Was Asgard party to the Milesian Accords?"

"The various 'nine worlds' are all part of the Glaswold, more or less." Einar paused as Pixel handed him another beer, and he took a long drink. If the stout was having any effect on him, it didn't show. "When the Accords went into effect, it became much harder to get from the Glaswold to the Dunwold and the dunnies started destroying the remaining known pathways."

"Dunwold? I get that it refers to the, for lack of better term, mortal world, and you refer to us as dunnies, but what is Dunwold?" Liam noticed the buzz of the potent beer seeping further into his mind.

"It means the 'Brown World,' probably because it's so pocking full of shit." Einar seemed amused by his own explanation, then his face turned somber again. "So when the paths between the worlds closed, the Gothi and the rune-wrights lost their power—their ability to call on magic—same as their Celtic counterparts. And they weren't the only ones affected; magic was cut off all over the world."

"So if this all happened ages ago, why do you need a druid now?" Liam rationalized getting a little drunk was helping keep his mind from getting overwhelmed. Part of him wondered if he'd really gone insane and was holding a conversation with his empty garage.

"There's a provision allowing the Exiled Folk to challenge the Accords. Our champion gets to fight their champion, and if we win, the paths between the worlds reopen." Pixel sounded as though she was explaining the town council's plan to annex a stretch of land, not a mind-bending shift in reality.

"Because it worked so well last time?"

Pixel frowned. "Last time our side got cocky. The lords thought with the ringer they had slipped in as champion there was no way they would lose to the Milesians, iron weapons or no."

"What, a god of war?" Liam ran through the list of Celtic gods of war and battle, as well as those with reputations of being badasses. Then his list went on to heroes. "Cu Chulainn?"

"If only they had gone with Cu Chulainn, but no, they had to get cute and used a dragon."

Liam coughed on his beer. "A dragon? Dragons are real?" He looked to Einar for confirmation. The dwarf shrugged. "How the heck did the Milesians beat a dragon?"

"Their champion was pocking Saint George," Einar grumbled.

"Einar is generalizing." Pixel added another bottle to the work-bench. "His name was Giwargix, and his story got rolled into the Saint George legend. Saint George the martyr never fought a dragon, but as time went on the story of Giwargix defeating the dragon was added to the tales about Saint George, and the site of the battle in the stories moved to Libya, or Lissa, to fit in better with the saint's hagiography."

"So I deliver this challenge, and your new hero takes on their champion, and if you win then what, the fairy folk and supernatural creatures can invade the mortal world?" As insane as it all sounded, Liam was pretty sure he didn't want to be the guy responsible for the equivalent of Armageddon or Ragnarok.

"It will let magic back in the world." Pixel sounded like one of those sad commercials for homeless pets. "And while a lot of the exiles won't want to come back, there are some who miss the Dunwold. But it won't be an invasion or a supernatural apocalypse, it'll be a homecoming."

"Don't forget if you can't make the pocking sword, we're at the anvil without a hammer." Einar belched loudly.

"Right, the magic sword that a god is going to teach me how to make." Liam looked over his shoulder toward the door into the house. "You know, I think I can use some tequila after all." He rose from his chair and started across the garage. "So who's this hero?"

"You wouldn't know her," Pixel replied. "But she's descended from Cu Chulainn."

* * * * *

Chapter Three

Erin

"Hey sweetheart, can we get another round?"
Erin Donnelly didn't need to turn around
to know the request came from the table of
four southern boys between the jukebox and the pool tables. They
were all clean cut, with button-up shirts and khakis, looking like they
were on their way to a Bible meeting or a conference for an uptight
but not quite lucrative profession. They were all smiles and thank-
yous with their Lexington drawls and white teeth, but they had been
watching her as though she was dancing on a pole, not waiting tables.

"I'll be right there," she called sweetly. Despite the expectation
that they would end up being cheapskates, she carried on as though
she'd get a decent tip out of the table. Dante's Pub was a small hole-
in-the-wall bar off the I-275 loop around Cincinnati, and it was a
slow night, so she had to work for every dollar she could.

"Those Kentucky boys giving you any trouble?" The bartender,
Ray, was also the owner. He looked over Erin's shoulder as she approached the bar. Normally cheerful and outgoing, he became serious if he thought someone was hassling one of the staff, his 'work
family.'

"Nothing I can't handle, Ray," Erin replied as she typed in the
order for four Budweisers. She wouldn't have considered trying to

43

sic Ray on the khaki quartet, even if they were being out-and-out jackasses. Ray was an older, slender man with a large nose and a small tuft of a beard clinging to his pointy chin, in no way intimidating. "They've kept their hands to themselves."

Ray snorted as he pulled four bottles from behind the bar, popping them open and setting them on her tray. "I ever tell you about the time my friend Ian and I rumbled with a bunch of drunk bikers?"

"Maybe once or twice." Erin had heard the story numerous times, in various iterations, depending on the audience. Ray was a consummate storyteller, and he had several favorites he loved to share over and over, and every time was as if he was telling the tale for the first time.

Erin picked up the tray, affixed a pleasant smile to her face, then pivoted toward the table where the four men ogled her like she was wearing a bikini, or less. Erin mentally sighed; she would have expected this kind of attention if she was a 22-year-old blonde party-girl, not a 31-year-old single mother working two jobs. Sure she was fit, but her attire, jeans and a Dante's t-shirt, certainly wasn't provocative.

"Here you go, boys." She set the beers in front of each of the men and collected the empties. "Let me know if you need anything else."

"Oh, we will, darling," the oldest of them said, a 40ish looking man with horn-rimmed glasses. He flashed a toothy smile while his compatriots, all 20-somethings, looked amused, as though they were sharing some inside joke.

Erin could guess the nature of their jokes, feeling their eyes on her as she walked away. She circled behind the pool table to check on the only other table she had remaining. The occupants of the booth were the ones she would have picked to be troublemakers when they walked in. A man and a woman, both tall and lean with long blonde hair, dressed in black leather, they looked like they could be twins.

Instead of being trouble, they were polite and kept to themselves. They had ordered glasses of mead, which fortunately Ray actually stocked from a local winery even though this was the first time Erin remembered anyone ordering it. Surprisingly, they hadn't drawn the attention of the other patrons, including the four Budweiser fans. They had spent the last hour nursing their drinks and conversing quietly.

Erin glanced at the clock behind the bar, an old neon-rimmed one that blended in with the other illuminated beer signs, wishing the minute hand would speed up. Only 15 minutes were left in her shift; the slow night had made it drag on. She glanced up and noticed the leather-clad blondes had left. They had paid for their mead when she brought it, so at least they hadn't skipped on her.

Erin started cleaning up the booth, a quick task as there were only the two glasses and a folded up piece of paper. When she scooped up the paper, she realized it was actually money folded up in the shape of a swan. She almost hated to unfold the little origami bird, but regretted it less when she discovered it was a ten-dollar bill.

She returned to the server station at the end of the bar to finish up her closing duties, making sure everything was stocked and arranged for tomorrow. The racket of several chairs scooting on the floor caught her attention. Horn-rimmed-glasses and his buds were all getting up from the table. He gave another grin and nodded back toward the table.

"Keep the change, darling."

46 | JON R. OSBORNE

"Thanks, come again." Erin returned a polite smile, hoping they wouldn't take her suggestion. A quick glance at the table showed a pile of bills with the check, so at least they weren't running on their tab. She waited until the door closed behind them before going to collect the money and clear the table. She half expected to find a business card or a phone number; it wouldn't be the first time. But all they left was a paltry tip, five bucks for two hours of creepy leers.

"They stiff you?" Ray asked as she sorted the money, separating her tip from what was due the bar.

"No. Not big on Christian charity, but they left a little something." Ray sometimes kicked some money back to the waitresses who got jipped by a table of cheapskates who rang up a big tab. While this job didn't pay a lot, she didn't take advantage of Ray's good nature because she knew that money came out of his pocket, and it wasn't a deep pocket to begin with.

Ray took the money for the tab and rang it into the drawer. "You might as well get home to your son. Hector and I will finish up."

"Thanks Ray, I'll see you Friday." She fished her purse out from behind the bar and headed to the door, making sure it was set to lock behind her. She could hear Ray begin another story for Hector as the door clicked shut behind her.

The parking lot next to the bar was darker than she liked. The light intended to illuminate the lot was prone to vandalism, and the building itself obscured the closest streetlight. There was enough glow from various sources to navigate by, so it wasn't pitch black. She swung wide of a van in the lot, checking its side as she passed it on the way to her car. As she closed on the car, she reached for her keys, then heard the crunch of shoes on gravel.

She turned to face the khaki quartet as they approached from around the van, two coming from the back, the other pair having circled it to try to get behind her. They were all showing their pearly whites now as they closed, the biggest ones in the lead.

"Now Missy, why don't you come along for a ride with us?" Glasses' drawl thickened with a slight menace. "My boys don't need to get rough."

"I don't think so," Erin replied icily. A small part of her was afraid. Someone who wasn't at all afraid of an ambush by superior numbers was a fool, she thought. But being afraid made her pissed. She knew that the six-foot brick wall separating the parking lot from the adjacent alley wouldn't be a challenge for her thanks to weekend parkour courses. But she wasn't about to choose flight from these smug assholes. She was furious and all about the fight now.

The lead pair came at her simultaneously, probably practiced or at least well coached, hoping to quickly grab and neutralize her. She did the last thing they expected and closed, taking three steps to the one on the left, angling away from the other. She batted his outstretched arm up, driving her elbow into his solar plexus as she side-stepped past him, seizing his wrist, turning, and cranking the arm hard over her shoulder. She was rewarded with a crunch from his elbow and a howl of pain as his arm bent at an unnatural angle.

Erin released the mangled arm, continuing her spin as the partner fought his own momentum to turn back toward her and get around his hurt comrade. He managed to change direction in time to catch the heel of Erin's boot to his jaw as her spin kick connected. Number two dropped like a sack of potatoes, his eyes rolling back in his head. She planted her feet and pushed off toward the remaining two.

Glasses' remaining goon brandished some sort of stun gun, which he sparked threateningly. A snap kick sent it flying and probably broke a couple of the fingers that had been holding it. A throat punch muffled the cries of pain. Glasses tore open the side door of the van, having back-pedaled as she closed. He started to reach into the van then froze at the metallic click of a gun being cocked.

"Your hands come up anything but empty, I will end you," Erin snarled, holding the .357 Ruger LCR aimed squarely at his heart. She was tempted to pull the trigger anyway, there wasn't a jury that would convict a woman jumped by four men for putting one down. Despite her blood boiling, she knew what a hassle it would be. Plus, something in the back of her mind told her this was more than four drunks looking to grab a woman off the street.

He turned slowly, holding both hands up in the air. Somehow he mustered a smile that made Erin want to punch his teeth in. "Now darling, no need to go all Second Amendment."

Erin stepped sideways, making sure she was clear of any of the men should they decide to renew their attack. It seemed unlikely, as one clutched his arm whimpering, another lay unconscious on the gravel, and the third was gasping for air. Still, getting cocky was a sure way to snatch defeat from the jaws of victory.

"Well done." The melodious voice came from the shadows in the corner of the lot. The two tall blondes from the bar stepped into view as though the shadows parted for them. "You live up to expectations, Miss Donnelly."

Erin readied to bring her gun to bear on the new arrivals, taking another step back to widen her field of view. "Who the fuck are you?"

"First of all, we're not with them," the woman said, nodding toward the khaki squad. "The rest is probably a discussion best not held in a parking lot in front of the dogs of Avram."

"Fuck you, faeries," Glasses growled, his smile disappearing. "Get your leather asses off our world."

The male blonde smiled. "All that repression. What has you more excited, being dominated by a woman or seeing a beautiful man like me?"

"Not now, Derek." The woman rolled her bright blue eyes. She turned to Erin. "Seriously, we should take this inside."

"What about them?" Erin gestured at Glasses with the gun, which made him flinch. "We need to wait for the police."

"Waste of time." Derek strode over to Glasses and held out his hand. "Give me your keys."

Glasses reached into his pocket and Erin had to resist the urge to fire, her finger frozen on the trigger. Glasses handed a set of keys to Derek, glaring the whole time. Derek turned them over a few times in his hand before splaying his long fingers open to show an empty palm.

"Where did the keys go?" Erin asked. She hadn't heard them hit pavement, she couldn't see where he had pocketed them.

Derek shrugged and smirked. The woman sighed.

"Later." The woman strode over to Glasses and slugged him in the jaw, dropping him to the pavement. She gestured for Erin to follow and headed back toward Dantes' front door. "Let's talk."

Throat-punch had stopped wheezing and was now working hard at not attracting any attention. The others posed zero threat. Erin slid her pistol back into the purse holster and followed the woman.

Derek blew a kiss to Throat-punch, then joined the others heading toward the bar.

Ray looked startled when he saw them approach through the glass, having been in the middle of counting the till, something Erin wished he would do in his office and out of sight of passersby. He set the money down and came around the bar, eyeing Erin's companions as he reached for the door lock.

"Is everything okay?" Ray asked, not hesitating to open the door.

"That's complicated." Erin looked over her shoulder at the two blondes. "I'm hoping to get some answers."

"Sorry to trouble you," the woman locked eyes with Ray. "We need to talk to Erin. You and your employee can leave."

Ray blinked twice, then cocked his head. A slow smile spread, exposing tobacco-stained teeth.

"Oh, you're good." He continued to smile and bobbed his head. He backed up to a bar stool and took a seat. "I don't know if that was hypnotism or some sort of binding, but I'm impressed. But you're not going to pull some sort of vampire mind control bullshit on me."

The woman's eyebrows furrowed while the man, Derek, was obviously suppressing a chuckle behind his hand.

"Hector, puedes salir," Ray called back to the kitchen. While his Spanish wasn't perfect, he could get his meaning across if he kept it simple.

"Jefe, I am not finished," Hector answered over running water.

"Esta bien. Miguel can finish in the morning."

The water turned off, and after a few moments of rattling glasses, Hector emerged from the back. He looked over the four people, wiping his hands on his apron and shrugged. Pulling the apron off, he went for the door, giving the blondes a wide berth. "Buenas no-ches, Jefe, Erin."

"Buenas noches." Ray waited for the door to close. "Okay, what's really going on?"

The blondes exchanged looks. The man shrugged and went to lock the door.

"This could take a while," the woman said. "It is not a simple tale."

"It rarely is." Ray fished a pack of cigarettes out of the pocket of his faded Hawaiian shirt, followed by a lighter. Reaching behind the bar, he retrieved the ashtray he kept hidden for after hours. As far as Erin knew, none of the employees had ever complained about Ray's occasional flaunting of smoking bans once the doors were locked at the end of the night. "Let's start with who are you? Though I'm guessing 'what' wouldn't be inappropriate as well."

"I'm called Izzy, my brother Derek." Izzy paused. Ray had obvi-ously thrown her off balance. "We represent the Summer Court of Iberia."

Ray chuckled, puffing on his cigarette. "Izquierda y Derecho. Left and Right."

Erin was confused, as much by what they had said as by Ray's re-action. This sounded more fanciful than even his best yarns. "How about we talk about why four Bible thumpers tried to kidnap me."

Ray stiffened, the cigarette dangling dangerously close to falling. "Say what? Have you called the cops?"

"A waste of time and a bunch of questions you don't want to deal with," Derek sneered, crossing his arms. "Besides, the Av-ramites probably have people among the law enforcement agencies."

"Avramite - that's the second time you've said that word." Erin fought the urge to pace while adrenaline worked itself out of her system. "What does it mean?"

Izzy pulled out another bar stool. "The Avramites are beholden to the forces behind the Abrahamic religions, the followers of the so-called One God." Ray's smoky snort elicited a hint of a grin. "Their minions are being tasked to prevent the challenge to the Milesian Accords, the pact which drove the Folk of the Old Gods from the world, and their magic with them."

"What does it have to do with me?" Erin still couldn't bring herself to sit, and barely managed not to shake. "I'm not into religion."

"You are the descendant of Cu Chulainn." For a change, Derek actually looked solemn. "You are destined to be the Champion of the Exiled Folk and fight the Avramite champion for our right to return to the world."

Ray almost lost his cigarette again as he gaped. Erin turned to him. "Ray, do you have any idea what they are talking about? Who this Kookoolin that is supposed to be my ancestor?"

Ray took his cigarette between his fingers, tapping off the ash. "Cu Chulainn, the champion of ancient Ireland. I'm guessing the Milesians they are talking about have something to do with the Irish Invasion myths. I'm more into Wicca and shamanism; it sounds like you need a druid. I wonder if my buddy Ian is up."

"We have a druid," Izzy said.

"Assuming the others didn't botch their task," Derek remarked, admiring his fingernails. "It has to be that druid and this warrior."

"Wait a minute, I've been out of the Army for a couple of years, and even then I wasn't a Ranger or Green Beret." Erin shook her head. She'd actually practiced martial arts since she was a child, but she had never competed in tournaments or such, even when she dabbled in MMA after the Army. "Sure, I may have a couple of black belts and know my way around a sword, but I'm not this so-called champion."

"Don't sell yourself short. I can kick my brother's ass, and I bet you could as well."

"I might enjoy that." Derek waggled his eyebrows. "But we also have someone lined up to train you for the fight."

"So if she's this champion, what's up with the Bible Thumpers?" Ray took a drag and puffed out a smoke ring. "Were they trying to off her before the duel?"

"Fortunately there are rules, otherwise they could simply take her out with a sniper." Izzy shifted on her stool. "They can't kill her, or they forfeit. But they could try to dissuade her from taking up the challenge."

"Shit!" Adrenaline returned as Erin looked at the others in alarm. "If they know who I am, could they know about my son?"

* * * * *

Chapter Four

Tim

"T immy!"

Tim Donnelly looked up from his tablet. Mrs. Adair was hard of hearing, so she practically shouted when she spoke. Fortunately, she wore headphones when she watched television, large padded ones that looked ridiculous when contrasted with her blue-grey hair and cat's-eye glasses. But she liked them because she could turn up the television as loud as she wanted without the neighbors complaining.

"Timmy, have you seen the remote?"

Tim scanned the floor, spotting the remote control on the carpet next to Mrs. Adair's overstuffed recliner. Setting aside his tablet, he retrieved the remote and handed it to her.

"Thank you, sweetie!" The old woman beamed a smile. "Did you finish your homework?"

Tim nodded, knowing she wouldn't hear his reply. He had actually finished two hours ago and had been reading up about a new game coming out. It wasn't as if his mom could afford it, or the game system required to run it, but he kept up on news about the game. Maybe one of his friends would get it and let him play.

It was lucky Mrs. Adair hardly charged anything to watch Tim while his mother worked. He'd tried to convince his mom that he was old enough to stay home alone, but at 12 she wasn't buying it. At least Mrs. Adair lived in their building and on their floor; if he needed something he could duck across the hall to their apartment.

A noise in the hall caught his attention as he retrieved his tablet. His first thought was that his mom had gotten home from work as it was about that time. He flipped on the security display next to the door, which showed the view of the camera perched on the frame above Mrs. Adair's door. Tim had installed the camera and monitor himself, cobbling it together out of salvaged electronics. His mother had insisted the maintenance guy actually hooked up the power and drilled the pass-through for the camera's cable, something about not wanting to lose her deposit if the building burnt down. Mrs. Adair had complained the peephole was too high and was hard to see through with her glasses and was overjoyed with Tim's solution. The camera let her easily see who was at her door or snoop on who was passing by in the hall.

The screen flickered to life. Instead of his mother, two strange men were at the door to his apartment. One had his back to the camera, hunched over as though he was trying to see through the keyhole. The other watched down the hall toward the stairs. Both men were dressed in khakis and button up shirts. They didn't look like criminals on the cop shows Mrs. Adair watched while she complained about the decline of society, but he had a gut feeling they were up to no good.

Tim held his breath when the lookout turned his gaze to Mrs. Adair's door. A quick glance at the old woman confirmed she was still engrossed in her show, oblivious to the outside world. Movement on the monitor caught his attention. The hunched over man was straightening up as the door swung open to Tim's apartment. Should he tell Mrs. Adair, call the cops, or call his mom? He went for his school bag and fished out his phone, then returned in time to see his mother appear on the monitor, entering the apartment.

Tim undid the chain and deadbolt, then cautiously opened the door. There was a crashing noise and muffled shouts, followed by sounds of a scuffle similar to a WWE match going on in his living room. Tim was torn between seeing what was happening and ducking back into Mrs. Adair's apartment. A few tentative steps took him to the doorway of his apartment, the door half open.

The door suddenly flung wide open, one of the men standing there clutching his face as blood seeped between his fingers. Tim shrank back as the man's wild-eyed gaze passed over him. Then his partner slammed into the man, yelping in pain and clutching an arm that looked as if it had too many joints.

"Go, go!" The man with the mangled arm snarled through gritted teeth. Neither of them seemed to notice Tim as they fled down the corridor to the stairs.

"Tim!" Mom had her handgun out and was pointing it in the direction of the escaping intruders, who had almost fallen over each other in their haste to descend the stairs.

"Mom, what's going on? Who were those men?"" He knew to stay away from her line of fire and watched as she lowered the pistol. He realized there were two more presences in the darkened apartment. "Mom, who else is with you?"

"Why don't you grab your things and tell Mrs. Adair goodnight, then I'll see what I can explain."

Tim nodded. Returning across the hall, he packed up his tablet and charger, then walked over to where Mrs. Adair could see him.

"What is it sweetie? Is your mother home?"

"Yes, Mrs. Adair." Tim gestured to the open door. Fortunately the gun wasn't visible as the old woman craned her neck to get a look into the hall where Erin waited. "Good night, Mrs. Adair."

"Good night, Timmy." She waved to Erin. "Good night, Erin."

Tim collected his bag and closed the door behind him, then followed his mother into their apartment. The coffee table and an armchair were overturned, and a lamp was in pieces on the floor. But much more interesting were the two tall, blonde, leather-clad people standing in the darkness. Their eyes reflected the light spilling in from the hall like cats' eyes, but bright blue.

* * * * *

Chapter Five

Liam

"Good morning."

The lilting musical voice cut through the fog in Liam's brain. Somehow, despite the mouth full of cotton and the head full of broken glass, Liam caught the whiff of flowers. Forcing his eyes open, he was greeted by brilliant violet eyes and a smirk.

The girl from the bookstore. Bits and pieces coalesced from his memory. She had been at his house last night. There was beer, then tequila. Now she was in his bed, and he didn't remember how either of them got there.

"Did we?" Liam managed to croak.

"You were in no shape to screw," Pixel giggled.

"Then why are you in my bed?" There were four guest rooms in the farmhouse, although a couple of them might have required excavation to use for guests as they were repositories for books and castoffs from various hobbies.

Pixel patted him on the chest. "Maybe I was hoping to pounce on some morning wood. Or maybe I wanted to make sure the key to our plan didn't choke to death on his own vomit in the middle of the night."

"I don't throw up." He caught himself watching as she slid out of his bed, wearing one of his t-shirts, and stretched. He tried not to notice as the hem of the shirt rose, exposing more of the swirling tattoos running up her right thigh.

"I need to clear my head." Liam forced himself to sit up, relieved to find he was at least wearing his boxers. He closed his eyes and let the dizziness subside before slowly standing. "I'm going to take a shower."

"Want some company?"

He tried to give the lavender-haired girl a baleful look but only managed a grimace as he shuffled toward the master bath. "There's another bathroom down the hall."

He ignored her pout as he closed the solid wood door behind himself. Blood shot eyes greeted him in the mirror as he tried to re-assemble the memories of the previous night. He contemplated the aspirin in the medicine cabinet, then decided to wait until he could brew some herbal tea downstairs. He hated to take the easy way out, and he would have rode out a mild hangover as a lesson to himself.

The shower was cold on purpose. It helped wake him up and push away any lingering slivers of memory of a warm form curled up against him. Other bits of the evening came back to him, and discussions of returning magic to the mundane world threatened to increase the pounding in his skull.

Stepping out of the shower and drying off, he wrapped a towel around himself and cracked open the door leading to his bedroom. There was no sign of Pixel, so he shucked the towel and hurriedly dressed in sweats and a t-shirt.

His head still ached, and his balance still felt a little wobbly, but the best thing would be to get some breakfast and hydration, lots of hydration. As he reached the stairs, the smell of cooking bacon wafted up to greet him. Gingerly descending the broad wooden staircase, he followed the smell to the kitchen. He wasn't really hungry, but knew he needed to get some food. Plus bacon!

"Good, you're up," Einar said from the stove, where he was managing a pair of cast iron skillets. "I was afraid she'd pocking left you for dead."

"We didn't sleep together," Liam managed to rasp.

"We did." Pixel handed Liam a glass of orange juice.

"I mean we didn't have sex."

Einar flipped pancakes onto a plate. "I don't care if you diddled her. Get your pocking head on straight."

"You said diddle." Pixel giggled.

"What is it with you two and sex?" Liam gulped the orange juice.

"He's repressed, like most dwarves."

"And she's horny like a cat in heat, like most fae." Einar slid bacon from the other pan onto a serving platter.

There was a knock on the kitchen door that led to the back porch, which then swung open half way with a loud creak. "Liam, are you decent?"

Susan Moore, one of Liam's oldest friends, poked her head around the door. Seeing Einar and Pixel, she immediately looked puzzled. "Did I come at a bad time?"

"Oh, hey Susan." Liam's mind tried to scramble through the remains of his hangover for a story to explain Pixel and Einar. He'd met Susan back during his Wiccan phase, and while many had thought they should hook up, they had never crossed that line, remaining friends over the years.

"Hi!" Pixel rounded the kitchen table. "Are you Liam's girlfriend? That'd explain why he's being such a prude. Apparently he's into bigger boobs."

Susan eyed Pixel up and down. Liam knew Susan would recognize the 'Here Come The Mummies' t-shirt that Pixel was wearing as a dress. Liam had bought the shirt at the first Mummies concert he had taken Susan to. Susan arched an eyebrow and turned toward Liam, crossing her arms. "Having a mid-life crisis?"

"What?" It took a moment for Liam's mind to catch up. "No! I didn't sleep with her."

"Technically—"

"I didn't have sex with her."

"You might as well, then you can quit pocking denying it."

"Not helping." Liam turned back to Susan. "This is really complicated. This is Pixel, and the guy wearing my aunt's apron at the stove is Einar."

"When did you get a cat?" Susan suddenly lost interest in Pixel and was looking past Liam into the dining room. Susan loved cats but couldn't have one because of her landlord. She'd tried in the past to convince Liam to get a cat so she could have one via surrogate.

"Huh? I don't have a cat."

"That's Scooter," Pixel said without looking.

Liam turned around. A chubby black and white cat was grooming himself on the huge dining room table. "Yeah, that's Scooter. He's new."

Susan passed Liam, approaching the cat cautiously. "Can I pick him up?"

Liam looked at Pixel, who shrugged. "Maybe...he might be skittish."

The cat stopped grooming to regard Susan with bright green eyes.

"Where did you get him?" Susan reached cautiously for the feline, tentatively lifting him and supporting his hind feet.

"He, um, showed up, and I kind of let him in." Liam still hadn't figured out how to explain Pixel and Einar, let alone a brownie who had apparently turned into a cat. He looked into the dining room where Susan held Scooter snuggled up to her ample bosom.

"I guess he likes boobs too," Pixel muttered.

Susan looked up from the purring cat. "So, you were going to tell me about your house guests?"

"Liam met me at his book store," Pixel offered. "He's a druid."

"Really?" Susan sounded disappointed. "Using the occult to lure in girls. I would have expected that from Potts."

"The creepy Internet pseudo-druid?" Pixel scoffed. "If he's a druid, I'm the washer-woman at the ford. Besides, Liam didn't lure me. I followed him."

"Stalked might be a better term." Liam took a drink from his orange juice.

"Alright, hotcakes are ready. You better eat up before it pocking gets cold." Einar plopped a pair of serving platters on the wooden kitchen table.

Even with the hangover, the food smelled good. "I didn't know your people were such good cooks."

Einar stripped off the apron and hung it over the back of the chair. He was still wearing the jeans and wife beater he'd had on under his biker leathers yesterday. Liam was grateful he couldn't smell him over the aroma of breakfast; it might have wrecked what little appetite he had. "You can't work a forge all day on an empty belly, and cooking isn't so different from smelting. You mix ingredients to the right proportions, then heat them up just right."

Susan cradled Scooter in one arm as she pulled out a chair. "So Pixel followed Liam home from the bookstore? Not at all creepy." She turned to Einar. "How do you know Liam?"

Einar's busy eyebrows shot up as he looked from Liam to Pixel.

"He's my uncle." Pixel pulled plates off a stack, setting one in front of herself and one in front of Liam. With a spatula, she doled out hotcakes to both plates. "He's a prude and was afraid I'd take advantage of poor Liam."

"Really? You take advantage of him?" The corner of Susan's mouth crooked down in skepticism. In Susan's lap, Scooter stirred and sniffed toward the bacon, his nose twitching. Liam wondered if Susan's vegetarianism would keep her from feeding the cat.

"Ja. He's uptight as shite and can't hold his liquor." Einar loaded his own plate. Scooter's gaze followed as Einar added bacon alongside his hotcakes. "She would have rode him like pocking Sleipnir if the tequila hadn't put him down for the count." Einar looked up to find everyone staring at him in awkward silence. "Syrup?"

"Gods, please, yes." Liam reached for the offered pitcher. As he poured the maple syrup on his pancakes, he muttered to himself. A memory from last night was trying to surface through the haze of his hangover. "Gods, gods, there was something about…"

A deep gonging noise shook the whole house. The glasses and plates in the cabinets rattled. Susan somehow managed not to dump the cat from her lap when she jumped, while Liam's fogged brain was trying to parse how the heck they were having an earthquake in the middle of Illinois. The New Madrid fault? There had been a lot of talk a decade or so previously about it.

"Gofannon's here," Einar said, skewering a slice of pancakes. "You had better let him in before he gets impatient and tests your wards."

Liam got up, instinctively heading for the front foyer. Through the old lace curtains, he could see a silhouette on the porch, the outline looking as though Einar had been blown up to seven feet tall. He was dimly aware of Susan following him as the front door boomed as though struck with a battering ram.

Liam threw open the stout oak door. The door frame was filled by a huge muscular man clad in a dark grey tunic and scorched leather apron, his black beard gathered in a pair of braids, and his long hair pulled back. Flint grey eyes peered down, seemingly unaware of the smoke rising from his skin. Liam heard Susan gasp.

Liam remembered yesterday's demonstration with the wards. Unlike Einar, the newcomer wasn't being pushed back. Liam wasn't sure if it was a result of relative mass or due to whatever power the new arrival had. "Please come in!" The smoke ceased, and the huge man strode through the door.

"You are the Druid!" The hulking man bellowed, clapping Liam on both shoulders. "Gofannon is pleased to meet you, Cathbadson!"

The thunderous voice had brought back Liam's hangover-induced headache, but he tried to smile instead of wince. "A pleasure to meet you, Gofannon. Welcome to my home." He extended his hand.

Gofannon looked down at the proffered hand, then seized it and pulled Liam into a back-pounding hug. "Good! Druid offers hospitality."

"Oi! Gofannon, get in here if you want some pocking breakfast!" Einar called from the kitchen.

Gofannon strode past, following the smells of breakfast. Susan grabbed Liam on his shoulder, still tender from the greeting. "Liam, what the hells?"

Liam could hear Gofannon exchanging pleasantries with those in the kitchen. He wondered if his neighbors could hear, they were only half a mile away. "Susan, that is Gofannon."

"Yeah, I heard. All of Eureka probably heard." She gestured toward the kitchen. "But who is he, along with your new girlfriend and her ZZ Top uncle?"

"You don't understand, and I know it's hard to believe; heck, I needed a bottle of tequila to bludgeon it into my brain. That is Gofannon, as in the Welsh aspect of the Celtic smith god."

"Bullshit."

"Do you believe in the gods?"

The question brought Susan up short. She had professed belief in the myriad of cultural gods as long as Liam had known her. "You're not saying that he is *the* Gofannon, the Welsh smith god from the Mabinogion."

"And he's sitting down for breakfast in my kitchen. Or at least some sort of physical incarnation of him is; I'm not exactly sure. I never expected to have to reconcile my beliefs regarding the gods with a physical presence pounding on my front door. Last night was kind of an info dump over a lot of booze." Liam headed back toward the kitchen. Gofannon had helped himself to Liam's plate and was digging in heartily. At least pancakes kept him from bellowing. Liam grabbed a chair from the dining room and pulled it to the end of the kitchen table.

"This is some sort of game or something, right?" Susan asked as she followed him, still holding Scooter, who gazed longingly at the platter of bacon. "Like that LARP those college kids and old hippies play out in Rutledge Woods?"

Liam scooped hotcakes and bacon onto his new plate. "So, how do you guys want to explain this?"

"She's not your girlfriend?" Pixel asked, scrutinizing Susan. Her eyes had the weird lambent glow. He wondered if his wards would protect Susan from glamours, or if they only applied to him.

"No, but she's one of my best friends, if not my best friend." It wasn't the first time someone had thought Susan was his girlfriend; she took such assumptions in stride. "I trust her."

Einar swallowed a mouthful of pancakes. "Is she a pocking Avramite?"

"No, she's a Wiccan and has been as long as I've known her."

"The Druid speaks for her." Gofannon scarfed down another mouthful of bacon. "It is good enough."

"Mrreow."

"Well, since Scooter agrees." Pixel shrugged, turning back to her breakfast. "As long as she can keep a secret."

"Right, she's not going to put this up on that Twit Book or whatever Internet shite these dunnies blather on," Einar grumbled, returning to his pancakes.

"You can't breathe a word of this, Susan." Liam fixed his gaze on her. "I'm serious. This sounds nuts, I know, but I'm dead serious."

Susan returned to her seat. From her lap, Scooter stretched out a paw toward the bacon, falling several inches short. "What? Okay, fine." She pulled a couple of strips from the pile and set them in the cat's reach, then wiped off her fingers. "I promise I won't tell anyone, though from what I'm getting, no one would believe me."

"The wrong people would," Pixel said. "Dangerous people."

"Yes, the Avramites must not learn of this plan." Gofannon emptied half the bacon onto his cleared plate. Though his voice was still deep and loud, at least he was no longer bellowing. Also, his accent, which had been thick enough to cut with a knife, had abated a bit. "They already suspect."

"Suspect what?"

"In a nutshell," Liam explained, "there was once a lot more magic in the world, and the old gods and their folk dwelt in the mortal world, the Dunwold as they call it. Then the Abrahamic powers and their followers moved in and tried to push out the Folk of the old gods by war." Liam paused, only to realize Gofannon had also drank his orange juice. "Both sides decided to settle it by a battle of champions; the Folk were outsmarted and lost."

Liam was acutely aware that Gofannon had stopped eating and was staring at him, but forged on. "There's a provision in the agreement that allows the Folk to challenge the Abrahamic, the Avramites, after enough time has passed. Another match up, champion versus champion."

"Oh, and I suppose you're supposed to be this champion?" Liam tried not to let Susan's sarcastic tone ruffle his feathers. Einar stifled a chuckle with pancakes.

"No, he is the Druid." Gofannon clapped Liam on the back. "The Druid is as important to our challenge as the Champion."

"There's all sort of rules and rituals tied up in the whole Milesian Accords." Liam wondered if his spine was bruised. "Plus there's some prophecy in the mix that says it needs to be a druid of a particular bloodline, and the champion needs to be of a particular bloodline for the new challenge to succeed. That's where I fit in, my many-times removed ancestor was the progenitor of the druid bloodline."

"What about this champion?" Susan's tone was still doubtful. "Where's he?"

"She's not here yet." Pixel got up and poured a glass of orange juice, bringing it to Liam. She patted him on the shoulder as she set it down, watching Susan as she did.

"Well, at least this insane prophecy is egalitarian." From her lap, Scooter thumped the empty space in front of him with his paw. "Goddess, Liam. Haven't you been feeding this cat?"

"He loves bacon."

"Who doesn't love bacon?" Einar forked some of the dwindling pile of meat onto his plate.

"Me, for one. I'm a vegetarian." Despite her statement, she retrieved two more strips for Scooter.

"Vegetarian? What in Jotunn's Pox is that?" Einar asked around a mouthful of bacon.

"It means I don't eat meat."

"Prophecy does not care if you eat meat." Gofannon belched loudly.

"Egalitarian is not the same as vegetarian," Pixel remarked as she took her seat. "Egalitarian means that it doesn't discriminate based on gender. Such as the champion being a woman."

"Why would that matter?" Gofannon patted his apron over his belly. "And I learned this English language only a week ago."

Liam managed to scavenge the last couple of hotcakes. "Gofannon has to teach me how to make the sword the champion is going to use for her duel."

"Well, at least you didn't build that workshop in the back of your garage for nothing." Susan stroked behind Scooter's ears, eliciting a purr. "I mean, you ended up making what, half a dozen swords?"

"What?" Gofannon sat up straight, the chair creaking as his weight shifted. "He has only made six swords?"

"Probably more like five and a half." Liam snagged the last of the bacon. "The first one had a flaw; I'm thinking some impurities caused the end of the blade to break off."

Gofannon turned to look accusingly at Einar. "You said he was an apprentice smith. An apprentice would have made half of a hundred swords."

"I said he was like an apprentice." Einar wiped bacon grease and maple syrup from his moustache. "I told you he would need a lot of training in a pocking hurry."

Gofannon glared at the dwarf with grey eyes, clenching his fists.

"That's why we needed you, Gofannon." Pixel batted her eyes at the hulking smith-god. "If anyone has the skill to do it in time, it would be you."

Gofannon looked mollified, leaving Liam to wonder if her whammy worked on gods—at least their physical forms—or if Gofannon was a sucker for flattery.

Gofannon leaned back in his chair, causing it to creak. "I suppose you are correct. No offense to Volundr, Einar, but if any smith can tutor our druid in the time we have, it is I."

* * * * *

Chapter Six

Lee

"You lost them?"

"Yes." Pastor Haskins was unsure what honorific to use, so he used none. He looked down to keep from meeting the speaker's gaze. Even so, Haskins could feel his fury.

"Your men were given a simple task, Lee." Mikha'el rose from his seat, a makeshift throne behind a dark wood desk that dominated the dimly lit office. "You assured me they were up to this task."

Haskins gulped, still looking down. "It seemed a simple task." He bit back the 'my lord' he almost added on. It seemed sacrilegious. "Grab a waitress and her son, bring them to you. Simple. But she beat the shit out of four men, and then two more who were to grab her son. My contacts are looking for her, but the same factors keeping my men out of jail keep her from wider suspicion as well."

"The answer is simple." Mikha'el stepped forward from the shadows behind the desk. His brilliant blue-white eyes had a cold light of their own. "Sacrifice one or more of your men."

"Sacrifice them?"

Mikha'el sighed, a very human gesture, and took a step closer. Haskins resisted the urge to retreat. The Servant of the Lord had six inches on the pastor. Even though Mikha'el wore what looked like

71

the finest of Italian suits, there was no mistaking the powerful form underneath. "Yes. She shot and killed one."

Pastor Haskins could feel the heat of Mikha'el's presence and sweat beaded on his brow. "But she didn't even shoot at them, she only threatened them."

"Lee, do I really have to spell it out for you?" Mikha'el's anger rose palpably. "Kill one or more of your men. Frame her. Let the secular authorities do the legwork to bring her in. If she's in jail, she cannot accomplish her mission, and we win."

Haskins wilted from the blazing anger, no longer able to stand his ground. The gloomy office offered little space to withdraw. "But, but that means murdering one of our own. Isn't that a sin?"

"It is no sin to die in His Glory. You chose your men because of their...less than sterling characters. If nothing else, this will ensure their entrance to Heaven." Mikha'el withdrew back to his throne, the anger on his otherwise chiseled features abating. "Unless of course you think you cannot make good on our bargain. What the Lord has given, the Lord can take away. Cancer is such a horrible road to take to Heaven, full of suffering. With it in remission, your wife can remain with you for a long time. How long had your doctors, with their science, given her? Mere months?"

"I'll get it worked out, we'll find the heathen *benayim*." Lee practically fled the Servitor of the Lord's presence, shaking as he left the office for the large darkened room outside. His mind was reeling as he skirted the dusty stage dominating the center of the room, tracking the exit by a flickering, illuminated sign.

Detaining a couple of people a short while to keep them from interfering in the Faith; that was one thing. But killing his own people in cold blood, how could he order such a thing? And even if he did, would his men obey? He'd have to find another way, for Christine's sake. If his men could succeed without drastic measures, surely Mikha'el would be pleased. If they could kill the heretic champion—the *benayim* as Mikha'el had called her—it would make the task so much easier. While Lee balked at the idea of murdering his own men, trading the life of an enemy of God so Christine would be spared was totally acceptable. But when Lee had initially broached the idea, Mikha'el's rage had been terrifying. There was some sacred proscription against utilizing the most expedient means.

Once outside and in his truck, Lee pulled out his phone, bringing up a contact, and dialed. "Jimmy? It's Pastor Lee. You got any more info for me?"

"Pastor?" the man on the other end of the line moaned. Jimmy was one of the group that was supposed to grab the waitress. "Darn if we didn't run into an army."

"What do you mean? You said the waitress kicked your asses."

"Yeah, but Mark and Jeremy said there were others at the apartment when they tried to grab the kid."

Haskins wiped his hand across his forehead. "Why didn't you tell me this last night?"

"I dunno, everything was still kind of fuzzy when I talked to you." Jimmy paused. "Now that I think about it, there were a couple with her in the parking lot, when we tried to grab her. They didn't help her during the fight; they might have shown up right afterward. Noah called them fairies, I figured because they looked all metro and done up in black leather."

Haskins leaned back in the truck seat. Some of the *nukraya*, the heathen alien minions of exiled pagan gods, had come up from the underworld. Lee had been told about them; they were perversions of the Nephilim and angels. Noah knew a lot more about the subject, so he had probably figured out what they were. The *nukraya* had been sent from the underworld to help the *benayim*, as well as to aid someone referred to as a druid, or *hartummin*. Lee missed the days when he thought angels dwelled in Heaven, demons lurked in Hell, and only Man walked the Earth.

"By the way, Pastor Haskins, it would have been helpful to know she's some kind of fucking ninja." Jimmy said something unintelligible to someone in the background.

Lee Haskins looked back at the building where Mikha'el held court, a rundown former strip club. He really didn't want to go back in there without some good news. "Were any of you seriously hurt? I'm talking life threatening, something we could use to get the police looking for her?"

"A broken arm, some cracked ribs, a messed up knee," Jimmy replied. "It would be kind of hard to go to the cops and complain how this one waitress messed up four of us."

Lee mulled Mikha'el's order. Faking someone getting shot in the scuffle at this late juncture would be a lot harder than the Servant of the Lord understood. Mikha'el was powerful, but his experience in dealing with mundane matters was lacking. There were a lot of considerations if they wanted to frame the waitress for shooting one of the boys. They'd have to make sure there was no contradictory security footage, figure out how to fake ballistics, how to pin the gun on her. Who would get shot.

"We think she's left town. Her car is still sitting where it was last night, at the bar, with the tires slashed." Jimmy paused and conferred with someone in the background again. "But last night the boys saw a black Dodge Charger they had never seen before while casing the apartment building. It's gone now. We're thinking the fairies had the Charger."

Lee's spirits rose with a spark of hope. "Did you get the license plate number?"

"Sorry, pastor. The boys were in kind of a hurry when they lit out of there last night."

"Okay, since we have an idea of where they are heading, it's still a help." Lee began scrolling through his contacts. "I know someone with some pull in the state police; we can get them to be on the lookout for the car and the woman."

* * * * *

Chapter Seven

Erin

"Where are we?"

"We just passed Indianapolis," Derek answered glumly. "Don't worry, you didn't miss anything."

Erin yawned and stretched, careful not to disturb Tim. He dozed against the door on the opposite side of the back seat of the Dodge Charger. What they had hurriedly packed had been tossed in the trunk of the car. Izzy had assured her it would be over a month before the landlord got curious about the rent, but Erin got the feeling she wouldn't be going back to the apartment.

She also hadn't asked where Derek and Izzy had gotten the car. It looked almost new and well cared for, a car that if stolen would quickly be reported. Fortunately, Izzy had kept to 5 miles over the speed limit, slow enough to not attract any attention.

"How long?" Erin squinted, trying to gauge the height of the sun behind them. They had left Cincinnati at almost six in the morning and Izzy had taken them down several country roads before getting onto I-70 toward Indianapolis. Erin guessed it was around 8:30.

"Sooner if my sister didn't drive like an old woman," Derek muttered.

"If we drove straight there, about two and a half hours." Izzy looked at her in the rearview mirror. "But we don't want to drive straight there. Plus we'll need a pit stop."

"So if this druid is so important and powerful, why does he live in Peoria?" Parts of the discussion while packing last night came back to Erin.

"For the same reason we found you in Cincinnati. People destined for greatness rarely start off in some place awesome." Izzy smiled at her in the mirror, eyes hidden behind sunglasses. "Like you, he has a lot of work to do to realize his potential. Unlike you, his home is hard to divine."

"Hard to divine? What, they're going to look for him with an Ouija board and Tarot cards?"

"It means despite his amateur status, this druid has actually managed to tap into some power and ward his dwelling." Derek turned back to face Erin. "It cannot be found by supernatural means. In fact, creatures not of the Dunwold cannot even enter his home without his permission. For someone with no training, his mystical defenses are quite impressive."

"Hence the detours," Izzy added. "So we don't lead the Avramites to him the old-fashioned way."

"If he's so hard to find, how did you find him?" Timmy muttered groggily. He slowly sat up and rubbed sleep from his eyes.

"Because we've had people watching his family since we faked his great-grandfather's death and made it look as though the branch of the family ended," Izzy replied. "With any luck, they are expecting us to meet with some distant cousin in Toronto."

"So what happens once we meet this druid?" Last night Erin had been more concerned about what needed to happen to get Tim out of harm's way. Despite her fatigue, she was now trying to think forward.

"We need to touch base with his team and talk about the next step." Izzy had returned her attention to the road. "No point in getting ahead of ourselves if something else has happened to toss our plans in the bog."

"I don't suppose our druid is like those Hellenic American druid fellows we met in Columbus?" Derek chuckled throatily. "They were quite accommodating. Open to new experiences, if you know what I mean."

"What does that mean?" Tim asked.

Derek caught Erin's baleful glare as he looked back toward Tim. "It means they were friendly and open to different points of view."

Erin held her breath, letting it out when Tim let the question drop and turned back to watch the passing cornfields and billboards. She wasn't sure if he pieced together Derek's implications, but she knew her son was smarter than most people gave him credit for.

Erin spotted the sign for a travel stop, a combination truck stop/restaurant/travel store. "There's a good place for a pit stop. Tim, are you hungry?"

Tim nodded against the window.

"Too busy, too many people." Izzy nodded toward the approaching exit. "We'll take the next one, then parallel on U.S. 136. There will be a gas station and a convenience store in Lizton."

"What, you memorized the route?" Erin hoped it wouldn't be too long before the gas station. She needed coffee, among other things.

Derek held up his phone. "Google Maps. My sister may be taking us on a tour of Podunk Midwest, but Google is everywhere."

Tim perked up, peering at the phone. "How come he gets to have a phone?"

Tim and Erin had both been instructed to leave their phones, wrapped in aluminum foil and with the batteries removed, back at the apartment. That had led to a half hour argument with Tim, who only relented when he was allowed to save data from his phone to the SD card he could take with him.

"Because the people looking for you don't have my account information to track me through the cell towers." Derek peered over his sunglasses. "If you're good, maybe I'll let you use my phone's wifi to connect your tablet to the webs."

"You mean use your phone as a mobile hotspot to make an Internet connection." Tim crossed his arms. "Define good."

"First of all, no snotty correcting me about Dunnie techno-babble." Derek pushed his glasses back up. "No whining, no complaining, and do what your mother tells you."

"Deal." Tim looked closely at the phone's screen. "And let me guess, no programs or apps that require location services."

Derek cocked his head toward Izzy.

"Correct," Izzy said. "In fact, my brother should let you set it up. It will be a lot less frustrating for everyone. But do it after our pit stop."

"So no Monster Hunters." Tim leaned against the window. "And that wasn't a whine, it was a statement. Monster Hunters requires you to sync your account with your GPS location."

"You said this druid has a team. How many people does he have?" Erin hoped it was a lot, based on the siblings' paranoia.

"Besides the Druid, three," Izzy replied. "Four if the big guy has arrived."

"That's not much of a team." Erin quickly tallied six men who had already come after her and Tim. She was hoping for better odds.

Izzy shrugged behind the wheel. "Too many folk crossing over to the Dunwold would risk attention, especially since we have a *deiw*, what you might call a god, crossing over."

"He's not much of a god," Derek added. "Gobain, even in his various incarnations, is pretty obscure. Even a lot of so-called pagans don't know of him."

"But he has the specific expertise we need for this mission." Izzy paused to watch a van with a plumber's logo and contact information in faded paint pass on the left. "I'm pretty sure this incarnation is Gofannon, his old Welsh aspect."

Derek snorted. "He doesn't get top billing, like Thor or Apollo. He's not in comic books or movies, and he's not one of the cool gods or goddess, like you-know-who."

"Who?" Tim appeared to have forgotten about Monster Hunters.

"If I wanted to say her name, I would have." Derek lowered his voice. "But I don't want her to hear me and realize I'm not one of her tragically want-to-be-hip Wiccan fan boys."

"Don't let her hear you talk like that; she'll have crows peck your eyes out." Izzy pointed at an upcoming sign. "Here's our exit, the town is a couple of minutes from the interstate."

Two minutes later they were pulling into a gas station with Nascar logos on the canopy, and a live bait sign planted in the grass alongside the road. While Izzy took care of gassing the car, Erin and Tim went inside. The building was fairly modern, with actual public restrooms as opposed to the key-locked roach box she had feared. At least the facilities looked as though they had been cleaned in the last day, maybe two.

After taking care of business, Erin went in search of the coffee smell that had greeted them. Spying the coffee and drink station, she bee-lined for caffeine. Filling the largest cup, Erin looked around for Tim. She found him hunched over in the snack aisle, poring over short cans of Pringles, his hands already full of junk food.

She resisted the urge to admonish him. He was tired, hungry, and probably scared. A little junk food wouldn't hurt him, but he shouldn't eat himself sick, especially on a road trip. "Tim, do you really think an armload of junk food is a good breakfast? Maybe you should pick a couple and have something more substantial."

Tim looked over at the hot food counter, where wrapped breakfast sandwiches languished under heat lamps. "I wouldn't vouch for their food safety, Mom. We don't know when the next pit stop will be. This is to last a while, not just breakfast."

"Fine, but don't waste money on those half cans." Erin picked up a full can of crisps and handed it Tim. "Here, we can share."

"Excuse me, ma'am?"

Erin turned at the deep voice, years of dealing with asshole customers helping her keep her face a mask of pleasantness. A state trooper, complete with hat and mirrored sunglasses, stood behind her. "Yes?"

The trooper nodded toward the gas pumps. "Are you in that black Dodge Charger?"

Erin nodded. If he was asking, he already knew, she thought. Options whirred through her mind as her pulse quickened.

"Your right front tire is low, you might want to get that looked at. It can be a stretch between pockets of civilization out here." He touched the brim of his hat. "Have a nice day."

"Thank you, officer." She watched as the trooper passed Derek and Izzy without even reacting to them. With their sunglasses, she couldn't see if they were watching the trooper or not. Letting out a breath, she tried to calm her racing pulse.

Tim looked up at her. She could tell he wanted to ask questions, but knew better than to do so here. She grabbed another can of Pringles, a bagel which didn't look too stale, and a banana that was mostly yellow, juggling them with her coffee. "Let's go check out."

Tim nodded, silently following her to the register, where he piled his haul of junk food on the counter.

"On a bit of a road trip?" the worn woman behind the checkout rasped. Her nametag had 'Joan' on the label, which was peeling at one end. She looked like she'd eaten more than her share of junk food and desperately needed a cigarette. "Where you folks headed?"

"Toronto," Tim piped up before Erin could answer.

"That's nice." She didn't say anything else as she scanned the pile into a pair of plastic bags, save for Erin's coffee and Tim's Mountain Dew. "That'll be $23.47."

An advantage of being a waitress, most of her money was actual cash. Erin had already been warned against using her credit cards on their trip. Counting out the exact change, Erin handed one of the bags to Tim.

"Have a nice day," Joan rasped, scraping the change into her hand.

"Thanks, you too." Erin picked up the other bag and her coffee and led Tim back out to the car. A state police patrol car pulled out onto the road and headed north back toward the interstate. Erin looked, and the front right tire was low, not quite flat.

"We'll air it up before we hit the road," Izzy said behind her, causing her to jump and almost spill her precious coffee. "Probably caught a nail or something."

"Maybe you don't need that coffee." Derek grinned as he passed her. "You're jumpy enough."

While Izzy rolled the car over to the air pump and fed it quarters, Erin watched Tim pick through his haul, pulling out a package of Twinkies and some beef jerky to go with his Mountain Dew.

"You're not going to be napping after that." Erin glanced up at the sun. "Hopefully, later on we can get some real lunch."

Tim smiled, because on a road trip 'real food' meant something like McDonalds as opposed to macaroni and cheese. But as much as Erin knew Tim would appreciate the change of menu, their money wouldn't hold out long eating fast food and gas station snacks.

"We'll probably reach our destination around lunch time," Izzy announced as they turned onto U.S. 136, heading west. "We might stop for more solid food, or at least hit a grocery store to bring in provisions. If it's any consolation, all of this is as big of a surprise to the Druid as you, Erin. No one expected this."

* * * * *

Chapter Eight

Liam

"This is terrible."

"It's not that bad," Liam protested, clicking on the light over the workshop in the back of his garage. He turned back to Gofannon. "I've made swords here before. The forge and smelter are outside in their own building so I don't burn the whole house down. These are the grinders and the woodworking gear I use for the hilts."

Gofannon looked across the chaotic array of machines and tools, shaking his head. "I recognize nothing. Much has changed."

"Well sure, a lot of tasks which were done by hand you can do with machines a lot quicker and easier." Liam led the smith-god past a belt-grinder to where his finished swords hung on the back wall. "But the end result is the same."

"You know how to use all this pocking crap?" Einar asked, following Gofannon. "It looks well used."

"Yeah, well, most of it was well used when I got it." Liam took down one of the swords. "I do okay with what the family left me and my salary, but some of my hobbies haven't been cheap."

"Especially when you keep picking new ones," Einar said.

"True. I'll be the first to admit I've had trouble sticking to things." Liam handed the sword, hilt first, to Gofannon. "That's the second one I made."

The sword looked like a toy in the smith's hands as he turned it over and looked down the length of the blade. In the dim lighting, his eyes glowed like smoldering coals as he took the end of the blade in one hand while holding the hilt in the other. When he flexed the blade, a spider web of red cracks appeared along it, then the blade snapped. Sighing, he handed the hilt and broken blade back.

Liam suppressed a flash of anger, reminding himself who he was dealing with. He set aside the pieces of the shattered sword and took another one off the wall. "This was the third one I made."

Again the glowing eyes and the testing flex. This one showed fewer glowing red fault-lines, but after a bit longer the metal gave way. Einar winced as Gofannon shook his head.

"This is the last blade I made." Liam picked it up from where it leaned against the wall, the last in line. "I, um, never got around to making a hilt for it."

Gofannon took the proffered blade. This time the blade showed a few flecks of red but didn't snap. The god peered down its length again, then sniffed it. "Dwarf, are you familiar with this steel?"

Einar sniffed at the blade, then ran his finger along it and licked the tip of his finger. "It's some modern dunnie alloy."

"It's high-carbon steel sandwiched with a nickel-steel alloy." Liam was relieved to see at least one blade had survived. "I actually had to go to a metal shop to do the pattern welding, since I don't have a powered drop-hammer."

"Why not?" Gofannon was still studying the blade.

"They're expensive, even used, and not exactly easy to find." Liam had heard of eBay and Craigslist but had never used them. It seemed too easy to get ripped off.

"I'll get Pixel on it," Einar said in response to Gofannon's glance. "She knows all this pocking modern online crap."

"How did you learn?" Gofannon handed the blade back to Liam.

"I took a couple of classes, watched some videos, and then tried it out." Liam set the blade down on the closest workbench, regretting he had never hilted the sword. "Over the course of a year, I made these, and a couple others. My first one snapped, another I gave to a friend for ceremonial use."

"It is a shame you did not keep working," Gofannon said. "In a few years you could be a decent smith."

"I'm guessing we don't have a few years."

Einar shook his head.

"Then it is good I will teach you." Gofannon looked around. "So show me your forge and anvil."

Liam led them through a side door to a small cinder block building surrounded by gravel. Opposite sides of the building had large metal doors. Once Liam swung them open, a cool breeze began to pass through, taking away some of the summer heat. Inside was Liam's forging and smelting gear, as well as a pair of anvils, one made from a slice of railroad track and the other a traditional looking anvil.

"Much better." Gofannon gazed across the setup, his arms crossed. "You built this?"

"Mostly. I had a couple of guys help me with the roof in exchange for steaks and cold beer."

"A currency I can understand," Einar said approvingly.

"It'll take me a few days to get everything up and running." Liam brushed dust and ash from the lip of the forge.

"Why so long?" Gofannon looked puzzled.

"I'll have to do it around work. I don't have another day off for six days." Liam looked at his watch. "In fact, I need to be going in about an hour."

"We don't have time for that," Einar said. "You'll have to quit your job. Your boss is an ass-boil from what Pixel said, so it's just as well."

"He is an ass-boil, but I need to pay the bills." Liam looked across the fields surrounding his farmhouse. "The rent I get for the acreage doesn't make ends meet, and it's not as if jobs are plentiful around here."

"You have new job now," Gofannon rumbled. "You are Druid."

"That's not exactly a paying gig."

"Yes it is," Einar countered. "If I understand right, it's pocking good pay."

Liam froze. "What do you mean? No one said anything about pay last night. Or did they? The last half of the tequila bottle is pretty damned fuzzy."

"Well no, we didn't discuss it last night." Einar dragged a finger through the dust on the anvil. "We didn't want you to take the job for the gold. We wanted you to do it because it's your destiny."

"Gold?" Liam's head swam. Even if they gave him a pile of gold, he couldn't walk into the First Peoria Bank with a handful of gold and not raise questions, lots of questions.

"Ja. Your weight in gold to make the challenge, then a twentieth of that per year you remain First Druid, then half as much per year once you retire."

Gofannon nodded. "Druid is important job."

"So there's more, even after the challenge?" Liam leaned against a cinderblock wall. "Assuming your champion actually wins."

"If she loses, we're all probably pocking dead."

Gofannon nodded again.

"What's there to do after the challenge? I mean, the Exiled Folk win, they come back if they want. What do you need me for?"

"As the First Druid, you will be, how do you say, arbiter for magical matters." Gofannon clapped Liam on the shoulder. "And there will need to be someone to teach other druids. It is a great honor."

"It sounds like a long commitment." Liam had the feeling the Tuatha weren't the only ones to get hosed by the fine print. How could he teach others when he barely grasped what was going on, himself?

"Look, Pixel knows more about that end of things. Me, I need enough money in my pocket to cover dinner and a few stout drinks." Einar turned to Gofannon. "Can you believe they have money made of pocking parchment?"

"Probably something they got from the Romans." Gofannon shook his head. "Maybe the Druid should speak to Pixel so we can get on with things."

* * * * *

Chapter Nine

Tim

"**A**re we there yet?"

"Tim, does it look like we're there?" his mother replied.

Tim stifled a sigh. A sigh might count as complaining and revoke his access to Derek's hotspot. Even if he couldn't play Monster Hunters, there were other games to keep his mind from the tedium of cornfields and more cornfields, punctuated by the occasional farmhouse or dilapidated barn. They'd left the interstate again and were paralleling it on what was generously called a highway.

"We're about 15 minutes from the turn-off at 117," Izzy said. "After that, it's about 5 minutes to Eureka."

"Pizza Hut or Uncle Roy's Ice Cream Parlor?" Derek looked up from his phone and waggled his eyebrows. "I wouldn't try Uncle Roy's special of the day, if you know what I mean."

Izzy sighed and Mom shook her head. Tim considered asking what Derek meant, but figured he'd get another vague non-answer.

"I like pizza." Tim didn't often get to have pizza, and when he did it was usually the school lunch version of it. He wanted real pizza with gooey cheese and a crunchy crust, not that flat, bland school lunch pizza that looked as though it was run over by a truck. "Please, Mom?"

91

"Given how appetizing Derek made the ice cream place sound, we might as well."

"We'll also pass a Subway at the intersection with 117, though I think it's one of those shops built into a gas station," Izzy offered.

"Ooh, foot longs." Again with the eyebrow waggling.

Tim held his tongue. Pizza sounded so much better than a sandwich, but he was afraid if he pleaded his case too hard it would steer his mom in the other direction.

"That does sound healthier," his mother conceded. Tim's heart started to sink. "But if we went to Pizza Hut, you could buy pizza for this druid and his team. Seems like the polite thing to do."

"Pizza Hut it is then. Derek, why don't you text Pixel and let her know we'll bring them pizza? Find out if anyone has any preferences."

"Hopefully Einar doesn't already have a side of beast spitted over an open fire." Derek tapped at his phone, then waited expectantly for the chime announcing a response a couple of minutes later. "She likes that idea. Someone there is a vegetarian, so we should take that into account."

Izzy sighed. "No one said anything about the Druid being a granola crystal-waver. If he's a new-age fluffy bunny we might as well turn around."

"Is he vegan or vegetarian?" Tim remembered one of his friends at school had a sister who had suddenly announced she was vegan. She was proud of the fact that she wouldn't eat anything that came from an animal. He stopped going over to the friend's house for dinner, as it was either something bland or his friend's sister yelling how no one cared about her feelings or the planet. Going home to a

A RELUCTANT DRUID | 93

pot pie or peanut butter and jelly was a lot less fuss. "If he's vegan he probably won't want pizza because of cheese."

Derek texted and quickly received a response. "Cheese is fine, and no, it's not the Druid who is a vegetarian. He eats meat but she doesn't know yet if he eats…oh my. We should pick up some booze if we can. Beer, tequila, and if possible something flammable."

Izzy shook her head. "Einar."

"Who's Einar?" Tim suspected he wasn't the vegetarian. At least pizza hadn't been vetoed.

"A boozing dwarf from Asgard, which I know is redundant." Derek sniffed. "Lacking in manners and hygiene, though he is into leather and a passable cook."

"If he's a dwarf, wouldn't he be from Nidavellir?" Tim had read a few books on the Norse myths after seeing Thor at the movies. He'd found the writers of the movies had taken a great deal of artistic license with Norse legends.

"I use Asgard to refer to the Nine Worlds as bound by Yggdrasil." Derek held his slender hand up, spreading the fingers like branches. He wiggled a pinky. "Nidavellir is one of those worlds."

"My son is well read." Erin looked over at Tim proudly. "Even better read than I knew."

"So is the Druid's team like a sports team, or is it like in an online first-person shooter game?" Tim was eager for the subject to be something besides himself. "You know, where different people have different roles to play in a fight."

"You're not supposed to be playing those kinds of games, Tim." The proud smile evaporated; disapproval was heavy in his mother's voice. It's not as if he could play those games often. They couldn't afford a gaming system or computer good enough to run them, not to mention his neighbors might notice the increased bandwidth in their wireless networks. Helping a few of them set up their networks meant he had their network passwords, and he tried to spread around what bandwidth he borrowed, but a game would suck up too much.

"The latter is closer, or one of the groups used in Realms of Quests, but not quite the same. I assume you're familiar with Realms of Quests?" Derek waited for Tim's nod, then he continued, "In the online game, things fall pretty evenly across the team members. In this case, picture the Druid as the tank, the one who has to square off against the boss monster. In this case, the job of everyone else on the team is to ensure the tank succeeds."

"That sounds more like the Champion. She's the one who will have to do the fighting." Izzy cast a glance at her brother. "And since when did you play online games?"

"Do you have any idea how many over-compensating repressed closet-cases there are in online games? I can't resist trolling them." Derek waggled his eyebrows. "I know the analogy isn't perfect. I'm framing it in reference to the Druid and the Folk working with him."

Izzy sighed, then looked at Tim in the mirror. "The druid has a mission, and it's his team's job to make sure he has what he needs to succeed. Just like we're your mother's team."

"Only two people?" Tim looked from Izzy to Derek. "Doesn't seem like much of a team. No offense."

"Out of the mouths of babes," Derek chuckled.

"You're on your mother's team also," Izzy said.

"Really?" Tim perked up. So far he'd felt like a coincidental passenger swept along by events. "What's my job?"

"To make sure your mother doesn't have to worry about you." Derek actually sounded serious.

Tim slumped back to the seat. That didn't sound fun. He didn't voice his opinion; Derek had a broad notion of what constituted whining.

"I know it sounds boring, sweetie, but it is important." His mother turned to Derek. "Besides, it's only for a little bit, right?"

"Only a few months."

"A few months!" Erin looked from Derek to Izzy. "I can't afford a few months. I can't really afford a few days, but Jesus lunatics are after us."

"He doesn't have anything to do with it," Izzy said.

"He who?" Mom was getting worked up into a rant, but it seemed derailed. Tim had used the same change-the-subject tactic in the past with mixed results.

"Jesus. Despite what many so-called Christians claim, he isn't party to this conflict."

Derek nodded in agreement. "Fortunately, the people who fervently believe in Yeshua and his precepts are not the ones using his name to justify their bullshit."

"So Jesus is real?" A lot of Tim's friends believed so, then again a few years ago they believed in Santa Claus. While he had outgrown Santa Claus, he was still making up his mind on the whole God and Jesus thing. He'd read the Bible and found it frustrating.

"In the same manner as the other gods, yes." Izzy looked in the mirror again. "But there is a difference between the historical Yeshua of Nazareth and the god-form Jesus."

"What do you—" Tim felt an icy cold panic. His attention was drawn ahead. "STOP!"

The car slewed on screeching tires, jarring to a halt barely before the intersection and sending anything not strapped down or secured slamming forward. A semi-truck full of hogs blew through the country road intersection, ignoring the stop sign, horn blaring, passing close enough to rattle the car.

"Tim, are you okay?" His mom was wide-eyed and had an arm in front of him.

Tim nodded numbly. The chill was gone. He looked down the road where the semi had rumbled off in a cloud of gravel dust.

"It's lucky you spotted that truck, Tim." Izzy let off the brake and put the car back in motion. "See, you're an important part of the team."

Tim nodded, his heart pounding in his chest, still watching the receding truck. He looked forward to find Derek regarding him.

Derek raised an eyebrow. "Interesting."

* * * * *

Chapter Ten

Iblis

"Interesting."

The witch looked up from the crystalline scrying dish, her pale face seeming to float in the shadows, illuminated by the candles under the dish. "How so, Master?"

Iblis chuckled, looking off into the distance. "The whole Exiled Folk resurgence almost ended with a freak accident. Yet somehow they avoided their fate."

The woman brushed back a lock of dyed black hair, her fingernails painted black as well. "If they avoided it, was it really their fate?"

"I suppose not, Raven." Shadows cast his chiseled features in relief as he turned toward the scrying dish. But all of the auguries Iblis had seen had placed the Exile Champion in dire peril at that place and time, before she was to face Giwargix. He could sense his witch's fear, her brown eyes large with apprehension, afraid that despite the powers he had gifted her, she had somehow failed him. But he had read the signs himself; he had rarely seen them so specific. A cruel master might punish her to vent his own frustration, but Iblis knew it would be counter-productive. He needed his valuable servants clear-headed, not cowering in expectation of his wrath. Besides, it wasn't in his interest for the champion to die so soon. He wasn't disappointed, just surprised.

Raven reached for her tarot cards and closed her eyes. Shuffling them, she opened her eyes and began drawing cards from the deck, laying them on the candlelit table in front of the dish. "There is something new, a new power in play. I think that is what...warned them. They were warned, and now...now..." The witch scanned the cards spread on the black tablecloth. "Now it's gibberish."

Iblis peered at the cards, then beyond them, into the Other, looking for the quantum tendrils connecting them to the fate of the subject in question. There were none, not even the faintest glimmer of information. The cards were merely random pieces of paper.

He turned to the map, spread across a wooden desk. Based on readings with the dowsing crystal, the Champion had been headed west, into Illinois, but even those readings had gotten vaguer. Pins, then circles had marked the readings. Now they could be heading west on I-74, or maybe north on I-39. He had no idea if this marked a destination, or a bump in the road. Something was occluding the occult senses he had bestowed on Raven, which ironically were more potent than his own senses, even if he had a better understanding of what he saw. But what or who could mask such a large area?

"The druid." Iblis smiled.

"We've never been able to divine anything on him or her, Master."

"And that's why we're losing track of the Champion now." Iblis tapped Illinois on the map. "She is going to meet the Druid, somewhere in the middle of Illinois."

"So we've lost her?"

"Only for now, my dear Raven." Iblis continued to smile, a smile that could light up a room or make men quail in fear. "Our intelligence guesses the challenge can't happen at least for a few more months, most likely Samhain. So unless the Champion remains sequestered with the Druid, she'll pop back up on our radar. Meanwhile, we now know where to narrow our search for the Druid."

Raven collected the cards and neatly stacked them. "But nothing we've used has been able to show us the Druid. Either they're warded against scrying, or where they live and work is warded. Possibly both."

"Yes, and that indicates a greater degree of skill or power than we expected. However, we will use a tool greater than any used by witch or warlock to find someone." Iblis picked up a large smartphone. "The Internet."

Raven raised a pierced eyebrow. "But we don't know the name, or even the gender of the Druid."

"Oh, it won't be a quick Google search, but now that we know an area, especially one that is mostly rural, I can put people to work." Iblis gazed down at the map. "After all, how many druids can there be in the middle of Illinois?"

* * * * *

Chapter Eleven

Liam

"They're here!"

Liam turned as the door slammed shut behind Pixel, then looked out the open garage door. A dusty black Dodge Charger turned into the gravel driveway, grinding to a halt. The rumbling engine went silent, then the doors creaked open. The first to emerge were a pair of tall, slender blondes, both clad in black leather and wearing sunglasses. It took Liam a moment to realize one was a man and one was a woman, probably siblings, if not twins. Watching them for moment, Liam realized they both wore long knives or short swords, the sheaths strapped to their thighs, and a trio of throwing knives on the other side.

A boy, maybe 11 or 12, climbed out from the back on the passenger side. He looked tired and bored, clutching some sort of electronic tablet and shouldering a cumbersome backpack. No one had warned Liam there would be kids. He didn't mind kids, but they often seemed to lack any sense of self-preservation when it came to anything sharp or flammable. Plus, if something went wrong, it could add new legal wrinkles.

A woman emerged from the back door of the driver's side. She looked normal, though harried. While the twins were taller than Liam, she was half a foot shorter and athletically built. Her black hair was pulled back in a ponytail that had started to come loose, and her eyes were puffy with dark circles. As Liam took in her face, a flash of recognition went through his mind. It had been more than a decade, but he recognized her.

"Erin?" Her eyes went from appraising her surroundings for potential threats and escape routes to Liam's face. He took a step forward so she could see him better. "Do you remember me?"

"You?" Despite her obvious weariness, he could see a variety of warring emotions play across her expression, before settling on bewildered. "What are you doing here?"

"Oh good, you know each other," the blonde man said with a faint Spanish lilt.

Liam walked out onto the driveway, half expecting her appearance to be a glamour. "You could say that. We only met once, 13 years ago at a pagan festival in Ohio."

Erin nodded, still apparently puzzled. "Why are you here, Liam?"

"This is my home." Liam tried to remember her last name, then remembered they had only exchanged first names that night. No last names, no phone numbers, and the next morning she was gone with the morning mist. "Gods, you're the Champion?"

"Izquierda, Derecho, glad you could make it!" Einar strode out to meet them. He gestured back toward Liam. "This is our pocking druid, Liam. Sounds as though he already knows the Champion."

Erin's mouth fell open, then she started laughing. "Of course you're the Druid. As if this couldn't get any more messed up."

"I don't know what you've gone through to get here, but my paradigm has been getting its ass kicked as well." Besides, Liam thought, she was the one who slipped off without even saying good-bye.

Erin put her hand on the boy's shoulder. "Liam, this is my son, Tim. He's 12 years old."

Liam felt as though the wind had been knocked out of him. He looked at the boy, who regarded him with blue eyes, the same deep blue as Liam's left eye. Liam looked up and met Erin's bright green eyes and raised an eyebrow. She nodded mutely.

"Maybe we should take the pocking reunion inside." Einar furrowed his bushy eyebrows and glanced meaningfully toward the blondes and then back toward the garage.

"Oh, right, the wards." Liam straightened slightly. "Izquierda and Derecho, welcome to my home, I invite you to enter."

"Aren't you all formal? You can call me Derek." The tall blonde man looked over the top of his sunglasses at Liam. "Too bad you're so vanilla, you're kind of cute, in a scruffy Dunwold sort of way. No wonder Pixel wants to jump your bones."

"Derek, seriously." The blonde woman rolled her eyes behind her sunglasses before addressing Liam. "Maybe you should rescind my brother's invitation so we can see how much hair he loses trying to pass through your threshold. I'm Izzy."

"Nice to meet you." Liam shook her hand as he stored the remark about uninviting in case it ever became useful.

"Do we have to be invited in, or can we take in the pizza and eat?" The boy dragged the toe of his shoe in the gravel.

"Oh, sorry. I had to specifically invite them in so they didn't burst into flame or something. But you and your mom are welcome." Liam caught Einar nodding out of the corner of his eye. Liam had been careful not to make blanket invitations. "Do you need help with anything?"

"Please tell me you have some pocking alcohol." Einar walked toward the car. "Nice ride by the way, 2012?"

"Yes, it's a 2012. Don't ask what my brother did to get it." Izzy walked around behind the car and popped the trunk. "Pixel was quite specific in regards to your request. Plenty of beer, whiskey, and tequila. We would have got here sooner but Derek had to harass the clerk."

"A man that quick to drop the 'fag' word is probably holding something in." Derek smirked and bounced his eyebrows. "I gave him something to think about. Bet he dreams about me."

"Do you mind?" Erin glanced from Derek to her son.

"I swear, you're worse than the pocking Twyleth," Einar muttered as he lifted a carton emblazoned with a beer logo from the trunk. "Izzy, I don't know how you put up with him."

"Tim, would you do me a favor?" Liam pointed toward the door in the back of the garage. "Can you go in there and let Pixel and Susan know we are bringing in the pizza?"

The boy shrugged, then nodded. "Sure."

Once the kid was out of earshot, Liam turned toward Derek. "I agree with Erin. Watch what you say in front of the kid."

Erin stepped up to Liam, green eyes flashing. "It's not your place to say. It's mine." She turned on Derek. "But he's right, knock off the lewd comments in front of my son."

"Okay, okay." Derek held up his hands in surrender.

"Let's take the food in before it gets colder," Izzy suggested, reaching into the backseat. "Or we could stand out here and bicker about my brother's poor manners, and who should call him out on it."

Derek pulled a box of rattling bottles from the trunk and followed Einar. "Fine, make me the bad guy. I like being bad."

Izzy rolled her eyes and handed a stack of pizzas to Liam, then she turned and leaned back into the car. Liam couldn't help but notice that the leather pants left little to the imagination. He quickly looked away and noticed Erin watching him. No point in denying it, he thought, and gave her a half-shrug as he carried his burden toward the door. A kick to the pedal he'd mounted under the step popped the door open, something he'd cobbled together during his carpentry phase.

In the kitchen, Pixel was fussing over the kid, probably in danger of jump starting his puberty, while Einar and Derek argued about where to put the booze. Susan had retreated to a corner, watching Pixel suspiciously while surreptitiously peeking at Derek.

"Susan, can you show Derek where the liquor cabinet is?" Liam didn't think the hard liquor would last long with this bunch, but he didn't want it sitting out on the counter. She nodded, mutely gesturing for Derek to follow her, probably worried she'd blurt out something embarrassing. "Einar, can you put the beer in the fridge in the garage? You know, the one we emptied last night?"

"This bit won't last long," the dwarf grumbled, stomping back out the door.

"That's why there are three more cases in the trunk." Izzy stepped aside to let Einar pass.

"I'll help him get the rest of the beer," Liam volunteered and started toward the garage.

"Sit, Druid." Izzy gestured toward the table. "This is your home we are invading. Besides, Einar will waste several minutes drooling over my car."

"Whose car, dear sister?" Derek leaned against the doorframe from dining room. "After all, I was the one who obtained it." He gave a knowing smirk and arched an eyebrow.

Erin set down the last of the groceries. Liam hadn't even heard her come in. "So, do we crowd around the kitchen table?"

"There's an actual dining room past Derek." Liam gestured toward the doorway. "It'll be tight, so let's leave the food on the kitchen table and everyone can fill their plates and take them out. I'd recommend doing it before Gofannon comes in from doing whatever he's doing at my forge." He knocked on the refrigerator. "There's some soda and ice in the fridge for those who aren't lunch drinkers or nursing a hangover. Also, I think there's a little coffee left from breakfast."

Liam turned to the coffee maker to find the pot brimming with fresh, hot coffee. "Or there's a whole pot." Susan had already set out plates and napkins; she knew what his cupboards held almost as well as he did. Liam wondered if she had made the coffee as well.

The door from the garage banged open, Gofannon filling the frame. "Splendid! I was told there was food!"

"Wow." Tim craned his neck. "You're huge. Are you a giant?"

Behind Gofannon, Einar sputtered indignantly. The smith grinned, then flexed a bicep as big around as Liam's thigh. "No, lad, I am just strong from good food and hard work." Gofannon picked up one of the pizza boxes, examined its contents, and carried the pizza, box and all, into the dining room.

"He'll be back for seconds, maybe thirds," Liam whispered to the newcomers. Not waiting for a repeat of breakfast, he grabbed a plate of pizza and poured himself some coffee. Susan gave him a reproaching look as he passed her going into the dining room. As the host, he probably should have waited until everyone else had filled their plate, but he was getting his appetite back. Plus he really needed to sit down and collect his thoughts.

Gofannon was seated at the head of the table, on the stoutest chair he could find, a bulky wooden antique that Liam's grandfather had built. The smith had the pizza rolled up like a burrito and was already halfway through it. Liam sat at the opposite end, that way he could wait for the others to sit down before eating without getting his lunch poached.

"Druid, what is that you are drinking?" Gofannon sniffed the air, setting his half pizza down.

"It's coffee." Liam held up the mug. "It helps clear your head and wake you up."

Gofannon waved dismissively and went back to work on his pizza. "I am awake. A meal deserves ale or mead, not some herbal soup."

The table filled in, with Pixel at his right and Susan on his left. Both women seemed to be watching each other out of the corner of their eye but rarely looked directly at each other. Liam felt as if he had missed something, possibly while they were in the kitchen and he was out back having his handiwork, tools, and work ethic critiqued by a god of myth.

The table was silent for several minutes except for the sounds of eating and the kid getting admonished for trying to emulate the smith by rolling up a slice and cramming it into his mouth.

"So, I guess the big question, especially for us 'dunnies,' is what happens now?" Liam had waited until everyone was almost finished before broaching the question. He was curious to see how much

Erin knew about what was going on, not to mention the discussion he wanted to have about Tim, but he was saving that for private.

"We already told you, Druid. You must make swords." Gofannon punctuated the statement with a belch that brought a giggle from Tim. "Lots of swords, you need much practice before you forge the Champion's sword."

"He's making me a sword for this duel? I have a sword, a decent high-carbon steel one." Erin looked over at Liam. "No offense, but it doesn't sound like you're much of a swordsmith."

Liam quenched the urge to bristle at the comment, especially since it was true. "You're not wrong. That's why they brought a smith-god to tutor me. Evidently, I need to make you a magic sword."

"Cool, like Excalibur or Anduril?" The kid looked up from his tablet. He looked at his mother. "Can I have a magic sword?"

"Tim, let's see if he can make the first magic sword before asking for more." She looked back at Liam, scrutinizing him. "Do you really think you can make one?"

"Twenty-four hours ago, I would have laughed at the notion." Liam realized it hadn't even been a whole day since his world had turned upside down. He looked at her squarely. "A lot has changed since then."

"Liam can do it, we have faith in him." Pixel put a hand on Liam's arm. "Don't we, Gofannon?"

"You said the fifth sword passed the test." Einar pointed at Liam with an empty beer bottle. "How many pocking blades does an apprentice need to make to get that good?"

Gofannon regarded Liam before answering. "Usually at least one dozen, maybe two."

"We need to take Erin to train with Scathach," Izzy said as she looked from Erin to Liam. "Like the Druid, she has much to learn."

"But she has more of a start," Derek muttered.

"Where is this Scathach?" Erin asked. "Springfield? Des Moines?"

"She dwells in Dunos Scaith, the Shadow Fortress. We believe it is to the west." Izzy looked at Liam then Pixel. "Can the Druid go to the Murkwold?"

"Maybe. He can definitely draw on the Gwuedd, to the point his wards can physically stop those not of the mundane world." Pixel nodded over at Gofannon, who was lamenting the lack of pizza in the Glaswold as he finished the last pie-turned-burrito. "Even the big G was stopped. Maybe he could have busted through, but that's also with the Druid not having any training."

"You mean the druid sitting right here?" Liam set down his coffee mug. "What's the Murkwold? A shadow realm of some kind? And are we talking about physically going there, or vision-walking?"

"The druid is smarter than he looks," Derek noted. "Physically Other-stepping runs the risk of detection. Going on a little vision-journey won't even make a ripple."

"Thanks. I think." Liam added more items to his mental list of things to ask about later. "It's been a while since I've done any vision work, and I had pretty mixed results. Sometimes I had trouble turning off my brain and getting into a trance. When I did, what I saw was often chaotic, like when you dream. Some of my peers had really coherent, lucid visions. My spirit-guide hit me with a stick in one."

"I suspect some of those peers, if not most of them, were fudging their results," Izzy remarked. "Going into the Murkwold, the spirit world as you might call it, is rarely cut and dry. A lot of 'seekers' go in with preconceived notions and desires, so they subconsciously shape what they see to get the desired outcome. Some probably not so subconsciously, for fear of looking like a failure when they don't have a cool story about meeting their patron goddess."

"You mean like the cool one you don't want to name?" the kid chirped. Liam glanced at Erin to see if she had a reaction to her son being party to this occult discussion of spirit worlds and gods. She didn't seem to notice. She looked exhausted, food colluding with fatigue to lull her to the brink of sleep.

"Do we have time for the Champion and her son to get some rest?" Liam nodded toward Erin. "You look like you could pass out right there."

Erin blinked a couple of times, looking around as though she had forgotten where she was. "Yeah, I caught a nap while we were driving, but it's been a long day, night, whatever the hell it is."

"I have a couple of guest rooms which are pretty much cleared out, the other two I'll have to move some books and stuff around." Liam pointed to the large staircase toward the entrance, visible from the dining room. "There's a bathroom at the top of the stairs; give me a minute, and I'll pull some fresh towels out of the linen closet."

"Already taken care of," Pixel said. "The other rooms are ready as well."

Liam looked at Susan, who shrugged and shook her head. Someone had been busy while he was showing Einar and Gofannon his workshop and forge. He did a quick headcount. "Even so, looks like a couple of people will be roughing it if everyone stays here."

"Well, I'm not playing slumber party; I have to go to work." Susan stood up, looking pointedly at the grandfather clock ticking away in the corner. "Don't you have to work today, Liam?"

"Oh yeah." Liam smiled. "I guess I should be on time when I tell Clark I quit."

* * * * *

Chapter Twelve

Erin

"What time is it?"

Erin realized there was no one in the room to answer her question. She blinked in the dim light, the evening sun baffled by a pull down blind and heavy curtains. She spent a moment searching for her phone before she remembered she had left it behind in Cincinnati. Her gaze fell on an old analog clock on a dark wooden nightstand. It read half past six; she'd been asleep for five hours.

She sat up and stretched. After lunch and the hot shower, she was asleep as soon as her head hit the pillow. She felt as though she could go back to sleep but knew she shouldn't, or she would screw up her sleep rhythm even worse than it was. Plus, she wanted to check on Tim.

The room smelled slightly musty. Erin suspected the furnishings, decorations, even the bedclothes were all older than her, and the room was almost never used. The druid, Liam, had said something about inheriting the old farmhouse from an aunt, but she couldn't see why he would live in such a huge house alone. He wasn't married, didn't have a girlfriend, and didn't have kids. It seemed like a lot to take care of and rattle around in by yourself.

She slid out of bed and found the clean jeans she had laid out after her shower. As she slipped them on, she realized the pile of dirty clothes she had dumped on a stuffed chair was gone. Had someone come in here while she was sleeping? She checked the door, it was still locked from her side, but she assumed Liam had a key. She pushed aside the image of him creeping in while she was sleeping, looking at her and collecting her dirty clothes. As if she didn't have enough to worry about.

She opened the door, and it slowly creaked open on big antique hinges. She stepped into the hall and could faintly hear voices downstairs. She could distinguish Einar's Nordic accent and Gofannon's rumbling bass, but that was it. She went to the room next to hers and knocked on the oak door.

"Tim, are you decent?"

"Yeah, mom," was the muffled reply.

Erin turned the knob, and the door creaked open. Tim was sitting on the bed, an old book in his lap tipped toward an antique lamp. While he still looked tired, he had his color back, and his eyes didn't have dark circles under them.

"Wow, nice bedhead, Mom."

Erin caught her reflection in a large mirror mounted on top of the dresser. Going to bed with her hair wet had predictable results. She set to work trying to pull it into a manageable ponytail. "What are you reading?"

He held the book up so she could see, even though the cover didn't really tell her anything. "It's a cool book about the history and myths around Merlin."

Erin didn't want Tim to get sucked into this weirdness. On the other hand, at least he wasn't whining about the lack of Internet. Derek had turned off his phone's hotspot shortly before they arrived at the farmhouse, which had released Tim from his no-whining agreement. So far, he'd been good—a trooper considering the circumstances—but he was only 12. He wasn't over the whininess that came with childhood but was starting to blossom into adolescent rebellion. Fighting a mythical dragon-slaying knight seemed less daunting than being the mother of a teenager.

Like the room Erin had been in, this bedroom was furnished with relics of decades past. The big difference was one wall was almost covered by bookshelves. While some of the books looked as old—if not older than—the furniture, most looked like more recent additions. Almost all dealt with mythology, folklore, and history.

"Are you hungry?" While she wasn't particularly hungry herself, there were times her son seemed like a bottomless pit.

Tim looked thoughtful for moment, then nodded. "I could eat. If that Gofannon guy left us any food."

"I'm going to see what the plans are for dinner."

"Okay." Tim nodded as she headed for the door. "Mom?"

"Yeah, sweetie?"

"You know the Druid. Is he a good guy?"

Erin turned back, Tim was regarding her with deep blue eyes. "Actually, that's how we know each other. Even though he didn't know me, he stood up for me. He probably didn't need to, but he didn't know that."

"Cool. Because it sounds like you've got to work together."

"Yes, it does look that way." Erin turned and slipped out the door, creaking it most of the way closed. She wondered how long it would take Tim to figure out the truth about Liam, assuming it didn't get blurted out. To give Liam credit, he'd held his tongue, but Erin wanted to tell Tim herself before he found out, either by putting two and two together or having someone else blab it to him.

116 | JON R. OSBORNE

"Well, someone looks better," Derek said from an overstuffed armchair as she entered the living room. Gofannon took up an upholstered loveseat all on his own, while Einar sat at one end of a couch that looked half a century out of style.

"I feel better, thanks." The flat-paneled television they were watching looked out of place amid the archaic furniture in the room. A news program played at low volume, probably from a local station, based on the interest in corn and soybean prices. "Where's everyone else?"

"Izzy drove Liam and Pixel to the city so that Liam could tell his pocking boss to bugger a goat," Einar replied, watching the fertilizer commercial that punctuated the news program. "Then they were going to swing by some stores and pick up more provisions and what not."

"Yes, the Druid went from living as bachelor to having a..." Derek said, looking at Erin with a grin. "Having a house over-flowing with people."

"Maintaining my corporeal form takes much sustenance," Gofannon added.

"I would avoid standing near any open wells if I were you," Derek chuckled.

"What do you mean?" Erin asked. Tired of standing, she sank onto the opposite end of the couch. At least it didn't smell as musty as it looked.

"Just that Susan or Pixel might push you in." Derek smirked. "Evidently they both can do the math."

Erin glanced back through the doorway toward the stairwell. "Well, no one discuss 'math' where my son can hear. I want to talk to Liam first, and if anyone is going to tell Tim about it, it will be me. Are we clear?"

The smirk faded. "Crystal."

"It's not my pocking business."

"What are all of you going on about?" Gofannon pointed at the television. "They are going to divine the weather without entrails!"

The growl of an engine and the crunch of gravel heralded the return of the Charger. Erin went to a window and peeked through lace curtains. The black Dodge came to a halt in a cloud of dust. Izzy climbed out of the driver's seat, then waved up toward the window. Liam climbed out the other side, followed closely by the purple-haired girl. Liam squinted in the setting sunlight, then turned toward the trunk of the car.

Erin let the curtain fall and headed for the kitchen, intent on going through the door to the garage. The cat, Scooter, watched her from the kitchen table. She thought about shooing him off the table until she was distracted by the cleanliness of the kitchen. Any sign of lunch or breakfast was gone; the double sink was empty, clean, and scrubbed white. There wasn't a trace of grease on the stove, and even the towels that hung from the oven door looked freshly laundered. None of the men she'd left in the living room seemed the kind to do household chores.

The door to the garage popped open, and Liam caught it with his shoulder as he carried in a cardboard box full of groceries. He waited until Pixel grabbed the door behind him before continuing up the steps into the kitchen.

"Oh, hey, you're awake." He set the box on the kitchen table, which was now devoid of cat. "How are you feeling?"

"Better, thanks." Erin was keenly aware of Pixel's attention. She leaned close and whispered, "Do we have time to talk? Just the two of us?"

"Sure. Follow me." He gestured toward the door.

"I'll get those lazy bones to help." Izzy left for the living room.

Pixel started to follow Liam, but he shook his head. "Give us a few, okay?"

Pixel nodded, then pretended to be interested in the groceries as Erin followed Liam into the garage. Liam opened a door in the side of the garage and went out past a small concrete block and corrugated steel building. He led Erin past the building and a patio dominated by a large grill, then down a stone-lined path. He stopped beside a pond in the shadows of a large stone structure composed of two upright slabs with a third slab across the top, same as the Greek letter *pi*.

Liam leaned against one of the upright slabs and closed his eyes. Erin wasn't sure who should speak first as she tried to nail down the thoughts fluttering about her mind.

"He doesn't know," Liam said, finally breaking the silence. A breeze swirled around the stone structure, ruffling his hair.

"No, he doesn't." Erin sat on a stone bench, the coolness of the stone palpable through her jeans. "Until today, I didn't know...actually I still don't know your last name."

"Knox. William Robert Knox. But Liam, because everyone seemed to be Bill when I was a kid, and Liam seemed a lot more...Celtic than William."

"William Wallace?"

"Touché." Liam looked back toward the house. "So, are you going to tell him?"

"I'm not sure. I never expected to see you again." Erin crossed her arms. Even though it was still an hour or two until sunset, the wind brought the temperature down. "I tried to find you. But the people who ran the festival told me they had listed people by different names and couldn't help me if I didn't have a last name."

"Half the people there were probably listed under Raven Moon-Child." Liam grinned, looking off into the distance. "And I actually registered under my legal name, which didn't help. No one seemed to know who you were. I asked around after you disappeared."

"That's because my friends had talked me into going to this, and I quote, 'hippy festival' where we could get free booze and weed. I'd told my parents I was spending the night at my friend's in Dayton. In the morning I slipped out because I had to get home."

"I thought you were 18?" Liam's gaze returned to her.

"Oh, I was, but not by a large margin, and my parents were over-protective. So you can imagine their joy when I turned out to be pregnant."

"You told me you were on the pill."

Erin cocked her head. "Do you remember that, or is it what you told yourself after the fact? We were both a little drunk and a little stoned."

Liam stood up from the stone. "I remember. It was May 3rd, you were wearing a red and rust gypsy skirt, a tied-up white blouse, and a black and red bead necklace. You had a temporary tattoo at the base of your spine that was kanji for Ohayo Neko."

"My mom thought the tramp-stamp was why I got pregnant. I'm pretty sure she thought it was the first time I'd had sex." Erin shook her head, remembering, and was impressed with the clarity of his recollection. "Mom was furious until Tim was born. As soon as she saw him, she forgot she was pissed off."

"So what now?"

"I need to tell him. Even if someone doesn't let it slip, he'll figure it out sooner or later. I don't want him to think I was keeping the truth from him." Erin let out a long breath. "With everything else going on, I just don't want to dump too much on him."

"He seems like a smart kid. He probably gets that from me." Liam grinned, and in the fading light, she saw him as she had all those years ago. "However you want to handle this, I'm onboard."

* * * * *

Chapter Thirteen

Lee

"I told you to handle it."

"I *am* handling it," Pastor Haskins protested. He was glad Mikha'el was staring off into the darkened club as opposed to affixing that baleful gaze on him. "It was too late to fake one of the boys getting shot by her and have the story hold up under police scrutiny."

That was true, much to Lee's relief. He suspected the Servant of the Lord could sense any falsehood uttered before him. The boys in the team who hit the tavern had made up a story about bikers to cover their own injuries. For whatever reason, the bartender didn't say anything to contradict the story. He told the cops he had seen the boys in the bar, bikers had been in and out all night, but he didn't know anything about a scuffle with bikers.

An anonymous tip was dropped about two tall blondes breaking into the waitress' apartment and fleeing in a black Dodge Charger. Cops showed up at the apartment to find it tossed and evidence of a scuffle. The fellows hurt in the fight got medical attention from a sympathetic doctor so their injuries wouldn't attract attention.

"We've got law enforcement looking for the woman, her son, those two faeries helping her, and their car." Lee waited for a response but was met with silence. "We have a possible hit near the

Indiana-Illinois border, a state trooper thought he saw a car and a woman who matched the description."

Mikha'el turned, the glow in his eyes dimming. "Really? When was that?"

"This morning, about eight hours ago. As soon as we got that, we put eyes on the bridges crossing the Mississippi out of Illinois. Even if they stick to back roads, there's only so many places to cross the river. Also, we've got someone watching for her to use her credit card, and for her or her son to log onto any sort of social media that might peg a location."

Mikha'el smiled and turned to look back into the darkness. "Yes, you mortals and your obsession with digital connections. If only you were as fervent in your faith to the Lord as you were to your tweets, likes, and shares. Continue your search, Lee."

"Yes." Haskins half-nodded, half-bowed as he took a step back before turning and descending the short stairs leading from the stage. Reaching the floor, he looked back. Mikha'el gazed into the distance, his hands steepled in front of him. The throne Mikha'el sat on was in a pool of light cast by a spotlight, the back of the seat against a tarnished brass pole. Lee hadn't ventured a guess as to why the Servant had a throne assembled on an old strip club stage.

Lee retreated through the darkness, finding the door by the illuminated exit sign. A cool evening breeze greeted him as he reached the parking lot, stirring trash and a few feeble weeds that pushed up through the cracked pavement. His truck was the only vehicle in the lot. He took out his key fob and chirped it as he approached, still juggling a dozen thoughts, when an old Cadillac with a broken headlight bounced into the parking lot.

Four men burst from the car, all in dark clothes, save for the occasional glint of gold chains. One of the men stepped to the truck's door, blocking Lee from opening it, as the other three surrounded him.

Lee rubbed his temple. He'd been afraid of this ever since Mikha'el had inexplicably picked this location for his headquarters. "You boys really don't want to be doing this."

"Who you calling boy?" One of the men flicked out a knife. "You hurry up and cough up your wallet and your phone, and we might not see if you bleed red, white, and blue."

The other men laughed malevolently, unaware of the white mist coalescing behind them. The mist gathered into a man's shape and congealed into what looked like living marble, with a drape of cloth around the waist to cover its modesty.

"Trespassers." The voice hissed like air escaping from a deep metal barrel. "Flee and the Lord will be merciful."

All four of the men turned. "What the fuck?" One of them produced a gun.

The alabaster seraphim held out an empty hand, and a sword swirled from mist into its grip. As the gang-banger tried to bring the pistol to bear, the marble blade lashed out, severing the weapon forward of the grip and taking the gunman's trigger finger with it.

Panic broke out as the four thugs clambered over each other to pile into the Cadillac. The marble form took a step forward and swung. The windows and tops of the open car doors on the passenger side were cleaved from the vehicle, and they clattered to the pavement in a rain of metal and glass. The vehicle leapt into motion even as the passengers struggled to close the remains of the doors.

Great white wings erupted from the seraphim's back, and it crouched to take flight as the car left sparks on the curb.

"Let them flee," Lee said. "It will better serve the Lord if others learn the peril of trespassing here."

The white form turned to Pastor Haskins. Its eyes were the same stone white as the rest of its being. "As you say. We serve the Lord Jehovah." The seraphim swirled away in a cloud of mist.

Lee looked around. The lot was partly obscured from the street by the building itself, and what little traffic zipped by showed no interest. Taking out a handkerchief, he picked up the finger and dropped in in the nearby storm sewer. "Won't be sewing that back on."

Then he set to picking up the pieces of the gun with the same handkerchief and sent them to follow the finger, along with the handkerchief itself. Looking off in the direction the Cadillac had fled, he shook his head.

"You boys better say a prayer, because the Lord was merciful tonight."

* * * * *

Chapter Fourteen

Liam

"Hoping you'll get lucky tonight?"

Liam looked up from the remains of his dinner. Pixel was leaning on his shoulder, whispering in his ear. He turned toward her. "What?"

Her face was really close, and as usual, the aroma of flowers accompanied her. "I notice you're not drinking anything alcoholic. Trying to make sure you don't pass out again?"

Liam bit his lip to keep it from twitching. His nerves had been buzzing with energy all afternoon. He'd assumed it was a combination of nerves and elation from quitting his job at the bookstore. But now Pixel's proximity was stirring another kind of vigor. He was glad he was sitting at the table as he tried to get his mind back on track. "I don't want to try to do vision-walking while drunk. I'll have a beer beforehand to calm down, and, depending on what we see, I might need more afterward."

"You know, we should be skyclad for this to work," Derek remarked from across the table, grinning over a glass of mead.

"That's a good idea," Pixel said. She still hadn't moved, and Liam had to banish the image of her naked as the room somehow seemed warmer.

126 | JON R. OSBORNE

"What's skyclad?" Tim asked from the end of the table, bringing Liam back to Earth. "Is it some sort of shaman thing? Do you change into a bird?"

"It's bollox, is what it is." It was going to be difficult enough to focus. He was supposed to lead himself, Izzy, Derek and Pixel on a vision walk to search for the location of Dunos Scaith. The last thing he needed was the distraction of everyone being naked. He'd participated in one skyclad Wiccan ritual when he was younger; it made him self-conscious and uncomfortable. He suspected the practice was invented as an excuse to get attractive young neophytes naked rather than removing so-called barriers to magic. "I don't have a problem with ritual garb as a framing tool, but we're not getting n…skyclad."

"Good," Erin remarked over her beer. "Even if I'm not part of this pow-wow, I don't want people running around…you know."

"Afraid you'll see something you like?" Derek smirked.

"Oh my god, skyclad is naked," Tim blurted. He realized everyone at the table was looking at him. "It made Mom embarrassed, and Derek liked it, so it had something to do with sex."

"Smart kid." Liam chuckled. He looked across the table at Erin. "He's quick to put two-and-two together."

"Laugh it up, Druid Prude," Pixel whispered, her breath warm on his ear, before moving away and returning to her seat next to him.

"So what should we do while you guys are on your spirit trip?" Erin asked. Liam didn't blame her for being eager to change the subject. Einar and Derek were both still laughing over Tim's outburst.

Liam nodded to Erin. "You'll need to watch over our physical bodies while we're mentally on walkabout."

"Makes sense." Einar nodded. "She is the pocking Champion."

"What do you expect to happen?" Erin looked worriedly from Liam to Izzy.

"Hopefully nothing," Izzy replied. "But we'll be in a trance and unaware of what's going on around us. Half the reason for taking my brother along is so he won't be tempted to draw on us with markers while we're out-of-body."

Tim giggled, earning a reproachful glance from Erin.

"I have no idea how long this will take, assuming it even works," Liam said, trying to wrestle the conversation back on track. "Typically, I'm used to it taking half an hour to an hour. But given the nature of what's going on, and the fact I've never vison-walked with glassies before..."

"Glassies?" Einar looked up from his beer. "What the pock is that?"

Liam shrugged. "You keep calling us 'dunnies,' so it seemed appropriate."

Einar opened his mouth to protest, then furrowed his eyebrows in thought. Finally he nodded and went back to his beer.

"Anyway, the point is don't disturb us if you don't have to. I expect us to talk aloud, and though everyone has had their bar for weirdness raised the last 24 hours, expect it to sound weird." Liam focused on Erin. "You won't be seeing what we see, and I'm not sure if talking to us will jar us out of the trance or not."

"Is it dangerous?" Erin asked.

Liam looked to Izzy, Derek and Pixel. None of them committed to an answer. "I'm going to go with maybe. We know there are forces working against us; I have no clue if they can get into this playground. There are enough mystic traditions associated with Abrahamic religions that I wouldn't rule it out."

"A good assumption." Izzy nodded. "Kaballists, Santerians, assorted miscellaneous mystery cults. The Avramites are not without mystical resources."

"Okay, so once you figure out where this Dunos Scaith is, then what?" Erin turned to Izzy. "I go there for a training montage?"

"In a manner of speaking." Izzy laced her fingers together. "You will need to train with Scathach for seven subjective years."

"Seven years!" Erin stood, the chair almost tipping over. "I can't be away for seven years!"

"I didn't think we had seven years," Liam added. Not that he had anything to do, since he had quit his job, but no one was talking about him going away for years; they had brought the tutor to him. "Can't Scathach come here like Gofannon did?"

"She could, but she won't," Derek replied. "Besides, this works to our advantage. Time doesn't flow the same for various ynswolds, or pocket dimensions as you might call them. Think Tir Na nOg and Avalon."

"Exactly." Izzy leaned forward. "Spending seven years with Sacathach will only pass as seven weeks in the Dunwold. The last time she took someone into such tutelage was your ancestor, Cu Chulainn."

"But it will still be seven years to me! I'll be seven years older, I'm not immortal like you guys."

"Technically not immortal," Pixel remarked.

"I am not immortal," Gofannon said. He was still working on what was left of the brats Einar had grilled for dinner as the burgers and hot dogs had already been depleted. "But I do not usually walk the Wold. In the Dunwold, the Folk and gods can age, just slowly. So when we go back home, we cheat."

"Don't worry, we thought of that." Einar got up, went into the kitchen, and came back with a cloth covered woven basket. "In fact, it might be a bit of overkill for the situation, but the Aesir were very cooperative when it came to the prospect of returning to Midgard."

Erin looked at the basket Einar placed in front of her, then pulled the cloth to one side. "It's an apple?"

"Not any old apple; those are Idunn's Apples, and—where's the other pocking apple?" Einar asked, glaring about before his gaze settled on Pixel.

Pixel glanced over at Liam and shrugged. "You said it was a spare."

Liam remembered the golden apple Pixel had given him while they were waiting for dinner. It had been delicious and sweet, and eating it felt like drinking a Red Bull. He realized now his surge of energy hadn't just come from handing his keys to his old boss or the excitement of magic being real. He turned to Pixel. "You fed me a magic apple?"

"It only seemed fair," Pixel said, gesturing toward Erin. "She's getting one."

"The other was in case she insisted on taking her pocking boy along!" Spittle punctuated Einar's anger as his face flashed red.

"Mom, what's pocking?"

"Not now, Tim. What does this apple do, and why would I give a magic apple to my kid even if I ate one?" Erin's eyes kept getting drawn back to the apple in the basket, and Liam remembered his fascination with the apple Pixel had handed him before he devoured it.

"Idunn's Apples will keep a mundane from aging for seven years." Izzy kept her voice composed and measured, trying to be a calm in the rapidly spreading storm. "This worked out conveniently for us, as while in Dunos Scaith, you would have aged according to your subjective time. With the apple, instead of coming back seven years older, you would come back the same physical age you left. If you had insisted on taking Tim with you, and we still had the second apple, the same would apply to him."

"You mean I'm frozen in time for seven years?" Liam did the quick math, calculating he would still physically be 39 on his 46th birthday. Not too huge of a leap, he could pass it off as looking young for his age. But he also remembered some less than pleasant side effects from various stories that came from messing with the flow of time. "What happens after seven years? Do I age to dust if I don't keep eating magic apples or drinking magic mead or something else to halt my aging?"

"Nothing so dramatic." Izzy kept her voice even and reassuring. "You'll start aging normally. If you eat another, your age will freeze again for seven years. But it's exceedingly rare for mortals to be given this boon once, let alone repeatedly."

"And you don't just pocking hand them out!" Einar's face was still red, and a vein throbbed on his temple as he stared daggers at Pixel. "Especially by nicking them from your supposed allies!"

"It is a shame. We could have made Bywodd Medd with the apples," Gofannon stated matter-of-factly. "It is easier to spread the magic of the apples around, even if not as potent. That is how we cheat back home."

"I don't want to be stuck as a kid," Tim lamented. "I'll never be old enough to stay home alone."

"I think I should pop some popcorn," Derek said with a laugh.

"Not helping, brother," Izzy said as she glowered at Derek, quenching his mirth. Then she turned to Einar. "Einar Jarnskegg, calm yourself. No impugnment of your honor or trust was intended. Remember, we're all on the same team." The bright blue-white eyes turned on Pixel, who seemed to wilt. "Some are a little enthusiastic and forget their boundaries."

Pixel fled, and the door to the garage slammed shut behind her. The dining room fell silent, and no one looked at each other. Liam's mind whirled; it seemed as though every time he'd come to grips with his world being turned upside down, the script got flipped again. Now he had been slipped the mythological equivalent of steroids. He wondered if there were any effects they didn't know about. He was reminded of the stream of potential side effects that followed every pharmaceutical commercial.

"We need to stick to the plan," Liam said, taking a deep calming breath as he looked up. "Einar, for what it's worth, I'm sorry about Idunn's Apple. The important thing is we still have one for Erin so she doesn't lose seven years in her training. We need to find Dunos Scaith, and right now our best lead is vision-walking to the Murkwold."

"I still haven't agreed to this seven-year training regimen," Erin protested. She was still staring at the apple.

"Fair enough, but we can still look for Scathach," Liam said, conceding. His heart was still pounding in his chest. "I'm not going to be able to focus on vision-walking with everyone riled up. I've got enough on my mind and feel like I drank a triple espresso on top of a Red Bull."

"That'd be the pocking apple," Einar muttered, still fuming. "It will make you feel like a pocking youth, probably why she stole it."

Liam gave the dwarf a reproachful glance. "Einar, I need you to drop it for now. I'm going to see if I can find Pixel and talk to her."

Einar scowled for another moment then finally nodded. "As you say, Druid."

* * * * *

Chapter Fifteen

Erin

"So are we done with the arguing?"

The smith god broke the silence after Liam left to track down Pixel. Erin was having trouble focusing on the squabble; her attention kept straying back to the apple. She wasn't even sure she believed in magic apples, and she had a harder time swallowing the notion that she was going to go on some sort of seven-year training retreat, and it was only going to be seven weeks for everyone else. It had to break the laws of physics or something, she thought. Time doesn't work like that.

"What happens if I don't go to this Scathach?" Erin looked around the table, covering up the apple. Removing it from her sight seemed to quell the magnetic pull it exerted. "Even if I believe this whole time warp thing, it's still seven years to me, seven years away from my son."

"If you don't train with Scathach, I doubt you'll be ready to face Giwargix," Izzy said, holding Erin's gaze with her cool blue eyes. "Giwargix will kill you, the Druid, and everyone else with you. Then the Avramites will hunt down your son, hoping to snuff the line of Cu Chulainn before he has children.

"Alternatively, you could walk away and spend the rest of your lives on the run as the Avramites hunt you both down for the aforementioned reason. They won't care if you refuse the challenge. They can't take the risk of your descendants deciding to take up the challenge."

"I thought you said there were rules so they couldn't just whack me?" Erin suspected they were trying to scare her into taking up this fight, and she wasn't about to be conned.

"That's true," Derek said, his voice devoid of its usual humor. "Until the day after Samhain. Then the challenge is over and you are no longer considered Champion. You're merely another mundane, and they can arrange an accident, assuming they don't settle for blatant murder. Then they'll make sure Tim doesn't carry on the line."

"Mom, you have to fight this Giwargix guy." Tim's eyes were wide and Erin cursed herself for not waiting until he was out of earshot to have this conversation. "These Avramite guys have already chased us out of our home, out of our whole life, same as they did to the magical folk and the old gods. If you won't stand up to them, who will?"

Erin got out of her chair and began to pace. Tim was right. They would never be able to put their lives back together with khaki Nazis breathing down their necks, having to always look over their shoulders. Plus, she realized Tim was twice as valuable a target, as he also carried Liam's bloodline as well. Since Liam didn't have any other kids, that left Tim as the only one to carry on both of them. Even if Erin didn't buy into it, the Avramites believed, and that was enough. People were willing to commit all sorts of atrocities in the name of religion. She'd seen it in person while on duty in the Middle East.

"If we win, what's to stop them?" Erin stopped and crossed her arms. Part of her was still fighting the notion of going on a seven-year mission. Seven years doing what? Wax on, wax off, hoping she didn't come back and find her son was almost 20? "What if they decide to get revenge? The challenge is over if they lose, so they could come after us then."

"If you win, the equations change, the balance of power shifts," Izzy said, watching Erin pace from her seat. "They'll have a lot to worry about, and you can take your payment and disappear if that's what you want. We'll help you vanish."

"The druid's weight in gold buys a lot of groceries," Einar added, his anger finally subsiding to the point he could make civil conversation. "It buys schooling for your son; I'm told you dunnies pay an arm and a leg for that."

"I'm supposed to roll a wheelbarrow full of gold into a bank?" The idea was ludicrous, Erin thought. There were all sorts of laws and regulations around selling gold; she couldn't shave a sliver off a bar at the grocery store or plunk a bar of gold down at the Bursar's office at a college.

"Nothing so primitive." Derek sniffed, looking slightly offended. "We've been laying the groundwork for the last 13 years. It's all handled through legal accounts and holding companies. I'd advise the per annum payment as opposed to the lump sum, it will be more favorable from a tax standpoint, plus a 529 plan to save for Tim's college."

"Are you speaking English?" Gofannon pushed aside his plate and scanned the table for any remaining food.

"A foul dialect known as legalese," Derek replied with a smile. "People are shocked when they find out I can actually string together multi-syllable words for something other than a bawdy limerick."

"Plus, between your training and the power that will be at the Druid's disposal, not to mention all of the blessings that will be heaped upon you by the Exiled Gods and their folk, you will be quite well protected." Izzy tapped a long, slender finger on the oak table. "I'm not going to throw the whole destiny thing around, but it seems you and Liam are meant to help us. I mean, what are the odds of you crossing paths 13 years ago, when we realized the challenge was coming, only to be the two people needed to bring it to fruition?" Erin narrowed her eyes. She resisted saying anything that would let the cat out of the bag to Tim. She didn't even want the cat to poke its nose out before she had a chance to sit him down. At least Izzy was respecting her wishes.

"Mom, if you go away for seven weeks, where will I stay?"

"He can stay with the Druid," Izzy suggested. "After all, this house is huge, especially once all of us aren't camping in it. It is well warded against divination and intrusion by supernatural entities. It's probably the safest place for him."

"We'll see." Erin held Izzy's gaze. "I think I need to talk to Tim first, and we should probably get Liam's input as well. How long do we have until this vision quest thing?"

"It depends on how long it takes everyone to settle down," Izzy replied, looking at the tall windows faintly lit by the last of the setting sun. "I know he wanted to wait until it was dark outside, and he wanted a fire in the fire pit out by the dolmen."

"I'll take care of that." Einar stood up and headed for the garage. "Maybe I can chop some wood and take out some...frustrations."

"Tim, let's go in the living room while the others clean up from dinner," Erin suggested. She was still struggling with what she was going to say but couldn't put it off any longer. "We need to talk."

* * * * *

Chapter Sixteen

Tim

"I know there's been a lot to take in the last day and a half."

His mom had made the understatement of the century, Tim thought. They were sitting in the old stuffed chairs in the living room. Like almost everything in the huge house, the chairs were probably older than his mother. They reminded him of Mrs. Adair's apartment and had a faint musty smell.

"I have something to tell you," his mother continued. "Something important, and I wanted to make sure you heard it from me."

"Something worse than you leaving me with strangers for seven weeks?"

His mother flinched; she hadn't expected that. Part of Tim knew it was unfair; she was being swept along by events as much as he was, but a bigger part of him resented it and wanted her to know.

Erin leaned forward, her elbows on her knees. "If I do this, if I go on this training mission, you'll stay with your father."

It was Tim's turn to be jolted in surprise. He tried to parse what she had said, looking for something he had missed. "But you said you didn't know who my father was. That he was some guy you met once and never could find. You don't even know his whole name, only his first name, William."

"That's right. After the night you were, um, conceived, I never saw your father again and didn't know how to find him." His mother glanced back toward the dining room. "Until I saw him today."

Tim followed her gaze. The dining room had emptied out as all the others got ready for the vision-walking ritual the Druid was going to do. But it was obvious who she was talking about. She'd acted as though she recognized the Druid when she saw him in the garage, and the Druid recognized her. "You mean Mr. Knox? The Druid is my dad?"

"Yeah." Erin looked halfway between laughing and crying. "Of all the insane, crazy things going on today, we got out of the car, and there he was, your father."

Tim pushed himself back in the deep chair, holding onto the arms. For all his life, his father had been this mystery man who haunted the edge of Tim's dreams, never coming into focus. Over the years, Tim had made up various stories for himself about who his father was, but he knew they were just stories. Now his father was a real person, not a figment.

"Does he know?"

Erin nodded, her eyes moist. "He found out today. It turned out he looked for me, but he never knew I was pregnant. So this is a big surprise for him as well. At first I didn't know if I was going to tell you. With all the other lunacy going on, it seemed like a big bomb to drop on you. He totally respected that and told me he'd abide by whatever I wanted."

"You said he was a good guy." Tim wasn't too keen on the idea that his mom had considered keeping it a secret from him, but decided that since she had told him, he couldn't hold it against her. "Is that why you decided to tell me, or were you afraid Derek would blab?"

"The last part may have been a little true." His mother chuckled, causing a tear to spill free. "But mostly because not only did you deserve to know, Liam deserved to not have to keep it a secret. He doesn't have any other children, then suddenly his 12-year-old son is sitting at his table, and he's having to bite his tongue."

"Do I have to call him Dad?"

"Only if you want, sweetie." Erin wiped her eyes and took a deep, steadying breath. "If you don't want to call him Dad or something, I'm sure Liam will be fine."

"Are we going to live here?" Tim looked up at the high ceiling where an old fan hummed. The house didn't have a wireless network. Tim didn't think it even had broadband. Were druids like the Amish, Tim wondered? "I mean after you beat Giwargix so the Exiled Folk can come back to the regular world. Once your mission is done, are we going to stay here with Liam?"

Tim watched as his mother's gaze swept the room, from the tall wood-framed windows, the dark antique bookcases that filled one wall around the television, to the large wood-lined doorways that led to the dining room and staircase. Her eyes returned to him, and she shrugged.

"I don't know. I hadn't thought that far ahead. There's certainly enough space, but who knows?" She shrugged again. "First I wanted to break the news to you. I haven't even broached the idea with him, and I don't know yet if I want to. What if he doesn't want us around, what if we don't get along, what would I do here in the middle of Cornfield, USA?"

"Do you think he doesn't like kids?" Tim had noticed there was nothing in the house for kids. No games, no toys, no movies, no televisions in the bedrooms; everything was for old people. "Is that why he hasn't had any other children?"

Tim knew some of his mother's boyfriends hadn't stuck around because of him. None of them had been mean to Tim; they just didn't seem to want a kid around, even the couple of them who pretended to like him to get in good with his mom. Tim could always tell the fakers, with their phony smiles and bogus platitudes. It usually took those guys less than a month to slip up and for his mother to see them for what they were.

Mr. Knox, Liam, hadn't struck Tim as fake. It was obvious at times he didn't know how to talk to a kid, but Tim liked it when the Druid had talked to him like a grown up. It was way better than treating him as if he was six years old, Tim hated when adults talked down to him.

"I don't think so," his mother replied. She had to have noticed how this house was like a museum, full of antiques and books and nothing for anyone under 30. "I'm guessing he isn't conventional and hasn't had a lot of luck in relationships. Kind of like me."

"That's weird. Pixel likes him, and that lady Susan likes him."

His mother raised an eyebrow. "Really? And how would you know that?"

"Well, Pixel practically hangs on him, and when Liam isn't watching, she's looking at him all googly-eyed." Tim tried to pantomime the expression, along with melodramatically-clasped hands. "And Susan was watching Pixel all squinty-eyed, kind of like when Mrs. Adair was spying on the new foreign family who moved into 4D, and she didn't trust them." He imitated the squinting scowl for good measure.

His mother smiled. "Sweetie, I'm pretty sure Liam and Susan are only friends; from what I understand they've been friends for a while. She's probably being suspicious because all these new people showed up with a crazy story. I mean, we're in the middle of it, and I'm not convinced. So far, all we know is that some people believe enough to risk kidnapping and burglary."

"What about Gofannon? He's a god, right? And if it isn't real, why would they pay you a bunch of gold?"

"Tim, 'Gofannon' could just be a big guy who has played too much Realms of Quests." She looked around the room. "They can claim they have gold, but have you seen any gold?"

"What about the apple? Do you think it's magic?" Tim remembered how mad Einar got about Idunn's Apple. Someone wouldn't get so angry about a plain old apple.

His mother got up and went to the dining room, returning with the small wicker basket. She set it down on the coffee table, another example of the old-fashioned and worn furniture spread about the farmhouse. Pulling aside the white cloth cover, she picked up the apple. The fruit was larger than a typical apple, and golden-yellow as opposed to red, but nothing about its appearance screamed supernatural. Somehow, Tim was certain it was magical, and a voice in his mind agreed with him. He realized the house agreed as well. The house had allowed the apple in because the bearer had been invited.

Tim tried to think of a way to tell his mom that the house thought the apple was magic without it sounding sillier than it did. He realized the feeling of being watched he'd had through the day wasn't paranoia; it was the house watching him. No, watching over him, as though it was some sort of protector. Liam had to invite the Glaswold people, the 'glassies' as he'd quipped, for them to enter. Tim and his mother hadn't needed an invitation because they were regular people, though Tim had felt a tingle as he stepped across the threshold of the garage.

Tim looked up and saw his mother dreamily looking at the apple, the way he'd seen an overweight kid in his class look at an ice cream cone after being on a diet for two months. Then she reached out and took a bite. She closed her eyes and sighed, a bit of juice dribbling from the corner of her mouth.

"Mom, should you be eating the magic apple?" Tim remembered how pissed Einar had been, but he'd brought this apple for his mother. She took another bite and made a contented noise as she chewed. She seemed oblivious as she took another mouthful of the fruit.

Tim sniffed the air, it smelled like apple to him. The flesh of the apple, exposed where Erin had bitten, looked the same as a regular apple. He debated taking stronger measures to get her attention, maybe even try to grab the apple away from her.

'Let her finish,' something in his mind said. 'It was meant for her.' He sat back and watched as his mother devoured the apple down to the thinnest spindle of a core under the stem. He never saw any seeds. That made sense to him; people couldn't plant their own magic apple trees.

Setting the core in the basket, his mother licked the juice from her fingers and leaned back in her chair, sinking into the upholstery with another contented sigh.

"Mom?" Tim prodded after a minute.

His mother's eyes fluttered open, as though she was waking up from a dream, and she looked around for a confused moment. "Did I doze off?"

"Kind of. You know the magic apple we were talking about?" Tim pointed at the basket. "You just ate it, and it was like you were sleep-walking, except you were eating instead."

Erin leaned forward and picked the core up out of the basket. As she examined it, the core dissolved into a shower of gold dust and dissipated. She looked to Tim and then back at her hand that had held the apple. "Oh, shit."

"What did it taste like?" Tim asked. "Because you ignored me and kept eating it."

"It was…" his mom stopped; whatever she'd been about to blurt out was something she didn't want to say in front of Tim. "It was really sweet and delicious, like cotton candy and a birthday cake, all rolled into one. In fact, I think I'm getting a little sugar buzz."

"So now do you think it was magic?"

Erin smiled. "Ask me again in seven years. Come on, let's take care of the dishes before they do this vision-quest thing."

Tim reluctantly pushed himself out of the chair and followed his mother. The dining room table had already been cleared off, so they continued into the kitchen. Tim looked around but didn't see any dishes in the sink or any of the serving plates that had held the grilled food. What was left of the chips had been clipped shut and were neatly lined up on one of the counters with the grilling tongs clean and dry next to them. Scooter, the cat, sat in the middle of the empty table, regarding them with unblinking eyes.

Erin looked around, confused. "I didn't see anyone do dishes."

"Aw, darn." Tim hoped she wouldn't find an alternate chore for him to do.

* * * * *

Chapter Seventeen

Liam

"**S**o we're not getting naked?"

Liam and Izzy both glared at Derek while Pixel giggled. Liam considered the latter a good sign. It had taken half an hour to get Pixel settled down, with her apologizing and sobbing on his chest until his t-shirt was wet. After assuring her that he wasn't pissed, the crying had eventually subsided. Liam had made sure to keep his face away from hers, lest his lip start twitching again.

Fortunately, Einar had arrived with a load of chopped firewood and dumped the split logs within arm's reach of the fire pit. He and Pixel eyed each other until Einar announced that, although he wasn't happy, he would have given Liam the apple if the kid wasn't going to use it, so he wasn't mad. Liam suspected Einar was still mad, but he was grateful the dwarf was willing to swallow his anger to keep the peace.

Liam had returned to the fire pit after changing into his ritual robe, a plain brown hooded robe that an ex-girlfriend had made for him back when he was doing group rituals for the pagan community. The only adornment was the same ogham as his tattoo, which went around the cuff of each elbow-length sleeve. She had made the robe loose fitting and practical, more like a long tunic, with a couple of different mantles to wear over it depending on the occasion and

145

weather. On a warm summer night, like tonight, he had forgone the mantle; he didn't want to be distracted by sweating under the layers.

A leather ring belt was cinched around his waist. It normally held a pouch for miscellaneous ritual supplies, a frog for a mead horn, and a short sword if the occasion called for it and the local ordinances allowed. Tonight the belt was empty, as they weren't doing an actual ritual.

Liam had brought along his staff, a stout oak branch that was as tall as he. The wood had a natural contour where he gripped it, bearing it as a walking stick as he approached the fire pit. A gust of wind followed him, fanning the small blaze already crackling, the flames illuminating the dolmen in flickering light. He had used the staff as a ritual implement in the past and wasn't sure why he'd brought it now, other than instinct.

"I told you we're not going skyclad," Liam said. Izzy and Derek were wearing the same black leather outfits they'd been wearing when they arrived, while Pixel had changed to a loose, short lavender sundress that seemed to disappear when she was silhouetted by the firelight. "I'm still buzzing, but I want to try and see what we can accomplish. I'm a little rusty, so if it doesn't work tonight, we'll try again. If nothing else, this will be good practice."

Liam walked to a patch of short grass between the fire pit and the dolmen. Three stone benches were around the fire pit, with the side facing the dolmen unobstructed. Wind ruffled the grass as he approached the dolmen, the eight-foot-tall menhirs and the capstone atop them all salvaged from an abandoned project a couple of counties over. Three years ago, he'd spent all summer digging the pits that the uprights sank into, a third of their length buried. Once they were in place, Liam had convinced a professor at the state university to test out his pet theory on the construction of megalithic monuments like Stonehenge to get the capstone in position.

He placed his hand on the smooth limestone slab, which even after the day's heat was cool to the touch. Sure, they weren't the same kind of stone as Stonehenge, but the stone being local seemed more important; it tied the dolmen to the history of the land as opposed to it being a random sculpture.

Liam turned back toward the others, who were watching him expectantly. He didn't know what was scarier—that nothing would happen and he would let everyone down, or that something *would* happen, further shaking up his world.

"I'm going to take us through a guided meditation to get us into the right mindset to do the vision-walk," Liam said. He paused, letting his thoughts catch up. "The big thing for the four of us doing this vision-walk is to focus on finding Scathach and Dunos Scaith. Hopefully, we'll get a clear enough vision or portent to interpret in the real world. I'm hoping you supernatural folk will be able to interpret something we see. I've only used this for spiritual purposes, not to try to find something in the physical world."

"Do you need a barrister for your disclaimers?" Derek quipped. He gave a slight grunt when Izzy elbowed him in the ribs.

"Liam, you can do this." Pixel placed her hand on his forearm, looking up at him with her glowing eyes. "You know magic is real, and your wards prove you can do it. You have Cathbad's blood in you."

"Remember, Druid, as the time of the challenge approaches, the curtain between the worlds grows thinner." Gofannon pinched his thumb and forefinger together. "Magic is getting easier to pull into the Dunwold; you draw on the Gwuedd. How do you say in English?"

"The closest term would be the Weave," Pixel replied. "If you picture magic as a web of energy, the more strands you can draw on, the stronger it is. It's not a perfect analogy, but close enough."

"The same as ley lines?" Tim asked from one of the benches. He'd been silently watching the proceedings. Liam wished he'd had a chance to talk to Erin and find out if she'd told Tim.

"To a certain degree," Izzy answered. "Most Dunwold...mystics view ley-lines as much more singular, distinct structures intersecting at mystic and historical loci. The Gwuedd isn't so rigid or constrained, but only the most powerful strands left traces in the Dunwold where magic once flowed before it was cut off."

"But..." Tim looked confused for a moment, struggling to find a word. "Liam can pull these strands into our world?"

Liam caught Erin's eye, and she nodded. She'd told Tim, and Liam realized Tim wasn't searching for a term; he was trying to decide what to call him.

"Ja, but he has to be careful," Einar interjected. "If he does too much, the pocking Avramites will sense it and narrow down where we are. We're pocking lucky this place is obfuscated from magic senses, but if he makes too much noise, they'll hear."

"And that's why we're trying to do this on a more mental plane." Liam smiled at the lunacy of how it would have sounded 48 hours ago. Part of him still wondered if he had gone mad or had fallen and hit his head on the garage floor. Another part was afraid this was really happening. "Instead of breaking reality and punching a hole into another dimension, this is more like using a scrying font or, at worst, an astral projection."

Gofannon nodded. "Much less noise."

"All right, let's get this started." Liam kicked off his sandals, leaving them by one of the benches, and he walked in a circle on the grassy patch, kneading the grass with his toes as he walked, feeling the turf beneath his feet. He finally sat down cross-legged on the side closest to the fire pit, facing away from the fire and toward the dolmen, which loomed in the flickering shadows. He wore his old black martial arts uniform pants under the robe, which kept him from being distracted worrying about his modesty.

Pixel sat to his right, her legs folded under her. A slight breeze brought the ever-present aroma of flowers, despite the odors of grass and smoke wafting in the air. Izzy sat to Liam's left and Derek sat across from him, both cross-legged. In the dim light, their eyes shone a pale blue, more like a cat's eyes than Pixel's glow.

Liam pulled the staff into his lap, balanced across his thighs. Reaching out, he took the hands of those next to him. Pixel's felt small and warm as she clasped his hand, while Izzy's felt cool as she draped her long fingers across his palm. Across the circle they took Derek's hands; somehow Derek resisted the urge to make some sort of joke.

Behind him, Liam could hear people taking seats on the stone benches, the occasional faint rustle of movement or whisper of a breath audible over the crackling of the fire. Liam took a deep breath and tuned them out. The fire, the night sounds of birds and insects, all became background noise as he started leading the group through the breathing exercises to ground and center.

Liam could feel the energy buzzing within him from what was presumably the apple, but as he grounded, seeking a connection to the energy of the earth, it subsided, replaced with what felt like a deep hum as he sank mental roots into the land to anchor himself.

He began the actual guide meditation itself, following his instincts as he improvised from his original script. Dream-like, he could see their circle of four and the dolmen, now illuminated by moonlight. In the waking dream, the four of them stood and silently walked through the opening between the menhir, with Liam leading the way with his staff.

Liam looked around; the fire and the observers were gone. Past the dolmen, at the top of its small hill, the farmhouse shimmered with pale light. Even though the outline was unmistakably his home, the impression in his mind was more of a fortress or keep, almost as though the house was carved from stone as opposed to constructed from wood and glass.

"Why can we see my house?" he asked, hoping that speaking in the vision wouldn't yank them out of it and back to their bodies.

"Certain things extend across the boundaries between the worlds," Izzy replied. Her voice was slightly fuzzy, like someone talking on the other side of a door. "Your home, the dolmen, are such things. Fortunately, your home hides itself and the surrounding land from denizens and travelers through the Murkwold. We can only see it because you invited us."

Liam looked around. The landscape was indistinct, all shadows and moonlight. There was no glow from the direction of Eureka, the closest town, or Peoria, which should have been off to the west. The stars were faint blurs, and the moon was a bright smudge in an otherwise dark sky, but Liam couldn't see actual clouds.

Liam looked at his staff, puzzled. It looked the same as it had in the real world. Part of his mind told him they were still seated in a circle in the light of the fire, holding hands. But here he was, walking around.

"If you imbue enough energy into something, it manifests with you, as with your clothes." Izzy gestured to herself. She was still clad neck-to-toe in black leather. Derek and Pixel were also dressed in the same clothes they wore in the mundane world. Liam looked down to see he was wearing his familiar robe. "Some of it also has to do with self-image."

"Hence why I am so beautiful," Derek said with a smirk.

"So we're manifested in the Murkwold." Liam looked around again, seeing nothing new. The only landmarks were the house and the dolmen. West would be the face of the house with the garage door, he thought. "Now we need to find where Dunos Scaith is, or find Scathach and somehow figure out where they are in the Dunwold."

"Perhaps this will help." Derek opened his hand. Perched on his palm was an origami owl. "The owl is both a nocturnal bird of prey and a symbol of wisdom. Focus on it, and it may lead us to what we seek."

Liam gingerly took the folded paper bird and placed it in his own palm. Holding the paper owl in front of him, he whispered in Irish. "Find the way to Scathach so that the blood of Cu Chulainn and Cathbad may fulfill their destinies."

Closing his eyes while in a dream seemed redundant, but Liam did so, reaching for the tendrils of magic that permeated the fabric of the Murkwold. He could feel it flow up his staff, and into the hand clutching it. It felt like electricity moving in slow motion but was not painful. The energy went up his arm, across his body, and flowed down his other arm, to the hand holding the paper bird. With a rustle of paper, the owl stretched its wings and took flight, leaving a trail of blue-green sparks behind it.

For a second, all four of them stared at the fading trail of the owl before willing themselves into motion. As they chased after the fluttering owl, each step seemed to slide across a mile in the real world, as occasional natural features swelled up before them only to disappear behind them in the next stride.

"Well done, Druid," Derek remarked as they stepped across the Mississippi, its ancient flow scarring the landscape of the Murkwold. "I was not expecting such immediate, or animated, results."

"You didn't know it would do that?" Liam got the sense they were crossing the state of Missouri as he answered, heading into the shadowy prairies of Kansas. In his peripheral vision, Liam spotted spirits flitting by and fought not to be distracted by them.

"I merely intended it to be a focus," Derek replied. Liam realized they were slowing relative to the Dunwold as the moonlit horizon began to grow jagged, marking the approach to the Rocky Mountains.

The origami owl circled Liam three times then fell dormant, tumbling to the ground at Liam's feet. Liam retrieved the bird and looked around. "Does that mean we are there?"

A blood-curdling yowl split the darkness ahead, causing Liam to jump and Pixel to clutch his arm. Ahead, in an inky dark patch, there was a swirling commotion. Dim moonlight revealed the form of a great winged cat, green light spilling from its open jaws and its eyes, its shoulders as high as the top of Liam's head. Before the feline, a pitch-black void extended tendrils of darkness, grappling the cat and trying to drag it toward its dark maw.

Liam cursed himself for not wearing his sword as Izzy and Derek pulled their own weapons and closed, hacking at the tentacles. They were rewarded for their effort with grasping strands of darkness lashing out at them, trying to drag them in as well.

"Liam, that's a shadowcat, a sentinel of Dunos Scaith," said Pixel, who practically clung to his side. "They are only solid in the shadows."

The moon was still a white blur overhead, providing barely enough illumination to cast shadows. Liam stared at the white blot in the sky, unable to resolve the usual lunar features. But he knew it was there. He just needed to focus its light. Holding aloft his staff, he called on the magic running through the landscape of the Murkwold, intentionally drawing it to him. If this was a vision, he merely needed the will to shape it, similar to lucid dreaming. He felt a tingle in his feet and the magic began to flow up his legs. He mentally ushered it up his extended arm and into his staff. A point of brilliant white light manifested at the end of his staff, focused moonlight. Gesturing toward the struggle, he willed the light to be released. An incandescent blue-white beam bathed the area.

The effect was immediate. The shadowcat faded to a dim outline, and as it did, the grasping tentacles slid through its intangible form. The void lashed out with a pseudopod of darkness toward Liam. Liam could feel the void's palpable anger now focused on him. The tendril dissipated under the harsh light, as did those grappling Izzy and Derek. Like a fireworks snake, the incinerating tendrils traced back to the pool from which they emerged.

The black, tar-like substance of the pool smoldered and began to char as it tried to retreat from the light. Crumbling to ash, the dark mass evaporated, leaving a murky, water-filled depression. Released from their captor, Izzy and Derek fell back into the brush surrounding the pool.

"And you had doubts, sister." Derek picked himself up and brushed himself off, looking at Izzy with a raised eyebrow.

"I think any qualms have been put to rest," she answered, regaining her feet. "He truly is O' Cathbad."

Liam released his concentration on the light on the end of his staff. The terrain fell back into dimly lit shadows, and the winged feline form coalesced.

"Thou are the Druid O' Cathbad?" Liam wasn't sure which startled him more, the cat uttering intelligible words from its glowing maw, or him getting the gist of what sounded similar to old Irish. The 'thou' term was his best guess, it struck him as different from traditional second person conjugations.

"Ta'im," Liam replied. "I am the descendent of Cathbad."

"The druid, its tongue is strange," the feline hissed, or at least as close as Liam could piece together.

"The Dunwold has changed much," Izzy interjected. Liam noted that the term Dunwold remained intact. He wondered if there was some sort of committee of elves and gnomes who hashed out these terms. "The druid is to challenge the Milesian Accords."

"Truth?" The cat cocked its head, for all the world looking like a common cat, barring the glowing eyes. "It has been too long since this one has walked on the wold of the ancestors. What brings thou to Dunos Scaith?"

"We seek to bring the Champion to Scathach," Izzy said. She sheathed her sword, as did Derek. "She has much to learn before she faces the champion of Avram."

"This one will not hinder thou passing." The great cat turned its glowing green gaze to Liam. Liam caught himself wondering if most supernatural creatures had glowing eyes. "This one owes the Druid O' Cathbad a debt. If the flower-girl cowering behind the Druid is the Champion, doomed are the Exiled Folk."

"Oh, I'm not the Champion," Pixel said, peering out from behind Liam. "I'm the Druid's…um…"

"The Champion is on the Dunwold," Izzy interrupted. "We need to find the passage from the Dunwold to Dunos Scaith so that we can bring the Champion there physically."

"This one cannot help the Left Hand." The shadowcat yawned, emerald light spilling from its maw onto the shadowscape near it, and stretched its huge, black, feathered wings. "This one cannot go to the Dunwold; this one can only be called there."

"What was the creature that was attacking you?" Liam looked around for any more motes of shadow that looked darker and deeper than the rest. "Is it native?"

"That one was Duvaryg. Druid people approaching distracted this one."

"Sorry about that." If this shadowcat could see them coming, Liam wondered what else had noticed them.

"This one was at fault. This one was not vigilant." The cat looked toward the pool of still water. "*Dengw* of Duvaryg hunt the unwary."

"Think of smoky chunks of black anger come to life," Pixel added. "Sometimes they form around the sites of great battles; sometimes they are drawn to the site of a potential battle."

Liam looked around, trying to find some sort of landmark that would narrow it down more than the Rockies in Colorado. "Is the portal or doorway to Dunos Scaith nearby in the Dunwold?"

"There is a path."

"And where is it?" Great, another supernatural entity that decided to be a jerk by answering questions literally and without explanation.

"On the Dunwold, it is near the summit of the Mountain of War."

Liam looked at Izzy, Derek and Pixel in turn. They all shook their heads. Of course this thing wasn't going to know what landmarks were called on a modern map. It didn't even know how to use proper pronouns. Liam leaned on his staff and furrowed his brow. His eyes were drawn to the same pool at which the shadowcat was gazing, and Liam realized he was seeing something reflected in the surface of the water.

'SSECCA DETCIRTSER'

It was a reflection of a sign, actually two signs, alongside a road.

'RESTRICTED ACCESS'

'OFFICIAL GOVERNMENT BUSINESS ONLY'

'WARNING'

'U.S. Air Force Installation'

"Fucking Mountain of War." Liam rubbed his temple. "Of course Scathach would put her fortress on top of gods-damned Cheyenne Mountain."

"What are you seeing in the pool?" Pixel stepped close to him, trying to follow his gaze. Even in the Murkwold she smelled like flowers.

"There is a sign next to a road." Liam looked to Izzy and Derek. Both looked in the pool and shook their heads. "It's for an Air Force installation, the only one I know of is the old NORAD base under Cheyenne Mountain."

"Well done, Druid." Izzy nodded approvingly. "You're right, it would make sense for Scathach to put her home there."

"Hopefully the entrance isn't in the facility itself," Liam said. It could prove really problematic if they had to sneak Erin into one of the most secure facilities on the planet.

"Sounds like a challenge to me." Derek grinned.

"Well, since our friend said 'summit,' hopefully there will be a service road or state park trail that will get you close enough." Liam hadn't read anything in detail about Cheyenne Mountain, or he'd already know the answer. Liam turned to the shadowcat, who watched with typically feline disinterest.

"What is your name?" Liam asked.

The shadowcat's pupil-less eyes affixed on Liam. Liam heard the reply in his mind and realized only he was privy to the creature's answer.

"This one is called Erolas. Use the name wisely, Druid O' Cathbad."

* * * * *

Chapter Eighteen

Erin

"They're back."

Erin looked down at her son. Tim's hushed whisper had barely been audible over the popping of the fire, even though the local wildlife went silent as soon as Liam and the others started their...what? Meditation? Ritual? Even the breeze circling the clearing barely made a noise.

At first the four of them spoke distinctly, with Liam doing most of the talking as he guided or hypnotized them through some breathing and focus exercises. That part she could understand, then they started some sort of guided dream-walk. After a few minutes, the volume of their voices began to decrease, until there was only the occasional murmur. Erin stalked around the perimeter of the grassy area, her nerves buzzing and blood racing, making it hard for her to sit still.

Something must have been happening in their shared dream five minutes ago, as they all twitched and their expressions changed from placid to intense. Liam's brow had broken out in sweat as his brow furrowed in concentration. Erin had tensed, considering trying to wake them, but Einar had caught her eye and shook his head. The clouds chose that moment to part, bathing the four vision-seekers in pale moonlight, and the wind kicked up.

She had circled back to the fire pit when Tim made his announcement. Looking back at the quartet, nothing seemed different. Their expressions had gone slack again a couple of minutes ago, and none of them moved. Erin looked back to Tim, who was staring at the four.

"They just came through the dolmen," Tim whispered.

Erin looked at the structure, the stone slabs casting deep shadows in the moonlight, but she saw nothing else. Then Liam let out a soft moan and mumbled something unintelligible. Izzy and Derek both opened their eyes; Erin noticed the first thing they did was sweep the area behind the other. Then Pixel stirred, releasing Derek's hand and rubbing the back of her neck.

Liam drew a deep breath, then blinked. "Whoa."

"Well done, Druid." Izzy released her hold on Liam and Derek, then stretched, cat-like. Erin caught herself admiring the lithe muscles under the tight leather as Izzy continued the stretch as she stood. "I thought this would merely be a warm up."

"Indeed." Derek also gained his feet, flexing his limbs as he did so. Erin averted her gaze, the last thing she wanted was for Derek to think she was watching him. "I would qualify tonight as a spectacular success."

"Liam, are you okay?" Pixel's question drew her gaze back to Liam, who still remained seated, the six-foot long stick across his lap. Erin realized with a tinge of annoyance that the purple-haired girl was still clasping Liam's hand.

"Yeah, I'm okay." Liam nodded, then rolled his shoulders. "I feel as though I plugged into a light socket. I'm still tingling but a little drained."

"I'm not surprised," Pixel said as she scooted over next to him, adding to Erin's irritation. "You channeled enough magic to pull moonlight into the Murkwold, and did it with your spirit-form a long way away from your corporeal body."

"How far away?" Erin asked, sick of being a bystander.

Liam turned his head and looked up at Erin. His eyes still had an unfocused look, like someone half asleep. "Colorado Springs. So roughly a thousand miles, give or take."

"You mean you were a thousand miles away from here?" Tim ran over, circling around to get in front of Liam. "Did you fly, or did you turn into birds and fly? Or did you teleport there, like on Star Trek?"

Liam smiled, and his eyes focused. "It was more like walking, but each step we took was like driving a mile here. It was hard to judge. There aren't a lot of landmarks in the Murkwold, and no road signs."

"Cool. Do you think you could walk across an ocean? If you were at the North Pole, would you get cold?" Tim hunkered down in front of Liam. "Can you take me there?"

Erin saw Liam's eyes flick in her direction, but he didn't break his composure.

"Let me get good at it first, then we'll see. There are other things in the Murkwold, that's why we call it the spirit world or something similar. We need to see where it's safe, and I need to get some practice before I try to take tourists. When I first learned how to ride a motorcycle, I got good at it before I would let anyone ride on my bike with me. Okay?"

"You can ride a motorcycle?" Evidently Tim had just awarded Liam some cool points.

"Ja, and he can almost fix them." Einar chuckled at his own joke.

Liam twisted around to face the fire pit, breaking the hold with Pixel in the process. "Shouldn't you be helping Gofannon drain the hard liquor that arrived today?"

"What is this hard liquor?" The hulking blacksmith suddenly stirred. "Is it frozen?"

"No, the pocking dunnies think it's strong." Einar stood from the bench and cracked his knuckles. "But when it comes to drinking, they're almost as lightweight as elves and faeries, some more so."

"Oh, really?" Derek asked with a raised eyebrow. "You think you can keep up, dwarf?"

"I am not cleaning up after this," Izzy interjected. "But I wager a bottle of mead on my brother."

"Can I contest in this drinking?" the smith asked, interested now.

Erin wondered what it was about supernatural beings and booze.

"That's not pocking fair," Einar protested. "After all, you're a god. You have more mass than the sidhe and I put together." When Gofannon's mustache drooped in a frown, Einar quickly added, "But you can keep up with us as a spectator."

"Splendid!" Gofannon boomed.

"Why don't you guys head to the garage and start your booze challenge?" Liam nodded toward the house. "I think Erin, Tim, and I need to talk."

"Ja, enough of this pocking mystic reindeer-shit for tonight." Einar turned toward the house. "Let's see how many shots it takes for a xanoso to kiss the floor."

"Good luck with that, dwarf," Derek retorted. "You'll be combing the remains of your defeat from your beard in the morning."

Their banter continued as it faded. Erin looked around and saw Pixel lurking at the edge of the firelight, watching Liam. Erin felt another pang of irritation. She wasn't sure what was going on be-tween the purple-haired girl and Liam, but Erin didn't feel inclined to include her in private family business. Erin cleared her throat, getting Liam's attention, then nodded toward the girl, resisting the urge to ask him to send his pet sprite inside. Liam realized what Erin was getting at and returned her nod.

"Pixel, why don't you head to the house?" Liam planted one end of the walking stick in the ground, using it to push himself upright. "We'll be along in a little bit." He brushed grass off his robe and stretched his legs, probably stiff from sitting on the ground for an hour.

"Surely it's okay if I stay." Pixel directed this to Erin, affixing her eyes on Erin's. She gave Erin a half-grin as she held her gaze.

Erin felt a buzz at the back of her head. Had she wanted the girl to leave? Then the annoyance flared again, and the buzzing was muf-fled.

"Knock it off!" Liam stamped the butt of the staff on the ground, and the buzzing vanished entirely. The wind gusted around him. Pixel took a step back, blinking. "You don't pull that glamour stuff on our people, understand?"

"Sorry. I just…sorry." The girl spun and practically fled toward the house.

"Wow, did she try to put some sort of charm spell on Mom?" Tim was watching where the girl had disappeared along the path winding around a hedge toward the house.

"Something similar," Liam answered, moving toward one of the benches by the fire pit. "It's probably closer to a form of hypnosis. They call it a glamour, and she is too loose with when and on whom she uses it."

"Is that why her eyes glow?" Tim followed Liam, and Erin fell in behind Tim.

"I'm not sure. They seem to glow a lot, especially in dim light."

"Wait, Tim, you said her eyes glowed?" Erin's annoyance was bordering on outright anger; that little bitch had tried to hypnotize her. "I didn't see anything."

"Really?" Liam straightened his robes as he settled on the bench. "I want to do a quick experiment; humor me. The two of you stand back-to-back."

Erin shrugged, then complied, as did Tim, who seemed much more eager.

"Okay, without looking at each other, I want you to hold a hand up to show how tall you think Einar is."

Erin held her hand up. Einar was a touch shorter than her, so it was an easy estimate.

"Keeping your hands at that height, turn toward me."

Erin kept her hand aloft and turned 90 degrees toward the fire. Out of the corner of her eye, she could see Tim turning as well. Erin realized Tim was holding his hand about even with her chin.

"That's interesting." Liam looked from one hand to the other. "Okay, you can put your hands down. So it looks as though Tim can see through their seeming, an illusion they use to tweak their appearances."

"Is it because you're my father?"

A grin spread across Liam's face. Seeing it caused Erin's anger to fizzle out, she'd always hoped if she ever found Tim's father, he'd be happy about it, if nothing else for what it would mean to Tim. Seeing Liam's smile told her all she needed to know.

"Probably. It turns out we are descended from an ancient druid. Evidently you got some of the mojo in addition to my left eye."

"Cool!" Tim sat on the bench next to Liam. "Does that mean I'll be able to do magic like you do?"

Liam chuckled. "Tim, I'm still not sure how I do this magic, or what all it can do, so it's hard for me to guess. Plus, your mom is descended from Cu Chulainn, the biggest bad—um the toughest warrior in Irish legend. Those are some pretty good genes to have as well."

"How about you concentrate on junior high before worrying about becoming the next Harry Potter." Erin took a seat on the next bench. "So, as you've guessed by now, I told Tim who you are."

Tim nodded. "She said you didn't know about me or how to find her."

"That's right. The campground where we met, it was really a festival, but they didn't do a good job of keeping track of who was who or making sure everyone registered." Liam looked a bit sheepish. "Plus, I didn't have a cell-phone yet, so I didn't do the obvious thing and ask for her phone number right away."

"Are you like one of those Amish people?" Tim lowered his voice conspiratorially. "Is that why you don't have cable or wifi or video games?"

"No, I'm not Amish, or anything like that, though I've been accused of being a Luddite," Liam responded. "I'm not good with technology, and it never really held any interest for me. I have enough hobbies as it is, and I can't imagine adding videogames and computers to the mix."

Erin could see the resemblance between the two of them as they sat side-by-side in the flickering firelight. It was especially strong around the eyes; they had the same eye shape and the same brow. She was tempted to ask Liam if he had any pictures from when he was Tim's age.

"Can I ask you something?" Tim asked, his expression serious.

"Of course," Liam replied. "I'll answer it if I can."

"If you had known about me, would you have tried to find us?"

"Absolutely." Liam looked over at Erin. "One of my regrets was my parents passed on before I could give them grandchildren. I can't say how things would have worked out—your Mom and I were a lot younger—but I would have done whatever I could."

Tim looked satisfied by the answer, smiling as he turned his gaze to the flames, probably trying to imagine what it would have been like to have a father around instead of being raised by Erin's parents while she was in the military on deployment.

"So was this your parents' farm?" Tim looked up from the fire.

"It belonged to my aunt and uncle. They had no children, so they left the house and the farm to me in their will." Liam glanced back toward the house. "I think they'd be surprised by some of my guests, but I think they hoped having it would prod me to fill it up with a family. I rent out the farmland to cover taxes, insurance, and most of my bills."

"I think the house wants you to fill it up also," Tim said earnestly. "I think it's kind of lonely."

"Well, it's been only me rattling around in it for six years, so it would seem pretty lonely." Liam turned to Erin. "So, can we go back to the house without you throttling Pixel? I know she's clingy; I think she's appointed herself my babysitter, as it were."

Erin sighed. She hadn't pictured wrapping her hands around the girl's slender neck until then and had to banish the image. Plus, she felt as though she'd drank a triple espresso; maybe a drink or two would help her calm down before calling it a night.

"Sure, I promise not to wring her neck," Erin replied. "But if she tries that Jedi mind-meld crap on me, all bets are off."

"Mom, Jedi do mind-tricks, Vulcans do mind-melds," Tim said, sounding exasperated. Erin absorbed a bit of pop culture through osmosis, but she couldn't keep track of all the vagaries. Each one was their own language, a nerd patois, as it were.

"So was that a mind-meld or a mind-trick?" Erin glanced over at Liam, who shrugged as he stood up. She guessed he knew even less about such matters than she did.

"Definitely a mind-trick," Tim replied matter-of-factly. "I mean, she's no Jedi, but it was just like a mind-trick. I wonder if George Lucas got the idea from the magical folk?"

"He's the guy who invented Star Wars, right?" Liam waited for them to stand, then led them up the path toward the house.

"Yeah, he is, though a lot of people are mad at him about it." Tim walked between Liam and Erin as they wove through the hedge then the gate next to a garden. "I don't know why they're mad, I thought Jar Jar was funny."

"I'll defer to your expertise." Even though he didn't need it, Liam tapped the large walking stick on the ground as he marched toward the house. Now visible, Erin could see a few windows lit up on the ground floor as well as the garage.

Liam led them around the garage to where the big doors opened onto the driveway. Izzy and Pixel both looked up as they walked in. Erin could only guess what the conversation had been about— probably what a bitch she was. Erin had flashbacks to high school.

Maybe women being catty to each other was something that transcended the mundane realm.

"Hi! The guys are inside starting their drinking contest." Pixel beamed a smile as though nothing was amiss, even though five minutes ago she was on the verge of tears and Erin was ready to find out if her roots were purple. Yup; same as high school.

"No drinking contest for me," Liam said, holding up his hand and shaking his head as he crossed the garage for the door that led into the house. "But we'd better have a quick powwow before they get too blitzed to remember English."

Erin followed, wondering if he was going to lay down ground rules about no using magic powers on, what was the term, dunnies? Erin wondered if Tim was affected by their glamours since he seemed to be able to see through their illusions.

At the steps into the kitchen, Liam triggered the garage door to close and turned to Tim. "See, not Amish, or Mennonite, since I think they can have electric lights but not fancier technology."

"Maybe tomorrow you can take me on your motorcycle?" Tim had admired the Yamaha as they passed it.

"First, we'd need to see if it's okay with your mother." Liam ticked off a finger, then added another. "Second, I need to finish putting it back together since I was working on it when everything got turned upside down."

"You mean when we showed up?" Tim asked.

"No, when Einar and Pixel showed up, and we went through a bunch of—" Liam glanced at Erin then back to Tim. "They told me about all this stuff that was going on."

"And then we practically had to carry him up the pocking stairs." Einar's laughter came from the dining room. "And he was all, no if

I'm Irish I can hold my fecking booze. I thought he was going to chuck over the railing!"

Derek's chortle was quickly drowned out by Gofannon's booming laugh. The fact Liam was now standing in the doorway to the dining room did not cause their mirth to abate. Erin could only guess at Liam's expression since she was behind him.

"And that's why I'm not touching the hard liquor tonight," Liam remarked as he circled the dining room table. "As much as I want some after our little trip, I'll settle for a beer. Maybe three."

Einar booed while the other two continued laughing, then all three threw back a shot of what Erin presumed was whiskey. A bottle of Old Tom Horan was on the table, already half empty. She snatched up an empty shot glass and thunked it down on the wood next to the three empties that had just smacked down.

"I'm not going to pretend I can keep up with you, but I could really use a shot."

"There we go!" Einar roared in approval. "If she fights like a champion, she should drink like a champion!"

"Maybe a little *vino veritas* will thaw her out?" Derek cocked an eyebrow and suddenly the room felt warm.

Erin accepted the shot and downed it. Pretty similar to Jameson, she savored the mild burn as it went down. She immediately had second thoughts about drinking in front of Tim before quickly realizing this wasn't the weirdest thing he'd seen all day by a long shot.

"Sweetie, do you want a soda?" Pixel asked Tim, who silently nodded.

"While you're at it, could you get me a beer?" Erin asked. Two could play the "nothing happened" game, Erin thought. Plus, her shot glass had already been refilled, and she wanted to break the cycle.

"Sure." Pixel smiled sweetly and ducked into the kitchen, quickly returning while the round of whiskey went down.

"Thank you." Erin accepted the beer and made sure her shot glass stayed out of Derek and Einar's reach, who were taking turns pouring. She quelled a flash of annoyance when Pixel handed Liam the other beer then hovered at his elbow.

"Alright, while we're all here and still somewhat sober, let's talk about sleeping arrangements." Liam took a draw from his beer to hedge against the awkward silence that followed.

Erin turned her bottle around. It said 'Kiss the Anvil Stout,' by Harter Brewing. She took a drink, it was a malty, potent stout with hints of honey and chocolate. Very tasty, and probably much stronger than an amateur would guess. This could be more dangerous than the shots.

Liam continued, wiping some foam from his mustache, "Tim and Erin each have their own rooms, and I have mine of course. That leaves two more bedrooms, plus crash space in the living room." He took another drag from his bottle.

"Why don't you and Mom sleep together?" Tim asked innocently. "It would free up a room."

Erin fought to keep from coughing beer out her nose. From the way Liam's eyes watered, he was having similar difficulties, or perhaps he had inhaled some of his beer. Pixel scowled without looking at anyone, and Derek smirked behind his hand, fighting to keep from laughing.

"I mean, since you're my father, it's okay, right?" Tim added, confused by the reactions.

Liam caught Erin's eye even as he caught his breath; his expression said it all. 'Help?'

"Tim, Liam and I haven't seen each other in a long time. When people have been apart for so long, they don't automatically…" Images formed unbidden in Erin's mind that caused her pulse to quicken, mostly drawn from the night Tim was conceived. It was a long time ago, she reminded herself, pushing aside the memories that had derailed her explanation.

"They might as well," Derek muttered to Einar. "I've never seen two people in greater need of getting laid."

If looks could kill, Pixel would have slain Derek on the spot while Einar guffawed.

"Your mom is right. We haven't seen each other in a long time, and we haven't had time to talk about anything like that," Liam said, his voice slightly raspy as he tried to clear the last of the stout from his airway. "It's best if she has her own room, and since she's the Champion, I don't think anyone would dispute it."

There were nods around the table even as another round of shot glasses were filled. Derek went to the liquor cabinet and opened it. Bottles of alcohol were lined up from today's shopping trip. He grinned and selected a bottle of Patron. Erin made sure her glass was well out of reach. The last thing she needed was to add tequila to this mix.

"Gofannon, as a host, I'm sad to say none of my beds are large enough to accommodate your physical incarnation." Liam gestured toward the living room. "I've pulled a couple of futons out of the basement that should make a passable pallet."

"Do not concern yourself, Druid." The hulking man sniffed at the shot Derek handed him, before downing it. Erin caught herself from recommending salt and lime; she didn't want to get swept up in their drinking challenge. "I have rested in much more primitive accommodations, besides, how could your Dunwold carpenters anticipate someone of my tremendous physique?"

"How indeed? I'll let the rest of you decide who gets a bed, and who gets a couch. There's plenty of linens, blankets, and pillows, so hopefully we can make everyone comfortable." Liam took another long drink from his beer then set it down on the table. "With that, I'm going to change out of this robe. I'll be right back."

Erin stifled the urge to follow him. What was wrong with her? Was nostalgia making her so horny, or something else? Ever since she ate that damned apple, she felt as though her blood had been running hotter. She wondered if anyone would notice if she slipped away for a cold shower?

* * * * *

Chapter Nineteen

Liam

"**L**iam, are you awake?"

Liam contemplated feigning sleep and quickly dismissed it. If the lilted accent didn't give it away, the floral scent told him Pixel was in the room. Had he drifted off, and she crept in? He thought he had locked the door behind him, or had she been lurking in here when he entered the room, and he didn't notice?

"Yeah, I couldn't sleep." That was true. Even though part of him was wiped from their little adventure in the Murkwold, not to mention the rest of the emotional roller-coaster of the day, he couldn't get his mind to turn off, and his cells still buzzed like he'd chugged an energy drink. He'd hoped the booze would have taken the edge off, but it just gave him a different kind of buzz.

Liam rolled over to face Pixel. He could see her silhouetted against the moonlit window, the pale light washing through the fabric of her dress and highlighting Pixel's slim figure. Her eyes were gleaming despite the fact that the moon was behind her. She drew up her sundress and shed it, discarding the garment out of sight. Even in the dim light, Liam could tell she wore nothing else, and he felt himself instantly get aroused.

"You know, I'm not in any danger of choking." Liam couldn't pull his gaze away as she slid into the bed next to him, an arm's length away. Part of him tried to order his body to scoot away, while other parts prodded him to edge closer, leaving him frozen in place. "I only had a couple of beers and a couple of shots, not like last night when I tried to drown my brain cells in tequila."

"I know," Pixel replied, propping herself up with her elbow. Liam's eyes had adjusted to the dark enough to clearly see her perky breasts. He was thankful the swirling tattoo disappeared under the sheets. "I was looking out for you. I probably should have done a better job the first night, but you seemed determined to get plastered."

"In all honestly, tonight would have been the night I expected to get blitzed." A war waged as Liam fought to decide between doing what he thought was right and what his body thought was natural. She was practically throwing herself at him, so there was nothing wrong, right? But how old was she? Was she reading more into this? And was it the right thing to do now that Erin had shown up after all this time? "Between what we experienced in the Murkwold, and all of a sudden I have a son, it's an awful lot for a sober brain to take in."

The glow from Pixel's eyes muted. "Is it important for you? I mean Tim being your son?"

"I'd never thought about children before today, not in any serious way." This line of discussion was helping him compartment off what his body was goading him to do. He felt like he was a teenager again, flush with hormones, and wondered if it was Pixel's doing. "I haven't had a lot of girlfriends and never any kids. Then all of a sudden Erin reappears with my son. It's as if this whole crazy thing was to bring us back together."

"Or that your fates were so strongly intertwined that you and Erin were drawn together, and she bore you a son to ensure you would help her." Pixel edged closer. Her fragrance was even stronger and her warmth was palpable. Her voice lowered to whisper, encouraging him to lean closer to hear. "It doesn't mean your future is with her."

Liam's blood pounded in his ears. Could that be true? Had the Fates merely brought Erin and him together 13 years ago to make sure he would aid her in her role as Champion because she was his son's mother? Liam closed his eyes and collected his thoughts. He needed some space before he gave in to a rash impulse. Idunn's Apple was still making his blood run hot and the last thing he wanted to do was succumb to some spur of the moment whim that would come back to haunt him.

"I need to get some air." Asserting his willpower, Liam rolled out of the bed away from Pixel. He didn't look back; if his escape hadn't pulled the sheets down from where they had been draped over Pixel's hips, he was certain she would have slid them down in a last bid to tempt him. Liam grabbed the same gi pants he'd worn under his robe, finding them by memory where he had discarded them in the darkness.

"Do you want some company?" Pixel asked. Out of the corner of his eyes he saw her eyes flare brightly in the darkened room, threating to outshine the moonlight. If she was trying to glamour him, it shed off his will like water. He was in greater danger of succumbing to physical temptation than mystic compulsion.

"No, actually, I think I need a little bit of time to myself." Pulling on his gi pants, he made sure to turn away so she couldn't see part of him really wanted to stay. Liam snagged a t-shirt from on top of the dresser and headed to the door. It was locked from the inside, as he thought. "I have a lot of stuff to process. Don't wait up, one of us should get some sleep."

Liam tried to go through the thick oak door from his bedroom as quietly as possible, but the door creaked before it clicked shut. Relieved that Pixel hadn't decided to pursue him, he slipped on the t-shirt. Then again, he hadn't kicked her out of the room, so she would probably still be there waiting for him when he eventually returned. What would he do then?

His eye drifted to the door of Erin's room across the hall and immediately he felt flush. No, he was in no state to talk to her. He considered hopping in the shower to take the pressure off and cool down, then thought better of it. He was getting too caught up in what was going on. He was letting the apple and magic and chaos get in his head; he needed to ground himself and get focused.

He quietly padded down the staircase, wincing as the odd step creaked, and crept past the living room doorway. Someone else might have thought there was a bear growling in there, but Liam knew it was Gofannon, snoring away on his pallet. Peeking in, Liam could make out Einar on one of the couches, his snores drowned out by the smith god. That left Izzy and Derek and the last guestroom. Liam decided to assume one of them was on the floor and not dwell on it.

As Liam passed through the dining room, part of his mind registered there should have been empty bottles and cups to pick up. The drinking challenge, and the drinking that had followed it, had left an impressive debris field, but the table was clear, the wood looked polished, and the room was tidy. When the gathering broke up, Liam hadn't noticed anyone lingering to clean up. Had Pixel done it, biding her time to pounce?

Deciding it didn't really matter, Liam went through the kitchen and into the garage. He went to the fridge and opened it, and was relieved to see the case of Harter's Stout still had a couple of bottles left. Liam hoped Cripes' Liquor Store wasn't sold out so they could replenish tomorrow. He retrieved a bottle from the carton then decided to grab the last one as well.

Exiting out the door by the smith workshop, he followed the gravel path past the forge shed. He walked the winding path through the hedge to the dolmen, guided by memory, moonlight, and as he grew close, the glow cast by the dwindling fire.

"You couldn't sleep either?" Erin asked, looking into the flames flickering in the fire pit.

"No, I couldn't settle down." Liam knew it would be a bad idea to mention Pixel's part in his restlessness. The glances he'd caught between the two women had left him thinking it was just as well Pixel wasn't on Erin's team. What happened in his bedroom had clarified why Pixel was antagonistic toward Erin. He wasn't sure why Erin felt that way; perhaps it was purely reactionary. "If you want, I can go somewhere else."

Erin looked up from the fire. "No, it's okay. If nothing else, it kind of brings us full circle. Besides, you brought beer."

Liam sat down on the bench next to her, handing her one of the stouts. He immediately caught a whiff of strawberries, the same as when they had met all those years ago, only stronger. He realized her raven-black hair was damp and no longer pulled into a braid; she had recently showered. He resisted the urge to sniff her hair. Mostly.

"Well, minus the two old guys hoping to get you drunk." Liam gestured to the empty benches. Thirteen years ago he'd met her around a similar fire pit, although it was ringed with simple logs as opposed to benches. A couple of members of the local 'community' had spotted a nubile and naïve college girl, already separated from her friends, and had moved in like wolves on the hunt. "As I remember, they were trying to lure you off to their tent."

"I didn't need your help, you know," Erin said, facing him. Her eyes were so green, a bright pale green with gold flecks, not like his deep green right eye. "Though it was kind of cute, you rushing to the rescue of the 'fair maiden.' Especially since you were so earnest about it."

The night came back to Liam crystal clear, as did almost everything he experienced. All he had to do was focus on the event in question, and it was like watching a movie in his mind. "You know they had laced their mead with Everclear? I mean, I told you they did."

"I remember." She inched closer on the bench; the fire crackled, and the air seemed to grow warmer despite the breeze ruffling Liam's hair. "I told you I could have kicked their asses. At the time, I was already working on my second black belt. I expected them to get grabby sooner or later."

Liam held her gaze. Even behind the fierceness in her expression, there was something else, the same as back then once he'd chased off the two old pervs. He felt his lip twitch and tried to squelch it. "Their plan was to get you so drunk it wouldn't have mattered, black belts or not."

"And you took it upon yourself to stand up to them." Erin's face was only inches from Liam's as she leaned in, her eyes still locked with his. "Even though you didn't need to."

"I had to," Liam responded. His lip twitched again. Then his lips found hers, all hesitation melting, the same as when she had gone back with him to his tent all those years ago. They embraced and drew each other together. Liam pulled Erin onto his lap as they continued to kiss, making out like passionate teenagers. Her hands went behind his neck as his drifted down her back.

Erin was wearing a t-shirt for some bar in Cincinnati. Liam found the hem and pulled it off.

* * * * *

Chapter Twenty

Iblis

"What is that?"

Raven's exclamation roused Iblis's attention, drawing him back to the here and now. He turned to face the table where the witch was leaning over the scrying bowl, seeking more clues to the Druid's whereabouts. There had been a ping in Peoria, an impression of a middle-aged man and books—lots of books. Then the reading had been lost, the confounded druid once again elusive.

"What do you see?" Iblis asked as he glided toward the table, his footfalls silent as he stood at the witch's shoulder. Raven seemed transfixed on the bowl, but no images appeared on the water's surface.

"Power."

Iblis realized there was light in the bowl's water, separate from the flickering candles. The first pulse he saw was dim green, reminding him of the glow sticks favored by ravers. Another pulse, a little stronger, a little lighter. A few moments later, there was another burst of light. Iblis closed his corporeal eyes and opened his mystic senses, his third eye. In the distance, magical energy thrummed against the barrier between the physical world and the magical one.

He debated shedding his body for a better perspective. Despite the increasing intensity and tempo of the surges, something was keeping him from getting a more precise fix. Was one of the other interested parties resorting to forbidden magic, as he was, or exercising an angelic talent? Perhaps they had found the Druid and were trying to flush him out or batter down whatever had kept him out of sight?

Raven moaned, and again Iblis had to yank his awareness back to his physical shell. Like a deer in the headlights, she continued to gaze at the pulsing bowl, the glow brightening from emerald green to almost white, each flash illuminating the whole room. Iblis sniffed the air, quickly recognizing the scent of the woman's arousal. His eyes slid down to her chest, where her nipples were clearly visible through the thin fabric of her peasant blouse.

His fleshly form responded. He had no qualms against engaging in some carnal pleasure with his minions, but there was a time and place for everything. Pulse, pulse, pulse. He imagined himself bending the witch over the table, hitching up her skirt, and giving her the fucking she obviously craved, pumping in and out…in time to the strobing light. Then the pace quickened, each accompanying burst of radiance brighter than the last.

His eyes snapped back to the table as he recognized the tempo. The bowl flashed blindingly white then exploded. Shards of glass peppered the room, and the water erupted outward. Raven recoiled as her face was drenched, and a line of red dots blossomed across her blouse right under her breasts.

Some of the shrapnel struck Iblis where the front of his long coat was open, and he registered the sting as it pierced his skin. Spots bloomed in front of his physical eyes as well as his mystic one, overwhelmed by the sheer magnitude of the flare. He closed his body's eyes, he didn't need them for the moment. He needed to see where the torrent of magical energy had punched through into the physical world. If he could find the breach and correlate it to its location, he might be able to track down the Druid, or whoever had caused this momentary metaphysical nova.

Iblis turned off his other physical senses to give all of his attention to the mystic plane. He slid out of his body, letting it collapse in a heap to the floor. The ether of the spirit world was still illuminated by the afterglow, but even that was fading quickly as the barrier between worlds sealed itself. The same pact the Abrahamic factions had imposed on the exiled pagan factions now stymied Iblis as the fabric of reality mended itself faster than he could regain his senses.

With the equivalent of a sigh, Iblis slipped back into his body, still unceremoniously splayed on the floor. Raven was wailing, one hand clutching her body as the other probed her face. Iblis stood, straightening out his clothes. Taking stock of his corporeal form, he concluded his injuries were superficial at best. There was the tinkle of glass falling to the already littered floor as it was pushed from his body.

"Raven, listen to me." Iblis said, placing a reassuring hand on her shoulder. "You're going to be all right, but I need you to calm down." He didn't know, but he wanted her to quit making so much racket. He sent a little of his energy into her, dampening her pain receptors while triggering her pleasure centers. That settled her down, and she sagged back into her chair.

Iblis cupped her chin and lifted it slightly so he could inspect her eyes in the dim light. There didn't appear to be any physical damage. Reaching down, he pulled the bottom hem of her blouse up. A line of small wounds tracked across her torso, from where the shards of glass had blasted parallel with the surface of the table. Even with the faint illumination left in the room, he could see the glint of glass, the fragments had not pierced deep.

"Stay still. I will call someone to take you to a doctor, we'll get you fixed right up." In truth, as with his own injuries, the shrapnel wounds looked superficial. Some tweezers, some ointment, then slap some bandages on them and let them heal.

"My eyes, I still can't see."

"It's like a really bright flash bulb going off; you'll be fine given time," Iblis lied. Well, maybe lying was too strong; unfounded speculation was closer. He might have to expend some mojo to help her if he could. She had tapped into something powerful and primal. He had chosen her well, and it would be a shame to start over from scratch. "Though it might be quicker if we bring in some of your coven; some collective positive energy will speed your recovery."

Raven nodded weakly. Most of the people in her coven were fluffy-bunny crystal-waving Wiccans, but there were a few who both showed promise and seemed pliable enough to embrace a more pragmatic viewpoint, where philosophy wasn't as important as results. Raven had been the best combination of talent and flexibility, plus she had desperately craved validation. Turning her to Iblis' goals had been easy.

Giving Raven one last pat on the shoulder, Iblis rose and left the room, his shoes crunching on glass. Once in the hall, he took out his phone and dialed.

"Bruno. I need you to come to my office on Eckler. I have an...associate who needs to see a doctor. No, not an overdose. No, not a gunshot." Iblis sighed. "It's not life-threatening, but she needs some broken glass plucked out. Oh, and she's blind, but I don't really expect him to deal with that. Tell him a light fixture blew up in front of her, but a filter kept her from catching glass with her face. Thank you."

Iblis shook his head as he dialed another number. Now he had a bit more information to give his basement trolls, who were scouring the Internet for clues regarding the location of the Druid. Maybe with a bit more data they could actually turn up something useable. How well could he hide in someplace like Peoria?

* * * * *

Chapter Twenty-One

Erin

"**M**om, are you awake?"

Erin stirred groggily. Even with the world turned inside out, some things didn't change. "What is it, Tim?"

"Einar's making breakfast, if you want some," Tim called through the door. "Also, no one knows where Liam went. Is he, um, in there with you?" Somehow her son managed to sound awkward and hopeful at the same time.

The events of last night came back. Erin looked around the bedroom, dimly illuminated by what sunlight filtered through the blinds and drapes. She was alone in the bed, in the room. She was wearing her t-shirt and sweats from last night. She took stock of herself. There was no hangover, though she was sore in other places; the ground and especially the stone bench hadn't been forgiving last night. A sniff confirmed she was desperately in need of a shower.

She cracked open the stout oak door. Tim was alone in the hall. Erin let the door swing open farther. "Liam isn't here, I'd assume he'd be in his room."

"Okay. No one has seen him, and people were whispering that you and he might be…um…that he might be here." Tim's face flushed red. "And I don't think Gofannon knows how to whisper.

Pixel said I should come up here and let you guys—well, I guess you—know about breakfast so it wouldn't get cold."

"Okay, sweetie, I need to grab a shower, and I'll be down." Erin looked across the hall to where the door to Liam's room stood ajar. "I'm sure Liam will turn up."

"Mom?" Tim squinted. "Is there grass in your hair?"

This time it was Erin who fought not to blush with embarrassment. "Why don't you go downstairs and make sure Gofannon doesn't eat all of the pancakes while I clean up? I'll be down in a bit."

Tim nodded and hurried off. As he thumped down the stairs, Erin ducked into her room and looked for clean clothes. Her clothes from yesterday were cleaned and neatly folded on the dresser. Surely Liam didn't skulk around in the early morning hours covertly doing laundry. Shrugging, she fished a different shirt and panties out of her bag. Even if they were clean, she didn't want to wear the same ones twice in a row.

Padding to the bathroom next door, Erin lingered in the shower, not only to make sure the detritus of last night's activities had all been washed away, but to give herself time to think. What had come over her? She hadn't had too much to drink; she'd been a bit buzzed but still in her right mind. She'd thought Liam was the same, a bit less reserved but not drunk.

Was it the so-called magic apple? She mentally rolled her eyes at the notion. It was probably a perfect storm of all the chaos and emotional upheaval of the day, nostalgia for that night long ago, and the fact she hadn't been laid in almost two years. Once she framed it in her mind, it made perfect sense.

But would Liam see it the same way? Was he out there buying her roses and planning their wedding? He had struck her as somewhat old-fashioned, certainly not a member of the current app-driven hook-up generation. She got the impression he hadn't had a girlfriend in a while. Hopefully that meant his part in last night was fueled by pent up physical desire and not unfulfilled romanticism. And she didn't want to get Tim's hopes up. He was obviously excited they had found his father, but now he was really hoping they would become a family, white farmhouse already set up. Is that what she wanted? No. She didn't want to become some Norman Rockwell housewife, staying home and baking pie.

Then again, if what Izzy had told her about the financial reward for this insane endeavor was true, she wouldn't have to worry about scraping by while working two jobs. She would have the luxury of looking for something she *wanted* to do, not what she *had* to do in order to make ends meet.

She'd have to keep Tim and Liam from getting ahead of themselves without being too harsh. She wanted time to choose her path without being pigeon-holed by others' expectations of her. Of course, she could be over-estimating Liam's romantic notions. Maybe this was just a booty call, a friends with benefits kind of thing to him? Erin had wondered if that was the case with his friend Susan. Maybe he was more practical about sex than she was giving him credit for?

Finishing her shower as the heat began to fade from the water, Erin toweled off and dressed in the bathroom, then dropped her dirty laundry in her room before heading downstairs. From the top of the stairs, she could both smell the aroma of bacon and coffee and hear the rumble of Gofannon's bass drowning out the other voices.

Everyone was crowded in the kitchen around the table. Well, everyone except Liam. Pixel eyed her as she entered then looked past, almost as though she was expecting Liam to be following on Erin's heels.

"There's our Champion," Einar called from the stove. He was wearing an apron over black jeans and a blue sleeveless t-shirt, his hair held back with a blue bandana. "What will you be having in your omelet?"

"Oh, cheese, mushrooms, and ham if you have them?" Erin asked as she scanned the counter for the source of the coffee aroma, spotting it half-hidden behind Derek as he leaned on the counter instead of sitting at the congested table.

"Sleep well?" he chuckled as Erin reached past him for the pot. One of Derek's eyebrows crooked up along with the corner of his mouth. Did he know, Erin wondered. More importantly, what had he already said?

She resisted the urge to sigh as she filled her coffee cup. While her body had returned to the energized state from last night, though a bit diminished, her mind still wasn't wide awake.

There was a clatter from the outside door in the garage. "I can't believe you slept in your yard." Susan's voice came clearly through the screen door. "The bugs probably ate you alive."

Liam's reply was an unintelligible mumble. Erin wondered if he was drunker than she thought. She had slipped away when he dozed off after the third round of love-making, leaving him snoring in the grass. She had assumed he would eventually wake up and find his way inside and had half expected to be awakened by him climbing in bed with her. The kitchen felt a bit warmer as she entertained the thought.

Susan paused at the doorway, taking in the scene before she re-membered Liam was right behind her. She stepped aside, standing next to the counter on the other side of Derek. Derek, of course, was looking down Susan's blouse out of the corner of his eye.

Liam stepped in, his attention on the food at first, then he spotted Erin, catching her eye. She could tell he was suppressing a goofy grin. She suddenly had an image of Einar baking a wedding cake. She needed to talk to Liam in private before he opened his mouth and made promises she wasn't sure she'd want him to keep.

"You've got grass in your hair," Tim piped up, and Erin held her breath, trying to see if the gears were turning in Tim's mind.

"That's what happens when you're wiped out and decide the grass by the fire is as good a place as any for a nap," Liam answered, both groggily and cheerfully. "Einar, are you making omelets?"

"Well I'm not baking a pocking cake," the dwarf replied. "What will you have in yours, druid?"

"Gods bless you, I'll take any meat that you have, cheese, mushrooms, and spinach if we have any." Liam opened a cupboard and pulled out a mug with some sort of weird stick writing on it.

"Einar, I bless you," Gofannon pronounced over a fork of fried potatoes.

"*Thokk*. Someone hand me a plate for this omelet." Einar held out a hand. Even though Pixel was the closest, it was Izzy who handed a plate to Einar.

Pixel was staring at Liam, her face set in stone. Had she figured out what had happened? Erin wouldn't have put it past the purple-haired girl to sneak down to the fire last night to spy on them.

"Hey." Liam wedged himself past Derek, ostensibly to reach the coffee maker. Derek wrinkled his nose and stepped aside. Liam smelled of smoke, grass, sweat, and a tinge of sex. Erin found herself afraid he would kiss her there in front of everyone. Part of her hoped for it, her blood stirring at the memories of what had happened by the dolmen, but she stuffed that part into the back of her mind.

"Hey." She gave him a half smile, trying to strike a balance between friendly and encouraging. Flicking her eyes in Tim's general direction, she whispered, "We should probably talk."

Liam glanced over her shoulder in Tim's direction, then nodded silently.

"Druid, I think you need a bath more than you need breakfast," Derek remarked.

"You are pretty rank, Liam," Susan added. "I can smell you from here. You might make people lose their appetite. Well, except for him." She nodded in Gofannon's direction.

"Go ahead, Druid. I'll feed this to the ever-eating smith and make you up one fresh when you come back," Einar said as he flipped the omelet in the cast iron pan. "Just don't dally; I don't want to be making breakfast come lunch time."

"Fine, I'll be right back." Liam set down the coffee cup and made eye contact with Erin. For a split second, Erin was afraid he was going to invite her to join him, and she had to squelch the voice in her mind suggesting she take him up on it. To her relief, and maybe a tiny bit of disappointment, he merely grinned and left.

Pixel started to move in the same direction, but Izzy stepped in her path. There was an exchange between the two women in a language Erin couldn't understand. Was it Irish, Welsh, something older? Derek looked amused, obviously following the discussion, while Susan looked confused. Einar added something in the same language, though his speech was a bit slower and punctuated with "pocking."

"Fine." Pixel slumped back into her chair, casting Erin a baleful glance.

"So what did I miss last night?" Susan asked, scanning the floor then peeking around the corner into the dining room. Erin tried not to blush while avoiding eye contact. She hadn't parsed how she was going to deal with what had happened with Liam, let alone have it come up for discussion in committee, especially in front of Tim.

"My father spirit-walked to Colorado," Tim responded between slurps of orange juice.

Susan's gaze snapped from the floor, where she still seemed to be looking for something, to Tim. "Your father? And he did what?"

"Tim is Liam's kid." Was that a touch of vindictiveness in Pixel's voice? "Surprise!"

"Pretty cool, huh?" Tim was oblivious to the subtle snark in Pixel's voice. "And last night he took Pixel, Izzy, and Derek on a spirit-walk to Colorado, where they met a shadow-cat and found out where Scathach lives." Tim had obviously been paying attention, Erin noted. He had spent the evening quietly watching and listening as the others discussed what had happened, ostensibly playing on his tablet.

"Liam never said anything about having a kid." Susan looked over at Erin, who couldn't avoid her gaze without being obvious. If nothing else, it certainly deflected any interest in what had happened last night down by the fire pit after everyone else had gone to bed. "In fact, he'd sometimes get a bit sentimental about the fact, as though he was letting someone down by not carrying on the family line."

"Liam and I met at a festival 13 years ago," Erin said, her eyes flicking to her son. "You can do the math. We didn't hear from each other and couldn't find each other until yesterday."

"Well, I guess that gets me off the hook," Susan remarked obliquely. She went back to looking at the floor.

"Off the hook?" Now Erin was curious about what she was searching for.

Susan nodded, turning around to peer into the dining room. "A few years ago, right after Liam inherited this place from his aunt and uncle, I joked if he didn't find someone and have a kid by 40, I'd have one for him. Guess I dodged that bullet. Where's Scooter?"

"Well, you do have child-bearing hips," Pixel muttered. Derek choked on his coffee while Izzy scowled.

"I beg your pardon?" The cat and Liam's children, real or hypothetical, appeared to be forgotten. Susan's eyes narrowed as she glared at Pixel. "And what are you, sixteen?"

"Um, weren't you looking for Scooter?" Tim pointed past Susan to the dining room table, where the tubby black and white cat sat, unblinking.

Still scowling, Susan retrieved the compliant feline. Returning, she glowered at Pixel over the top of the cat's head, who bumped her chin for attention. "So what was this about spirit-walking? Liam used to do vision work back before he went solitary."

Erin realized after an awkward moment the question was directed at her. When none of the others stepped in, she replied, "Liam took them into the spirit world to look for someone named Scathach."

"What's her real name? Liam almost has a phobia regarding using modern technology like the Internet." Susan shifted the cat to better free a hand for petting. "It would probably be more practical to use Google and Facebook. Is she local?"

"No, she's in Colorado," Tim reminded her. "A shadow-cat guards her fortress."

"Did you participate in the vision-seeking?" Susan asked with a frown.

"No." Tim sounded disappointed. "I heard about it when they got back to their bodies."

"I wasn't part of the spirit journey either," Erin said. She had the impression Susan was judging the involvement of a child Tim's age in the occult matters. "I watched over the three of them plus Liam while they did their thing."

"I want to meet a shadow-cat," Tim said, pushing the last couple bits of omelet around his plate.

"Don't be so pocking sure about that," Einar replied from the stove, pouring Liam's ersatz omelet onto Gofannon's plate. The huge man had been oddly silent the whole time, but heartily dug into the fresh omelet. "They're willful, vicious creatures that see people as potential lunch or tools. They miss being able to lurk on the Dunwold and will try to trick or bargain with people to get here."

"So did you guys smoke a little something, or I don't know, maybe pop some mushrooms to help with these visions?" Susan looked around the room. It was obvious she still had doubts, but Erin still had doubts, and she'd had a ringside seat.

"Susan, you have a choice," Izzy spoke up, her tone matter-of-fact. "You can either accept what is going on is real, or you can assume we are mad and have swept Liam, Erin, and Tim up in our delusions. If you think the latter, you should probably leave."

"I'm not saying I accept everything at face value—at least not yet—but if you guys were lunatics, I wouldn't abandon Liam either." The cat head-butted Susan's chin in response.

"Well, since you're here and not running in terror, do you want some breakfast?" Einar asked, picking up a couple eggs from an open carton. Erin realized her own omelet was getting cold and picked up the plate from the table.

"Sure, I don't object to eggs. Did I see mushrooms and spinach?"

"Ja." Einar began picking up ingredients. "Do you want cheese as well?"

"Please," the woman said with a nod. "I'm fine with dairy as well."

"Tim, if you're done, why don't you put your dishes in the sink, and you can go play on your tablet in the front room?" Erin figured an opportunity to stick his nose in his tablet would entice him, as Erin had maintained a "no electronics at the table" rule. Sometimes she thought her son went through withdrawal when deprived of his electronics.

"Sure." Tim collected his plate and silverware, taking them to the old fashioned double sink, then returned for his half-full glass of orange juice. "Don't talk about anything cool without me," he admonished at the doorway to the dining room.

Susan moved to the vacated chair, settling the cat in her lap. She plucked a couple strips of bacon from the nearly emptied platter on the table and set them down in front of Scooter. The cat reached out and snagged the closest one, dragging it to the edge of the table, where it contently munched away.

"Susan, would you like some coffee?" Erin offered. If she wanted to know more about Liam, especially from a woman's insight, Erin realized Susan would be the best source. She was good enough friends with Liam to freely walk into his house, had known him for years, and was obviously fond of him. Had they ever dated? Was Susan's offer to Liam more than mere idle humor?

"Please," Susan said as she half-twisted in the chair. "Mugs are in the cupboard to the right of the sink, above the coffee maker."

Pixel bit back some sort of remark, possibly because Izzy nudged the back of her chair. Susan studiously ignored the purple-haired girl while accepting the coffee from Erin.

"So who are the bad guys?" Susan asked after she sipped the coffee. "If I'm going to buy into this, obviously it isn't a one-sided deal. You guys are challenging these Milesian Accords you mentioned yesterday, and it sounds like someone wants to stop you."

"Pocking Avramites," Einar grumbled as he flipped the omelet.

"I think she is asking us to be more specific," Derek noted. Erin considered shooing him out of his spot along the counter so he'd quit peering down Susan's top. "As in, do we know who is acting against us on the Dunwold?"

"Obviously they, the Avramites as we call them, realize the game is afoot," Izzy added. "They sent toadies to try to kidnap Erin and her son, probably to blackmail her into not accepting the challenge and becoming the Champion."

"Not only that, one of them knew us—Izzy and I—for what we are. That implies more than merely telling some Bible-thugs to go and do a snatch and grab." Derek laced his fingers as he spoke. "And we have to remember, some of our opponents can tap into the Gwuedd."

"Gwuedd?" Susan asked. "That sounds Welsh." She picked at her fried potatoes while waiting on her omelet, probably looking for signs it had been 'contaminated' by meat. Fortunately for the cat, her injunction against eating meat did not appear to extend to feeding Scooter as much bacon as he could beg for.

"It is," Pixel said, breaking her sullen silence, "although it is somewhat simplified over time. The Exiled Folk use a mish-mash of languages as terms were settled on over the centuries to make a common lexicon. Of course, the Avramites will have their own term for what we would translate as 'magic,' calling it divine power or something else more palatable to their supposedly monotheistic dogma."

"So the Christians, Jews, and Muslims have magic?" Susan was distracted as a steaming hot omelet on a plate was set in front of her. After a dose of pepper and a test bite, she continued. "Why don't they use it?"

"When they won the original Challenge, cementing the Milesian Accords, they made it almost impossible to access 'magic.'" Izzy noticed her brother's gaze, reached out, and nudged him. "You hear about miracles, faith healers, and such. While much of it is fraud or superstition, there is a kernel of truth. Also, there are the Elohim, which you probably know of as angels, and their descendants through mortal bloodlines, Nephilim. The latter are not to be taken lightly, and the former are outright frightening.

"Luckily, the servants of Yehovah who walk the Dunwold are few and far between," Izzy continued. Erin caught movement out of the corner of her eye and saw Liam standing in the doorway from the dining room, listening intently. "And because of the way the barrier worked, it is—well, was—difficult for them to draw on their power."

"But because the Challenge is approaching, both sides will be able to draw on more power," Liam said as he entered the kitchen, retrieving his coffee mug from the counter. He smelled faintly of

Irish Spring and Old Spice, a vast improvement. He took a gulp of his coffee, then warmed it up from the pot.

"Here, Druid, take my seat," Izzy offered, standing and clearing her own place setting.

"Thanks." Collecting an empty plate and silverware, he took Izzy's place at the kitchen table. "It sounds like we're having a real meat and potatoes discussion about what we're up against."

"If I'm going to hang around for this, I need to know who the Black Hats are," Susan said, stroking a temporarily-sated cat. "Can they use their magic to figure out where you are?"

Izzy looked thoughtful, her pale blue eyes rising toward the ceiling. "I think we are warded here. Liam has woven potent protections around this house, and even the land. So as long as they aren't compromised, it should be difficult for the enemy to find anyone here."

"That's why we had to track him down at work," Pixel offered. "It was the only place he would stay put long enough that wasn't here."

"So what, you guys followed me home from Word Nerds the other day?" Liam asked, scooping the remaining potatoes and bacon onto his plate. "I'm surprised I didn't notice you."

"Actually, I tried to glamour Kyle into giving me your address," Pixel said, sounding a bit guilty. Erin wondered if it was the same mind-trick Izzy had tried on Ray. "He didn't know it, but he knew what kind of car you had, so we followed you in an Uber."

"Glamour?" Susan asked, looking around. "Someone want to fill me in?"

"Some of what you might call the sidhe, seelie, gwyllon, and so forth have an ability to compel mundane folk," Izzy volunteered.

"It's often called glamouring, which gets confusing because of glamours or illusion charms."

"You'd think the pocking Council of Lexicony would have sorted it out, what with all the other words and terms they wrangled over," Einar grumbled as he flipped Liam's omelet.

"As my sister learned, not all dunnies can be glamoured," Derek chuckled. "At least, not by her."

Erin remembered Ray's remarks, and she wondered what made him able to resist. Normally a beautiful woman like Izzy wouldn't need magic to convince Ray, but he not only shook off her 'glamour;' he knew it for what it was.

"Yes, there are a few people with the right talent, willpower, training, or stroke of luck who can resist being glamoured." Izzy nodded to Liam. "The druid is one, and I suspect the Champion is as well, especially given their bloodlines."

"So why didn't you compel me to leave and forget about all of this?" Susan asked. She caught Derek's gaze and scowled at him. "I'm sure you have all sorts of fun with this glamour."

"Me?" he replied with mock innocence, then arched an eyebrow. "What's wrong, afraid I'll charm you out of your blouse?"

"Not funny," Liam growled, the bemused grin he'd worn since staggering into the house evaporating. "You try compelling her, I'll punch your teeth down your throat. Are we clear?"

Derek's mirth vanished as the room fell into a stunned silence, Izzy looking daggers at her brother. "Crystal clear," he answered evenly. "My apologies, Susan."

"Here, let's feed the Druid before he gets cranky." Einar held the cast iron skillet toward the table. "Help me out, Gofannon."

"Hmm, yes." The smith had seemed distracted, took hold of the sizzling pan without benefit of the handle, and unceremoniously dumped the omelet onto Liam's plate. "Here you go, Druid." He then returned the skillet to Einar, who took it by the handle. "Before you get cranky, whatever that means."

"Your hand." Susan stared at the hand Gofannon had used to grip the hot skillet. "Isn't it burnt?"

Gofannon scoffed. "By something as paltry as a cooking fire?"

Liam dug into his omelet as though he hadn't just threatened someone with bodily harm. Not that Erin blamed him, Derek was kind of a creep, and the notion of being able to hypnotize someone on the spot made him extra creepy. Even as an off-handed jest, the intimation that he could do it to take advantage of Susan had brought out the same 'white knight' she remembered from the campground 13 years ago. No; stop thinking about it, she reminded herself. Even after rounds of sweaty sex in the grass last night, dwelling on when they got together began raising her pulse.

Erin decided to go check on Tim, her breakfast finished. He was in one of the antique stuffed chairs in the living room, tapping away on his tablet, his brow furrowed in concentration. She sat in the chair adjacent to his, watching for several minutes in silence, enjoying the quiet. The kitchen wasn't large, and all of the people talking over each other was getting on her nerves. She probably should have stayed, she admonished herself; Susan was actually asking good questions.

And there was still the big question, the one she wanted to discuss with Liam without any of these supernatural folk kibitzing. If they went through this and won, what would happen then? Would there be some sort of war between the two sides? Hadn't a war started the whole thing to begin with? Would there be Dereks in bars and alleys, waiting to glamour unsuspecting women? What about more exotic and frightening monsters from folklore?

She glanced back toward the kitchen, where Einar's Nordic cadence was drowned out by Gofannon's booming voice. Had Liam blurted out what had happened last night? Maybe they were making plans for lunch; these Exiled Folk seemed obsessed with food and drink—especially the drink.

Erin hadn't realized she had dozed off until she felt a hand on hers. Blinking, she saw Liam kneeling by her chair. She stole a glance at Tim's chair, which was now vacant.

"Sorry, maybe I shouldn't have woken you," Liam whispered. "But you wanted to talk, and quiet time is hard to steal at the moment."

"Yeah. I dozed off, no big deal." She looked around, trying to figure out where everyone was. Einar and Gofannon were easy to pin down, the others less so. "Is there somewhere private?"

"Sure, follow me." He took her hand as she stood from the chair and guided her to a hall past the staircase.

Should she pull her hand back? Probably, if she didn't want him escalating things. Another part turned traitor, causing her to question her resolve, remembering last night. Was the damned apple to blame? She would have thought any physical longing for mere intimacy would have been sated. Was it love?

No, absolutely not. She liked Liam, she decided, but didn't love him. She hardly knew him. As with her last few and far between 'romances,' she needed to keep him at arm's length and not risk getting too attached, or letting him get too attached.

He led her into a small den. An antique desk, probably at least as old as the house, dominated the middle of the room. Two walls were lined with laden bookshelves, and a modern office chair behind the desk looked anachronistic, especially compared to the décor adorning what little wall space wasn't covered by books.

Erin spotted a watercolor painting of a stone dolmen with flowers blooming around the bases of the stone menhirs, which of course reminded her of the previous night.

"My mother painted it," Liam said at her shoulder, his breath warm against her ear. "I'm pretty sure I get my Cathbad blood from her side of the family."

"Is that why you built the monument?" Erin was aware of his arms encircling her. She unconsciously leaned back against him before she realized her body was turning traitor to her well-thought-out logic.

She felt his nod, his beard tickling at her ear. "At least part of it. I felt since I had the means to do it, I should. I couldn't do something on a grand scale, like Stonehenge, but I thought if I could build the dolmen, I could honor my mother and the gods at the same time." Then his lips brushed her neck, a soft nuzzling kiss. "But you didn't want to go somewhere private to talk about stonework, did you?"

The next kiss, right below her ear, almost melted her knees. Dammit, she wasn't a hormone-addled teenager. She turned to face him, wishing she hadn't opted for the yoga pants and a t-shirt after her shower. If he glanced at her chest, he'd see not only how turned on she was, but that she wasn't wearing a bra. Maybe he wouldn't notice—his eyes were locked on hers, and his goofy half-grin from earlier had returned.

She'd rehearsed a speech, but his lips found hers. One of her hands reached behind his neck, the other behind his back, pulling herself closer, grinding against his erection through his sweat pants. One of his hands slid from her ass up under her t-shirt, slowly sliding up her side toward her breast, excruciatingly slow.

"Wait," she panted, untwining their tongues. His hand froze, barely cupping her breast. She tried to gather her wits, then leaned forward to whisper in his ear. "Does that door lock?"

She'd save her speech for later.

* * * * *

Chapter Twenty-Two

Mad Dog

"You sure this is the place?" Mad Dog gave his partner an irritated glance. "No, I picked it at random." The hulking biker shook his head. They had been given their instructions by e-mail and their down payment by Paypal. "Now keep your eyes peeled. This guy should be coming out any minute."

"How do we know that?" Mikey asked. Mikey wasn't happy about the lack of details regarding this job. Then again, he was called Mikey because he didn't like anything. The bald biker was almost as big as Mad Dog and showed more ink, his tattoos running down both arms almost to the wrist.

"Because it's the intel the client gave us." Mad Dog tried not to sound exasperated. Mikey was an old friend and his most reliable partner-in-crime. "We make sure this guy is the Druid, and we grab him, stuff him in the van, and take him to the place the client told us."

"What the fuck is a druid? Is it like Merlin or Gandalf?" Mikey scowled. "Sounds like some stupid nerd bullshit."

Mad Dog bit back a retort. Mikey was a real estate agent who covered his tats with long sleeves and played fantasy sports when he wasn't hanging out with fellow bikers. The nerd dig seemed ironic

206 | JON R. OSBORNE

coming from a guy who crunched numbers for fun. "It's some sort of hippy priest, which means he should be a pushover."

"Is that him?" Mikey actually managed not to point, using his eyes to direct Mad Dog.

Mad Dog followed Mikey's gaze. The guy matched the description, vague as it was, and was coming from the right place. The briefing had warned the target might have allies in the immediate area, but he looked alone at the moment. The middle-aged man appeared to be distracted. That was perfect as far as Mad Dog was concerned. He gestured for Mikey to follow him as they broke cover from their lookout spot.

"You the Druid?" Mad Dog waited until they were almost on top of the distracted man before asking.

The man looked up, confused for a moment, juggling books and car keys. "Why yes, I'm a druid. In fact, I'm the senior druid for the Middle Illinois territory."

Mikey swooped in from the druid's other side. "Sounds like the right guy to me." Mikey grabbed his arm. "And I hate to be wrong."

"What's this about?" the druid asked. He began to protest as they hauled him into the white van. Mad Dog slugged the guy in the gut to knock the wind out of him before he had the presence of mind to yell. The middle-aged man doubled over and wheezed. Mikey shoved him the rest of the way in, then climbed into the van.

Mad Dog took a quick look around as he circled to the driver's door of the van. No one seemed to be paying attention. Good. This job seemed pretty risky, grabbing a guy in the middle of the day, but looked clear.

"Get his cell phone." Mad Dog said as he climbed into the driver's seat and fired up the van. The man in the back groaned as he feebly tried to hang onto his phone. One last check that they were in the clear, then Mad Dog casually pulled out of the parking lot. "Remember, we're not supposed to hurt him more than we have to. Keep him quiet for an hour, but if he gets out of line, knock him back into line."

"Got it," Mikey growled. It was really theater for their victim; Mikey knew damn well they were to deliver this druid guy as intact as possible. If the guy got the message that he wouldn't get roughed up if he didn't cause a fuss, hopefully he'd behave for the hour drive.

"What's this about?" The question was labored; he still hadn't caught his breath.

"Don't know, don't care," Mad Dog replied. "Someone wants to talk to you pronto."

"Guess he didn't think an engraved invitation would convey his urgency," Mikey added. Nerd words for sure, Mad Dog thought.

* * * * *

Chapter Twenty-Three

Iblis

"So, this is the Druid?"

The man had been dragged in by the two bikers and unceremoniously shoved into a chair. Sunlight filtering through a dusty window dimly lit the room, a small office in a non-descript shared building that was half vacant. A shady lawyer, a 'health supplement' peddler, and a house flipper were the other tenants. His kind of people, Iblis thought.

"That's what he said," the bigger of the two bikers replied. "Said his name was Taliesin, sounds like a druid to me."

The other biker shrugged.

"Very well, gentlemen. Mr. Taliesin and I are going to have a little chat. I won't need your services anymore, at least for this job." Iblis pulled out his phone and tapped the icon that would complete the payment from a shell account to their Paypal account. The big biker's phone chimed. He glanced at it and nodded to his partner.

"So, Taliesin is it?" Iblis asked.

The man mutely nodded, trying to draw his eyes away to look around the room, no doubt hoping to get some idea of where he was. "Who are you?" he finally asked.

"That's a good question. I go by many names, many titles, all given to me." Iblis smiled, his perfect white teeth brighter than the weak daylight. "You may call me Iblis. I'm going to go out on a limb and

209

guess you gave yourself the moniker Taliesin. An impressive name, to be sure, but not yours. So what is your name, druid?"

"Potts. Don Potts, Taliesin is my craft name."

"A craft name? That's quite Wiccan of you, Mr. Potts. Then again, doing some research, it looks as though a lot of you neo-druids didn't fall far from the Wiccan tree." Iblis rested his forearms on the edge of the table, his hands in front of him touching finger tips. "Where are my manners? Mr. Potts, would you care for something to drink? My assistant made some fresh coffee."

The druid nodded. "Yes, please." Nothing like fear to reinforce good manners. "What is this about? Are you from the Chicago group? We can work something out regarding the whole Illinois Pagan Council thing; you didn't need to get rough."

Raven entered the door behind Iblis, carrying a cup of steaming coffee and a small plate with sugar, sweetener, and those disgusting fake creamers. Iblis didn't know how mundanes actually drank the pseudo-dairy liquid plastic. She set everything down in front of Potts, leaning across the table to give the man a good view down her blouse. The druid's eyes flicked up to quickly inspect the cleavage. Silently, if not somewhat stiffly, she left the way she came. Her eyesight had returned when she awoke, and a couple of the shards had required stitches, but nothing important was punctured. A few days, and she would be as good as, well, not new, but as close as she was going to get.

"I'm not from Chicago, Mr. Potts. I'm from someplace rougher, and no, I'm not here about some Internet political drama between a bunch of goddess worshippers playing at magic." Iblis kept his tone calm and melodious, despite his growing irritation. He was quickly suspecting the basement trolls had pointed him to the wrong druid. "Tell me, what do you know about the Milesian Accords?"

"I've heard of the Milesians, the final wave in the invasion cycle myth of Ireland." Potts sat up a little straighter. "The Milesians were descendants of Noah, according to the tale, and displaced the Tuatha de Danann, driving them into the underworld." The man pushed up his glasses and picked up the coffee, sipping it tentatively.

"But you haven't heard of the Accords?"

The man shook his head, blowing on his coffee to cool it before taking another sip. "Does it have to do with the invasion myth? I've never actually read the Lebor Gabala Erenn." He quickly added, "It's on my reading list, but I haven't found a translation I liked."

Iblis was now almost certain he had the wrong druid. While the man seemed well learned, in a puffed up, self-important way, he should have been contacted by one or more of the Exiled Folk. At least two had contacted the Champion before she dropped off the radar. This pseudo-scholar almost certainly couldn't be responsible for the explosive backlash last night when Raven tried to scry the source of the power surge.

"Let's talk about your druidry." The trolls had fed more information to Iblis' phone as he talked to Potts. "What is this Druidic Fellowship you belong to?"

"The DFA? I mean, the Druidic Fellowship of America? I'm the senior druid for the Middle Illinois Territory. I'm hoping to become the Midwest High Druid when Hern Starbrow retires at the end of the year." The man puffed up even more, apparently forgetting he'd been abducted for this interview.

"Really, you people and your silly names," Iblis mused aloud, scrolling through the pages the trolls had sent him. "How can you take yourselves seriously, calling each other Rainbow Moonwaffle?"

Potts bristled. "You sound like that little purple-haired snot who turned up, asking around about druids."

Iblis' finger froze on the screen. Maybe having this self-important pseudo-druid dragged in wasn't a waste after all. Iblis wondered if he would even need to compel the man to divulge what he knew. "Tell me more about the purple-haired snot."

"Sure, she turned up at our last Pan-Pagan Meet Up, asking questions about druids." Potts leaned back in his chair. "She was cute, though I'm not sure if she was jailbait or not. I know a couple of the guys and at least one of the girls wanted to find out. Me, I'm not going to take that kind of risk. Anyway, she started in with this whole thing about craft names being silly, and druidry not being a party game. Party game! Can you believe that?"

"Shocking."

"I know, right? No respect for her elders. Well, since I wasn't scheming to give her a poke, I let the young bucks fuss around her. Then they started coming up to me and asking if there were any other druids to refer her to, one after the other." Potts sighed, crossing his arms. "I figured they were competing to try to get in her pants. Finally I got sick of being pestered and told one of them to send her to Knox."

"Knox? Is he one of your DFA druids?"

Potts scoffed. "Yeah, as if he could complete the study course. It's 18 months long; that's a commitment. No, he's this loner who hangs out on the fringe of the pagan community and claims to be a druid but has no grove. He's a hypocrite to boot, giving people flak about craft names when he uses one."

Sounds as though this Knox had gotten Potts all bent out of shape. Who needed compulsion when good old human wrath, envy, and pride would do? "Really? What does he call himself?"

"Liam, trying to sound Celtic, when his real name is Bill."

"So…his real name is William, but he calls himself Liam?" Iblis resisted the urge to face palm. "But he gives you grief for calling yourself Taliesin when your given name is Donald?"

"Exactly!" Don took a drink from his coffee. "Anyway, I don't know if the little bitch found him or not; we never saw her again. Just as well, the boys were ready to come to blows over her."

"So where did you tell her to go look for this Mr. Bill Knox?"

* * * * *

Chapter Twenty-Four

Tim

"What do you think you're doing?"

Tim looked up from his tablet, then realized Izzy wasn't whispering at him. She was on the other side of a closed door that went from the living room to the front foyer. However, the transom was open. Yes, this house was so old it had transoms. That would put her in the hall behind the staircase.

"Nothing." The other voice was Pixel's, even whispering he could make out her musical accent. He liked listening to her talk.

"You're spying on the Druid and the Champion." Izzy's voice was more cultured, with a hint of a Hispanic accent. Tim recognized the trilled "R" from his Spanish class. But now he was more interested in why Pixel was spying on his mom and dad. For that matter, now he was curious what his parents were up to. They kept looking at each other funny during breakfast when they thought no one was looking, including each other. "That's rude in any situation, but especially in your host's house."

"They've been in there a while. I think they're…" Pixel's voice trailed off. They're what, Tim wondered? He'd assumed they were talking about the mission, or more likely, since they weren't including anyone else, they were talking about Tim. Tim had already figured out he'd have to stay here when his mom went away to train. She

215

was probably giving Liam a list of rules and things not to let Tim do. Yeah, it would take a while; the list was long.

"So what if they are?" Izzy hissed. "To quote my brother, which I can't believe I'm doing, I've never met someone in greater need. This will bring them closer together, which is what we need."

"It's not what I need," Pixel protested. Tim was still trying to fill in the blanks. What did who need?

"Yes, everyone knows you're panting to jump the Druid's bones. You've done everything except jump on the breakfast table and take your top off." Tim flushed at Izzy's statement. He wasn't sure why, or at least didn't want to admit it to himself. "I swear, you *morwynion flodyn* are in rut until…"

There was a prolonged silence that left Tim wishing for a camera like the one over Mrs. Adair's door. He started to type the phrase Izzy had used into a Google search on his tablet until he remembered he didn't have Internet access.

"So, is that it? You're hoping he'll claim you?" Izzy's tone was accusatory. "Or are you after the seed of *An Chéad Draoi* for the *lledrith*? Because we can't afford to have him weakened so you can sate your cravings."

"I wouldn't do that to him! How could you think I'd do something like that?" Pixel sounded defensive, and it reminded Tim of when his mom caught him doing something he shouldn't; and he tried to deny it. Did it mean she would hurt Liam? "I'm here for the mission. I just hoped that maybe I could solve one of my problems in the process. I certainly didn't count on the Champion being his ex-girlfriend."

"It was a surprise, though to be honest, it's not much of a shock. The Fates work in mysterious ways. But this has given them both a personal stake, rather than an abstract cause. If nothing else, they'll do it to protect their son. That means leave them be and stick to the mission. For that matter, make sure you leave the Druid's witch friend alone."

"Fine. Do you want a crack at him before me?" Tim could almost hear Pixel's pout through the transom.

"He's a little soft for me. Frankly, I'd pick the Champion, though I don't know if she rides on that side of the field." Tim wondered if Izzy was speaking in some sort of code. As far as he knew, his mom didn't ride horses. Did Liam have horses? This was a farm, after all.

Pixel made a noise of disgust. "That's right, you and your brother aren't too picky about which team your bedmates play for."

"And Einar calls the Druid a prude. I'm going to make sure my brother hasn't recovered from the Druid's rebuke and returned to harassing Susan. Remember what I said, leave them be."

"Fine." There was the sound of rapid footsteps retreating up the stairs, Tim presumed Pixel's, which was confirmed when Izzy strode into view, passing through the adjacent dining room toward the kitchen. Tim watched her leather-clad form with fascination until she disappeared around the corner.

Setting his tablet aside, Tim climbed out over the over-stuffed chair and crept into the dining room, hoping the wooden floor wouldn't creak and give him away. Surprisingly, it remained silent. Peeking into the hall, he saw that no one was there. One closed door doubled back into the living room. Another under the stairs was probably a closet. At the end of the short hall were two more of the stout wooden doors. One was ajar, obviously leading to a small bathroom, as an old fashioned sink was visible from where he stood. The other door was closed, as was the transom above it.

He cautiously padded to the door, looking back over his shoulder, half expecting to see Einar or Derek. The thick wood muffled his parents' voices, and what little he could hear was fragments of speech that didn't sound like whole sentences. Were they arguing about something? About him? He glanced up at the transom. The weird little crank must be on the inside. Tim looked around, torn between getting caught and wanting to know what was going on.

A click above him drew his attention, as did the sudden sound of his parents' voices through the transom. Peering up, he could see the transom was now open a crack, maybe an inch. The sounds were mostly moans and grunts, punctuated with single words, underscored by a slapping sound. Tim fled in embarrassment, willing his mind not to put together the pieces of the puzzle.

"What are you up to, boy?" Tim almost plowed into the barrel-chested dwarf as he rounded the corner into the dining room. One of Einar's caterpillar-like eyebrows arched in suspicion.

"Nothing!" Tim realized he answered too quickly. "I was looking around to see if I could find a router, there's no wifi signal here, and I can't get on the Internet."

"Come along, maybe the Druid's friend knows something." Einar guided him toward the kitchen, where Tim could hear Derek and Izzy going back and forth in some foreign language.

They both stopped when Tim entered the kitchen, but before they did, Tim thought he heard a few familiar sounds from his Spanish class. It didn't sound quite Spanish, and even if it was, they were speaking way too quickly for him. Susan was still sitting at the table, looking as though she was intent on ignoring them while she sipped her coffee and read a newspaper.

"You know it's rude for you to carry on in your Galixo in front of the Druid's friend?" Einar asked. He scowled as he followed Tim into the kitchen.

"It's fine," Susan said as she looked up from the paper and set down her coffee cup. "I'm not part of the Scooby Gang—the inner circle—whatever you call your supernatural club. Besides, they're only bickering about whether they should say something to Pixel or leave it be since Liam and Erin…" Tim recognized the pause as what happened when an adult realized he was in the room. "Since they're getting along so well."

Izzy was stone-faced while Derek tried to hide his surprise with his trademark smirk. Tim wondered if Derek practiced his smirk in a mirror.

"Or maybe not," Einar muttered.

"You speak Galixo, or more likely Galego?" Izzy finally said to break the awkward silence that had settled over the room.

"Galician and Portuguese branched off from each other in something around the Fourteenth Century. While I'm guessing what you are speaking is older, there are enough similarities for me to pick up the gist," Susan said, picking the coffee cup back up. "I may not have some ancient bloodline, but I'm not stupid." She took a sip. "That and I dated a guy from Brazil for three years."

"Tim, why don't you ask Susan your Internet question?" Einar suggested.

"Oh, I, um, was looking for a router." Tim knew Derek had already talked about the lack of Internet here being a good thing and hadn't been willing to turn on his phone's hotspot. "I thought maybe there might be one, and it wasn't turned on, or something."

"Sorry, sweetie, but I'd be surprised if Liam knew what a router was, let alone had one." Susan gave Tim a sympathetic look. "I'm afraid your father is a bit of a Luddite. He seems to think that all the Internet is for is to carry on arguments without having to actually face the person you're arguing with, or spreading rumors about people without having to look them in the eye. I helped him make a Facebook page, and I don't think he's checked it for over four months."

"Sounds like he has a lick of sense, after all," Einar said. He opened the fridge, then looked at the ornate clock on the wall opposite the sink. Sighing, he closed the refrigerator. "Too early," he mumbled.

"Tim, we've already discussed the Internet." Derek's voice lacked its typical humor.

"I could use a VPN and make sure location services are disabled in the browser and any apps." Tim hoped it didn't get to his mom he knew some tricks to keep from being tracked on the Internet. Then she'd want to know why he had learned to hide where he'd been on the net. While better than his father, his mother didn't even know about incognito browsing and deleting cookies.

"I don't know much about the web business, but I'd have to agree with Derek." Einar leaned against the fridge, looking around the room. "The best thing about this place is that it is hidden from our foes. We don't want to compromise it."

"If I'm going to be stuck here while my mom is gone training, I'm not going to have anything to do." Tim knew he was getting dangerously close to whining territory, but it didn't sound as though Derek was going to hook him up anyway. "The TV only has five channels."

"Maybe we could go to town and rent some movies?" Susan suggested. "I know he has a DVD player hooked up to the television, though he almost never uses it."

"You know how we used to entertain bored children where I came from?" Einar asked as he stood up, crossing his arms. "We'd give them chores."

* * * * *

Chapter Twenty-Five

Liam

"I'm surprised they haven't sent a search party."

Liam nodded in agreement. He was especially surprised Pixel hadn't come looking for him. He had expected a knock at the door at any moment. Hopefully, she'd stop trying to creep into his bed, especially if Erin was there. That could get awkward.

He looked around the room, one of the last places he would have expected to have a tryst. Papers and books from the antique cherry desk were scattered on the floor in front of it, other furniture was in disarray as they had improvised to make up for the lack of a bed or even a comfortable horizontal surface. Out of the corner of his eye, he spotted the transom, cracked open an inch. He was positive it was closed earlier; he'd checked it when he locked the study door, and it only opened from the inside.

"Do you think they know?" Erin asked. Liam turned around in time to catch a glimpse of her breasts as she pulled on her t-shirt.

"Maybe that's why we haven't been pestered." Liam had already found his own t-shirt and was putting on his sweats. "It's only been a little over an hour. What does it matter if they know?"

Erin didn't answer as she searched the floor for her yoga pants. Liam found himself praising the gods again for yoga pants as she bent over and retrieved them from behind the desk.

"I mean, they already know I'm Tim's father, so they already know we've been together." Liam wondered if they had been audible through the transom. The way the house was laid out made the study fairly private, and the furnishings and drapes helped baffle the sound.

"I don't want people…getting ahead of themselves." Erin tugged up the leggings. "For example, Tim might jump to the conclusion we'll suddenly become a classic nuclear family. Hell, you already have a white picket fence out front."

"Would that be so bad?" The same thought had occurred to Liam. "We could even get a dog."

Erin froze, then gave him an inscrutable look that wiped the happy grin from his face.

"No dog then." Had he overstepped some bound? Maybe her M.O. was to not get attached, to take off before there were any entanglements.

"Look, Liam, I like you." Liam heard the unspoken 'but,' hanging over the conversation like a cartoon anvil. "But I don't love you. When this whole craziness is sorted out, I want you to be in Tim's life if we can make it work. I think it would be good for him, and I think it would probably be good for you."

She stepped close to him, while he was resisting the urge to sag against the closest piece of furniture. "But just because we had sex, it doesn't mean we're going to get married, nor do I expect either of us to make a commitment."

"Oh, sure. I understand." So, what, she wanted to be friends with benefits? He'd thought their attraction—the passion—implied something more. But he wasn't going to give voice to the thought; it would be sure to chase her off. "I mean, we're both adults."

"Good. I'm glad you understand." She smiled and kissed him on the cheek. "I'm going to get cleaned up."

Liam nodded, and Erin slipped out the door, peeking into the hall beforehand. Even with the turmoil going through his mind, he caught himself admiring her ass as she left. He needed to button that shit up, he thought, at least until he'd come to terms with her reticence about having a deeper relationship.

He straightened the study as he collected his thoughts, trying to organize his mind as he did his books and papers. Once he had returned everything to where they had started before he and Erin used the desk for a less than scholarly purpose, he started filing the books into the bookcases. It helped him focus and push aside the roiling emotions. Categorize, organize, file away. Twenty minutes and as many books later, he felt better. At least that's what he told himself as he climbed the stairs and went to his bedroom.

Placing his hand on the solid oak door, Liam's gut instinct told him she was in there. Not Erin, but Pixel. Part of him didn't want to deal with the fairy-girl right now. But he couldn't keep dodging people, even her. He twisted the tarnished brass knob, and the door creaked open.

He half expected her to be in his bed, waiting for him in a lurid pose, eyes glowing. Instead she was standing at the window, similar to last night, but looking out. She was wearing the black jeans and pink crop top she'd had on at breakfast. A corner of Liam's mind wondered where all these supernatural folks kept their clothes and did their laundry?

"I suppose you're mad at me too." She kept looking out the window. Liam didn't know what was so impressive about the view; it was soybean and corn fields stretching off toward the horizon with the odd farm building, tree, or windmill dotting the landscape.

"No, I'm not mad at you." Liam collected some clean clothes from his dresser. "I don't know why anyone else is mad at you. But I do have a lot on my mind right now, so don't take it personally."

She half-turned toward him, so he could see her face in profile. Her eyes glistened with wetness, but they didn't have redness or dark circles to show she'd been crying. "Anything you want to talk about?"

"Thanks, but I need to process some stuff."

She nodded before Liam closed the bathroom door. It seemed silly to take another shower, but he didn't want to go around smelling of sweat and sex, and she was about the last person he wanted to talk to about this, considering last night. The mystic Armageddon seemed simple compared to all of this soap opera bullshit. Liam distracted himself by making a mental list of every blacksmithing and sword smithing book he had in the house, as well as any relevant tools he should gather up.

Dressing after his shower, he found his bedroom empty. Good, he needed to not get sidetracked. He brought his list of questions back to the front of his mind. They mostly revolved around what he was expected to do, what the nature of their foes was, and what could be expected afterward.

Descending the stairs, he spotted Tim in the living room, playing on his tablet. Good, that meant the kid was probably oblivious to what Liam and Erin had been up to. The dining room was empty, but he could hear voices in the kitchen.

Izzy, Derek, Einar, Susan, and Pixel were in the kitchen. Liam guessed Erin was either in her room or the upstairs hall bathroom.

He had no idea where Gofannon was, though the Smith-God would probably reappear once it was time for lunch.

"All right, let's talk business," Liam said, crossing to the coffee maker and looking for a fresh mug. He realized someone had done the dishes, and his Ogham mug was on the drying rack. Picking it up, he filled it with coffee and turned back to the rest of the room. "How long do we have?"

"Until Samhain," Izzy replied.

Liam frowned. November 1 was roughly ten weeks away; if Erin needed seven weeks of real world time for training, it didn't give them a lot of leeway.

"So I have to be able to forge a magic sword by then, with Gofannon tutoring me." The physical part of the work didn't concern Liam, it was what constituted a 'magic' sword. He wished he could slip off into an otherworld to stretch out time. "Anything else special about this sword?"

"Well, it should be made from a meteorite." Einar drummed his fingers on the table. "It will help pierce the Milesian champion's armor. The only trouble is meteor iron is resistant to magic."

"So I need to make a magic sword out of metal that is resistant to magic?" Liam didn't even bother to resist the urge to roll his eyes. "Swell."

"You'll need to find something you can infuse in the metal to carry the magic." Einar sounded as though he was suggesting Liam try a different oil for his motorcycle. Liam shelved the rest of that line of questioning until he could talk to Gofannon. Surely a smith god would have some ideas on the matter. "Where is Gofannon?"

"Once the food ran out, I think he wandered out to your forge," Einar said. He nodded in the general direction of the out building housing the forge. "Probably melting your motorcycle down or something."

Liam resisted the urge to check on his motorcycle. "And once the Champion finishes her training montage, where do we go to deliver the challenge? Ireland? Wales?"

"Georgia," Izzy replied.

"So we have to face off against St. George in what, Atlanta?" A long drive, but it beat a trans-Atlantic flight, Liam thought.

Derek chuckled. "No, the country Georgia, near the Black Sea." Liam waited for him to admit he was joking, only to finally realize he wasn't. Good thing he'd kept up on his passport. "The first challenge was in Ireland. The second one, well, I don't know how the location was picked, but we have to assume it was for a reason. Maybe St. George, as they call him, is a narcissist and wanted to live in a country named after him."

"It's not the historical person the Catholics refer to as St. George," Izzy reminded them. "It was around the same time, and the story of Giwargix slaying the dragon of the old gods was rolled up into St. George's legend."

"Yeah, we've covered the whole hagiography thing." Liam was more worried about how he was going to get a magic sword and magic people into the former Soviet Union. "So, do you have a plan to get us there?"

"Hopefully by then it will be worked out." Einar said. He looked up at Liam. "If not, this whole pocking thing is for naught."

Liam turned to Izzy and Derek. "Okay, assuming we're going ahead with this, what is your plan to get Erin to Scathach? And what are the odds of the Avramites interfering, since you'll no longer be under my home's obfuscation?"

"If we can use the interstates, it should take us two days," Izzy replied. "We could do it in less, but if we travel when there's more traffic, we won't stick out. A lone car on the road in the middle of the night is easier for police or some other suborned persons to pick out. As part of regular traffic, not so much. We could also take back roads. They're less likely to be watched, but it will add another day of travel time."

"How soon can you be ready to roll?" Liam asked. Was he actually committing himself to this course of action? If Erin took off in pursuit of this, for the lack of a better term, quest, there was no way Liam could leave her hanging. Even after the emotional gut punch she had given him.

"So eager to be rid of us, Druid?" Derek grinned. "As soon as it is decided, we are ready. My sister and I travel light."

"We should talk to Erin and see if she's ready to embark on the next leg of our journey," Izzy added, looking meaningfully in the direction of the living room.

"You should also make sure she's committed," Liam remarked dryly. "You might assume her intentions and be wrong."

Derek raised an eyebrow, and Izzy narrowed her eyes. Susan put a hand on Liam's arm. "Do you need to talk about something?"

"Not now. Later." Susan was his greatest confidant. If there was anyone Liam could talk to about what he was feeling, it was her. But he didn't want to dwell on his issues and shoved them back into their mental box. "Finally, after it all goes down, and we win, then what? I don't want some happy homecoming bullshit. After almost two millennia, what are the old gods and the Exiled Folk going to do?"

"Part of that will be up to you, Druid," Izzy said, looking solemn. "You will be *An Chéad Draoi, Y Drwydd Cyntaf,* the First Druid. You will have a great deal of say in the matters of magic going forward."

"So, I become the Druidic Pope?" Now Liam understood the ongoing part of the salary offer. Evidently, his role didn't end with the challenge. "Thàt's going to go over well. You can't get pagans to agree on who should bring a main dish or a dessert to a potluck, let alone thrusting some random stranger on them as a pagan pontiff."

"Do not confuse religion and magic," Derek said, as serious as Izzy. "While they are interconnected, they are not interdependent. You could end up with some very dry magi who approach magic in the manner of science. By and large, the bulk of the religious will not have the mental capacity to learn magic."

"What do you mean by 'bulk?'" Liam asked. Even if only one percent of the world's population could do magic after the Accords were brought down, that left millions of potential magic wielders. What would that even look like?

Izzy and Derek looked at each other before she answered. "Keep in mind, this is only a guess, but somewhere in the neighborhood of one in one hundred thousand to one in a million. That's based on what we know from before the accords. Given the Dunwold's obsession with science, it could be even less as mundane folk won't be able to wrap their minds around the idea of magic. After all, magic appears to seriously bend or outright violate the laws of nature."

Liam wondered if it was too early for a beer. "And being First Druid means what, I get to say who can use magic and who can't? I have to teach others how to use magic?" Either way sounded like a lot of work and responsibility. "And it means people coming to me, or after me, because of this."

"People will develop talent with magic without your approval or teaching, unless you put that in the new accords." Izzy leaned forward on her elbows. "You see, if we win, we don't merely light the Milesian Accords on fire and toss them in the ash can, we replace them with new accords that lay down the general rules for magic and how outsiders—supernatural entities—interact with the Dunwold."

"And you thought you were simply going to have a make a sword and learn a speech," Derek said. His smirk had returned. "I hope that one of the two dozen hobbies you've dabbled in over the years included lawyering."

"I don't think he ever actually tried that one," Susan muttered into her coffee. "Liam, if you screw this up, you could screw up the whole planet. Dragons razing cities, faeries stealing children, clowns lurking in woods, that's real nightmare fuel. Are you sure you're up to this?"

Beer sounded more and more tempting. "No, I'm not sure. Every time I turn around, this whole thing gets crazier and more complicated. What if I said 'no more magic?'"

The siblings both blanched. Apparently the idea hadn't occurred to them; maybe they assumed he would naively go along with what they wanted. Maybe if he cut off all magic, he'd protect the world from incursion by the myths and legends of a dozen or more pantheons. Liam gave voice to his next thought. "Would it cut off the Avramites from their power as well?"

Izzy chose her words carefully. "While it would indeed cut off mystical or divine influence, and keep angel and tuatha alike from treading the Dunwold, there would be other, harder to quantify, ramifications. Imagine the world without inspiration or faith. Please do not act rashly, Druid."

"There is plenty of time to think on this, Druid," Derek suggested. "As my sister said, do not be rash. It would be a shame for the world to suffer because you had a fit of pique." Derek turned to Izzy. "Perhaps we should find Erin and discuss travel plans?"

Izzy nodded, scooting her chair back on the linoleum. She regarded Liam momentarily, as though debating whether to add any final words, then silently followed her brother out of the kitchen.

Liam waited several seconds, filling time by replenishing his coffee. It wasn't beer, but he wanted a clear mind. "What do you think, Susan?"

"Other than this whole thing is madness?" Susan shook her head. "I can't believe I'm saying this, but to a degree, I agree with them. If this is real, if you really can somehow write the rules for magic if you girlfriend beats St. George—"

"She's not my girlfriend," Liam snapped. Then quieter, he added, "She made that abundantly clear."

"Liam, I'm sorry." Susan took his hand. "Then I definitely agree with the sentiment of not making a hasty decision, not while you're hurting and possibly resenting the world. Look, I'll help you with this, if you want. If it'll help me with my tomato plants and herb garden, a little magic might not be such a bad thing."

"I guess not. After all, for a druid, I'm pretty mediocre at the whole green thumb thing." Actually having some help on this, coming up with these new accords, sounded like a good idea. Liam felt overwhelmed, which was usually when he decided he was tired of whatever he was working on and looked for some new hobby to distract him. That wasn't a luxury he had now.

"So, do you want to talk about the other thing?" Susan asked, her voice low. "Do you want to talk about what's going on with Erin?"

Liam sighed. He didn't really want to talk about it, but he knew he shouldn't bottle things up. Maybe actually talking about it would take some of the sting out, and Susan had heard his romantic woes before, and he had heard hers. "Are you sure you want to hear this?"

"Let's just agree I don't need a play-by-play of whatever went down last night after I left," Susan replied. "Because I can guess. Something happened after I left? And now she's changed her mind?"

"Pretty much." Liam collected his thoughts. He didn't want to ramble or rant. Once he was ready, he began to tell Susan what Erin had said to him about not wanting a relationship.

* * * * *

Chapter Twenty-Six

Iblis

"You've been most helpful."

"You're welcome, Miss Raven," the manager replied, oblivious to the fact Raven was using his tie as a leash. Iblis noted his servant was enjoying her power more and more. He'd best watch that, in case she got any notions about over-stepping her bounds. But for now, he let her run with it.

It had taken little for her to compel the tattooed kid at the front counter of the bookstore to take them back to the manager's office. The manager at first had been full of pompous authority, until Raven mesmerized him, along with feeding him the story that they were writers looking to interview the druid, this William Knox.

Unfortunately, Knox had little digital footprint. It was obvious he had taken pains to keep his personal information well hidden. The man didn't have a street address in the phone book, nor did he have one associated with his bare bones Facebook account. The basement trolls had not been able to trace an ISP to a likely home location. The few times he had posted anything online had been done at a public hotspot, such as the one here or at McDonalds.

None of Don Potts' contacts knew where Knox lived, either. Supposedly, when he showed up at events, he arrived alone and left alone, and he never had anyone over to his house. The best piece of intelligence Potts had yielded was where Knox worked.

"He quit yesterday," the manager droned, rifling through a file cabinet. "His file is gone."

Iblis resisted the urge to strangle the man. "Did you send it to your home office?"

"I don't remember," the man replied in a monotone.

Iblis glanced over at Raven. The witch was still moving stiffly, but had accompanied him without complaint. He'd noticed her make-up was a bit more Goth today. He wasn't sure if it was an affectation, or a side effect of what she had tapped into last night.

"Try to remember," Raven commanded him, putting her will and the power Iblis had bestowed on her behind the words. "What did you do with the files?"

"I don't remember doing anything with them," the manager, Clark, droned in response, looking slightly confused.

"I think he's been glamoured," Raven said, turning to look at Iblis. "Someone else got to him first and took the druid's file."

Iblis tamped down his irritation. In a way, this was good news. "Well, at least we know Potts was right on his guess. This Knox fellow must be the Druid we are looking for. A pity he quit, he won't be back here now."

"Knox will have to come in and pick up his pay check tomorrow," the manager stated.

Iblis clasped his hands. Of course this druid was too cagey to tie things together electronically by using direct deposit and online banking. But it meant unless he was willing to walk away from a whole paycheck, he'd turn up here tomorrow. Iblis debated; should he have Mikey and Mad Dog do the stakeout, or should he do it himself? If Raven couldn't compel the Druid, surely he could.

Then again, his presence might tip off the Druid. Iblis knew the Druid of the Exiled Folk would have some access to the magic of the Otherworld. Last night's excitement had borne that out. While Iblis didn't know how proficient Knox was in his mystic abilities, a couple of mundanes would fly under his radar, at least until it was too late. Based on the report of Potts' apprehension, he didn't expect Knox to put up much of a physical fight.

Iblis turned back toward the slack-faced manager. "Mr. Hayes, would you happen to have a picture of Bill Knox?"

Clark nodded slowly, then fished through a trashcan next to his desk. "Here you go. I pulled it down right after he quit."

The photo was a headshot, showing a scruffy-looking man with a sandy brown beard beginning to gray. The slightly rumpled company polo certainly made him look anything but intimidating.

"I like his eyes," Raven said, reaching toward the picture, drawing her fingertips over the eyes.

At first Iblis didn't know what she was babbling about. Ever since he had granted her a portion of his power, she'd been prone to the occasional nonsensical tangent. As he looked at the picture, he realized the Druid's eyes were different colors, one deep blue and the other deep green. If nothing else, it was a good way to prevent mistaken identity, Iblis thought. There might be plenty of Internet druids running around, but almost none would have heterochromia.

"He has power," Raven said, still gazing at the picture. "Ancient power. His progeny would be strong."

"Knox doesn't have any kids," the manager stated. Thank someone for small favors, Iblis thought.

"I could change that." Raven's whisper was husky. Iblis looked at the picture again. This Knox fellow wasn't particularly good looking.

Then he realized Raven wasn't attracted to his appearance; it was the notion of bearing his bloodline.

Iblis stroked his chin. Getting control of the bloodline had a certain appeal. Could Raven seduce the Druid? Could he keep the product of said seduction secret from the other interested parties, at least until it was to his advantage? Until now, it wasn't an option he had considered.

"Thank you for your time, Mr. Hayes." As if the man had any choice, Iblis mused. "We'll be taking our leave. Please keep our visit confidential."

"Confidential," Raven echoed.

"Of course." The manager's voice was still monotone. "Glad I was able to help."

"Of course you are." Iblis smiled, knowing his teeth could star in a toothpaste commercial. "Come along, Raven."

The witch obeyed, following him out of the small office and through the cluttered shelves of the bookstore. Once outside, Iblis placed a call to Mad Dog, giving him instructions and using his phone to snap a picture of the Druid's photograph from the store. Either way—whether Raven succeeded in seducing the Druid or not—Iblis would still want to have words with him.

Besides, how much of a fight was he likely to put up?

* * * * *

Chapter Twenty-Seven

Lee

"**Y**ou expect me to drive with that riding shotgun?"

Lee Haskins immediately regretted his words. While the seraphim did not take offense, he was afraid Mikha'el would interpret his reaction as impertinence. "He would attract attention from the mundane authorities and compromise the operation," he hastily added.

Mikha'el shifted his golden gaze to the alabaster form that stood silently next to Haskins. A white mist swirled around the seraphim, its cold, white, marble-like form replaced by a blue-eyed blonde surfer dude, wearing blue jeans and a red, white, and blue 'America!' t-shirt. The blonde man flicked out his hand, and a blue ball cap appeared in it, which he settled on his head.

"There. Jehoel blends in with the mundanes." Mikha'el's gaze returned to Lee, making the pastor repress a shiver. "Go west. Your minions have not reported our quarry crossing the river, but there has been a great disturbance near the city of Peoria. If you cannot intercept the Champion and thwart or dissuade her while remaining within the cumbersome rules of the Accords, perhaps you can find the Druid."

"Is Jehoel going to listen to me, or will he go off half-cocked and break the rules of the Accords?" Haskins was more concerned the seraphim's quick and brutal methods would lead to reprisals against Lee himself, or worse, his wife.

Lee tried not to wilt under Mikha'el's gaze, which finally shifted to the seraphim-turned-surfer-dude. "Jehoel, obey Lee Haskins as you would obey me. He speaks with the authority as a servant of our Lord. Do you understand?"

Jehoel silently nodded.

"There." Mikha'el turned back to the pastor. "Go. Do not fail me—do not fail Him—or all that has been given in His name will be taken."

"Of course." Lee glanced over at the surfer-seraphim, then nodded toward the door. "Let's go."

Joel, as Lee had dubbed him, silently followed him outside. Without being coached, the seraphim went over to the passenger side of Lee's truck and climbed in, closing the door as he settled into the seat.

"You know how to put on a seatbelt?" Lee secured his own before glancing over at his passenger. "You might be a stone-skinned servant of the Almighty, but local law enforcement won't know any different, and it will slow us down if we get pulled over."

Joel gazed at him a moment before securing his own seatbelt.

"See, that wasn't so hard." Lee fired up the truck and put it in gear. Even as he pulled out of the parking lot, he was running numbers through his head. It was around noon now, which put them on the far side of Illinois close to sundown. "Now, I have no clue if you need to eat, drink, or piss, so you'll need to let me know."

Joel didn't respond as they pulled out of the defunct strip club's parking lot. Lee couldn't say he was sad to leave the place behind and futilely hoped he wouldn't have to set foot back there again. A tiny part of him was tempted to say to heck with the mission. If the heretics won, Mikha'el would be stripped of his power, right? He wouldn't be able to make good on his threats, especially those to bring back Lee's wife's cancer.

But what if the Servant was actively keeping the cancer at bay? Would losing its power mean dooming Christine? Lee gave Joel a quick glance. If the seraphim could read his thoughts or pick up on his doubts, it gave no indication. It stared straight ahead, unblinking.

"That's creepy, you know?" Lee tried to focus on the road and the traffic as he made his way toward I-90. "You not blinking and all. I mean, it's not a big deal, people passing in cars aren't likely to get a good enough look at you to notice something's off, but if we have to stop somewhere, folks might take note."

"Do not stop," the surfer hissed, sounding like a church organ in a mausoleum.

"I'm flesh and blood, with the needs and weaknesses that go along with it. Plus we'll need gas in a couple hundred miles." Lee tried to repress the goose bumps. "If you have to talk, you need to sound more…organic. The less attention we draw, the better we can accomplish our mission."

"Is this better?" Joel's voice mimicked Lee's, an octave lower, the Kentucky drawl intact.

"Um, yes, that should be fine." It was almost creepier hearing a human-like voice issuing from the faux-surfer, given what Lee knew, but if it would keep people from getting too nosey, so much the better.

After several minutes of riding in silence, Lee turned on the radio. He kept the volume on the Christian station out of Akron low, barely loud enough to provide some background noise. Joel did not even seem to take notice.

"You understand our orders and what the rules are, right?" Lee finally asked.

"We may not kill the Druid," Joel said. "We may not kill the Champion. Endeavor not to draw attention to ourselves. Keep the Druid or the Champion from fulfilling their duty through compulsion or persuasion. Destroy any of the servants of the heretic gods found walking the world." Joel turned toward Lee. "Is this interpretation of His wishes correct?"

"As far as I can tell, yes." Lee noted the absence of any mention regarding protecting those who served the Lord. That meant in the seraphim's eyes he was expendable. Would Mikha'el still help Christine if Lee lost his life in service to the Lord?

* * * * *

Chapter Twenty-Eight

Erin

"So we leave in the morning?"

Izzy nodded in response to Erin's question. "There is no reason to linger, unless you wish to fight with the Druid some more."

"Or do other things," Derek added.

"We didn't fight," Erin protested. She should have known better than to sleep with Liam. Now he was acting all hurt, and she was the bitch for breaking his over-eager heart. "We just don't see eye-to-eye on some things."

"You mean like getting busy on his desk in the study?" Derek asked, his signature eyebrow arching.

Erin tried to fight down her rising flush, a combination of embarrassment and stirrings brought on by the memory. "That's none of your business! Don't push me, or I might walk off this little project of yours."

That erased Derek's smug grin. Izzy remained serious, as she had from the start. "Assuming my brother doesn't piss you off, yes, we should leave in the morning. Assuming you are okay with leaving your son with the Druid?"

"Yes. I think so, at least." Erin began to pace again. The bedroom didn't have a lot of space; huge antique furniture took up most of the floor. "It's not much different from a summer camp, and he'd get to spend time with his father. To be honest, it would be good for Tim. It probably wouldn't be bad for Liam either. If nothing else, knowing he has a son has given him a sense of purpose. It would be seven weeks or so from their perspective, right?"

Derek remained diplomatically quiet. "From their perspective, you are correct," Izzy said. "The Druid seems pleased to have a son, and this place is as safe as any you can find."

"And maybe your son can bring the Druid into the 21st century," Derek added. "I've met skilly-hobs with a better grasp of technology."

Erin continued to pace in silence. She knew Izzy was eager to get on the road, but they had a few weeks to spare until it was time for the challenge. Although getting under way would mean getting away from awkwardness with Liam, she didn't want to rush off on her son.

"We'll leave in a few days, but not tomorrow," Erin announced. She wasn't worried about Tim, at least not too much. Barring the lack of Internet connection, which Tim would undoubtedly complain about, she knew that her son was excited to have found his father. Hopefully they would bond, especially without her there to stir up drama between herself and Liam. She knew that she had hurt Liam by rebuffing him, but she didn't see any other way around it. Well, besides continuing to have sex. She felt her blood warm. Erin realized her thoughts were drifting off track and both the Iberians were staring at her.

"Anything in particular I should bring? Do we need to make a provisions run? If we are going to be at Dunos Scaith for seven years, what do we need to stock up on?" The seven years part was what bothered Erin. This would be worse than being deployed.

There would be no Skype, or letters, or leave. On the other hand, there would be no missed birthdays, or any of the other milestones that came with children growing up. Tim would look the same when she got back as he did now.

"Wait, what do you mean 'us?'" Derek asked. He sounded slightly alarmed, the mirth gone from his voice.

"I'm not going by myself," Erin said. She stopped pacing. She looked from one sibling to the other. "If I'm going, you two are going. I assume that won't be a problem?"

"Other than my fool of a brother making a pass at one of Scathach's granddaughters a century or two ago, no, no problem at all." Izzy turned to her brother. "I'm sure all will be forgiven, especially in light of the challenge to the Accords."

"I wouldn't bet my hide on that," Derek mumbled. "Remember, Champion, you're the one who insisted I come along, so you get to vouch for me."

"Of course, Derek," Erin said. She smiled sweetly. "After all, we have to have something to use as a training dummy."

* * *

Dinner was awkward, punctuated by long silences, even though everyone was gathered around the huge table in the dining room. Liam was cool but polite, merely nodding when Erin announced her 'team' would be hitting the road in a few days. At least Liam hadn't let his melancholy regarding Erin extend to Tim. Liam appeared fully engaged when talking to their son.

246 | JON R. OSBORNE

That was good, because Tim seemed to have endless questions, which went far to mask the uneasiness in the room. Fortunately, Liam seemed to have a good sense of what questions to defer to Erin. Could Tim hang stuff up in his room? Sure. Could he learn how to ride a horse? Check with your mother.

Even Pixel seemed subdued. Erin would have thought the purple-haired girl would be ecstatic that Erin was leaving soon and no longer competing for Liam's attention. Instead, she bordered on sullen, only speaking when spoken to, and with none of her characteristic exuberance. Oh well, that was going to be Liam's problem.

Susan had given Erin a few odd looks, but didn't seem hostile. It was obvious the woman had a rapport with Liam, and he had probably told her something, but unlike Pixel, there didn't seem to be a veiled resentment. Probably because, while Susan seemed comfortable with Liam, there was no indication they'd been intimate.

At least the drinking seemed to have abated. Well, except for Einar, of course. Erin had already decided to abstain from alcohol, in part because she was afraid her resolve to keep Liam at arm's length would crumble if she got a few drinks in her, especially if she dwelt on what happened last night by the fire pit, or this afternoon in the study, or…yeah, not drinking was definitely a good idea.

She was happy to see Liam had also refrained from drinking. She'd been a little concerned that upsetting him would have the opposite effect. She'd known enough men who, when they were angry or upset, went straight to a bottle, which almost always made things worse. Instead, Liam was sipping on some sort of herbal tea, which Einar described as foul.

Good, it meant Liam would still have a clear head after dinner when she wanted to have another talk about Tim, especially regarding the next school year, which should be starting in about four weeks. She knew she was mentally committing to them staying in Eureka for at least a semester, and she'd rather not force Tim to change schools half way through the school year. Assuming the world didn't end, of course.

Erin realized the other reason the table was so quiet, and why Einar was drinking alone. "Where's Gofannon?"

"He's puttering around in the Druid's forge," Einar replied, finishing off his third beer. "Said he wanted to stretch his smithing muscles."

Liam looked up from his tea and cocked his head. "Huh, I hadn't noticed him hammering. Does he even know how to use any of the gear out there besides the hammer and anvil?"

"He'd probably say, 'what else would I need?'" Derek quipped.

"I showed him how the blower on the forge works," Einar said. He belched and wiped the crumbs from his sandwich from his beard. "He didn't give a whit about your other equipment other than to point out that it needed to be oiled."

Liam shrugged. "Well, if it makes him happy, let him putter. At least we don't have to guard our sandwiches."

"Don't worry, the smith won't go hungry," Izzy said. "I took him three foot-long sandwiches and a family-sized bag of chips. He barely looked up from hammering away."

Liam got a suspicious look. "Where did he get the metal for what he's working on?"

"Maybe he made it with magic?" Tim suggested, wiggling his fingers in the air.

Liam furrowed his brow and looked at Einar. "Can he do that?"

"Not really." Einar wiped his mouth with the back of his hand. "Anything conjured would have no real substance. Now, if he had some tucked in an *alf-vassi*, I guess it's possible."

Liam seemed to perk up. "An elf-pocket? How does that work?"

Einar glanced over at Pixel, as if to see whether she'd join the conversation. When she continued to silently pick at her sandwich, he explained. "You make a space between the wolds, and you stick stuff in it. After glamours, it's probably the most popular form of magic for the Folk."

"That's true," Izzy said. She held up her empty left hand, then she reached under her right arm and drew forth a slender sword she had obviously not been hiding in her tight leather outfit. "It comes in handy."

That explained how the siblings travelled so light, Erin thought. It would be especially useful for stashing weapons out of sight. "How much can you fit in one of those?"

Izzy shrugged. "Only a stone or so. It depends on how much *bruxia*, magic, one has."

"Oh." Erin's idea regarding an extra-dimensional holster vanished. That would have been handy.

"So it moves with you?" Liam squinted as though looking for signs of these pockets.

"It wouldn't be much of a pocket otherwise," Derek remarked. "Skilly-hobs can sew them in garments, but skilled *bruxos* or *draoi* can tether them to their own persons independent of what they wear."

"So can my dad make one?" While Tim hadn't taken to addressing Liam as 'dad,' he had no qualms about using the term in the third person. Erin thought she saw a hint of a smile on Liam after Tim's question.

"I'd hope so." Einar leaned back in his chair. "He's going to have to learn a lot tougher magic than making an elf-pocket."

"Gods, I need a Magic 101 book," Liam said. He swirled his tea, watching the contents spin in his cup.

"That's what she's for," Einar replied. He poked a thumb toward Pixel, who finally looked up. "I know a little, and more in basic theory, but Pixel knows a lot more than I do."

"Hm?" Pixel looked up. "Yeah, think of me as your familiar. I'll help you get up to speed."

Erin had no doubt Pixel wanted to get familiar with Liam, then quickly tamped down the twinge of jealousy. If she was going to reject Liam's romantic attentions, why should she care if someone else was interested in him? Was it because the girl was so pushy about it? Because she was young?

"I heard you mention a skilly-hob," Susan said. She'd only finished half her vegetable sandwich and was wrapping up the remainder. "Is that some sort of crafting fairy?"

"Precisely," Izzy replied. "Though in general the term 'Ffolk' is preferred over fairy. They tend to specialize in certain crafts, especially soft goods, whereas dwarves tend to work in materials such as metal and stone." The double "F" was emphasized slightly to Erin's ear, but she didn't understand the significance.

"So the Land yields," Einar intoned, almost prayer-like. "That's not to say a dwarf can't learn skilly-stitching or a hob can't learn metalwork; it just seems to be their natural aptitudes."

"If my dad is going to learn to make magic swords, does that mean a dunnie can learn skilly-stitching?"

Einar chuckled. "No offense to your father, but the Druid will never be as good at the forge and anvil as most dwarves. He has a lot more *gwuedd* on the Dunwold than about anyone, which is important when you're making an enchanted weapon."

"If Liam is the only person who can wield magic, at least to any real degree, then who has more mojo or whatever you call it?" Susan was also drinking herbal tea. Unlike Liam, she had doctored it with sugar retrieved from a cupboard next to the refrigerator. It was again obvious to Erin the woman was familiar with the contents of Liam's kitchen.

"There are servants of the Avramite powers who walk the Dunwold, and some followers have been gifted with the ability to draw on the *sefir*, the divine spark of their gods," Derek explained. Erin had been surprised he passed on drinking, sticking with water. "Ironically, the more power that these empowered followers and various Elohim and Nephilim draw upon, the more Gwuedd leaks into the Dunwold.

"In a way, they made this challenge possible," he continued. "If the Avramites hadn't drawn so much power to influence various political and material agendas, we couldn't have crossed over so easily, and Liam wouldn't have as much access to mystical power as he does."

"Now I have to learn how to tap into this power," Liam said. He swirled his tea again. "Another thing to figure out."

Erin wasn't sure if the last remark was directed at her. Liam didn't look up as he said it, though she noticed Susan nodded.

* * *

After dinner had broken up, and Susan had taken her leave for the evening, Erin managed to corral Liam off by himself out in the garage. It seemed like a safe option, open enough that they wouldn't be pushed into close proximity, and it didn't have any tempting horizontal spaces…unless they cleared off a workbench. She hurriedly squelched that train of thought as she felt herself becoming aroused.

"Look, I know you're hurt by what I said earlier, and I'm sorry," she said. "But I wanted to talk some more about what was going to happen after this whole thing goes down."

"You made it pretty clear nothing was going to happen." Liam's replied, his tone flat.

"Right. No, I'm thinking more about Tim." Some of the defensiveness in Liam's stance ebbed, which Erin took as a good sign. She didn't want to have found her son's father only to drive him off from having anything to do with Tim. "The school year is going to start up before I'm back, and well before we do the challenge. I'd like him enrolled here."

Liam looked skeptical. "In Eureka? Aren't you worried he won't be challenged? He's a smart kid."

"What I want is for him to have a little stability, and for him to get to know you. So I'd prefer to keep him here at least a year." She stopped pacing to look out into the darkening night. "I'm sure you can find stuff to keep him challenged. Maybe you could teach him Irish, and he could teach you about Facebook."

That elicited a smile. "I don't know how interested he'd be in Irish, but I'm sure I can find him something. As for Facebook, I don't need to pick arguments with random people pounding furiously at their keyboards. They still use keyboards, right?"

252 | JON R. OSBORNE

"Some, although I think a lot are going to phones and tablets for their virtual jousts." Erin was tempted to settle into one of the lawn chairs; it would quell her impulse to pace. "If it's an issue, I can find us an apartment in town once the mission is over."

"If we can sort it out, I think you guys should stay here," Liam said. He spread his hands. "I have tons of space going to waste. You can have your own room."

"Do I have to keep the creepy doll?" Erin had thrown a blanket over the staring antique doll that occupied a small rocking chair in her room.

"Aunt Millie's doll? We could put it in the attic or even take it to the antique shop on Main." Liam looked in the general direction of the second story. "I was never a fan of that doll either. It gave me the heebie-jeebies."

He gave her a half-grin that made her glad she had opted to avoid alcohol. She admonished herself; he wasn't that cute, and she wasn't some school girl with a crush. Backsliding now would be a mistake. It seemed as though she was getting him to accept that even though their lives might be entwined, it didn't mean they had to have a romantic entanglement. Look at him and Susan, they were perfectly good friends without the emotional landmines that came with a sexual relationship.

Erin looked up when she realized Liam had repeated something she had missed while deep in thought. "I'm sorry, what did you say?"

"I said you guys should stay the year." He wandered toward the fridge on the far side of the garage. "No strings attached. We can see how things work out, if you want to stick around longer and see how Tim likes small town life."

Liam stopped at the fridge and popped the door open. Erin hoped he wouldn't offer her a beer. She needed to stay sober, she felt, and she was hoping Liam would also.

"I owe my liver a break after the last couple days," he said, holding up a can of diet cola. "While I enjoy good beer, I've probably drank more in the last two days than I normally would in a month. Do you want one, or would you rather have beer?"

"I'll have what you're having." Staying clear-headed was definitely for the best, Erin thought. Last night in the grass could be chalked up to a few too many drinks on top of everything else.

* * *

A few hours later, Erin was pacing in her darkened bedroom. Last night might be chalked up to booze, but she was sober this afternoon in the study. She was sober now, but she couldn't sleep. Was it the damned apple? Surely by now she'd sufficiently scratched whatever itch she had after going almost two years without sex, so she couldn't blame that.

She'd thought about tending to things herself, but as soon as she started the line of thought she realized she was at the door and ready to cross the hall. She froze, her hand on the doorknob. Was it some sort of spell? One of those glamours they had talked about earlier?

No, she was pretty sure it wasn't. In fact, they'd said she was resistant to such magic. She cracked the door open, alarmed at how loudly it seemed to creak in the quiet house. Erin paused, listening for any reaction. I should go back to bed, she thought; this is stupid. She closed her door and tiptoed across the hall, each floorboard seeming to be a squeaky tattle-tale, but there was still no sign anyone had heard her.

She paused again at Liam's door. What if Pixel was in there? Erin thought she had mollified any potential resentment on Liam's part, so hopefully 12 hours later he wouldn't have moved on to the purple-haired girl. Holding her breath, Erin turned the knob and gently pushed the door open. Of course it squeaked.

Slipping into the room, she made sure the door closed behind her. In the moonlight spilling in through the windows, she could see Liam sit up in bed. Thankfully, he was alone.

"I guess you couldn't sleep either," he said softly.

"No." Stupid, stupid, stupid, she thought as she padded to his bedside. "You have to understand, what I said earlier, I meant it. This doesn't mean anything beyond tonight."

"Well, I did say no strings attached." He pulled aside the sheet to let her slide into the bed. She'd half expected him to be naked already, waiting for her, but he was still wearing boxers.

She pulled off the nightshirt, aware the moon was silhouetting her. She eased onto the bed and scooted close to him, his skin warm in contrast to the breeze from the ceiling fan.

"Admit it," he whispered after the first kiss. "You were curious what it would be like in an actual bed."

* * * * *

Chapter Twenty-Nine

Liam

"Liam, are you awake?"

The accompanying knock on the door ensured he was awake. Liam realized he was alone, which was good, since it was Tim pounding on his door. At least he wasn't hungover.

"Yeah, buddy, I'm awake. Is the house on fire?"

There was a pause before Tim replied. "No."

"Okay, then tell whoever sent you that I'll be down in a few minutes."

"Okay."

Liam stretched and checked the clock. It backed up what the sun had told him, it was just after 10 in the morning. Glancing at the empty space, he was disappointed he had woken up alone, then he chastised himself. Erin had made it clear she didn't want an attachment. Maybe slipping away before he woke up was her way of keeping him at arm's length.

He flexed his back under the hot spray of the shower. While last night hadn't been as primal as the previous night at the firepit, it had been athletic. He was lucky he wasn't more than a little sore and fatigued; he wasn't as young as he used to be, even if he didn't feel his age right now.

Downstairs, he was grateful some of the French toast Einar had made escaped Gofannon's appetite, along with some ham. Liam figured he'd need to make a major grocery run when he went into Peoria to pick up his paycheck.

"Morning," he said. He gave Erin a smile, hoping it wouldn't be awkward. He filled his favorite mug with coffee and plunked down at the table.

"I thought you were going to sleep all day, Druid," Einar said as he set what was left of the French toast and ham in front of Liam. "Good thing for you Gofannon was eager to get out to your forge, or you wouldn't have had any breakfast."

"Thanks. I guess I needed to catch up on my sleep after the last couple of days." Liam dug into the French toast. It was only lukewarm, but he wasn't about to complain. Between Einar cooking and others doing the dishes, he was getting spoiled. He found himself wondering who was doing the dishes. He certainly couldn't see Derek and Izzy rolling up their leather sleeves to scrub pots and plates. "So, I need to go to Peoria to get my paycheck from Word Nerds, and I bet we need groceries."

"I should probably get some supplies for the trip," Erin said. She glanced in the direction of the living room, where Liam had seen Tim playing on his tablet. "Plus I might pick up some things for Tim."

"Do you want to give me a list?" Liam suggested.

"I don't know," Erin said. She smiled sweetly. "Do you want to pick up seven years' worth of tampons?"

"Or you could come along." Liam looked around the table. "Anything else specific anyone needs?"

"Ja, you're getting low on booze," Einar replied. He removed the apron, hanging it over the back of his chair. "And make sure you pick up some cream."

Pixel nodded. "Someone could definitely use some for all of his hard work."

"What do you mean?" Erin asked, looking puzzled.

Liam remembered the lore around brownies, and it clicked into place who had been cleaning up. It also explained the laundry. "I'll explain it in the car."

"Um, okay." Erin shrugged, but didn't push the point.

"Here," Pixel said, reaching across the table to hand Liam and Erin each a slip of paper. Liam looked at the slip; it had a long number written neatly on it, with an L in the upper corner. "Those are the accounts for your payments. They're at United Federal Bank, which conveniently has branches in Peoria. You'll probably want to visit to check the balance, establish credentials, and maybe take a little out for provisions if you want. I'm sure the tricksters that helped set these up and get your gold converted paid themselves a bit generously, so you might want to double check and make sure they didn't outright rip you off."

"I'm going out on a limb and guessing these are way too big to be covered by FDIC." Liam looked at the slip of the paper. "And what about tax ramifications?"

"I've got a bunch of printouts of legalese mumbo-jumbo." Pixel held up a pair of folders. "Read through these when you get the chance; I can't even begin to explain the accounting acrobatics they went through to set these up. I know you'll get corporate cards to access the money, but if you dump it into your personal accounts…well, it gets messy."

258 | JON R. OSBORNE

"Can using this be used to track us?" Erin asked. Liam hadn't even thought about that.

Pixel looked over to Izzy, who answered. "I am fairly certain these accounts will be safe. However, it wouldn't be a horrible idea to take out some cash for sundry expenses."

"Oh, and the big guy said you should pick up some pocking iron ore," Einar added.

"Where the heck am I supposed to get iron ore?" Liam wasn't sure there were any iron mines anywhere in Illinois. It wasn't like he could roll up and buy a couple hundred pounds of ore, even if there was.

"Take it up with him," Einar said, nodding in the general direction of the forge. "He said once the Champion was under way, you'd need to get cracking on making this sword of hers."

Liam wondered if Tim could use Google to find iron ore for sale. Supposedly you could find almost anything on the Internet. Then he had a better idea. "I'll swing by a junkyard. Why smelt raw ore when we can get some good steel and rework it?"

"Maybe for your practice, but he seemed set that the real thing would require some pocking smelting." Einar shrugged. "I'm not going to argue the point with him."

"Let me finish breakfast," Liam said, halfway through his French toast. "Then we'll head into town."

"I'll come along, in case there are any questions," Pixel said.

"I will as well," Izzy added. "Provisions for the journey and all that."

* * *

The drive to the city had been quiet, an Albannach CD keeping it from being silent. Pixel and Erin had both headed for the shotgun position, resulting in a brief stare down before the flower-maiden backed down and settled for the back seat with Izzy. The scenery certainly wasn't anything to talk about; drums and pipes provided a dissonant soundtrack for fields of corn and soybeans. Eventually, farmlands became punctuated by housing additions and the occasional church, the former growing more common the closer they got to the Illinois River.

"Welcome to Peoria," Liam announced as they crossed the bridge. "This is what passes for 'the city' hereabouts. We'll stop by my previous place of employment and see how much of my time Clark wastes before he coughs up my check." Liam predicted at least 15 minutes, maybe 30.

"I could always glamour him," Pixel volunteered.

"Druid, any chance you could retrieve any files that would lead anyone to your address?" Izzy asked.

"Too late, I already got his file from Mr. Stuffy-Manager," Pixel countered.

"Besides, I lived in East Peoria when I started working there, and switched to a P.O. Box in Peoria after my neighbors kept swiping my mail." The neighbors had probably been drug addicts trying to steal welfare checks. He didn't miss the neighborhood. "I never changed my mailing address once I moved into the farmhouse."

"What are the odds someone could track you down there?" Izzy asked.

"Well, I'm related through my aunt, so the surname isn't the same." Liam thought back to the estate proceedings. "You guys had to find me through my work, not the house, so I'm guessing it would be pretty hard. It would have to occur to someone to dig into it, let alone find something once they thought of it."

"That's a relief," Erin said. "Once you have your last check, you don't have to worry about anyone tracking you through the bookstore."

"Yeah, I tried to get Clark to have it sent to my P.O. Box, but he was his usual anal-retentive self." Liam instinctively guided the car, having driven this route hundreds of times. It was hard to believe he wouldn't have to do it anymore.

By habit, he swung around to the back of the store, where the employees had to park. By the time he realized employee parking was another thing he didn't have to worry about, it seemed like too much trouble to move the car back up front. Walking an extra hundred paces or so wouldn't kill him.

"I'll be right back." Liam almost turned off the car, then decided against it. The August sun was beating down on the parking lot, and the car would warm up quickly.

"Do you want me to come with you?" Pixel volunteered. "In case Clark needs whammied?"

And maybe make him cluck like a chicken, Liam thought. Amusing, but he was hoping to be in and out. "No, that's okay. But if I don't come out in 15 minutes, come in after me."

As it turned out, Clark thrust some paperwork on a clipboard at him. Liam flipped through the forms. "Clark, I'm not signing these until I get my last check. Now go get me my next to last check, please." He emphasized the last word, because Clark never used it.

"Fine, have it your way, Knox." Clark stomped off toward his office, fixing his tie as he went.

"Dude, did the chick with the purple hair track you down?" Kyle asked conspiratorially as soon as Clark was in his office. "She came in here again looking for you."

"Yeah, she tracked me down, and in answer to your next question, no I haven't."

Kyle looked disappointed for a moment. "Too bad, she was smoking. I'd love to see where that tattoo goes." He paused, then added, "Oh, and some Goth chick was in here yesterday asking Clark about you. I'd guess she was a Wiccan or something."

"Really? Do you know what Clark told her?"

"No, man." Kyle shrugged. "When I asked him about it, Clark pretended she had never been here."

The hairs stood up on the back of Liam's neck. "Did you get a name?"

"I think Clark called her 'Raven' when he was speaking to her," Kyle replied. "It was weird; I remember her asking me where he was, then asking me to take her back to his office. She asked about you and your file, told Clark to forget she was there, and left."

Raven. That narrowed it down to about a quarter of the witches out there. It sounded as though she'd glamoured Kyle and Clark. Great, the game was afoot.

"Here." Clark had returned with the check in an envelope. "You'll need to sign when you pick up your last one."

"Yeah, yeah." Liam took the check. It was freeing not to have to endure Clark's bullshit anymore. "Maybe if you treated your employees more like people instead of serfs they wouldn't leave as soon as they got a better offer."

Clark glowered for a moment, then stomped off again.

"I hope he doesn't take that out on you guys," Liam told Kyle.

262 | JON R. OSBORNE

"If he does, it was worth it." Kyle chuckled, looking in the direction of the slammed office door. "I think he's about to burst a blood vessel."

"Take care, Kyle. I'm sure I'll be in as a customer." That much was true; bookstores were a dying breed, and Liam wasn't comfortable shopping online. He tucked the envelope in his pocket without even looking at the check. He'd need to swing by his bank before they went to the United Federal branch where his and Erin's accounts were set up.

Rounding the corner, he was snapped out of his thoughts by someone calling out, "Hey, druid!"

Two bikers were approaching him from an idling van. "Come with us, and we won't have to get rough," one of them snarled.

Liam's mind whirled. One of them he might be able to stand his ground against, but there was no way he could fend off two of them. Maybe he could glamour them?

Hurriedly he tried to draw on the flicker of magic he thought he could feel below the parking lot. He had to resist the urge to wave his hand like the old man in that movie. "I'm not the Druid you're looking for."

"Oh really?" One looked to the other. "He says he's not the Druid we're looking for."

"Yeah, funny guy."

Shit. Liam went into a fighting stance, quickly sidestepping so the one on his right would have to come around his other opponent. The biker closest to him threw a quick grab, which Liam swept aside and countered with a snap punch to the man's jaw. Before he could capitalize on the opening, Liam was forced to back-pedal to avoid the partner, who was trying to grab Liam's arm.

"Look at that, Mikey. He wants to put up a fight." The biker wiped his mouth, then smiled. "We tried to do this civilized, Mr. Knox."

Liam realized he was taking the fight the opposite direction of where he wanted to go, toward the reinforcements in the car. Mikey circled to cut off his retreat toward the front of the store, taking out Plan B.

"You know my name, but I don't know yours." Liam tried to sound glib, but wasn't convinced he'd pulled it off.

"You can call me Mad Dog, Bill." Mad Dog grinned. "I'll give you one more chance to come along quietly."

"Hey, Mad Dog, want to bet 20 bucks you're going to get your ass kicked?" Liam angled back into the parking lot. Of course there were no customers, but that didn't matter now. He just had to keep their attention.

Mad Dog grinned again. "You might have gotten a good pop in, but you're no match for one of us, let alone both."

Liam grinned in return. "No, but she is."

Erin's boot caught Mad Dog right behind his knee. As it buckled, she grabbed his throat and slammed him to the pavement, his head bouncing off the asphalt. Stepping around the fallen biker, she closed on Mikey, who barely had time to register the threat before the one-two kick caught him in the gut, then the face. Reeling backwards and clutching his nose, Mikey didn't even defend against her kick to his knee, which drew his hands away in reflex in time for her to smash her elbow into his teeth.

Izzy was already standing over the first biker, who was obviously still seeing stars. She grabbed hold of his vest and hauled him to the waiting van, slinging him in like a sack of potatoes.

Erin gave Mikey one last kick in the breadbasket before looking at Liam. "Good thing we didn't wait 15 minutes."

"Um, yeah, thanks." Adrenaline was still pumping through Liam's blood. He followed Erin toward the van, which obscured them from any traffic that might pull into the parking lot. Pixel was already there as well.

"These two were watching you go into the store," Izzy explained. "When they suddenly seemed interested in something in your direction, we thought it better safe than sorry."

"Absolutely not sorry," Liam said. Sure, there might be a tiny primitive male part of his ego abashed at being the 'damsel,' but it was by far outweighed by the knowledge he would have gotten his ass kicked if Erin hadn't stepped in. "By the way, Erin, thank you. That was incredibly badass."

"You're welcome, and you're right." Erin gave him a quick grin.

"Now the question is, who sent these guys?" Izzy glared down at Mad Dog, who was trying to focus. "Why don't you grab his partner before he draws any attention?"

Erin and Liam both went to the other biker, who was weakly moaning on the asphalt, blood visible between his fingers. They each grabbed an arm and hauled him up while he feebly tried to resist, then half carried, half dragged him behind the van.

"Do you want to do the honors?" Izzy asked Pixel. "You are better at this than I am."

"Don't mind if I do." Pixel looked down at Mad Dog. Her eyes glowed. "Who sent you to grab Liam?"

"Liam?" Mad Dog sounded befuddled, as much by his skull bouncing off the parking lot as by the question. "We were supposed to grab Bill Knox."

Pixel looked to Liam.

"My given name is William," he answered. "I've gone by Liam since college."

"Who sent you?" Pixel tried to sound menacing.

"Iblis sent us."

This drew puzzled looks all around.

"Who is Iblis?" Pixel demanded.

The biker looked puzzled for a moment before answering. "He's the boss."

Liam started to get nervous about attracting too much attention. "So what do we do with them?" They couldn't hold them prisoner—like P.O.W.s in some metaphysical war—and he wasn't about to commit the obvious alternative.

"You didn't find Mr. Knox," Pixel instructed Mad Dog. "You were mistaken, and tried to grab someone too tough for you, who beat the crap out of you and your partner."

'Let's go,' Izzy mouthed once Pixel finished. Quietly, they left the two bikers and their van, returning to Liam's car. He was relieved to find they hadn't inadvertently locked the keys in the car with it running. Once everyone was in, he backed out of his spot and casually drove past the van as though nothing was amiss.

* * * * *

Chapter Thirty

Erin

"There are so many numbers."

Erin held the slip as if it were going to bite her. An hour of tedious paperwork and deflecting tiresome banking sales pitches, and she had the first real world evidence the Exiled Folk could deliver on their offer. She didn't understand some of the fiscal acrobatics involved, but a trust was paying her over the course of ten years, with the first payment already deposited.

She immediately moved a chunk of the money to a new college savings account for Tim. That way, he could get an education almost anywhere he wanted and wouldn't have to worry about racking up debt or subsisting on ramen noodles.

Especially since Liam had done the same thing. Like Erin, he had also named Tim his beneficiary in case something happened. The altercation a little over an hour ago had made that a stark possibility. Erin was still seething when they had reached the bank; the others had taken her effort to quell the rage as nervousness about this transaction.

Granted, dealing with this kind of money made her nervous. She kept expecting something to flash on a computer monitor, and federal agents to come storming in. The branch manager had certainly looked dubious when they walked in. A few screens of information later, he was all smiles, practically salivating at the chance to "help" them manage their money.

Liam had seemed to take it in stride. Obviously he had dealt with his family's estate, but it couldn't have been anywhere close to this kind of money. Otherwise he wouldn't have been working in that crappy bookstore for a boss who was a total jackass. He seemed blasé about the numbers and asked a few questions that wouldn't have occurred to Erin, then mentioned he would at some point need to see his accountant. Erin couldn't stop staring at the number on the slip.

"Any questions before we wrap up?" Liam's voice shook her out of her reverie. Looking up, she could see the banker was waiting with practiced patience, probably hoping she would ask something that would segue into one of his pitches.

Erin shook her head. "We can always come back or call if I think of anything."

"Oh, absolutely." The banker smiled, all white teeth, which reminded her of the quartet in the bar three days ago. Had it only been three days? "Feel free to call me anytime."

Erin might have taken his statement as a subtle pick up, except she knew he was really interested in her money, and what he could do to get a percentage.

Liam stood and reached across the table to shake the banker's hand. "Thanks for your help, Brad. We'll be in touch, and I imagine my accountant will want to talk to you at some point."

"Absolutely." Brad seemed fond of the word.

Izzy was leaning against the back of the car, watching traffic, with Pixel sitting next to her on the trunk of the car. Erin caught a bit of their conversation, but it was in the pseudo-Irish that seemed to be the common language for these Exiled Folk. Erin struggled with the smattering of Spanish she'd picked up through work.

She also didn't know how Izzy was not melting or burning to a crisp. What little skin wasn't covered in black leather was almost ghost pale, and Izzy was standing in the August afternoon sun. At least Pixel seemed to feel the heat. She looked ready to wilt, which gave Erin a tinge of petty satisfaction.

"Anything interesting?" Liam asked as he unlocked the car. He'd offered to leave it running, but Izzy insisted he keep the keys with him.

"Fortunately, no." Izzy stood and strode to the back passenger door. Erin realized her boots made no sound on the pavement. She wondered if it was something Izzy did, like a glamour, or if it was her boots. "A police car cruised by 15 minutes ago, but the officers took no interest in your car."

If Pixel was still annoyed at being denied the front seat, she didn't show it as she slid off the trunk, her pink sneakers softly crunching on the parking lot pavement. "I take it everything went okay?"

"Yeah." Liam started the car as soon as everyone was in. "The banker tried to sell us on everything under the sun, or we would have been done in half the time."

Erin still had the slip, along with the packet Brad had given her. She wasn't paying attention to the passing scenery. Peoria didn't look all that different from parts of Cincinnati. She was thinking about the next seven years. Liam had it easy. A couple of months' worth of work, and his part would be done. Sure, there was mention of something going forward, but it sounded like a cushy consulting job; how hard could that be?

But doing this would mean she and Tim were set for life. Seven years, from her perspective, is what it would take. Do it, win the fight, and she could do more to ensure Tim's future than working the next 20 years in shit jobs.

Erin looked up and realized they had pulled into the parking lot of some big box retail store. Fortunately, she had a wad of fresh bills in her purse, courtesy of her new account. She had written a list of things she and Tim needed—Tim for the impending school year and her for a seven-year trip. She was leery of trying the card she had been given as she still expected something to go wrong.

An hour and two shopping carts later, she still hadn't tried the card, despite Pixel's insistence it would be fine. Erin couldn't help but notice Liam hadn't tried his card either.

"Cash is always good," he said. The cashier had raised an eyebrow at all the liquor and beer filling the bottom of Liam's cart, revealed once the groceries had been sent down the conveyor. "Family reunion," Liam remarked, receiving a knowing nod in return.

Pixel had been saddled with one of Erin's carts so that Izzy could peel off and watch for anyone seeming to have an interest in them once they reached the exit. Erin checked the traffic, and Izzy was gone from sight. As their carts rattled across the pavement, Erin tried not to look around, worrying that every vehicle was about to erupt with assailants. By the time they reached Liam's car, the only person who had shown an interest was the old lady waiting for their parking space, scowling as she peered over her steering wheel.

"Really? You carry a full sized spare?" Erin asked. The tire ate up a large chunk of the space, ensuring they would have to load some of their purchases in the back seat.

Liam shrugged. "I hate those little donuts they give you and the crappy little jack." He shoved a toolbox and a bundle of jumper cables to the side, trying to clear as much room as possible before he started loading the booze.

The little old lady continued to scowl and chomped her dentures as Liam began arranging the groceries. "I think granny over there is afraid she's going to expire before she gets this spot," Erin said. "There's no prize for neatness."

"You think this is bad?" Liam asked, adjusting a few things before starting on the first of Erin's carts. "Be glad we didn't bring Susan. She has to group her groceries by storage requirements and type. Besides, Izzy needs enough time to get to the stoplight by the Hibachi restaurant."

He went to the back door and started loading bags into the middle of the back seat. "Good thing you're tiny, Pixel, otherwise you might have had to ride in Izzy's lap."

Liam took a quick look around the lot before climbing in and starting the car up. "Heck if I can see anyone scouting us; there's too much traffic in the parking lot. I hate big stores, but this let us get everything at once."

Finally relinquishing his space to the elderly woman, Liam cruised slowly through the lot, following the traffic toward the exit. Erin scanned the other vehicles, but none looked particularly suspicious. As they waited for the light at the exit to the street, Izzy climbed into the back behind Erin.

"It looks like we are clear, Druid." Izzy buckled herself in. "That or they are good, which, given what we saw earlier, I am doubtful of."

"Good. I assume you alerted your brother to what happened so they can keep their eyes peeled at the house?"

"I did."

"Okay, we're going to take a little scenic route, so we can make sure we aren't being followed." Instead of going back toward the river, Liam headed west. Following one looping road after another, they ended up on I-74 heading west, only to jump off at the next exit, heading north. Erin lost track of where they were as this new road curved around until they were alongside a lake, which was really a bloated portion of the Illinois River.

Liam was quiet, splitting his attention between driving and watching the rearview mirror. Erin sat sideways in her seat—at least as much as the seatbelt would allow—to give her a view out the back window without having to crane her neck. It also gave her a good look at Liam's profile. In the afternoon sun, his beard looked fuller, Erin realized it was because much of the gray that had peppered his chin and temples was gone, replaced by the same sandy brown as the rest of his hair. Had their fling prompted him to dye the grey out?

As she scrutinized him between eyeing the odd pickup truck or car following behind them, she realized the creases at the corners of his eyes were less pronounced. Usually bright sunlight had the opposite effect, harshly illuminating every flaw and trace of time. She knew over the years she'd watched a few lines appear as she hit 30 and tried not to obsess over their progression.

Erin flipped down the sun visor and opened the mirror. Her own lines were virtually gone. If she hadn't had each one memorized, she wouldn't have noticed anything. She turned her head, watching the light play across her face, expecting every line and crow's foot to reappear. Instead her skin remained smoother than it had been in years.

Izzy finally broke the silence. "Not to question your wisdom, Druid, but is your plan to drive through random farmland until potential pursuit dies of boredom?"

"That's my plan," Liam replied with a grin. "Or I want to cross the river up north at Lacon. I don't know what kind of resources this Iblis character has, but there's a half-dozen bridges across the Illinois from Peoria or just south of it. This is a little more out of the way and a lot less traffic."

"Back to Iblis, there's an Iblis who appears in Islam as the devil, who is also referred to as Shaitan," Liam explained. "According to myth, he was banned from heaven for refusing to bow to Adam."

"He could be a fallen Elohim," Izzy responded, without taking her gaze off the road behind them. "The trouble with fallen Elohim is you can never be sure where their agenda lies. Given the nature of Iblis' 'invitation,' we can assume he does not side with the Exiled Folk on the Accords. He may see the return of the Exiled Gods as diminishing his influence, or he could be concerned the new accords will banish him and his ilk from the Dunwold."

"I would have thought you guys would have been more up to speed on the opposition," Liam said. He cocked his head, as though listening to an internal dialogue. "He couldn't be Lucifer could he, or an aspect of him? Kind of like how our Gofannon is an aspect?"

"It is a possibility," Izzy conceded, nodding. "As far as our lack of intelligence, the Elohim and Nephilim on the Dunwold have mastered the art of working from the shadows. Their presence, if revealed, could cause quite an upheaval in the Abrahamic religions, actually diluting their power base."

"So, in theory, how tough would he be? Would he have funky powers? Could you kill him the old-fashioned way, with a bullet or sword?"

Izzy looked forward to meet Liam's eyes in the rearview mirror. "Pray we do not have to find out."

* * * * *

Chapter Thirty-One

Iblis

"You grabbed the wrong person?" Mad Dog nodded and glanced over at his partner for support. Mikey nodded also, more gingerly. He had a bloody mouth and a broken nose, wads of cotton turned crimson from stopping the flow. Both men had limps. "He looked up when we said 'druid.'"

"And he beat you up?" Iblis was annoyed. Men of clay could be so annoying. Earth was an appropriate name; these mortals wallowed dimly in the muck and their own refuse. "I thought the two of you were made of sterner stuff."

What Iblis had learned from Potts didn't lend a great deal of credence to the bikers' excuse. Knox had been described as a dabbler. While Iblis couldn't rule out his minions' version of events, as the Druid had supposedly sampled a couple of martial arts, it didn't seem likely he could hold his own against a pair of experienced brawlers.

"We were hit from behind," Mikey protested, slurring his words through what would probably need dental work. "One minute we had him boxed in, the next this chick was going kung-fu on my face."

"The druid was in front of you." Iblis waited for them to affirm the statement. "And you were hit from behind. By a woman."

"I don't remember a woman," Mad Dog said. Not surprising if he really did have a concussion from his skull getting bounced off the pavement as he had described. "We grabbed the wrong guy, and he kicked our asses."

"Fools," Raven barked from where she was perched on the corner of Iblis' desk. The corner of her mouth crooked up in a wicked grin. "You were ambushed and glamoured. The druid baited you out and had help."

"No way." Mad Dog shook his head, a little unsteady in doing so. "We grabbed the wrong guy. He kicked our asses."

"I think you are correct, Raven," Iblis said. He really needed more manpower; it would allow a larger and more subtle net. Obviously the Druid was well informed if he'd laid a trap for his men. Perhaps some sort of oracular talent that let him divine the time and place he would be attacked? Except it wasn't an attack, more like a robust invitation. Somehow, the Druid, or one of those otherfolk abetting him, had predicted it. "Did you at least get his license plate?"

The bikers looked at each other and shook their heads. Iblis stifled a sigh. It might have been another dead end, given how the Druid seemed to have covered his tracks so far, or it could have been the first solid lead on where to find him.

"Go have your injuries tended." Iblis dismissed them with a shooing motion, waiting for them to limp out of sight before flicking his hand at the door, which swung shut and latched with a click.

"Perhaps we should scry for the Champion again?" Raven asked. She remained on the desk as Iblis sank into the luxurious leather chair behind it. The chair was worth more than the rest of the furniture in the room put together, an indulgence on Iblis' part. "Since she is with the Druid, she could lead us to him."

"I had thought of something similar." Iblis closed his eyes. The woman had been the one to tear his men apart, not a druid with some amateur belts from a couple of strip mall dojos. Iblis had heard rumors about Mikha'el sending men to make a grab for her, only to have her hospitalize them. "However, we seem to only be able to locate her at cruxes, moments of great importance, and somehow she evaded her appointment with an eighteen-wheeler."

"The otherfolk are helping her as well."

"Of course, but it felt as if there was a last minute intervention. Who knows how many players we have on the board?" Iblis chuckled. "Or even what game they are playing."

"Maybe we should garner more mystical strength of our own?" Raven asked. Iblis recognized the tone in her voice. She craved more power and was trying to entice him into granting it. But he wasn't about to put all of his eggs in one basket.

"I think it's time to bring in a couple more of your fellow witches," Iblis said. He opened his eyes to see the disappointment play across Raven's face. Good, she needed to have a bit of wind taken out of her sails. "After all, haven't I taught you much more than your priestess, Moon-Bird, ever did?"

"Moon-Phoenix, and yes, you've taught me real magic, not platitudes that fall on the deaf ears of uncaring gods or hopeful self-delusions of positivity." She slid off the desk, kneeling beside his chair, placing one hand on his knee. "You've taught me about power."

Iblis smiled as she leaned forward between his knees, inching forward on her knees. Her hand slid up his thigh until it reached his belt and began unbuckling it. Iblis could have freed his swelling member with a snap of his finger, but he wanted her to do the work.

"You could teach me more about power," she said huskily, drawing down the zipper, looking up at him hungrily.

"Oh, I will teach you more about power, my dear Raven," Iblis murmured. Raven smiled before bending forward. "But not by simply giving you power. We'll bring a couple of your neophytes into our circle, and teach them as I have taught you. You will be over them, and collectively your power will be greater than anyone else's."

Iblis wasn't sure if she was listening anymore as she fell into a rhythm. He didn't really care. They would bring in a couple of the younger, more pliable members, ones more easily swayed and eager to take short cuts. He would grant them power the same way he had Raven, by imbuing them with some of his essence, which had the bonus that they would associate serving his carnal desires with gaining their own mystical strength.

Iblis smiled down at Raven, who met his gaze even as her head continued to bob. "I don't suppose you have any virgins in your coven?"

* * * * *

Chapter Thirty-Two

Lee

"I told you I need sleep."

Joel followed Lee into the hotel room. "I can operate the vehicle. This is a waste of our time."

At least there were two beds, Lee thought. Not that there was any indication Joel would sleep, but he didn't want anyone to think this was some sort of homosexual liaison. Even if it was in the middle of nowhere, at least as much nowhere as Galesburg was, and no one knew him.

"We don't need you getting pulled over by some state trooper trying to make quota and you chopping him into cold cuts." Lee tossed down his gym bag, which had a few changes of clothes and some toiletries. A red herring had cost them three hours, making a long drive already longer. Every time they had stopped, Joel had complained. The more Lee thought about it, the more it seemed like they were on a fool's errand. He wasn't about to tell Mikha'el that, though.

"I must eliminate." Joel headed toward the bathroom. When they had stopped at a burger restaurant built into a gas station, Joel had actually eaten after initially protesting he didn't need to do so. He claimed it was so he would not draw attention, but to Lee it looked like Joel actually enjoyed it after the first tentative bite.

"At least you're housebroken," Lee muttered, turning on the television. After hours of the same three gospel CDs, he wanted some noise and hoped there might be a slim chance there might be some hint in the news of the impending Armageddon.

"I heard that," Joel remarked as he closed the door.

Lee shook his head. After all, if the heathens won this challenge, it might as well be the end of the world. Every pagan god, troll, and spook would boil up from the underworld, ready to take revenge for almost two millennia of banishment. The news broadcast was really white noise, babbling about which politician had offended whom and what piss-ant third world nation was saber rattling now.

Did the heathens, the pagan gods, and the creatures Joel had referred to as *nukrayam*, otherfolk, actually stand a chance? Surely with God taking an active interest and dispatching members of His heavenly host, there was no way the otherfolk would win. But Mikha'el had never actually said the Lord had sent him and his fellow angels; he'd only *implied* it was the Lord's will. Was this some sort of test for mankind? Lee couldn't imagine why else the Lord would even allow a risk to the faith. Or was God's commitment to free will such that He would allow centuries of religious progress to be undone?

"Pastor Lee Haskins, I am speaking to you."

It took a moment for it to register that the talking head on the cable news channel had addressed him. "You're speaking to me?"

"Are you a *dobblegar* masquerading as Pastor Haskins?" The cable anchor looked into the camera, even as the news crawl continued to scroll under him. The price of oil had gone up again and there were protests on Wall Street regarding wealth inequality.

"No, of course not!"

"Then yes, I am speaking to you." The anchor adjusted his tie. "There have been two significant disturbances. One near where you currently are, the other to the west, near Colorado Springs." Behind the news anchor, a graphic appeared showing the state of Colorado with Colorado Springs indicated with a blinking dot.

"Colorado Springs?" Lee peered at the map, which lacked any detail. "What the heck is in Colorado Springs?"

"Cheyenne Mountain for one." The anchor pointed at the map. "And NORAD."

"So, what, the heathens are going to nuke the world?"

"Who can fathom what their archaic and blood-thirsty motives are?" the anchor replied. "It is hoped the Champion will be spotted along I-70, en route to Colorado Springs. You and Jehoel are to proceed west along I-70 in anticipation of the Champion and her allies being spotted."

"You said the other disturbance, whatever that means, was near us. Doesn't that bear checking out?"

The map pulled back to show the midsection of the nation, with I-70 a bright blue stripe. "We've been unable to pin down the location of the disturbance."

"You can talk to me through the television, but you can't figure out where this disturbance, in the same state as us, is located?" Lee resisted the urge to tap the screen over Illinois. "Wouldn't it make more sense to try to track down what is going on here?"

The anchor pressed a finger over his ear. "Your suggestion may have merit. Check back in the morning before departing for further clarification."

The news abruptly went back to North Korea's latest threat, the anchor's blonde partner reading the newest proclamation with a vapid smile.

"I assume you heard that?" Haskins asked.

"I did," Joel replied from the bathroom door.

"That means we have permission to spend the night here and get some sleep." Lee dug into his gym bag and pulled out a set of headphones he normally used to listen to inspirational tracks at the gym. He held the headphones out toward Joel. "Plug these into the television if you want to watch it while I sleep. A little mortal world knowledge might do you some good, but change the channel if they mention the Kardashians."

* * * * *

Chapter Thirty-Three

Liam

"See what you have wrought?"

Liam looked across the corn and soybean fields. The smoke hung on the horizon, illuminated from below by firelight as Peoria burned. He turned to the woman next to him, a woman he didn't recognize. She was a few years younger than him, probably about Erin's age, though it was harder to tell with the heavy black eyeliner, smoky eyelids, and dark red lips. She was dressed in a simple peasant skirt and a loose cotton blouse that made it obvious she wasn't wearing a bra.

"How is this my fault?" Liam asked.

"You brought them to our world," she replied, still looking west. The shoulder-less blouse revealed a raven tattoo on her shoulder closest to him. "You brought them from the past, and you upset the balance of things. Now dark creatures and darker magic set fire to the world."

"How was I to know this would happen?" Was that a dragon on the horizon, flying south toward Pekin? For that matter, where was everyone else? Was the challenge over? Apparently they'd won, but Liam couldn't remember any of it. Had something happened to him? "Who are you?"

"My name is unimportant, though some call me Raven." She finally turned toward him, her eyes were dark pools of brown. A choker with a small pentacle was on her neck; Liam realized the pentacle was inverted. "Like you, I learned about magic, only to have it stripped away by the Hibernian Accords. The accords you wrote, druid."

"Are you Wiccan?" Liam didn't remember writing the new accords. He vaguely remembered discussing the basic concepts but couldn't place how long ago it had been. Liam looked around and realized he didn't see his house or the farm. His best guess placed him several miles northwest. A small wooded hill was behind him.

"I am, and for a while, I truly *was* a witch." She stepped toward him. "But you took my power away, and you gave it all to the Others, those under the hill and beyond the veil."

"I don't remember doing that," Liam protested, his eyes momentarily drawn to where Raven's nipples were quite evident under the thin fabric.

"You can fix it." Raven held his gaze as she undid the knot holding the top of her blouse closed. Once untied, the cotton began to slide enticingly down. "It'll even be fun for the both of us. You'll just need to give me a little bit of your essence."

Liam took an unconscious step back. Despite his body responding to her charms, his mind knew there was something wrong. How could he screw up the whole world and not remember it?

"Get away from him, you bitch!" Pixel stalked out of the copse of trees that surmounted the hillock, her eyes blazing violet. Vines and gauze draped around her, barely enough to protect her modesty. As she approached, Liam caught wind of her floral fragrance, which did nothing to diminish the raging hard-on he had.

"What's wrong, fae? Afraid I'll get what you're after?" Raven taunted, crossing her arms below her breasts. "What are you, his familiar?"

Pixel glowered at the taller woman, moving possessively next to Liam. "That's none of your business."

"I see, he hasn't given it to you yet." Raven smirked, drawing a finger from her pentacle down to her cleavage. "Maybe he wants a woman, not a little girl?"

"Liam, this isn't real." Pixel appeared to ignore the jibe. "You're dream-walking in the Murkwold."

Liam ignored his physical senses and concentrated, feeling for the weave of magic he'd felt permeate the Murkwold. Connecting to it, he opened his eyes. The three of them were still in the same location, but there was no sign of fire, smoke, or dragons, and now it was night. The fogginess of sleep fell away from his mind.

"What a shame," Raven said. "We could have had so much fun." Raven shrugged off the blouse, exposing her breasts. "We still could, if you tell me where to meet you, druid. I give great familiar."

"You work for Iblis, don't you?" Liam remembered the afternoon and the bikers.

"For now." Raven extracted her arms from the sleevelets of the blouse, then discarded the garment. "That could change, with the right incentive."

"As if we would trust you," Pixel hissed.

"What does Iblis want?" Liam figured it didn't hurt to ask. Maybe if she was hedging her bets, she might slip something useful. Of course, he reminded himself, it was all likely a trap.

"He wants to meet with you, druid." She glanced south, and Liam resisted the urge to follow her gaze. "Perhaps he wants to make some sort of agreement that doesn't leave him powerless when you strip the scions of Abraham of their power and supplant them."

"Then why didn't he come himself?" Liam was actually glad he hadn't; he didn't know what kind of danger such a powerful being would pose to his spirit-form, and what kind of ramifications there could be for his physical body.

Raven shrugged, an exaggerated gesture obviously intended to accentuate her assets. "What's the point of having minions if you have to do your own legwork?"

"Because he's one of the Fallen." Pixel had remained firmly at Liam's side, her warmth palpable through his robes. It was only then that he realized he was wearing robes, or at least his spirit-form was. "And if he comes to the Murkwold, all of his non-Fallen colleagues might be able to find him."

"Well, as fun as this is, I'm feeling a little exposed out here talking to the enemy," Liam said. He looked around, expecting foes to come creeping out of the darkness. He put an arm around Pixel, who responded by snuggling up against him and putting her own arm around him. "Tell your boss to leave me and mine the hell alone before he inspires me to get real creative with the new accords."

Without waiting for a response, Liam stepped, carrying Pixel along with him as he crossed a mile, then another and another, each step taking him west. A score of steps had taken them across the Illinois River, its murky waters present in the Murkwold as well as the mundane world. After several more steps, he stopped and looked at Pixel.

"Thanks," Liam said. He checked for any sign of pursuit. "I'm sure we'll have a lot to talk about in the morning, but I don't think we should stay on walkabout."

Pixel glanced down at the bulge in his robes. "Are you sure you don't need help with that?"

"I'm going to wake up now." There was a disorientation, like falling in a dream, his body jerked, and then Liam was staring at the ceiling.

"What's wrong?" Erin mumbled sleepily. So far, she hadn't slipped away after joining him in bed. She had made sure to remind him that it was only sex, or co-parenting with benefits as he'd dubbed it.

"Either I had a really weird dream, or I spontaneously spirit-walked." He rolled on his side and snuggled up behind her.

"My god, are you horny again?" Erin sounded a little more awake and ground back against him.

* * * * *

Chapter Thirty-Four

Erin

"So you didn't sneak out in the middle of the night?" Erin realized where she was before the cobwebs had finished clearing from her head. She'd meant to sneak out before dawn, but their second round in the middle of the night made her oversleep. Part of her wondered, was it so bad?

"I overslept," she murmured, then she yawned and stretched languidly. It was warm and comfy in the bed; she was reluctant to leave it. But she had to, for many reasons, both practical and psychological. "It's almost nine."

"We could just stay here and see how long it takes them to notice." Liam's arm had been around Erin when she awoke, but he had pulled it back so his hand rested above her hip. He was making it easy for her to leave, but inviting her to stay. "We don't have anything pressing on the agenda."

"Other than evading people searching for us while getting to Cheyenne Mountain, and you learning how to make a magic sword, nothing at all." Reluctantly Erin slid out of the bed, stretching again in the cool air under the ceiling fan. She looked over her shoulder. Liam was watching her with a lopsided grin. "Didn't you say something about spirit-walking last night?"

The grin vanished, and he tossed off the covers to climb out the opposite side of the bed. "You're right. I thought it was a weird dream or nightmare at first, but I think I spirit-walked and ran into someone working for the Avramites."

"What? Who was it, those bikers again?" Erin didn't think those thugs were the mystic meditative types, but nothing seemed too absurd anymore. "Could they follow you?"

"No, it wasn't those guys, it was some witch who works for Iblis." Liam was looking straight ahead into empty air, his eyes unfocused. "She tried to trick me, make me think it was after the challenge, and I had somehow screwed up the world with the new accords. It was like something out of one of those end-of-world movies, but with dragons."

"What do you think she hoped to accomplish?" Erin asked. She definitely preferred dealing with goons she could punch rather than spirit-walking witches.

"She tried to seduce me, telling me I could fix it."

Erin remembered when Liam jumped in his sleep, waking her up. She also remembered what happened afterward. "Is that why you were horny? Because this witch was coming on to you?"

"What? What difference does that make?" Liam's eyes focused again and he looked at her, his brow furrowed. "Besides, you were the one that pointed out this was just sex."

Erin felt her blood pressure going up, even if it was basically what she had told him. "Why didn't you invite Pixel, you guys could have had a spirit-three-way?"

"Actually, Pixel showed up. She helped shake me out of whatever illusion Raven was using to mess with me."

"Raven? Did you get her number too?" Erin fought to keep her voice from rising.

Liam let out a sigh, probably both of frustration and to give himself an extra second to compose his answer. "Look, I didn't have sex with either of them, in the spirit world or the real one, so I don't know why you're mad at me."

Erin snatched up her clothes from the floor, spotted a robe hanging on the back of the door and threw it on. She gave Liam one more baleful glance before throwing open the door and slamming it shut behind her. Or at least she meant to slam it, the hinges somehow bound up and the door closed softly with a click. She stalked across the hall to her room.

Why would she be mad at him? Because he was dreaming about other women then waking up to poke her with his hard-on to get some relief? Of course she should be mad. She fished through her bags for clean clothes, tossing the dirty laundry into the hamper in the corner. She'd need to wash her clothes before she left, she thought. She wondered how quickly she could get everything together as she stalked to the bathroom.

Everything was pretty much set. She ran through a mental checklist in the shower, the exercise helping her diffuse her anger. They could hit the road as soon as she did her laundry, sooner if she was willing to hit a laundromat on the road.

No, it would leave them stationary longer than they needed to be, and she would have a last couple of hours with Tim before she set out. Was she still comfortable with Tim staying here? Despite his father being a bit of a clueless jerk when it came to women; yes, this was the best place Erin could think of for Tim. Liam had been insensitive, not malicious. To be truthful, he seemed to have a lot calmer temperament than Erin, even though she wasn't about to tell him that.

By the time she had dried off, she was committed to leaving this afternoon. Maybe this was just as well, having this fight with Liam. It clearly drew the line they were not a couple, and he shouldn't get attached to her. It was a reminder she shouldn't get attached to him, because Erin knew how that always played out.

Breakfast was winding down by the time Erin got dressed and calmed down enough to face Liam. Einar had cooked up corned beef hash, biscuits, gravy, and scrambled eggs with cheddar cheese. Liam and Pixel were at one side of the kitchen table, Derek and Izzy at the other, and Einar at the end closest to the stove, leaving Erin the other end.

"There's a fresh pot of coffee," Liam said when she walked in, interrupting whatever the others had been intently listening to him say.

"Thanks." She headed for the cupboard with the mugs. "I assume you told them about your encounter with 'Raven' last night."

"He did," Izzy replied for him. "It is disconcerting the Avramites have suborned some witches who actually have some talent."

"So does this mean they know where we are?" Erin filled her cup and took a whiff of the rising steam. The coffee smelled good and strong. "I was thinking we should get underway."

"I don't think she knew where Liam had come from." Pixel looked from Liam to Erin. "If she had figured it out, she would have gone right back to her master, as opposed to trying to get something out of him."

"She was trying to get more than information out of him," Derek remarked, sipping on his coffee.

"Very funny," Liam grumbled.

"No, that's not what I'm talking about, Druid." Derek smirked over his cup. "Well, a little bit. But her remarks regarding essence. I think she wanted, or at least wanted to imply, you could give her power in the process of congress with her. It's actually not uncommon among the Folk."

Erin leaned over the table between Liam and Pixel, a plate in hand, and loaded it. She glanced down at Pixel and wondered if that was the fairy's interest in Liam. Could screwing him somehow give her power, or sustain her like a succubus? Erin regretted all of her supernatural knowledge being based on a television show.

"So could Iblis have jumpstarted her, and now she's worried if the Avramites lose, she'll lose her mojo?" Liam asked. He carefully gave Erin the space she needed, whereas before he would have casually welcomed her brushing up against him. "She could be hedging her bets."

Erin stepped around to her seat, setting her plate and coffee down. "Or she's hoping to trip you up by pretending she's willing to switch sides."

"That's entirely possible." Erin was surprised to hear Pixel agree with her. Pixel picked up a half empty glass of orange juice, but didn't drink from it. "If she could have gotten something out of Liam, in more ways than one, and convinced him she was a potential ally, I'm sure her master would have been quite pleased with her. She is Iblis' familiar after all."

"What does that mean?" Erin asked, digging into the hash. She realized she was famished, probably from all of those nighttime calisthenics she'd been doing instead of getting proper sleep. "What's a familiar?"

294 | JON R. OSBORNE

"Sometimes a supernatural entity will form a bond with a person of the Dunwold, a person with a talent for magic," Izzy said. She set down her fork. "In exchange for knowledge and service, the dominant partner gives something to the familiar. The most common being essence, which helps the familiar remain on the Wold and makes them more powerful while the bond is intact. However, a powerful entity can take a human as a familiar, giving the familiar their essence and a portion of their strength, in return for some sort of service."

"So Iblis is giving this witch magical power in exchange for being his minion?" Erin asked between bites. She wished they were taking Einar on the road with them, so he could be their cook. Let Liam eat Poptarts and Cheerios; Tim would probably like it better.

"Most likely," Izzy agreed.

"Any way to find her, so I can punch her like I did those bikers?" Erin asked. She could tell Liam would have trouble bringing himself to strike a woman, even one who was a threat. His old-fashioned chivalry might be endearing, but Erin had no such compunctions. "We can put off leaving a day or two if it means I can kick her in the mommy-parts."

Liam looked predictably surprised; Izzy and Derek's faces were neutral, as was Einar's. Pixel looked like she was thinking furiously how to track down the witch. Eventually everyone shook their heads.

"Okay, then let's get on the road after lunch," Erin announced. She turned to Liam. "Do you have a washer and dryer here?"

Liam nodded. "In the basement. The door down is under the front stairs, and the green door by the fridge in the garage will take you there also. There's detergent on the shelf over the washer."

The door from the garage banged open. "Good, Champion, you are still here," Gofannon bellowed. "I have something for you."

The smith held out a small leather pouch, which looked diminutive in his huge, calloused hands. Erin took the pouch, curious. It felt empty, and looked big enough to barely fit her hand in. An odd, coarse black thread was stitched to form a line with little hash marks on it.

"Thanks." She didn't know what else to say.

"A skilly-hob from Scooter's holt made it for you," Gofannon said, grinning as though telling a joke. "Go on, reach inside."

Erin tentatively slid her hand in and immediately found a hard object that felt like metal and leather. Wrapping her hand around it, she pulled out a sword, the weapon emerging from the bag similar to a magician's scarves. Once the blade cleared the pouch, she held a yard-long, double-edged weapon. It flared out near the hilt, with a heavy blunt pommel below a grip big enough to accommodate both of Erin's hands, with a little room to spare so she could adjust her grip.

"You made me a sword?" Erin scooted back from the table, forgetting about breakfast. Standing up, she examined the weapon, one handing gripping the hilt while resting the blade on the back of her other hand. Ideally, she wouldn't touch the blade at all with her skin, but she was caught off guard.

"Yes. It is not as potent as the one Cathbadson will forge for you, but it should get you by for your training," Gofannon said. He caught a whiff of food. "Splendid, breakfast!"

Erin held the weapon out at arm's length, testing the balance, the center point of which was barely past the grip. Conscious of the confined space, she tentatively maneuvered the weapon to get a feel for its heft. "Will it go back in the pouch?"

"Of course," Gofannon replied. "Otherwise, what is the point?"

"Where'd you get the metal?" Liam asked. "You didn't melt down my motorcycle, did you?"

"Don't be ridiculous!" Gofannon boomed. "I used your practice blades!"

Erin looked back at the table. She didn't even mind that Gofannon was eating her breakfast.

* * * * *

Chapter Thirty-Five

Tim

"You'll be okay."

Tim nodded nervously in response to his mother. He was going to spend the next several weeks with his dad, but his mom would be gone for them. Whatever progress had been made toward his dad and mom being together, like normal parents, seemed to have been almost entirely undone.

They'd had another fight—that much was obvious. While they were polite to each other, which was more than could be said for some of his mother's break ups, they seemed to circle each other, avoiding getting close, even when they had to talk to each other.

"You're sure you have everything you need to get Tim signed up for school?" Erin asked. She stood on one side of Tim with Liam on the other.

Liam tapped a pile of papers on the desk. "Everything we need is here, and I've memorized them as well." Tim thought it was cool that his father had an eidetic memory, same as him. "Also, I've talked to a friend at the high school about getting some pre-work for him when he gets bored with the 7th grade material."

"Can I learn Irish?" Tim had already scoped out some books scattered around the house, but learning a language from a book would be tough. He could memorize vocabulary, but pronunciation and grammar required practice and hearing the language spoken.

Liam looked at Tim's mother, who seemed to be trying to think of a reason to say no. She had already vetoed him learning how to make swords, use swords, or ride a motorcycle. The jury was still out on riding horses, but since it turned out Liam didn't have any horses, it wasn't as pressing.

"I don't suppose it would do any harm," Erin finally said. "But I don't want it to interfere with your schoolwork."

"Are you sure, Tim?" Liam surprised Tim by questioning him learning Irish. Obviously, he didn't see the advantage of knowing the almost secret-language. Tim had seen his mother's irritation when Liam and the Exiled Folk spoke in Irish. Tim was tired of missing out on what was being said. "I would think Spanish, Chinese or Arabic would be a lot more useful."

"Not around here." Tim looked to his mother. "Besides, I won't have video games or the Internet here, and I don't know any kids. I'm kind of like John Connor."

"Who's John Connor?" Liam asked. "One of his friends from Cincinnati?"

"You know, from the Terminator?" Sometimes Tim thought his father was as old as this house. "John Connor, Sarah Connor, I'll be back?"

"It's a movie, and I think it's a television show," Erin explained. "Kind of appropriate when you think about it. A mother and son on the run from a relentless killer robot while facing their destiny. "

"I'll take your word for it." Liam didn't seem convinced. "And we'll need to see about chances to socialize with other kids."

"Please don't sign me up for soccer," Tim moaned. While he wasn't adverse to physical activity, he hated sports. Between coaches and the other kids, he was miserable when his mother signed him up for a youth soccer league.

"What about martial arts?" Liam looked from Tim to Erin. "Believe it or not, there's actually a dojo here in town that's pretty good. I went to it for a couple of years."

Tim tried not to hold his breath as his mother contemplated this new suggestion. She was chewing her lip, which meant she had a reservation, but she was juggling whether it was enough for her to say no. "There's kids in these classes?"

Liam nodded. "Not a lot of Internet and Xboxes out on the rural routes."

"Okay, but only if you keep your grades up and don't do anything stupid." She held her hand up when Tim started to protest he wouldn't do anything stupid. "You're a boy and almost a teenager. It's wired into your hormone-addled brain."

"It's only a couple of months," Liam said. He grinned and ruffled Tim's hair. "How much trouble can he get in?"

"I'll remember that when I come back, and the garage is burnt down." Erin looked down at Tim, then knelt down to hug him. It brought back a vague memory of when he was little, and she had gone away with the military and left him with his grandparents in Columbus. "Be good for your father, listen to him, and try to make some friends." After she stood back up, she wiped her eye, and Tim had to resist the urge to tear up as well.

Tim nodded, afraid if he said anything it would sound choked up. They all went out through the garage to where the Charger waited, rumbling in the driveway. Tim noticed it had a new license plate, this one an Illinois plate. The noon sun beat down on the gravel driveway and glared off the car's waxed finish.

"Take care of our son," Erin whispered, barely audible. Liam nodded, then they hugged awkwardly.

"We'll be waiting," Liam responded once they parted, his hand lingering on her upper arm a moment.

Erin nodded, stepped back a pace, and looked at Tim one last time. With a sniffle and a half wave to Tim, she turned and climbed into the back seat of the Charger. The car rumbled down the driveway, gravel crunching under the tires until it hit the country road asphalt. With a roar of its engine, it took off west, quickly lost through the corn in the adjacent field.

Tim stood, listening to the fading roar of the engine, then wiped his nose on his sleeve. He knew that would have drawn a rebuke from his mother, and it made him a little sadder.

"It's okay, you know," Liam said as he put a hand on Tim's shoulder. "If you need to cry, or need some time to yourself, there's nothing wrong with it, and don't let anyone give you that men don't cry bull crap. Remember, it'll only be a few weeks for us, and she'll be back."

"You don't think the Avramites will get her?" That was what really worried Tim about her being gone. The people chasing her might catch up to her, and he'd never see her again.

"Tim, your mom is a badass. You heard how she saved my butt when those bikers jumped me in Peoria?" Liam waited for Tim's nod. Even though he had heard the story before, Tim liked to hear his father tell it. "They had me dead to rights, and she was on them like a force of nature. It was maybe 15 seconds and she cleaned their clocks without even breaking a sweat. If anyone tries getting in your mother's way, they'd better have a good dental plan."

Tim chuckled and wished he had seen his mother in action. "Will you come to the martial arts classes with me?"

"Sure." His father led him through the garage, back toward the door to the kitchen. "Since your mom had to save my bacon, I should probably brush up. Assuming Gofannon hasn't found the ice cream we stashed in the freezer, do you want some? I've even got chocolate syrup."

Ice cream sounded tempting. Tim could tell his father was trying to put him at ease and cheer him up, but he really wanted some time alone to think and hopefully clear up the lump at the back of his throat. "Is it okay if I go up to my room for a while?"

"Sure, buddy. Whatever you need." Liam looked in the direction of the smithy. "I'm sure Gofannon is eager to yell at me and get me started on learning how to be a proper smith, not an amateur who managed to bang a few chunks of metal into vaguely sword shapes."

"Druid!" The bellow came from the direction of the smithy. "Are you done hugging yet and ready to get to work?"

"And that would be my cue," Liam said with a sigh. "But seriously, you need anything, interrupt us. Nothing is more important than you. Okay?"

Tim nodded. In a way, he was glad for the interruption. He had questions for his father, but he wanted time to process everything, and maybe let some things out where no one could see him. While Liam had said it was okay, his Papaw had taught him boys and men don't cry, so he felt he should go somewhere no one could see him.

"Are you okay, sweetie?" Tim hadn't seen Pixel when he walked through the dining room, but her lyrical voice was almost right behind him. While Tim wanted to like her, because she was pretty and seemed fun, he also knew that she was somehow competing with his mother for his father's attention.

"I'm okay," he answered, a bit more huskily than he intended. Stupid frog in his throat. "I'm going up to my room."

"If you need anything, let me know." She beamed a smile at him, her eyes glowing amethyst. He could feel her trying to influence him, to regard her as a friend.

"Okay, I will." Tim decided to file the information away. Was she trying to win him over to influence his father? He'd heard a remark that both of his parents were resistant to being glamoured by the Exiled Folk. Was that what she was trying to do to him? He turned and climbed the stairs.

She's no threat, the house advised him as his hand slid along the old wooden bannister. She wants—Tim didn't understand the concept the house conveyed—with your father. She is trying to win his favor through you.

Tim reached the door to his room. Was Pixel why his parents had fought? He remembered one of his mother's boyfriends had been seeing other women, which ticked Tim's mom off. He didn't want to think that about his father.

No, the house replied. The Champion spurned the Druid even though the Druid had rebuffed the Flower Fae.

Okay, Tim thought, so his father hadn't mucked things up by doing something stupid like cheating. Tim felt a little relieved. He'd seen enough men disappoint his mother over the years, and sometimes he thought it was because of him; they didn't want a stepson. Liam was his real father, though, and seemed to embrace the fact.

The distraction had derailed Tim's intent to vent his sadness in the privacy of his bedroom. Not that he wasn't still sad about his mother leaving for months, and maybe forever if the bad guys caught her. But now he wondered if he had been wrong to blame himself in the past?

You shouldn't blame yourself, the house told him. Take your father up on ice cream, it conveyed, knowing there was indeed still ice cream in the freezer. Don't blame the Flower Girl; she is an ally and doesn't act out of malice—your parents do not fight because of her. Well, mostly.

Why don't you have Internet? Tim thought back to the house. It would be a great distraction right now.

What is Internet? The house seemed confused.

* * * * *

Chapter Thirty-Six

Erin

"This will take longer."

"Yes, but we'll avoid Peoria and any potential lookouts at the bridges," Izzy replied without looking at her brother. "Interstates 70 and 80 both end up in Denver."

Erin had pretty much tuned out their bickering, a lump in her throat as she watched fields of corn and soybeans blur past from the back seat. She tried not to dwell on the time involved, but it loomed in her thoughts.

"How will I know time is really passing slower for the outside world?" Erin asked. While the notion of this being an elaborate trick seemed almost as outlandish as it did being true, the doubt still gnawed at the edge of her mind.

Izzy spared her a glance in the mirror. "After two weeks, we could step out and you can check your phone. If we are right, only a few hours will have passed. If we are wrong, it still will have only been two weeks you've been away from your son."

"She's not going to approve," Derek said. His tone had an edge of worry. "Scathach is loath to open the way to the Dunwold as it is, to do it again simply so we can pop out to check the time…"

"That or we turn around." Erin was sure the burner phone they had given her would hold a charge long enough if turned off. She quickly formulated a back-up plan; she'd need a couple of items at the next truck stop they hit.

"Very well," Izzy said. She nodded to Erin in the mirror. "After two weeks you'll probably be ready to kick my brother back to the Dunwold."

"At least I'll get out of being a practice dummy," Derek grumbled, drumming his long fingers on the dashboard. "Do you think Saidhe is still pissed? It *has* been quite a while."

Izzy sighed and rolled her eyes. "As usual, my brother's mouth, among other parts, got him in trouble. I know *that's* hard to believe. He seduced your progenitor's daughter. Saidhe's mother was Uathach, Scathach's daughter. I guess it would make Saidhe your many-great aunt."

Erin sat up a little bit. "How long ago was that?" The twins looked to be mid-twenties, thirty tops.

"I would say roughly the 16th century by the reckoning on the Dunwold," Izzy replied matter-of-factly. "He was young and impetuous, even more so than now."

"It was 500 years ago? How old are you guys?"

"We were born before the Reconquista in what became Spain, so roughly 600 years, maybe 650." Derek turned back and looked over the seat, smirking. "Fancy a roll with an older man?"

"How are you not insane or something, being alive for so long?" It boggled Erin's mind, the notion of living long enough to see years slip by like the cornfields alongside the highway.

"We experience time differently, especially when off the physical world of the Dunwold," Izzy said, sounding like a lecturer at the community college where Erin had taken a few classes before giving up on getting a degree. "It's hard to explain to someone fixed in experiencing everything day-by-day, minute-by-minute. Have you ever driven somewhere, and gone into a trance, and then realize you've been driving for a long time even though it seemed just like moments?"

"Sure." That was almost a blessing on convoy rides back when she was in the military, but that was something she could only do as a passenger. Spacing out while driving or on lookout meant your vehicle could end up ambushed or blown up by an IED.

"That is often how it is for those who dwell beyond the Veil. We can lose a year lost in thought the same as you would an hour." Izzy tipped her head toward Derek. "This *choucho* has gotten in trouble more than once because he wasn't paying attention to the passage of time."

"And you worry about it so much, I'm amazed you aren't a withered crone," Derek retorted. "Even when she was young, my sister was always so serious. She seriously needs to get laid. You know, since you're going to be stuck there for years, the two of you could keep each other company."

Erin fought down a blush. She'd never given serious thought to being with another woman, but seven years was going to be a long time, and her birth control would run out in a couple of months. She'd caught herself admiring Izzy's physique, the woman's tight leather outfit doing nothing to hide her athletic body. But would Erin actually be interested in getting physical with Izzy? The more Erin thought about it, the less resistant she became to the idea.

"Really, brother?"

"You're the one who said you fancied her more than the Druid." Derek arched an eyebrow. "Besides, I'm sure Pixel was pouncing on the Druid before the dust settled on the driveway behind us."

That brought a flash of irritation, dispelling some of Erin's embarrassment. "What is her deal anyway? Liam wouldn't come out and say it, but I'm pretty sure she threw herself at him at least once while he was drunk. Is she some sort of nympho?"

"She's not a nymph; a dryad would be a better analogy." Izzy said. She seemed grateful for the change of subject. "I don't know what you know about Blodeuwedd, but Pixel is one of her fae, a Flower-Maiden."

"That means as much to me as Tim trying to explain the game with the cards and monsters," Erin replied. "Maybe less; I haven't had to overhear any cartoons about this Blodeuwedd."

"Blodeuwedd was made as a bride for a Lleu, who had been cursed by his goddess mother to never have a human wife. She betrayed Lleu and was cursed into being an owl," Izzy said. She might have been reading from a book, from what Erin could tell. "It's actually much more complicated. Some refer to her as a goddess, others claim she is only an arch-fey. Either way, the maidens of her court, referred to as flower-girls or flower-fae because of Blodeuwedd's origins, are promised to powerful beings as familiars and fae-wives."

"So you could say it's in her blood to want to get busy with the most powerful magic wielder walking the Dunwold," Derek added. "Since she is unbound, the Druid's power is probably like a potent aphrodisiac to her."

"Liam doesn't seem 'powerful,' as you put it," Erin protested. She remembered him scrambling away from those bikers. He couldn't even glamour them, let alone anything more spectacular like turning them into toads or setting them on fire.

"That's because he doesn't realize it yet," Derek replied, taking a more serious tone. "Once he taps into his potential, he will be the most powerful human to wield magic since Merlin, Taliesin, or Cath-bad."

* * * * *

Chapter Thirty-Seven

Lee

"What are you doing on the floor?"

Lee looked down at the sprawled form of Joel. So much for not needing to sleep. The seraphim-turned-flesh twitched and snorted once before opening his eyes. Lee shook his head; who would have thought being flesh-and-blood would be so hard?

"I lost awareness," Joel said. He sat up and blinked.

"It's called falling asleep," Lee said, stepping past Joel to get to the bathroom while resisting the urge to chuckle. The seraphim didn't seem to find his predicament amusing. "Looks like while you have meat on your bones, you get all of the fun that comes with eating, sleeping, and pissing. I'm going to shower, you can have it after I'm done. Smells like you sweat as well."

At least Joel hadn't badgered him about getting on the road early, Lee mused as he had a quick shave and got in the shower. He'd actually gotten a full night's sleep for a change. Emerging from the bathroom after toweling off and getting dressed, he was startled to see Joel standing in the middle of the room stark naked.

"Where are your clothes?" Lee tried not to notice Joel's well-muscled physique. "You shouldn't stand around naked."

"My nudity is irrelevant, as we are the same gender." Joel stepped past him into the bathroom. "I will manifest new garments after I have cleaned off my body."

Lee shut the door after the seraphim and went about packing up in preparation to get back on the road. He flipped on the television to the same news channel he'd watched last night. A vapid looking blonde was excitedly talking about the latest fashion trend. If you asked him, the network should dress their female newscasters and reporters a bit more modestly. He could imagine young men watching, hoping to catch a glimpse up the women's skirts.

"Good morning, Pastor Haskins," the blonde on the television said with a brilliant white smile. "I trust you're ready to get on the road after your prolonged rest?"

"Sorry, Joel, I mean Jehoel, passed out, and I overslept," Lee said. He glanced back at the closed bathroom door. He could hear the shower running. "We'll be back on the road shortly. Speaking of which, should we look around Peoria instead of heading west?"

"Your suggestion was considered, but based on the latest intelligence, it is deemed you and Jehoel should proceed west along I-70." The map popped up behind the blonde, tracing a route south through Illinois until it reached St. Louis and turned west. "There are other parties investigating the Peoria area. It would be wasteful to duplicate their efforts."

"That's understandable." Lee finished packing and set his bag next to the door. "So head west on 70 and wait for orders?"

"Unless otherwise advised, proceed to St. Peters, Missouri, just west of Saint Louis," the blonde replied, pointing to a dot on the map. Lee's phone buzzed with a text message, a link in the message showing a location and address on his travel map app. "You will be picking up an additional agent there to help track down the heathen champion."

"Splendid." Lee heard the door open behind him and didn't turn around for fear Joel would be standing there naked.

"Jehoel, you are reminded that while using mortal flesh as a disguise, do not succumb to its temptations," the blonde commanded. "The mortal senses are insidious and seductive."

"Understood." Joel walked past Lee, who was relieved that he was fully dressed in jeans and a flannel shirt. Joel stopped and looked at the screen. "If there are no further instructions, we are prepared to depart."

The woman on the news channel went on to discussing the latest red carpet faux pas. Joel watched the television for a moment before going to the door and opening it.

Lee clicked off the television and set the key card for the room next to it. Grabbing his bag, he followed Joel out into the warm August day. He made a mental note to pick up some basic toiletries for Joel at the nearby truck stop. Along with temptation, Joel's mortal flesh came with sweat glands and bad breath. Lee started to head for his truck until he noticed Joel had veered toward the adjacent Cracker Barrel.

"We should have a meal before we depart," the seraphim said.

* * * * *

Chapter Thirty-Eight

Liam

"What time is it?"

Liam looked around, trying to gauge the time by the remaining sunlight. He had started working with Gofannon shortly after Erin and the twins had hit the road. It felt as though he'd been in the forge for eight hours, but it would have been dark. It looked closer to five or six.

"What does it matter, Druid?" Gofannon looked like he had barely broken a sweat, while Liam's arms burned, and his shirt was drenched. They had been heating and hammering various pieces of metal Liam had picked up from the junkyard, with Gofannon berating him for his hammer technique. "We have much to do before you are ready to forge the Champion's sword."

"I know, I know," Liam said. He set down his hammer, frustrated. The truck spring he'd been pounding refused to straighten. He realized he was hungry, hungrier than he would have expected for dinnertime. Maybe he had gotten too accustomed to the regular meals he'd been enjoying since his guests had arrived. Chalking up his appetite to the physical activity, he looked toward the house. "Besides, I should check on my son. His mother took off for a couple of months, leaving him with a dad he barely knows. Plus the kid is probably bored as heck, given I don't have the Internet or much of anything interesting to a kid his age."

315

"Give him chores. You keep a child out of mischief by keeping his hands busy and tiring him out." Gofannon's bushy black eyebrows knitted together as he scowled. "You have a farm, there must be plenty for the boy to do."

"I own the farm, but other people pay me to let them grow their crops in the fields." Granted, he could probably have Tim do things like mow the grass around the house, but it wasn't how Liam wanted to start things off. He certainly didn't want to assign Tim the kind of drudgery Gofannon was talking about. Liam wished Erin would have stuck around a few more days, so they could have hammered things like this out. "Plus, I'm guessing farming has changed a bit since you were familiar with it."

"I have never farmed, and I am here to teach you how to forge a sword, not raise your son." Gofannon set aside his own hammer and closed the air intake on the forge, starting the cooling process. "Go, see to your son. Truth be told, I could use a mouth to eat as well."

"Bite to eat," Liam corrected. Standing up and stretching, he realized he had forgotten to plan anything for dinner. He'd gotten spoiled because Einar seemed to enjoy cooking so much, and he was pretty sure Scooter had been cleaning up afterward. Liam added leaving a bowl of cream out for Scooter to his mental list of things to do as he walked toward the house.

As soon as Liam entered the garage, he caught a whiff of hamburgers and bacon cooking. He glanced guiltily at the dusty grill in the garage; he'd have to tell Einar about it. The dwarf might actually prefer cooking over a charcoal fire to the propane fueled stove. Opening the door to the kitchen added the scent of sizzling potatoes to the mix.

"Good, I was hoping you'd break soon," Einar said without looking up from the stove, where he was managing three skillets. "Track down Pixel and your boy; everything is almost ready."

"Sure." Yes, Liam was getting spoiled, and he warned himself not to get used to it. Once the mission was over, he expected Einar and Pixel would go back to wherever they came from. Well, at least Einar, Pixel might try to stick around. Liam found Pixel in the living room, flipping through an old family photo album.

"I hope you don't mind," Pixel said as she closed the album, looking a bit guilty. She had traded her black jeans and pink tank top for a pale lavender sundress. Liam tried not to notice. "There's a lot to learn from your ancestors, especially for you *dynion;* your lives go by so quick, so you have a lot of ancestors."

"That's okay, what's the point of having all those pictures if someone doesn't look at them?" Liam gestured over his shoulder toward the kitchen. "Einar says dinner is almost ready. Have you seen Tim?"

"He went up to his room shortly after his mother left." She set aside the leather bound book. "I wasn't sure if I should check on him or not; he hasn't come down since."

"I'll go get him. I shouldn't have let him stew this long; I lost track of time with Gofannon out in the smithy." Liam climbed the stairs, trying not to think of the various times Pixel had blatantly hit on him. He had a feeling that now Erin had left, Pixel's attempt to get his attention would renew, and he was conflicted on how to handle it. On one hand, Erin had made things clear: they were not a couple. On the other hand, Tim might react poorly to Liam taking up with someone other than Erin. Liam wasn't the only one who had gotten his hopes up when he thought he and Erin were making a connection.

Liam paused at the top of the stairs. He had enough to worry about, without adding relationship drama to the mix. The best thing he could do was refrain from any more romantic entanglements until this whole mess was done with. Maybe he'd add an extra lock to his bedroom door.

"Hey buddy, anyone home?" Liam knocked on the frame of the open doorway to Tim's room.

Tim looked up after a moment, engrossed in something on his tablet. "Oh, hey."

"Dinner is ready." Liam remembered it was possible to use tablets without an Internet connection and books could be stored on them. Maybe it was just as well he'd quit Word Nerds, between Internet shopping and books stored on electronic devices, traditional bookstores were going the way of the dodo. "Einar made burgers. Come on down when you're ready."

"Aren't you going to tell me to wash up first?" Tim asked. He set aside the tablet, puzzled.

"Do I need to remind you?" Liam assumed the boy knew to wash up first, but probably hadn't been involved in anything requiring extra caution. Liam, on the other hand, definitely needed to wash his soot covered hands and face. "I'm going to wash up. I'll see you downstairs."

Liam went into his room to use his bathroom to clean up and changed his shirt. Gofannon had worn his leather apron but no shirt while working at the forge, oblivious to the occasional spark spawned by their hammering. Liam wasn't about to be so cavalier about his own hide. Tossing his sodden shirt in the hamper, he quickly washed up as well as he could without opting for a shower.

Downstairs, he found everyone else already gathered around the dining room table, Gofannon already working on what looked to be his second burger, based on the crumbs in his beard.

"One thing I will say about being on the Dunwold, I never tire of the food," Gofannon boomed between bites.

Liam picked up a plate and helped himself to a burger from the pile and a serving of fried potatoes heaped in a skillet. Einar had fried the sliced potatoes in bacon grease, with what looked to be a dash of sea salt and black pepper. Liam topped his burger with a slice of cheddar and three strips of bacon.

"I didn't know if Susan would be joining us," Einar remarked, wiping crumbs from his own beard. "I know the dunnies make pocking fake meat, but we don't have any, so I didn't worry about it."

"She has some sort of coffee meet-up tonight," Liam replied as he fetched a beer to go with his meal. "It's twice a month on Tuesdays. She tries to get me to go and play nice with the other pagans, but half the time it's rumor-mongering and people taking offense at whatever crap someone said on the Internet."

"It might not be a terrible idea for you to start making some more connections," Pixel pointed out between nibbling at her burger. Unlike Liam, she had eschewed a bun, taking a knife and fork to her patty. "You'll be First Druid; pagans will be looking to you for advice."

"Which they'll dismiss out of hand because it doesn't agree with their world view, or conform to whatever author they're into at the moment," Liam grumbled. "Trying to deal with these people is like trying to herd cats. Everyone has their own idea how stuff should work and to heck with what anyone else says."

"Maybe that will change once magic and the old gods are let back into the world?" Pixel asked, sounding earnest. She hadn't dealt with the kind of people Liam had to put up with before mostly retreating from the public.

"It will probably make it worse. People with magic are as likely as not to lord it over those who don't," Liam said. He skewered some potatoes with his fork. "Those who don't will be pissy and whine about it. Who will they whine to, me? I don't want every wannabe Wiccan or videogame magician knocking on my door. How the heck am I supposed to manage that?"

"Get a pack of large, hungry hounds," Einar suggested, eliciting a giggle from Tim.

"Seriously, how much of this will I have to micromanage? Am I going to be Santa Druid, with a list of who gets magic? Am I going to have to spell out how everything works?" Liam didn't even know where to start.

"We don't have that kind of time, Druid," Gofannon rumbled, picking up his third burger. "Even if you didn't have to learn to forge a blade while untangling how your magic works."

"Besides, the more rules you have, the more likely it will be someone will find some sort of exploit no one predicted that will break the game, I mean system," Tim said without looking up from his food.

"Maybe you should have the boy come up with your pocking accords," Einar said with a chuckle.

Liam chewed on his burger thoughtfully. Maybe that wasn't such a bad idea. Not the whole kit and caboodle, as Aunt Millie would say, but maybe involving Tim wouldn't be crazy. The kid was smart and might see things in a way Liam or someone else would entirely overlook.

Pixel's musical laughter caught his attention. She knew how existing magic worked. Of course, she would be biased toward her own people and their gods, but someone with knowledge of the metaphysics and variety of "wolds" and their denizens would be crucial. Plus it would help keep her busy when she wasn't working with Liam, trying to help him learn how to harness magic.

Now he would need someone else more grounded and practical, someone who could be really organized. It had to be someone good-natured. Liam thought a lot of why the world was messed up was because jerks had consolidated power to elevate themselves with little concern for other people, a system he didn't want to perpetuate.

Liam pulled out his phone and dialed Susan's number.

* * * * *

Chapter Thirty-Nine

Lee

"**Y**ou have got to be kidding me."

Joel gave Pastor Haskins a puzzled glance. "Why would I be jesting? We are on an important mission for His Glory. Besides, I find humor difficult to understand, let alone engage in."

"What's your problem, collar?" the dog said, cocking its head and looking at Lee. It had emerged from the nearby bushes about 15 minutes after Lee had parked the truck in the truck stop's parking lot.

Lee almost fell to the pavement blurting out blasphemy. As it was, he backed up against the truck. While he hadn't seen the Doberman's mouth move, Lee had clearly heard its voice. He reined in his composure; given what he'd been through the past couple of weeks, ever since Mikha'el had come to him, nothing should surprise Lee anymore.

"Pastor, this is the agent we were told of, Qashmet." Of course Joel acted as though it was perfectly natural to be introducing a talking dog. "He is begotten from the line of—"

"Yeah, let's spare my whole half-breed family history. Mikha'el impressed on me the job was urgent." The dog looked from Joel to Lee, his tongue lolling in the heat. "You can call me Cash."

Lee looked around before addressing the dog. This part of the parking lot was bordered on one side by a clump of scraggly trees. At least the trees provided a little afternoon shade from the August sun, as well as obscured them from the road. With the truck behind them, it appeared he and Joel were hanging out in the back of a truck stop parking lot, not as though they were having a conversation with a dog. Great, Lee thought gloomily, I look like I'm having a homosexual tryst, not like I'm insane.

"All right, Cash. Mikha'el sent us to you, so what can you do? I mean, it's not as if you can bloodhound them down the interstate, is it?" Lee had a ludicrous image of them creeping down the shoulder of the highway, following the dog as he sniffed the pavement.

"That's pretty much it, collar." The dog turned back to Joel. "Do you have the article?"

"No, a courier will bring it to us in the morning," Joel replied, then looked to Lee. "Since we do not have their location, and can obtain it once Qashmet has an article of the Benayim's clothing, we can stop come nightfall. Preferably somewhere with a Cracker Barrel."

"Uh oh, someone is getting a taste for life in the flesh," Cash chided. "Better watch it, or you'll end up like my grand-pappy, humping mortals and whatnot."

"This mortal shell requires sustenance," Joel protested. "And, I have learned, sleep, as well. It is quite annoying."

"Welcome to how things work in the World of Man," The dog said. He trotted over to the truck door, which clicked open of its own accord, and hopped in.

"Get in the back seat," Joel ordered, a foot on the running board. Lee was glad he'd opted for the larger cab as he circled to the driver's side.

"Fine." The dog clambered into the back. "But it's not my fault if I get car sick."

Lee climbed in and started the truck as soon as the doors were closed. Silenced prevailed as he navigated his way through the traffic and back onto the interstate. Once they were cruising west again, he broke the silence.

"All right, I have to know," Lee said. He looked in the rearview mirror, where he could see Cash watching the passing farm fields. "A talking dog?"

"Qashmet is descended from a Fallen." Like the dog, Joel seemed to be watching the flat landscape speed by. "His progenitor is a Nephilim, the progeny of an angel who choose to walk the World of Man rather than bask in His Glory in the firmament. They wallowed in the sins of the flesh and lay with mortals."

"Yeah, grand-pappy was a shape-shifter and not too particular about what he got busy with." The dog met Lee's gaze in the mirror, intelligence in its eyes. "He may have been responsible for some of the werewolf myths out there. Down the line, I pop up, looking like a normal canine, but with obviously superior mental faculties. I don't know if this is some sort of joke or something, but I have the ability to track almost anyone if I have something personal of theirs. The more personal, the better; dirty underwear works best."

Joel wrinkled his nose and pursed his lips in disgust, but bit back a remark.

"So why haven't we done this from the get-go, instead of chasing our tails in the middle of nowhere?" Lee asked. If they had used

Cash to track their quarry from the beginning, they would have found them by now, and Lee would be on his way back to his wife instead of riding around with the cast of some quirky fish-out-of-water movie.

"Because Qashmet does not serve Our Lord as we do, Pastor Haskins," Joel said, his tone accusatory. "Qashmet's services had to be bargained for, like purchasing a salmon from a fish-monger."

"Funny how the Almighty is willing to bargain when he needs something," Cash shot back.

"He would not sully Himself by dealing with the likes of you directly. I cannot believe Mikha'el resorted to trucking with your kind." Joel turned to glower over the seat. "You are an abomination in the eyes of Our Lord."

"Not if I deliver," Cash replied. He matched Joel's glare, not quite going into a snarl. "Then Our Lord will grant me the form of his beloved Man, and I won't be stuck living out of dumpsters and handouts. You guys must have really screwed the pooch, figuratively of course, unlike grand-pappy. Too bad Mikha'el didn't come to me to begin with; I could have saved you a lot of time."

"It's going to be a long enough drive as it is without you two at each other throats," Lee interjected. He would love to explain to a state trooper why a surfer and a Doberman were fighting it out in the cab of his truck. "Let's make our way west until it's time to stop for the night and grab something to eat."

"I want real food," Cash said with a growl. "No doggie bags."

"And somewhere with milkshakes," Joel added.

* * * * *

Chapter Forty

Erin

"That's nice, honey."

Despite Izzy and Derek's protest, Erin had insisted on calling to check on Tim once they had stopped for the night. She had been worried Tim would be sullen, if nothing else, at the notion he was being left behind. Instead he was all fired up about something Liam had asked him to help on.

"I'll be working on it with Pixel and Dad's friend Susan," Tim said over the phone, excitement in his voice. "Dad seemed really interested in what I know about game rules and how different systems work. I have to read a lot of stuff, and Pixel has to teach us about the history of how things worked before. I think Susan is helping us so we don't over-run the world with dragons and unicorns."

Erin wasn't thrilled about Tim spending any more time than was absolutely necessary with Pixel. Even though Izzy had assured her there was nothing to worry about, the last thing she wanted was for Tim to get some puppy-love crush on the girl, which undoubtedly the fae would find some way to exploit. If nothing else, the girl would try to manipulate Tim to further her agenda with Liam. "Well, you start school next week, so I want you to make sure this doesn't interfere with your homework and studying."

Tim's sigh was audible. "Dad already said I have to finish my school work before I can work on the new accords, although in Irish the word for treaty, conradh, is closer in meaning, and yes, he said I have to keep my grades up."

"Good. You do need to keep your grades up." Especially because now Erin had the money to send him to any college he wanted. She caught Izzy's meaningful glance, the blonde woman pacing the hotel room they had rented for the night. Erin had been on the call too long, though she thought Izzy was being paranoid. Both phones were burners, pay-as-you-go inexpensive phones, which had been picked up in a big box store using prepaid credit cards, which had been, in turn, purchased with cash.

Erin nodded to Izzy, holding up a finger to let her know she was almost done. "I've got to go, sweetie. Love you."

"Love you too, Mom." Had Erin imagined a sniffle? "Bye."

"Bye, sweetie." Terminating the connection, she wiped at the moisture collecting under her eye before it could turn into tears.

"Sounds as though the Druid already has him busy," Derek remarked, sprawled on the other bed, still clad neck to toe in leather. "He's lucky Gofannon did not draft him to pump bellows or shovel charcoal."

"Liam has him working on some sort of project. It sounds almost like a game." Erin concentrated to recall the Irish phrase Tim had used. "I think he called them Conradh na Draoi."

"Conradh na Draoi?" Derek sat up, glancing at his sister. "The new rules are being written by a 12-year-old boy?"

"It sounded as if Tim was helping Liam. And of course, Pixel is involved. I'm not too keen on that," Erin replied. She noticed both Derek and Izzy were paying rapt attention. "And Susan, also, I guess, to keep them from getting too fancy with these rules. Something about dragons and unicorns. But Tim is really good at the games with really complicated rules that I can never understand. I try to pay attention when he talks about them, because he's really into them, but it's hard not to zone out."

"The Druid is having a child rewrite the rules of magic for him?" Izzy's voice was heavy with disbelief. She sank into the chair in the corner.

"Surely he's not talking about those Accords—the ones this whole fight is over?" Erin asked. She wished she had paid more attention when magical matters had been discussed back at the farmhouse. Like the rules for the card game about magic and monsters, when they had started going into mystic discussions, she'd lost track of what was going on, especially when they kept flipping to other languages. "Besides, those are already written; it's why there's this challenge to begin with."

"Yes, but the winner gets to write new rules regarding the use of magic and laws governing supernatural creatures on the Dunwold," Izzy said. She laced her fingers, deep in thought. "It will also have the terms for the next challenge, and the Avramites will be looking for loopholes they can exploit, same as we have the past several centuries."

"But the new treaty has to be authored by the line of Cathbad," Derek protested. "It was one of the time crunches we worried about regarding the Druid—whether he would have enough time to hone his skills, forge the sword, and write an ironclad treaty that will put the Avramites in their place."

"*Choucho*, Tim is of the line of Cathbad," Izzy mumbled from behind her hands, which now covered her face as though she were trying to ward off a migraine. "Anything he writes would be as valid as the Druid himself, unless Liam countermands it."

"Should I call him back and tell him not to do it?" Erin asked. Tim would be disappointed, but the twins seemed to think it heralded disaster. "Or we could tell Liam, and why."

"Let Tim write them," Derek said, his tone turning conspiratorial. "The various Powers will be expecting some ovate mumbo-jumbo mixed with some New Age optimism. They won't be expecting rules to tell them how to play their games, with measures keeping them in line. We can always look things over when we get back to make sure there aren't any glaring issues and convince the Druid to amend them."

"Are you insane?" Izzy dropped her hands and fixed her sky blue eyes on Derek. "We'll have a couple of weeks, at best, once we return from Dunos Scaith."

"We were going to want to look over them anyway," Derek countered, his grin contrasting his pragmatic tone. "There's nothing to guarantee Liam wouldn't have ended up writing something rushed with holes big enough to walk Baba Yaga's hut through. While we're in Dunos Scaith, we can work up a list of does and don'ts. We'll have seven years after all."

"Assuming Scathach isn't going to keep us busy." Izzy was no longer glaring, but still sounded unsure. "After all, as part of the bargain, we serve her the seven years she's training Erin."

"What?" Erin asked. She had never heard about the bargain. "You're, what, indenturing yourself for seven years so I can get this training?"

"Technically, only my sister," Derek said, his grin evaporating. "To be honest, I was hoping to wait things out on the Dunwold, so as not to stir up any lingering bitterness."

"Coward. You are coming with us," Izzy said. "If nothing else, it will help abate any grudge Scathach and Saidhe may have against you and our holt." Izzy rubbed a temple, as if warding off a headache. "Erin, think of it like your school loans, where students have to work many years to pay the debt incurred by their education. To be honest, it takes your *neacha* much longer to pay off their debt. We couldn't ask this of you, in addition to going through the training and taking up the challenge."

"Well, as much as I hate to say it, Derek makes sense," Erin said. She intentionally didn't look at Derek as she said it, but she could imagine his smugness. "Why don't the two of you write up what you think needs to be in the Conradh na Draoi, along with a list of things to make sure *aren't* in it? When we get back, Liam or Tim can use these to amend or even rewrite what Tim, Pixel, and Susan have written up. Heck, won't there be Exiled Folk at Dunos Scaith besides us, Scathach, and Derek's ex? We might find others to help us."

"We'll have to watch out for those seeking an upper hand in the new world," Izzy cautioned. "After all, it would be a mistake to assume the Exiled Folk are one homogenous people with the same agenda. We have assholes, just the same as the Avramites."

* * * * *

Chapter Forty-One

Liam

"**A**re you paying attention?"

Liam jumped at Gofannon's booming voice. "Of course, how could I not with you bellowing at me between hammer strikes?" For good measure, he parroted back what the smith-god had been lecturing him on, word for word but without the volume.

"Then why are you still doing it wrong?" Gofannon asked, His great, black, bushy eyebrows knitted together as he frowned.

"Because remembering words is easy; muscle memory takes practice," Liam said. His muscles reminded him he was out of practice; his arms were burning. Despite the breeze through the open doors at both ends of the smithy, the heat was sweltering, especially with the thick leather gloves and apron, as well as the safety goggles Liam slid down every time metal was being worked.

They had started right after breakfast, and the clock on the wall seemed to crawl. Even though his stomach told him lunch should have come and gone, it wasn't even eleven. If every day was going to drag on like this, it would be a long two months until Samhain. Liam immediately felt guilty for the thought; Erin was going to be working for seven *years*.

"Hotter! Work the bellows!"

334 | JON R. OSBORNE

"Why don't we use the blower?" Liam asked. He set down his hammer and pumped air into the forge. He understood Gofannon's case that to imbue an item, you have to work it more personally than you could with a tool like a drop-hammer, that each hammer strike put a bit of the smith in the blade. However, Liam thought the god was just being obstinate when it came to using the blower to stoke the forge over man-powered bellows. "It's not as though a smith usually pumps the bellows himself; that's what apprentices are for."

"That is…" The smith's reply sputtered as he pursed his lips, looking for a retort. "Fine. We will use your lazy excuse of a device to fire up the forge."

"Finally." Liam flicked on the blower motor and adjusted the speed until Gofannon was satisfied with the glowing coals. Of course, this heated the concrete-walled building even more, but at least the wind seemed to pick up.

"Now if you focus on your smithing as much as you do on your air conditioning, maybe we could make some progress," Gofannon grumbled, watching the piece of metal they had been heating turn a dull red.

"The blower has nothing to do with air conditioning," Liam said. He glanced up at the ceiling fans, which helped circulate the air, but didn't do as much to cool them off as the fairly steady stream of air coming through the doors. "We don't even *have* air conditioning out here."

"I am not talking about your *dunnie* machines," Gofannon replied without looking up. "You are calling on the sky to push air through here. Not that I mind a breath of cool air, but we are here for you to practice metalwork, not *lledrith*."

"I'm not doing it." Liam wiped the sweat beading on his forehead before it ran down into his eyes again. Impractical as it was, he wished for an air conditioner in the forge shed. "It's the way the air flows around the house."

"Cathbad was especially attuned to the sea." Gofannon used tongs to flip the metal over, peering into the blinding glow of the forge. "He could turn the waves to stone and walk across them. He was no, how you say, slouch, at the other realms, but the sea was his domain. You should talk to him, maybe it will help with your *lledrith*. He would tell you that you are influencing the sky spirits to move this air, not a convenient downdraft."

"How am I supposed to do that? He's been dead for what, a millennia and a half?" Liam picked up the hammer, ready for when Gofannon pulled the glowing metal from the forge and set it on the anvil. "Break out an Ouija board?"

"Druid, what are the three kindreds?" Gofannon withdrew the red-hot metal and swung it over to the anvil.

Liam took the tongs from the smith-god, holding the steel firmly on the anvil as he started hammering. "Gods, Spirits, and Ancestors. But how does that...well, shit, I'm an idiot. Cathbad is my ancestor."

"Exactly. Look to your ancestors for their wisdom and advice." The eyebrows furrowed again. "You are still gripping your hammer too high."

"It's easier for me to control that way." Liam knew not choking up on the hammer would lend more power to his swings. "So I can contact Cathbad? I wish someone had told me sooner. I have a ton of questions."

"So reach out to him." Gofannon scrutinized each hammer blow, watching how the metal reacted. "But do it when you are working with Pixel, not now. While you are at it, see if you have any smiths in your family tree."

* * * * *

Chapter Forty-Two

Lee

"You should answer the door."

Lee looked up from the Bible he had been reading. It wasn't his Bible; he had found it in the nightstand of the hotel room. He had flipped through it, skimming Jeremiah and then Isaiah while waiting for the courier. He'd turned the television to the news, which repeated the same loop of headlines they had droned on about last night. Now the anchor person was looking at Lee expectantly and pointed to the door.

As if on cue, there was a knock. Qashmet, who had jumped up on Joel's bed as soon as the seraphim went into the bathroom, rolled upright and looked eagerly at the door. Lee used the ribbon attached to the Bible to mark his place at Isaiah 54 and set the book on the nightstand.

Not sure what to expect, Lee opened the door cautiously. If he had been hoping for a celestial messenger with pearly white wings, he was disappointed. The young man standing there looked like a typical millennial, complete with a man-bun, long but meticulously-trimmed beard, and skinny jeans. A small gold cross was visible over his t-shirt, visible because his flannel shirt was unbuttoned.

"The personal possessions requested." The unnatural voice, sounding as if it came from a small church organ, caused Lee to take

337

338 | JON R. OSBORNE

a step back. The courier grinned, his eyes turning gold for a moment to match his cross. He held out a plastic bag stuffed with clothing.

"Hey, Ezra," Qashmet said as he trotted over, tail wagging. "So they've sucked you into this mess?"

"Hey, Cash." The courier coughed once, cleared his throat, and then continued in a normal voice, only notable for drawing out the vowels. "Mikha'el is pulling out all the stops, at least those he can get away with. If it was up to him, I think he'd bring down the Celestial Host and scour the Midwest, just to be sure. He is calling up every willing Nephilim and mobilizing them, assuming he can meet their price."

"Why are the children of the Lord's Servants so…mercenary?" Lee asked, puzzled by their attitude. The status quo of religion on the face of the world was at stake. "Surely you don't want the heathens to win?"

Ezra shrugged. "Things wouldn't really change for me. I'm not a cherubim; I'm just a dude whose grandmother got banged by an angel who came to ground. Or fell, either way. I'm not even a half-breed; I'm a mutt. No offense, Cash."

"None taken." The dog regarded Lee with those too-intelligent eyes, deep brown with flecks of gold. "You've got to see things from our perspective, collar. We're nothing unless someone high and mighty needs something done and doesn't want to stoop to doing it themselves and can't rely on the Sons of Adam to get it done. Then they'll throw us a bone and a few shekels. If the heathens win, the world will be too crazy for anyone to worry about us."

"All right, I've done my bit for God, Heaven, and two thousand dollars," Ezra said. He handed the sack of clothes to Lee. "I'm out. See you around, Cash."

"You too, Ezra." Lee hoped no one noticed the dog calling after the hipster as the latter strolled to a blue Prius.

"I take it our 'spoor' has arrived." Lee jumped, having not heard Joel walk up behind him. "Let's get breakfast, then get on with the hunt. The sooner we finish this mission, the sooner I can shed this fleshy shell. It is quite distracting."

"Perhaps if you wouldn't gorge it and luxuriate in corporeal sensations, you wouldn't be so distracted?" the television news anchor asked. "Do not dawdle. Intercept the Champion of the pagans, dispatch any *nukrayam* with her, and try to entangle her with the mundane authorities. Do not harm the pagan champion any more than necessary to defend yourself." The last statement was delivered directly to Joel, the anchor's eyes turning silver with the pronouncement.

"I remember my instructions and the rules of engagement during the time of the challenge," Joel said, sounding irritated.

"What of the other end of this puzzle, in middle Illinois?" Lee asked. "Is there anything still there?"

"Your mission is west, Pastor Haskins." The newsperson paused, holding a hand over his ear. "Contact your men in Ohio, send them to Peoria. It may prove useful to have more people there as the situation develops."

"All right, enough talking; give me the laundry," Cash demanded, jumping up on Joel's bed. Cash not getting a bed had been a point of contention last night until Lee and Joel had each given up half their pillows and a blanket for Cash to use as a nest.

Joel looked as though he was biting back a remark as the dog splayed his paws and wagged his tail excitedly. Not bothering to hide his disgust at what he suspected was about to happen, Lee dumped the laundry in front of the dog.

"Oh yeah, this is the good stuff." Cash buried his nose in the clothing, obviously laundry, and rooted around, sniffing loudly. "Oh yeah. Hmmm. You know, there are perverts in Japan that would pay good money for this kind of action."

"Well?" Joel crossed his arms impatiently. The talking head on the cable news remained silent, watching the proceedings.

The dog closed his eyes, sniffing again. "West, about 180 miles…let me see a map."

The television switched to a map, a dot showing their location between Kansas City and Topeka. Qashmet stared at the screen. "Scroll left, give me a satellite view." The map changed from a bland graphic to a photographic map. "Slow down, zoom in…a little more left. There, by Fossil Lake."

Another dot appeared on the map, roughly 180 miles from their current position.

"Are they moving?" Lee stared at the screen. They could be there in two and a half hours without drawing undue suspicion.

Qashmet closed his eyes again. "No, they are stationary, at least as far as I can tell. I can pin my quarry down within about 50 yards."

The map disappeared, and the talking head was back. "Excellent. You can reach them in two hours if you hurry. I advise you to hurry." The image wavered and the news anchor was talking about the same terrorist attack in Europe they had broadcast every 30 minutes.

"Don't forget to pack up the laundry." Qash gave the pile of garments a last sniff. "If they move, I'll need to home in on them again."

Joel looked down at the heap with obvious distaste, then plucked the clothes one by one into the plastic bag. Meanwhile Lee made sure he was leaving nothing behind, grateful he had woken up an hour before his roommate and had already showered and such. He had already packed his travel kit and dirty laundry, and his bag was by the door.

"I suppose you want to go to Cracker Barrel?" Lee asked as he hefted the gym bag to his shoulder.

"If you know, why did you ask?" Joel still had the sack of dirty laundry, holding it out away from himself.

"It's their thing," Qashmet said, trotting out the open door. "They love to state the obvious. At least this Cracker Barrel has outdoor seating, so we don't have to go through the fuss we did in St. Louis."

* * * * *

Chapter Forty-Three

Erin

"Damn it, Murphy!"

Izzy looked up from the flat tire. "Who is Murphy?"

"You've never heard of Murphy's Law?" Erin asked. She had trouble believing anyone who had been alive several hundred years had not heard of Murphy's Law.

"I have heard of it," Derek said. He walked from the back of the car, jack in hand. The device, typical of modern cars, looked too tiny to lift the Charger. "And things could be worse. With any luck, the gas station across the road can fix this tire, and we'll be on our way. According to Murphy, we'd have gotten this flat in the middle of nowhere."

"There certainly is plenty of nowhere out here," Izzy said. She loosened the last of the lugs holding the wheel on. "And we are still almost 400 miles from our destination."

"And Murphy drops the other boot," Derek muttered.

Erin looked up to see a state police cruiser grinding to a halt in the gravel parking lot. She patted her pocket where the elf-pouch was tucked. Nothing betrayed there was a three-foot-long sword somehow space-folded there.

The trooper stepped out of his cruiser, all polished boots and mirrored sunglasses. Erin briefly worried whether mirrored sunglasses would keep Izzy from being able to glamour the officer.

"Looks like you folks are having a peck of trouble." In other circumstances, Erin might have found the police officer handsome, in an old-fashioned way, though she wasn't sure about the moustache. But right now she wanted him to go away. He looked from the twins to Erin. "You need help with anything here, miss?"

"No, officer, just a flat tire," Erin said, trying to sound cheerful and not like a kidnap victim, which was what was probably running through the cop's head. Now she regretted not trying to convince Izzy and Derek to dress in something more practical and less noticeable than skin-tight black leather in the middle of August. Assuming there wasn't any sort of bulletin out on them, either from what happened in Cincinnati or from the opposition trying to track them down.

Izzy set the tire iron on the ground and stood up, carefully keeping her hands in view without being obvious about it. Erin suspected the trooper's eyes were tracking Izzy's hands from behind those shades, as well as where Derek had stopped with the jack. Derek also made sure the officer had a clear view of his hands.

"Thank you for your concern, officer," Izzy said, smiling disarmingly. Erin had never noticed how brilliantly white Izzy's teeth were. Derek was often flashing his when he upgraded from a smirk, so she shouldn't have been surprised. "There's really not much for you to do here, we have it well in hand and will be on our way shortly."

"You'll be on your way, shortly," the trooper parroted back. After a moment, he touched the brim of his hat. "There's not much for me to do here. You folks have a good day."

Erin realized she was holding her breath as he marched back to his cruiser, and she slowly let it out. The trooper climbed in, adjusted his hat, then started up the car. With a crunch of gravel, he pulled onto the blacktop road and headed toward town.

"Do you think he was suspicious?" Erin asked. She immediately felt silly for asking. Of course he was suspicious. "I mean, do you think he was looking for us or the car in particular?"

"It is hard to say," Izzy said. She stepped aside so Derek could put the jack in place and waited for him to crank the car high enough to pry off the wheel. "We have to assume the Avramites are trying to use mundane authorities to locate us, but we don't know how widespread their influence is."

"You don't think it's likely they could track Tim back to Liam's house?" After disappearing from their apartment in Cincinnati, and leaving it looking as though there had been some sort of struggle, the authorities might not need any outside influence to be looking for Erin and her son. Erin felt the urge to turn around and head back to Illinois.

"Not likely," Derek remarked as he worked the jack. "My sister and I, and to a lesser extent this car, are distinctive. There would be nothing to lead them to Liam's home, especially since he has gone to pains to make himself difficult to track down. They would need to know who he is to even start, and given Liam's magical protections from supernatural divination, your son is in the safest place he can be."

"As opposed to us," Izzy grunted, working the wheel loose now that the tire was finally off the ground. "Exposed and stuck. The sooner we get moving, the better."

As Izzy rolled the flat tire to the edge of the road, Erin looked around, half expecting to see some sign of pursuit or surveillance. There was nothing to see except the typical cluster of businesses sprouting up around an interstate exit surrounded by Kansas flatlands. Still, she would feel better once they were back on the road.

She followed the twins across the road, mindful of the sporadic traffic from the truck stop they were heading toward. Once they had reached the gas station, she looked west. She couldn't see the mountains yet, but could feel them looming over the horizon. Once they reached Scathach, they would be safe from pursuit. All they had to do was skirt around one of the top military installations in the country without arousing suspicion and find the way across to Dunos Scaith.

Then the hard part would come.

* * * * *

Chapter Forty-Four

Iblis

"**H**ow long were you planning on keeping this secret?"

Raven regarded Iblis for a moment before answering, her brown eyes revealing nothing. "I just told you, Master. It's no secret, especially since I learned little from the encounter."

"You encountered the Druid on the spirit plane, dream-walking. I would call it a significant development," Iblis countered, annoyed. Raven had sat on this information for two days, which was vexing; it meant she was trying to find ways to change the balance of power in their relationship. Maybe it was some sort of protest against his decision to bring in more witches from her coven. She must have felt threatened, thinking she would be replaced with a younger witch, both as Iblis' right hand and as his favorite play thing.

"But I have not been able to find him since. I may have been able to sway him with my charms if his familiar had not interrupted us." Raven drew a finger from the pentacle at her throat down toward her exposed cleavage. The corset she was wearing over a black silk blouse emphasized the asset, especially since the blouse was unbuttoned all the way down to her bra. "He seemed quite interested in what I had to offer him."

348 | JON R. OSBORNE

"Tell me more about this familiar." Iblis drew his gaze from her bosom, focusing on her face.

Raven let out a dismissive sigh. "Some possibly jailbait little wench, with purple hair and lingerie, like that plant-girl from those cartoons. Obviously, she doesn't measure up to me, but maybe he likes them young."

Iblis pondered the description. Obviously it was some sort of fae, but it was almost impossible to narrow it down to which court. Maybe she had gotten to the Druid and had put him under her spell, using less obvious charms to sway him? It didn't really matter, Iblis supposed. It explained Mad Dog and Mikey being glamoured. But it also made Raven or one of the neophytes less useful to tempt the Druid.

Iblis grinned. He knew this would annoy Raven, and hopefully remind her of her place. "Speaking of young, are our neophytes ready for tonight?"

Raven sighed and smoothed the short skirt that crept up her thigh as she perched on his desk. "Yes, Orliath and Gypsy will be here at nine. They're all excited to meet you, of course, especially once I showed them the candle flame trick. You could probably have Gypsy without even going through the whole ritual theatrics, though Orliath might need a little persuasion."

"You assured me they would both be pliant," Iblis said. The last thing he needed was the distraction brought about by some witch getting cold feet then running her mouth and drawing attention to him.

"Don't worry," Raven said. "Orliath is simply inexperienced— naïve you might say." She lowered her voice conspiratorially. "She might even be a virgin. I know she hasn't been with the few straight guys we have in the coven."

Iblis did enjoy a challenge, seducing a virgin both carnally and spiritually was especially rewarding. "And what about Gypsy?"

Raven made a dismissive noise, fidgeting with the hem of her skirt, making Iblis wonder if she was wearing stockings or hose. It was certainly a departure from her typical Goth-hippie-chic attire, not that he minded. "Shellie has been with all the single guys and a couple who weren't; it's how she got the nickname Gypsy. Going from bed to bed, backseat to backseat. Of course, she doesn't know that; she thinks it's because she dresses and dances like a gypsy, so she adopted it as her craft name." Raven gave a quick, wicked chortle.

"Sounds as though we're going to have fun tonight." Excited to have new toys to play with, Iblis had almost forgotten he was cross with Raven. "But let's go back to your encounter with the Druid."

"I already told you; he was dreaming on the spirit plane, and I was able to enter his dreamscape." Raven sounded irritated at having to repeat the information, but Iblis was curious to see if he could find any inconsistencies indicating she was hiding something or lying. "He was dreaming he had screwed up the world with the new pact. At first I played along until that little sprite showed up. Then he figured out I worked for you. He even knew your name."

The name he shared with mortals, Iblis thought. Of course, the bikers had probably spilled it when they were glamoured. Iblis had half expected some of the pagan minions to come pounding at his door, but they must not have gotten the location from Mad Dog and Mikey. Or they were afraid of a direct confrontation. "And you told him I wanted to meet with him?"

Another sigh, accompanied by a roll of her dark eyes. "Yes, he said stay the hell away, or he would make sure you regretted it when he wrote the new accords of magic."

"That won't do at all," Iblis said. He rubbed his chin. "Do you think one of our new girls might tempt him? If he prefers girls with a more youthful demeanor, that might be the route to take."

"Oh, I had him interested, and he was responding to me," Raven replied. "Besides, the newbies won't know how to spirit-walk yet."

"I'm sure you could bring them up to speed once they've been initiated, and I've granted them a modicum of power." Iblis watched Raven's face for tell-tales of the conflicting emotions that must be bubbling under the surface. She'd gotten quite good at hiding them, something he hoped she didn't pass on to her new apprentices. "And even though I'm not fond of sharing my toys, if one of them caught the Druid's fancy, I'd be willing to relinquish her to him in exchange for his cooperation. I'm talking about the new girls, of course. You are too important for me to part with, my dear Raven."

That actually elicited a smile. Sometimes the carrot worked better than the stick. Truth be told, once the new witches were bonded to him, Iblis could make one of them his familiar, his link to the mundane world and conduit for his magic. But it would mean starting almost from scratch, and Raven had an aptitude he was unsure the neophytes could match. Iblis would need to keep her lust for power in check and make sure she knew her place.

The trick was trying to find out what made the Druid tick. The dream was interesting; it meant the Druid had apprehensions, and he might be reluctant to impose a new set of magical laws for fear of leaving some flaw which would turn the supernatural loose on the world unrestrained.

Frankly, Iblis would rather keep the mystical realms and creatures hidden from the mundane world at large. It made life much easier for the few who walked the world like himself if the populace at large relegated anything fantastical to fairy tales and fools' whimsy. And the more mystical energy both sides expended in the growing conflict, the better for Iblis.

"Very well, Raven. Why don't you go and make sure everything is ready for tonight?" Iblis asked. He watched as she slid from the desk and strutted to the door, heels clicking on the worn linoleum of his office. "Let's make sure we have plenty of wine, fortified with a splash of Everclear. But not too much, we want them suggestible, not throwing up in the cauldron."

"Of course, Master." Raven turned and caught him staring at her ass under the skirt. That elicited another smile as she left.

With a gesture from Iblis, the door swung shut behind the witch. Intercepting the Champion had become dangerous. Her path was bound to cross with Mikha'el's minions and Iblis did not want to get tangled up in that mess. With the Druid, he could play a longer game. The fae might be a problem, as she was likely the Druid's familiar. Raven was an anchor and conduit for Iblis in the physical world; the fae would act as a tap to allow the Druid to draw power from other planes. While a sexual component wasn't necessary, given the form the fae had taken, Iblis considered it likely, as it would create a stronger, more intimate bond as well as give the fae greater sway over the Druid.

But the Druid was mortal, and as Iblis had learned over the ages, men were typically weak when it came to temptations of the flesh.

* * * * *

Chapter Forty-Five

Lee

"**D**ammit."

"Do not blaspheme, Pastor Haskins," Joel admonished.

"I didn't take the Lord's name in vain, though you two are making me sorely tempted," Lee said as he gripped the steering wheel, hoping they didn't blow by a state trooper as they roared along the interstate.

"What did I do?" Qashmet asked.

"You could have mentioned you need to keep sniffing to update where she is, as opposed to costing us 45 minutes of backtracking." Lee could have sworn Joel smirked as he yelled at the dog. "And you, Joel, you just had to have pie before we got on the road. Who has pie for breakfast?"

"It was on the menu." The grin evaporated from the chiseled face. "It should be a sin to advertise food that is not available."

"You know what's a sin? Gluttony!" Lee almost forgot who, or rather what, he was reprimanding.

"Chill out, collar. They haven't moved in 20 minutes; we're gaining on them." There was the rustle of plastic as the dog stuck his snout in the bag. "We're 30 miles away. As long as you don't get pulled over, we'll catch up to them shortly."

"There is the exit, one mile ahead," Joel said as they whipped by a sign. He might not be able to operate a GPS, but if Lee told him to watch for a road or exit, the seraphim was razor-focused on the task.

Lee dropped his speed and signaled to move over, trying not to get stuck behind a lumbering semi-trailer. He knew it would only cost him a few seconds if he did, but it was the principle. "It's easy for you to tell me to chill out, Cash. You don't know what I have at stake."

"Some sweet gig as a mega-church minister, with all the bible-study teeny-boppers you can handle?" the dog replied, slightly muf-fled by having its face buried in laundry. "Not that I'm judging. Once I'm bipedal and furless, I'll be trying to score as much poon as I can."

"Your obsession with the carnal pleasures is disgusting," Joel said, his gaze remaining fixed on the upcoming exit.

"Please; I saw you checking out the waitress," Qashmet said. He pulled his face free of the bag. "That meat suit is getting to you. You're wondering what it would be like to get biblical with a female. Or maybe a male, I don't judge; whatever gets your corporeal rocks off."

Lee guided the pickup truck onto the exit ramp, checking the signs to make sure he turned the correct direction. The last thing they needed was another time consuming misdirection. "For your information, I am doing this to save my wife from cancer. If Mi-kha'el had not healed her, she would have joined our Lord in Heaven by now. Call me weak, but I wasn't ready for her to pass on yet, and I don't think she was either."

"Perhaps it would have been better," Joel said. He glanced over, his blue eyes momentarily flashing gold. "She would be at peace with Our Lord, and you would not be beholden to another."

"That's rough, collar. For what it's worth, I'm sorry." The usual humor had left Qashmet's voice. "I can only imagine how Mikha'el is holding it over you. Which sucks, because it sounds like you're a good guy, even if you do have a stick up your ass."

"It is roughly 30 miles to Colorado Springs," Joel intoned. "If they are indeed heading for Cheyenne Mountain, it is an additional six miles across town."

There was more snuffling from the backseat of the cab, followed by a canine sigh. "Still in Colorado Springs. My guess is they stopped to eat, or they are shopping. It's too early for them to have stopped at a hotel."

Lee wished it was Qashmet with the opposable thumbs. He handed his phone to Joel, who took it, puzzled, as though Lee had handed him a live octopus. "Why don't you see what you can find out about the area? Maybe you can figure out where they are going? It's not as if they are going to roll up to the Cheyenne Mountain Air Force Base and glamour their way in, is it?"

Qashmet had actually been more informative over the trip than Joel or Mikha'el, and he proved informative again. "Why the hell would they go to the Crystal Palace? Despite what movies would tell you, it's not like they could go in, flip a few switches, and start Armageddon. They must need something out here for their champion. Maybe a weapon or something, and I don't think she's going to walk into the challenge with an ICBM over her shoulder. Though that would be funny."

"I fail to see the humor," Joel said, tapping the phone screen. Lee resisted the urge to look over, he was too busy watching for sudden intersections and speed traps.

"Come on, Giwargix puffs up all self-important, 'you cannot defeat me,' and she nukes him," Qashmet said with a laugh. "That's some funny shit. I mean, not for us, because we'd lose, but it would be the funniest thing I've seen since those coyote cartoons." He looked over the seat. "You want the colored wheel icon. Then type 'Cheyenne Mountain' in the search box."

"Who is Giwargix?" Lee asked. He had never heard the name before; then again, Mikha'el wasn't exactly forthcoming beyond what he absolutely needed to know to accomplish the mission.

"You know him as Saint George," Qashmet said, but then paused to look at the phone screen when Joel held it up. "Tap the button that looks like a bent arrow. Giwargix was the one who fought on behalf of the Abrahamic religions in the original challenge that led to the Milesian Accords. The pagans thought they would be cute and entered a dragon as their champion."

"Saint George and the dragon? The legend was born of the first challenge?" Lee had heard of the legend, but had never been curious about it. He had always assumed the dragon was a metaphor.

"Yeah, Giwargix, or George, not only kicked the dragon's ass, he skinned it." Again Qashmet made the rasping noise Lee associated with a laugh. "Then for good measure, our side arranged it so George had to stick around for the next challenge, which I'm sure made him good and pissed."

Lee looked over at Joel, who stared impassively ahead. "Why didn't you tell me any of this?"

"You did not ask," the seraphim replied. "It was not relevant to our task."

"Back to the question, why are they coming here?" Barring hijacking the country's nuclear arsenal, why else would the Champion of the heathens be heading to Cheyenne Mountain? "What is coming up on your search?"

"The first several entries are about the military installation," Joel said. He held up the device again to allow Qashmet to read over his shoulder.

"And I'm telling you that you guys watch too many movies. Scroll down." The dog scanned the screen. "Scroll again. Maybe they're going to the state park? It's right next to the Air Force base."

"You think they are going on a camping trip?" Lee thought that made as much sense as his nuclear apocalypse scenario. "They're not trekking halfway across the country to roast marshmallows."

"I concur." Joel nodded, a mechanical motion that looked awkward. At least he was trying to blend in. "Watch out for the police vehicle ahead."

Lee wasn't sure how Joel had spotted the county sheriff, but he bled off enough speed by the time they got to him they weren't worth the trouble. Lee could see the sheriff glance at his radar then at the pickup truck as they cruised by at three miles over the limit. The sheriff immediately lost interest, and Lee let out his breath.

"Collar, you need your flock to tithe better; this screen is tiny." Lee could see the dog squinting in the rearview mirror.

"Why don't you use my tablet instead?" Lee carried the tablet for scripture reading and sermon writing, but he hadn't had any reason to use it during the road trip. "It's in my bag, along with the charger and cord."

Lee heard his bag unzip and wondered how Qashmet accomplished it without thumbs. If he could work latches and zippers, why couldn't the dog use phones or tablets?

"Why did you not tell us you had a more appropriate device to begin with?" Joel said as he set the phone back in the holder between the front seats.

"You didn't ask." Lee could hear the dog rummaging through the bag. "Don't get slobber on my clothes."

"You need to do laundry anyway," Qashmet retorted before popping his head over the seat, the tablet clutched in his jaws. "Here, take it, Joel."

Lee wondered how the dog could speak with something in his mouth before remembering that Qashmet's mouth didn't move when he spoke. Joel daintily took the proffered device, obviously disgusted as he used napkins left over from their last pit stop to wipe the drool from the screen. A moment later a set of cords flopped over the seat.

Lee took the power adapter and plugged it into the socket under the radio in his truck's dash. "Take the little end and plug it into the matching hole on the bottom of the tablet."

"Remember that; it might come in handy if you want to indulge in more of the features of your meatsuit." Qashmet made the rasping laugh.

"I have neither the inclination nor time to engage in base acts," Joel scoffed as he compared the plug to the various ports. Lee resisted the urge to coach him, not wanting to take his eyes off the road. "There, it is connected."

Qashmet walked the seraphim through the next steps of turning on the tablet and bringing up its map application while Lee saw the mountain itself appear on the horizon, a dark lump through the afternoon haze.

"They have to be meeting someone," Qashmet remarked after he helped Joel zero in the map on Cheyenne Mountain. The dog looked meaningfully at Joel. "It's a shame we don't have a spirit-walker, like a witch or a shaman."

Joel wrinkled his nose in distaste, as though biting something bitter. "Those are all heretics and heathens."

"See, that's the trouble with you Elohim, everything is black and white." Lee saw Qashmet roll his eyes in the mirror. "You know, there are plenty out there your ilk condemn as occultists who believe in the Big Guy, because they take a different path."

"What are spirit-walkers and why would one be useful?" Lee hoped he had headed off an imminent theological debate, especially since he knew the dog liked to push Joel's buttons.

"The spirit plane lies parallel to the physical world. Some say it mirrors it, others say it's out of synch with the physical world and they occupy the same space, some sort of quantum shadow, whatever." Qashmet paused, probably to see if Joel was going to protest, but the seraphim remained silent, staring ahead. "Then there are deeper planes of existence, for example what we call Heaven, the otherworlds where the banished pagan gods and their ilk reside, and so forth. When one of the otherworlds interact with the physical world, there is almost always a sign of it on the spirit world, plus the denizens of the spirit world might have seen something."

Joel broke his silence. "More heresy, trucking with the dwellers in the dark."

"Don't mind him, he's being melodramatic," Qashmet scoffed. "Spirit-walkers can project themselves into the spirit plane, travelling out of their body, able to see the spirit world and interact with the beings there. Sometimes powerful ones go there and manifest their dreams. Back in the old days, rumor was a handful of them could actually step through the spirit world to cross huge distances on the physical world."

"That's ridiculous." It was Lee's turn to scoff. "People can't teleport. Even if you could solve the problems of the Earth's motion, the amount of energy required would be preposterous."

"Thinking like a scientist? Watch out, Joel might kick you out of the truck." The canine's chuckle sound similar to panting.

"I do not like scientists," Joel confirmed, stone-faced.

"Look, I don't know how it works, and it doesn't matter; no one has been able to do it since before the Milesian Accords," Qashmet continued. "The point is, if we had someone who could psychically project onto the spirit plane, they might be able to scout around and tell us if there is anything suspicious the pagan crew might be heading toward."

"Any chance of finding one of these spirit-walkers in Colorado Springs?" Lee was tired of this game of chase. He'd welcome the chance to get ahead of the opposition, even if it meant dealing with some crystal-waving hippies or wannabe witches.

"Here's a fun fact. Elohim, that's angels to you and me, can pass through the spirit world on their way to and from Shamayim, or as you call it, collar, Heaven." The dog looked pointedly at Joel, who still had his gaze fixed on the road ahead. "Which means our surfer buddy here could in fact step into the spirit world for a looksee. He just doesn't want to do it."

Joel suddenly turned, eyes blazing gold, his voice hissing steam in bronze and stone, as he berated Qashmet in some ancient tongue.

The dog actually yelped and back-pedaled. It was all Lee could do to focus on staying on the road, even though they were in a long straightaway.

"Joel, knock it off!" Lee shouted, half afraid the furious angel would summon the white marble sword and start flailing away. "Why didn't you say you could do that, and don't give me that 'you didn't ask' bull shit!"

Joel was still glaring over the seat to where Qashmet was cowering when his eyes reverted to sky blue, and his voice took on its mortal timbre. "Because it leaves me vulnerable."

"Vulnerable? You're the scariest thing I've ever seen, including a stint in Iraq." They passed a sign that read 'Colorado Springs—15 miles.' "If you can figure out where they are going, we can intercept them, instead of playing catch-up. Now spill, why don't you want to do this?"

"As I said, it leaves me vulnerable." It was the first time Lee had heard anything resembling fear in the seraphim's voice. "It will require me to split my essence between the corporeal shell and my celestial self. If either one is slain, then I truly die. Also, Elohim do not travel the spirit plane as easily as the spirit-walkers that Qashmet refers to. "

"Look, I can pull over so your mortal shell won't be in danger. It'll be worth it if we can get a jump on them." Lee spotted the sign for a grocery store coming up. "I'll pull into that parking lot, and you can do your thing."

Joel mulled it over while Lee slowed down and made the turn off the highway. "Very well, but do not let the dog molest my corporeal shell while I am gone."

"I wouldn't dream of it," Cash said with a panting chuckle, which caused Lee to spare an admonishing glance as he pulled into the parking lot. "Seriously, I won't mess with your body. I want this mission to succeed, or I won't get what I was promised."

"Do not move the vehicle while I am projecting," Joel said. He returned to staring straight ahead. "And I will likely need sustenance after I return, as it will be quite tasking."

"Do you want me to go into the store while you're on walkabout, or do you want me to wait until you are done?" Lee eased the truck into a parking space far enough away from others to keep people from pulling up next to him without looking suspiciously close to an exit on the edge of the lot.

Joel considered for moment. "Wait until I am back." He paused and then added, "I will need quiet."

Lee nodded.

Joel closed his eyes and leaned back in his seat. Not knowing what else to do, Lee took the tablet and examined the map, looking for routes to and around the mountain. He noticed there was an antenna farm near the top with a service road that looked promising. It would require going around behind the mountain, but would certainly be easier than hiking up the mountain.

As the minutes slipped by, Lee could hear Qashmet in the back seat licking himself. He didn't want to know what the dog was doing. After another 10 minutes, Joel convulsed in his seat several times. Lee risked a glance back at Qashmet, who somehow managed to convey the equivalent of a shrug. Lee debated risking waking up the seraphim, but the motion abated. After a few more minutes, Joel opened his eyes, which were glowing gold.

Joel blinked a couple times, and the glow abated, his eyes returning to the surfer blue. "I know where they are going."

* * * * *

Chapter Forty-Six

Erin

"D o you have any idea where we are going?"

"Of course we do," Derek responded as they walked from the storage facility where they had parked the Charger for two months. Everything in the car they thought they might need had been loaded into backpacks bought at a big box store; the remainder was locked in the trunk. Each of them had a copy of the key in case something went wrong. "Well, pretty much. We know it's up on the mountain; we'll know it when we see it."

"Do not let my brother's glibness alarm you." Like Derek, Izzy had traded her tight black leathers for more practical hiking attire. Erin couldn't help but admire the lithe muscle tone of Izzy's legs in the khaki shorts. Izzy hefted the backpack easily, even though it must have weighed fifty pounds. "When we spirit walked, we got a good look at the mountain itself. We want to get above the state park and the military base, behind the ridge running above them."

"So we're going to hike across town, then up the mountain?" Erin's own pack was as heavy as Izzy and Derek's, giving her flashbacks to her military days. Her attire was a bit more practical for off-trail hiking and was put together from clothes she had already packed, including a pair of her BDU pants from her Army days. Much more practical than shorts, Erin thought.

"Don't be ridiculous." Derek took out his phone. Unlike his sister, his khakis were full length and covered in pockets, despite his original threat to wear matching shorts. His pack was as loaded as Izzy's, and Erin felt a little guilty because most of the stuff crammed into all three backpacks belonged to her. Evidently the siblings had elf-pockets to take care of what little they carried. "We'll take an Uber to the state park, then hike from there."

As if on cue, a black Cadillac sedan rolled up to the office of the storage facility. It had the signature Uber 'U' displayed in the front window. The driver rolled down the passenger window.

"You called for an Uber?" It was an anachronism, since one didn't actually call for ride services. Derek checked his phone, comparing the picture on the app to the driver in the vehicle.

"Yes, we did." Derek picked up his backpack by the strap. "If you'd be good enough to pop the trunk, we'll load up and be on the way."

"Sure thing." The driver put the car in park, and the trunk opened with a metallic click. Getting out, the driver hurried to the back to help stow the backpacks. "I'm Paul, I'll be your driver."

It was obvious the middle-aged man had noticed Izzy's legs like Erin had. Paul smiled and gestured to take the pack, which Izzy handed over, suppressing a grin as the driver struggled with it.

"You guys are packed up." The driver was slightly out of breath as he closed the trunk. "You folks going camping?"

"We are," Derek replied, getting in the back seat behind the driver. "We're going to meet some friends in Cheyenne Mountain State Park. Are you familiar with it?"

Erin grabbed the back door on the passenger side, leaving Izzy to sit up front. Erin figured it wouldn't hurt to throw the guy a bone, and if he was distracted by Izzy's body he might not remember their faces. Izzy crooked the corner of her mouth, realizing what had happened, giving Erin a glance before beaming a smile at the driver and climbing in front.

"Sure, I know the park. It's right next to the Air Force Base." Paul tried real hard not to check out Izzy's legs again as he buckled up and set the climate controls on the dashboard. He almost succeeded. "Let me know if it gets too cold for you. So am I taking you folks up to the campground? It's not a problem, I've got a season pass."

"That would be splendid if you could take us all the way to the campground," Derek replied, obviously amused by the driver's fascination with his sister. "We were afraid we'd have to walk all the way from the gate, and, as you saw, we have a lot of junk in your trunk."

Paul glanced in the mirror, apparently trying to gauge if Derek was mocking him.

"My brother means we have a lot of camping gear." Izzy turned to look over the seat. "You could say he has too much baggage."

"No worries, I'll get you there." The Cadillac eased into evening traffic, with Paul dividing his time between the road, the GPS, and covert glances at Izzy. "Where are you folks from?"

"My brother and I are from overseas," Izzy said, turning her attention to the driver. "How much do you know about the Iberian Peninsula?"

"Portugal and Spain," Paul replied, focusing more on the road as the traffic grew heavier going through town. "And there's some speck of a place in the Pyrenees. An old friend used to talk about it. Ian claimed he walked from downtown into the mountains and back in a single day. You can do the same thing here. I don't know why you would, but he seemed impressed."

"Andorra," Izzy said. "What your friend described isn't exactly a feat, it's more of a testament to the diminutive size of the principality."

"If you say so; I've never been there." The driver looked at Erin in the mirror. "How about you, miss? You don't strike me as European."

"No, I'm plain old American." Erin didn't want to say where she was from, in case the driver had heard anything on the news. "I'm from Illinois."

The driver nodded. "I'm from New York, myself. Upstate, so I'm used to the kind of snow we get here in the winter."

The mountains loomed larger as they crossed town. Even when they were obscured by buildings or trees, Erin could feel the presence of Cheyenne Mountain. Was it Scathach or Dunos Scaith calling her somehow? She'd been to mountains before, but their presence wasn't on her mind like today. As they reached the highway running parallel to the mountains, it became almost impossible to hide them from view. By the time they reached the road heading into the state park, the mountain was in stark view.

"We're going to hike up that?" Erin asked. While it wasn't a sheer rock face, it certainly looked too steep to just walk up to the top.

"The state park trails will take you up onto the lower parts of the mountain; those are the slopes ahead of us and a bit to the south." Paul made a sweeping gesture with his hand. "They won't take you near the top. To be honest, the best way up there is the service road circling up to the antenna farm. But there's no camping up there; it's out of the park bounds."

Izzy gave Derek an accusing look. He made a dismissive gesture. "I'm sure we'll get high enough in the park for the views we want."

"So do you know which campground your friends are at?" Paul slowed as they neared the entrance station where cars stopped to pay their admission. The park employee looked at the Uber placard and shook his head. Paul flashed a card to the employee. "Hang on a sec."

Derek reached over the seat with a handful of money, which the driver took and passed to the attendant. Erin held her breath as the attendant leaned forward and peered into the car, then counted the money. She handed a few dollars and some coins to Paul, who held it toward Izzy.

"Oh, no, keep it." Izzy said with a smile. "My brother prides himself on being a good tipper."

"Thanks." Paul dumped the money into a cavity in the center console.

Derek consulted a map on his phone. "If you follow the road in about a mile, there should be a four way intersection with a service building on the right. Drop us off there since we aren't sure what site our friends will be at."

"Sounds good." The Cadillac wound its way through the park until the driver spotted the green-roofed building and pulled into its parking lot. The trunk popped with the press of a button and he opened his door. "Here you go."

Erin didn't make the driver wrestle with her pack; she pulled it out and shouldered it while he struggled with Izzy's. Derek also took pity on the driver and relieved him of the burden as soon as it cleared the trunk.

Paul pressed a business card into Izzy's hand. "When you folks need a ride out of here, give me a call. Or if you need anything else."

"Thank you, Paul, we will," Izzy replied, giving him one last smile. She turned to Derek as the driver returned to the Cadillac and departed. "Be sure to give him a decent tip, but not so good it would attract attention."

Derek tapped at his phone. "I think if you texted him your number, it would be better than any remuneration I could give him."

"Bite me, brother," Izzy said as she hefted her pack into position.

"Now we take a leisurely three- or four-hour hike. The good news is that the trail system will get us part of the way." Derek gestured vaguely southwest. "The bad news is that it only takes us part of the way. We'll need to hike cross country without attracting undue attention from the military."

"I thought we were avoiding the base?" Erin shouldered her own pack.

"Oh, we are, but they might get suspicious as we'll have to skirt the fence line." Derek consulted the map again. "Assume any fences we see are electrified."

* * * * *

Chapter Forty-Seven

Iblis

"It's good to be the king."

The three women looked at Iblis with confusion. He blamed a combination of alcohol and a lack of appreciation for the classics. He was still basking in having taken all three of the women. Raven had been right, Orliath had been a virgin, which was a special treat for Iblis. The willowy blonde had been reluctant at first, but between the fortified sacramental wine and his own considerable charm, he'd swayed her to yield to him.

Raven had suggested he simply compel Renee, or Orliath, or whatever name she chose to use. Iblis considered the suggestion vulgar, on a par with using physical force. It gave him no pleasure to force himself upon a victim. It was so much more gratifying to seduce his quarry, working down her resistance and parting her legs through his own charisma. Sure, he was totally willing to employ means to reduce his target's inhibitions, but he took pains to make sure they still had a choice in the matter.

As predicted, Gypsy had been eager, both to acquire magical potence and to please Iblis. What the girl lacked in experience, she made up for in enthusiasm and a spectacular rack. If Raven failed him, Iblis already knew who would replace her.

After he had initiated the neophytes, Iblis had thrown Raven a bone, so to speak. He didn't want her to feel left out and resentful, but he had to be careful how much essence he gave her. At least he had avoided impregnating her; the mystical energy involved would have increased exponentially and may have given him away to his former colleagues. The last thing he wanted was some angry seraphim kicking down his door.

"Does the king require anything?" Gypsy crawled toward him, still naked and sweaty from their earlier exertions. Iblis liked minions who were eager to please and gave her a charming smile, encouraging her. The king's scepter rose to the occasion.

Raven watched suspiciously as Gypsy began her ministrations. Orliath remained off by herself on the opposite side of the room, her eyes unfocused.

"Raven, perhaps you should take Orliath to get cleaned up." Iblis managed to make the suggestion without cracking his voice despite Gypsy's attentions as she bobbed between his knees. "Maybe some soothing tea."

Of course, soothing tea was a special blend not sold in stores. It worked wonders on anxiety and stress, just the thing to calm the girl down in case she was having second thoughts about yielding her maidenhood to Iblis. The last thing he needed was mortal authorities sniffing around and interrupting his work. Of course, if the tea and some positive reinforcement didn't work, he could always compel her not to tell anyone what had happened, but in his experience, naturally overcoming a conquest's qualms worked much better than artificially placed blocks. After all, he'd hate to invest his energy in her only to have her empty a vein in a bathtub.

"Yes, Master." Reluctantly, Raven left Iblis and Gypsy alone, guiding Orliath to her feet and taking her from the room. Iblis admired their asses as they left, the physical response encouraging Gypsy.

Iblis let his mind drift as he enjoyed the carnal sensation of Gypsy's efforts. The Champion and those helping her had headed west, and, as he had predicted, Mikha'el's minions were hot on her trail. Qashmet's reports had been brief; the Champion's party was heading toward Cheyenne Mountain for some reason, and Mikha'el had dispatched a seraphim to kill the fae helping the Champion, which would hopefully derail whatever her mission was in Colorado.

It was a risky gambit, Iblis thought. If the angel accidently killed or maimed the Champion, then the Avramites forfeited. Whatever orders Mikha'el had given his celestial lackey, things happened in the heat of battle. It certainly wasn't a gamble Iblis would have made. It was risky enough dispatching his thugs to try to collect the Druid, and Iblis had seen how *that* had panned out. As annoyed as he was with Raven for seeking out the Druid on her own, it could well have been the best route. Lure him in and find out if he could be swayed, or if nothing else, delayed. The carrot would likely work better than the stick.

Iblis had almost peaked when suddenly Gypsy stopped, causing his mind to concentrate on his corporeal senses, his body clenched just on the brink of release. Gypsy crawled up his naked body, making sure to drag her breasts up his chest as she locked her blue eyes on his. With a wicked smile, she lowered herself onto him, Iblis instinctively grabbed her and pulled her down.

She held his gaze as she fell into a rhythm. Only by sheer force of will did Iblis make the mental effort to withhold his magical essence as he physically released into her. Had the girl already figured out how the exchange between master and familiar worked? That the more sex they had, the more likely she was to receive a portion of his power? Or was Gypsy merely as wanton as Raven had claimed?

As if on cue, Iblis looked over Gypsy's shoulder and saw Raven in the doorway. Her hair was wet, and she was in a simple black shift. Her narrowed eyes were locked on Gypsy's back, who had slumped against Iblis after her orgasm had subsided. Iblis stroked Gypsy's chestnut hair as he met Raven's gaze. Yes, Raven needed this, to be knocked down a peg before she got too enamored with her own power.

Something clawed at the periphery of Iblis' perception, something unnatural. He almost dumped Gypsy off his lap, their physical entanglement forcing him to lift her bodily so he could stand. Setting the confused girl down, he cast out his senses for the source of his unease.

Of course, Raven had picked up on it as well. They both looked east, sensing something clawing its way across the landscape.

"What is that?" Raven whispered, her brown eyes wide and no longer glaring at Gypsy.

"That could be a problem," Iblis responded. Could Mikha'el be so stupid? Maybe frustration and anger combined with incarnating in the mortal world had taken their toll. Whoever was responsible was almost certainly trying to flush out the Druid. Depending on how the Druid responded, it could kill him in the process. Slaying the last of the line of Cathbad would have the same result as killing the last of the line of Cu Chulainn outside of the challenge, the forces of Abrahamic faiths would forfeit the challenge. Iblis was almost positive it wouldn't work out well for him unless he could disappear in the ensuing chaos.

Raven had closed her eyes, concentrating on the possible mystical threat. "We are probably safe, whatever it is; only the fringe will pass over us. I wouldn't want to be in Peoria when this hits."

Gypsy looked confused, still naked on the floor where Iblis had unceremoniously dumped her. "Master, what is happening?"

"Not now, dear. Grownups are talking," Iblis replied. "Raven, you're going to have to go into the spirit world. Odds are, if the Druid comes out to face this, he will be there as well."

"If he comes out to face this, I don't think he's going to be in the mood for a quickie, regardless of my rack." Raven's eyes continued to flick east, searching for a target. To her credit, she didn't spare Gypsy the contemptuous glance Iblis expected.

"That's not what I want." Iblis' mind whirled with possible permutations. Could there be other parties involved? Absolutely. Could this be a faction of the Exiled trying to frame the followers of Jehovah, Yahweh, and Allah for the Druid's demise, forcing the terms of the accords? Possible, but unlikely, as their culpability would almost certainly be revealed. Whatever was happening, Iblis knew he couldn't intervene any more than was necessary to protect his own physicality. That's why he had cultivated agents to act on his behalf.

"Then what do you want me to do?" Raven asked. Iblis wasn't sure if it was the urgency of the situation or Raven's desire to make sure Gypsy didn't supplant her; Raven had shed her attitude of rebelliousness.

"It's a good thing you are so charged up from tonight's festivities," Iblis said, still focused east, where the threat continued to close. "You'll need to spirit-walk ahead of this and render whatever aid you can to the Druid."

"In return for what?" It was apparent the gears had immediately started turning in Raven's mind. "Also, do you have demands or conditions? Or do you want him to agree to meet with you before we help him?"

At least she acknowledged where the power came from, Iblis thought. "No, I want you to do the unexpected. Help him with no strings attached." Hopefully it will be enough, Iblis thought.

* * * * *

Chapter Forty-Eight

Erin

"Are we there yet?"

Derek turned back toward Erin. "As a mother, you should know better than to utter that phrase."

They had been hiking for almost three hours. The first two had been on the trail systems, and then they had veered off upslope. They had been careful not to get too close to the fence marking the perimeter of the Air Force Base, so hopefully their climb hadn't set off any alarms.

Derek had taken the lead once they started cross-country, agilely picking his way as he scouted the best path. At this point, anyone in the park would have been hard pressed to spot them as a spur of the mountain obscured them from the campgrounds and hiking trails below. They had been climbing parallel to a stream bed, the steep drop barely manageable as the stream tumbled down the mountain.

Izzy had been quiet, marching behind Erin. Glancing back, it looked as though the blonde woman had hardly broken a sweat. Erin was breathing hard; the combination of altitude and exertion were taking their toll and leaving her wishing she had kept up her conditioning.

"Are you all right?" Izzy asked, concern apparent on her face. "We can pause for a moment if you need to catch your breath."

Erin resisted the urge to be stubborn and try to show she was tough. Nodding, she found a rock outcropping she could lean her pack against. "I'd forgotten about the elevation," she wheezed, pulling out a water bottle and sipping carefully. She guessed they had maybe an hour or so before the sun set, then maybe half an hour of twilight, depending on how much shadow the mountains cast. At least the weather was clear.

"If we follow this ravine up the rise ahead, then turn north once we are behind the ridge, it should put us close to where we encountered the shadowcat in the Murkwold." Derek pointed toward the ridge in question. It looked like another half hour to reach the ridge if they kept a decent pace.

After several minutes in silence, Erin hefted the pack back onto her shoulders and stood straight. "We're running out of daylight."

Izzy and Derek both shouldered their packs as well. "At least we don't seem to have drawn any government attention," Derek said as he began picking a path through the rocks and brush.

"Actually, I think a drone has been keeping an eye on us for almost an hour," Izzy replied from the rear. "They probably want to make sure we aren't trying to get above the upper tunnel entrance and come down into their perimeter."

Derek scoffed. "What would be the point? Even if we wanted something in the facility, rappelling down the bluff and running in the tunnel would just get us arrested. Outside of movies, who would be so stupid?"

Erin shrugged. "I was Army, so I know as much as you when it comes to this place. I would recommend that we pretend we don't know we are being watched. Nothing pisses off a security guard more than being flipped off like he can't do anything about your presence. It provokes them to come up with an excuse to nab you."

Forty minutes later, they had hiked above the ravine and crested the slope. The ridge rose to their right, running north. The terrain behind the ridge was flatter and easier to navigate than the eastern slope they had climbed. The shadows were growing long as the sun fell behind the mountains to the west. The blinking red lights of the antenna farm on top of the mountain were visible to the north.

Another 30 minutes of trudging uphill brought them to a cleft running between the easternmost ridge and the higher peaks of the mountain. Derek paused several times to get his bearings, comparing the outlines of the ridges and peaks to the skyline.

"I think we are here." Derek surveyed the crest again as twilight fell.

Erin looked around for some sign of how to get to Dunos Scaith. Would there be a portal or a hidden door carved in the side of the mountain? "What now?"

"Now I send the pagan filth to Hell," a voice rasped, like steam coming from a pipe organ. "And your mission ends."

Erin spun around, cursing herself for not hearing the strangers approach. Had they been lying in wait? The strange voice had come from a blonde-haired, blue-eyed surfer dude, who strode purposefully toward them. In another situation, Erin wouldn't have minded meeting the blonde man. With his chiseled physique, he could have modelled for one of those classic statues from the Renaissance.

An older man followed Blondie, probably fortyish, with glasses and a slightly receding hairline greying at the temple. A burnished bronze cross hung prominently from the older man's neck. Erin remembered Horn-Rimmed-Glasses sporting a similar cross. It couldn't be a coincidence. A Doberman trotted alongside the cross-wearer. Something about the way it looked over everyone, as though calculating the odds of a fight, bothered Erin. Its eyes were way too intelligent for a dog.

Izzy and Derek immediately produced their slender short swords, Izzy moving in front of Erin as they took up positions 90 degrees apart from the surfer. The blonde man looked from one sibling to the other, and his blue eyes turned into glowing pools of molten gold. White mist swirled around his right hand, coalescing into a sword that looked like it was made of white marble.

"We can avoid any need for violence," Cross said, holding up his hands. "Miss Donnelly, all you have to do is abandon this mad quest. It is never too late to seek the Lord's grace."

"Why would I do that?" Erin snarled. She could feel her heart pounding, not from fear but fury. "You people hounded my son and me, and drove us from our home."

"I'll admit some of my colleagues were a bit heavy-handed in their tactics," Cross said. He was obviously staying clear of Surfer and the gleaming stone sword. "But if you succeed in your mission—the mission these aliens have compelled or convinced you to undertake—my wife will die. It's as simple as that."

"Don't listen to him, Erin." Izzy didn't spare a glance toward Erin, keeping her attention on the blonde man. "These are the guys who tried to grab Tim. Kidnapping isn't exactly a 'Christian' act."

"Enough talking." Again the surfer's voice rang as steam forced through metal. "Die, pagan filth!"

He lunged toward Izzy, who barely managed to sidestep the strike. Derek sprang in with his own weapon, only to be forced to flinch back as the gold-eyed surfer reversed his stroke with alarming speed, as though his sword weighed nothing.

Erin reached into her pocket and the elf-vassi contained within, grabbing the hilt of her new sword. She drew the sword, the gesture awkward as she had to get the entire blade clear before she could bring it up into a fighting position. If Goldie worked for the Av-ramites, he couldn't hurt Erin without risking the terms of the challenge. The siblings had no such protection.

Cross seemed content to hang back and appeared to have no weapons. Erin tentatively relegated him to a non-threat; he seemed as alarmed by the surfer's attack as Izzy and Derek. The white stone sword flashed back and forth. Where the blade struck a boulder it sent stone chips flying, forcing Izzy to backpedal as she shielded her face from the spray of granite shrapnel.

Erin watched for an opening in the melee. If the siblings could draw Goldie forward, she could flank him, but they seemed deter-mined to keep her out of the fight. There was a loud pop and sud-denly Derek convulsed. It took a split-second for Erin to realize Cross had shot Derek with a taser. Derek tried to slice the wires free even as he fell backwards.

Izzy's attention was drawn to her brother, and in that moment the Doberman leaped forward, all fur and fangs, latching onto Izzy's throat and bearing her to the ground. Goldie closed on Derek, who was still trying to regain his senses after several thousand volts.

The dog yelped and scampered away, trailing blood as it released its hold on Izzy's throat. Her own weapon fell to the ground as she clutched at the wound, attempting to staunch the bleeding. Goldie strode to where Derek had fallen. Derek feebly raised his sword to try to block a weapon twice its size. Goldie smiled triumphantly as the stone blade traced an arc for the stricken *xanoso*.

"No you fucking don't." Erin's blade intercepted the death blow. Blooded roared in her ears as her counterstrike forced Goldie to back pedal.

"You cannot harm me," Goldie intoned. Nonetheless, he dropped into a defensive stance. "No weapon forged by man can harm me."

"And if you kill me, you automatically lose, mother-fucker," Erin growled, spinning her sword to an attack position, gripping it with both hands.

"Then it would appear we are at an impasse." The golden eyes fixed upon her. "Yield and I will spare the creatures you have been misled into befriending."

"Fuck you!" Instead of taking the obvious overhead swing, Erin reversed the stroke and came in from the side, stepping into the swing to add force to the strike. Goldie managed to twist his sword down and block, but it left him in too awkward a position to counterstrike. Erin lashed out with her steel-toed boot right for his crotch.

She felt as though she'd kicked a Buick, and instinctively jumped back as her opponent slashed for her exposed leg. That swipe left Goldie out of position and Erin forced him back despite the spike of pain in her foot when it bore her weight. The surfer dude assumed a defensive stance, his face impassive. For all his boasts about how she couldn't hurt him, Goldie sure acted as if she was a threat.

Erin pressed the attack, striking repeatedly, and forced Goldie to give ground. Goldie's eyes dipped to a boulder to Erin's right, his sword tracing an arch toward the rock. Instead of flinching back,

Erin closed her eyes and lunged, forward thrusting her weapon. Even as stone shards stung her, she was rewarded with her weapon striking meat.

Erin opened her eyes. Her left side had been peppered with stone shrapnel and was bleeding. The blade Gofannon had forged for her was sunk into Goldie's torso, below the sternum.

"Oh yeah, this sword wasn't made by a mortal man," Erin growled as the glowing gold eyes met hers. Sparks appeared around her opponent's wound, growing in number and intensity as his flesh began to burn away from the bleeding injury. The surfer's mouth hung open, working as though he was trying to say something. "So fuck you, asshole."

Goldie exploded in a gout of sparks, which whirled up into the darkening sky. As soon as her sword was free, Erin spun, looking for other threats, the blood rage still pounding in her ears. Cross and the dog had fled; Erin tamped down the urge to pursue them.

Derek had made it to his sister's side and was clutching the wound at her throat. "Get...Erin...Scathach...," Izzy managed to rasp. If she had been pale before, now she was ghostly white.

Derek turned to Erin, tears welling in his eyes. His sister made a gurgling noise and fell limp. "There's nothing I can do for her."

Despite the red creeping along the edge of her vision, Erin noticed there were new arrivals. She spun, bringing her sword to bear. Death demanded death, her blood roared.

"Stay your sword, Champion." The speaker was a striking red-headed woman, bearing a spear and a large round shield. She affixed fierce green eyes on Erin. "I am Scathach. I suspect I am the one you seek."

384 | JON R. OSBORNE

Derek looked up from his sister, tears trailing down his cheeks. "Please, don't let my past indiscretions keep you from helping my sister."

"Derecho, do you think me so shallow?" the warrior-woman replied. "Sadly, your sister's demise is not up to my whim, or I would save her."

"We can't just leave her," Erin said, fury still pounding in her blood.

"We won't leave her," Scathach replied. "If nothing else, she earned a warrior's funeral."

* * * * *

Chapter Forty-Nine

Liam

"Something is wrong."

Liam set down the book and looked for the source of his unease. His body was sore and tired from working in the smithy, then after dinner he and Pixel had spent three hours talking about different kinds of magic, with her explaining what she knew about how they worked. Liam wasn't sure where Pixel had gone; he suspected she was lying in wait in his bedroom. He also wasn't sure how he felt about Pixel's attention since Erin had brushed him off, and he had decided to read a couple chapters to calm his mind before going to bed.

Pixel had left him alone last night, and he hated to admit, part of him was disappointed. She had gotten more flirtatious once Tim went to bed, and Einar and Gofannon had disappeared. Liam had abstained from alcohol despite the suggestion to break out the tequila. He had been drinking more since this whole mess had started and thought he should cut back, especially since he had so much to do. He also didn't trust himself if he got drunk to maintain his resolve.

A distant flash to the east caught his attention through the window. It had rained an hour ago, bringing a welcome respite from the heat, but it hadn't stormed. The system must have picked up intensity as it rolled east. There was another flash of lightning. Something tickled at the back of his mind. As he watched, lightning arced from the clouds to the ground. It looked closer than the other two strokes.

Liam turned off the light and went to the living room, where larger windows gave a better view of the east. There was a sense of dread as he gazed east. Illuminated by lightning, he could see a boiling storm front drawing closer. Something was wrong, that wasn't an ordinary storm. Distant thunder rumbled.

Tim thumped down the stairs, eyes wide. "Dad, the house is afraid."

As if to punctuate, Scooter appeared on the back of the couch, glaring out the windows and growling. Everyone jumped when the weather radio in the kitchen went off. The electronic voice announced a severe thunderstorm warning and tornado watch. Liam listened as the radio droned out a list of counties that formed a swath from Interstate 80 to the north to Interstate 72 in the south. They were smack in the middle.

"Pixel! Einar! Gofannon!" Liam bellowed up the stairs. "Everyone up, we've got trouble!"

Pixel appeared at the top of the stairs almost immediately, wearing one of Liam's t-shirts. "What's wrong?"

"Something is coming." Liam glanced toward the windows again. "Some sort of freak storm, I don't think it's natural. Make sure Einar and Gofannon are up."

"I'm pocking awake," Einar said. He blinked under the light in the stairway. "What's the ruckus?"

"Get Gofannon, we might be in trouble." Liam heard the radio go off in the kitchen again, this time with tornado warnings.

Einar disappeared back into the upstairs hall as Pixel dashed down the stairs. Despite everything, Liam caught himself noticing her bare legs. She came over next to him, following his gaze east.

"There's something in the storm," she whispered after a minute.

"That's what I thought." Liam watched the lightning and listened for the accompanying thunder, trying to gauge the distance. "Weather in this part of the country goes west to east. Sure it might veer north or south, but overall, it almost always rolls east. I'm almost certain the rain that passed over us an hour ago is doubling back."

Gofannon lumbered down the stairs, Einar trailing behind him. The smith-god rubbed his eyes as he entered the living room then froze. "That is not good," he rumbled, looking toward the storm.

"The good news is we have one heck of a storm cellar; go through the laundry room." Liam gestured toward the back of the house. "I think my great-grandfather intended it to double as a bomb shelter. Einar and Pixel, take Tim there. If the power goes out, there's a generator. Gofannon, let's go see what we're dealing with, and if we can diffuse it or exorcise it."

"I should go with you," Pixel said as she caught Liam's sleeve. "I know more about magic than you and Gofannon put together. No offense, Gofannon."

"None taken," the smith said. He furrowed his brows. "Druid, why not simply wait this out?"

"Because if it's magical, it's probably aimed at me." Liam remembered the dream. "I don't want anyone hurt on my account if I can do something about it."

Gofannon shrugged but didn't protest further. "It is a shame I am not a thunder god."

"Einar and Tim, go to the cellar." Liam expected a protest from Tim and was surprised when none came. The boy cocked his head, as though listening to something, then reluctantly nodded. Heading for the door outside, Liam instinctively grabbed his staff from where it leaned at the end of his workbench.

Outside, the wind had picked up. The doors at either end of the forge shed rattled. Liam marched toward the rise where the dolmen stood. At least it hadn't started raining yet, he thought, as he gauged the distance of the storm. He guessed it was three miles or so away; flashes of lightning showed a boiling line of clouds stretching across the horizon.

Liam could feel something seething in the heart of the storm, looking for something to lash out at in anger. For a moment he considered taking Gofannon's advice and letting the storm pass by, but Liam steeled his resolve. The base of the dolmen was only ten feet higher than the surrounding field, but it was enough to give him an almost unobstructed view. Kicking off his sandals, he planted his feet in the grass and closed his eyes.

The wind whipped around them, carrying a few drops of rain with it. Liam tuned out the distraction, setting the end of his staff to the ground. He was aware that Pixel stood close to his right. With his mind, he reached for the weave of the Gwuedd, drawing the magic up through his feet and the staff.

Opening his eyes, he could see the Murkwold overlaid with the physical world. The storm appeared as a great malevolent beast, slowly clawing its way across the landscape, hateful eyes casting about. Liam really didn't want that gaze to fall on him. "What the fuck is that?"

Pixel took his free hand, and a spark passed between them. "It's a tempest elemental, a nasty living storm born of anger and magic."

"Then someone is really pissed." Liam held his breath as the baleful gaze swept past them. "How do we get rid of it?"

"I'm not sure. In the old days, I think druids would try to draw them out to sea," Pixel replied.

"That might work on an island, but we're out of luck here." There was no safe direction; any way the storm could be guided, there would be people in its path. Two miles away, it continued to laboriously draw closer. Green-black whirls appeared in the clouds as funnel clouds began to form. "It's fighting the jet stream and prevailing winds by going west. It looks like the elemental is holding the storm to the ground, hauling the front with it."

"That sounds smart, Druid," Gofannon bellowed over the wind. He was standing closer to the base of the hill, studying the storm. "Can you do anything with all of those words?"

A mile and a half away, the tempest loomed; twisters, backlit by bolts of lightning, reached toward the ground. Its furious glare now swept farther east, still looking for a quarry to unleash its ire upon.

"If we could call up wind from the west, we could probably halt its progress," Liam suggested.

"Wonderful, it would hang over us until you tire." Gofannon looked from the storm to Liam. "I do not like this plan."

"You'd wear out quickly trying to hit it head on," Pixel added. "It's using a lot of energy to come this way."

She didn't add the unspoken fact Liam had never tried something like this before. Liam wracked his mind while the tempest clawed closer. Weather systems contained an enormous amount of energy, how could he channel enough to even ruffle its clouds, let alone break it up?

Liam closed his eyes, looking only at the spirit world. He could clearly see Pixel at his side, and could make out Gofannon as a shimmery, hulking form nearby. Liam could see the tempest elemental clearer than ever, silhouetted against boiling clouds in the Murkwold. It reached forward a great, smoky limb that looked like congealed storm clouds, with arcs of lightning occasionally flashing up and down the appendage. It sank black talons into the earth and hauled its bulk forward. Watching in horrified fascination, Liam realized the elemental's mass wasn't dragging across the earth, it floated above the ground like a nightmarish parade balloon.

Liam became aware of a presence to his left.

"Hello, scion." Liam's mind painted a ghostly image of a man, middle-aged and in simple robes. As Liam, he bore a staff. Even though the image in his mind's eye was composed of black, white, and greys, the man's eyes were in striking color; one deep blue and the other bright green.

"Cathbad?" Liam whispered.

"More or less," the apparition replied. "You've gained strength from the gods and guidance from the spirits. Now it's time you gained some wisdom from your ancestors. You've realized you can't fight this thing toe to toe, at least not yet. You are going to have to get creative."

"If I could unmoor it from the Earth, it would get swept up higher where it couldn't hurt anyone." Liam turned from the ancestor spirit back the elemental. "I don't suppose you can give me a crash course on how to manipulate the wind?"

"You don't need one." Cathbad gestured upwards with his staff. "Do not move the wind, ask the Sky to do it for you."

Liam could hear a distant rumbling behind the roaring wind in the physical world. Ignoring it, he looked up into the sky. This is the spirit world, where I can walk a league at a time, he thought. I don't have to obey the laws of physics. Putting his arm around Pixel's spirit form, he stepped up.

Pixel yelped, clinging to him. Wind from below ruffled the clothes on their astral bodies as they remained aloft. Cathbad reappeared next to him. The elemental's gaze stopped sweeping the countryside, and it focused on Liam. It drew another hundred yards closer, straight toward Liam.

"Call to the Sky!" Cathbad swept his staff in an arc. "Let your fae-wife help you, adding to your call. Call as many zephyrs as you can."

A maw appeared in the elemental's bulk, full of lightning and hail. On the physical world, tornadoes snaked across fields, all bearing down on Liam's home.

"You can do this," Pixel whispered in his ear. Somehow he caught her floral perfume, even though his physical senses were a mile below him.

"Sky Above, come to my aid!" Liam yelled, holding his staff aloft. He could feel the Gwuedd in the sky all around him. He willed the energy to pass through himself, then he cast it out with his mind, imploring the zephyrs to bring their winds down to the ground and sweep below the tempest elemental.

A ripple passed through the air, like the surface of a pond after a stone has been tossed in. Dozens, then hundreds, then thousands of wind spirits whirled around him, carrying their breezes with them. Then, en masse, they dove toward the ground and swooped east.

Liam fought the panic as the equivalent of gravity caught hold of his spirit form and it began to plummet down. As the ground drew closer, he willed his body to take a deep breath and open his eyes. He jerked as his spirit entered his body, surprised not to find himself sprawled in the grass. His staff was still planted in the dirt, and Pixel leaned against him under his arm.

The temperature fell as a torrent of wind roared overhead. The storm seemed to snarl defiantly as the cold stream of air reached it and roared under it. The ceiling of clouds began to rise. Refocusing on the spirt world, Liam watched as the elemental reached forward with a limb, only to be unable to find purchase. It began to lose ground as it rose, the tornadoes dissipating as the funnel clouds stretched and lost contact with the ground.

Cold rain burst from overhead as the frigid air rushing above condensed the humidity. Pixel shivered against him, huddling against Liam for warmth. Gofannon seemed as little bothered by the cold as he was by the heat of the forge, running his huge hands through his hair as though it were a morning shower. Liam sensed a presence besides him and turned, expecting Cathbad.

"It looks as though you didn't need my help after all," Raven's spirit form muttered, unaffected by the rain.

"What are you doing here?" Liam demanded, immediately on the defensive. Had her boss sent the storm, and she was here to see what had gone wrong?

"You can see me?" Raven seemed surprised. "You fell out of the spirit world."

Pixel peeled herself off Liam, stepping around him to glare at Raven. Liam tried not to notice how the wet t-shirt clung to Pixel and revealed what she wasn't wearing underneath.

"Well done, Druid!" Gofannon turned around, frowning when he spotted Raven as well. "Who is that?"

Thunder roared from a couple of miles away. All along the front, clouds were breaking up and starting to drift east, dumping rain. In the center, still futilely scrabbling for the ground, the tempest glowered at Liam. Lightning filled the sickly green gaps that made up its eyes.

Liam felt the hair on his arms and head stand up. He shoved Pixel toward Gofannon while backpedaling. "Run!"

Liam heard his name called as the sky lit up, and everything went black.

# # # # #

ABOUT THE AUTHOR

At thirteen years old, Jon Osborne discovered a passion for two things—writing and telling stories. Instead of doing what a normal author-to-be would do and write stories, Jon wrote for his school newspaper and told stories through the medium of running role-playing games for his friends.

Journalism helped pay the way through college, and gaming garnered him lifelong friends. After college, journalism didn't pan out as a career, but Jon continued creating worlds and forging stories with his friends.

Fast forward almost 30 years; Jon is still a gamer who every now and then dabbles with writing. A long-time friend and fellow gamer who had found success as an author, Mark Wandrey, convinced Jon to submit a short story for an anthology. Jon's story was accepted, and it gave him the impetus to finish his first novel, "A Reluctant Druid."

Living in Indianapolis, Jon still games, and continues to write. You can find out more about Jon at jonrosborne.com. Fans who sign up for his mailing list will receive "Chapter 0" of "A Reluctant Druid" and be the first to get the news about Jon's newest books and stories.

* * * * *

Connect with Jon R. Osborne Online

Website: http://jonrosborne.com/

Amazon: https://www.amazon.com/Jon-R.-Osborne/e/B073PKR8GS

Facebook: https://www.facebook.com/jonrosborne/

Twitter: @druidoz

* * * * *

The following is an
Excerpt from Book Two of The Milesian Accords:

A Tempered Warrior

———————————————

Jon R. Osborne

Available Soon from New Mythology Press

eBook, Paperback, and Audio Book

Excerpt from "A Tempered Warrior:"

"I liked it better when you were armed."

Mysie looked up from the dirt of the practice field. She added, "You're more dangerous with your bare hands."

Erin extended a hand and helped Mysie up. They had been instructed to spar without weapons; Erin was eager to have the advantage for a change. During weeks of training in sword and staff fighting, which mostly consisted of getting beaten black and blue, Erin had focused on learning those weapons. Now she was getting to put a couple black belts to good use.

Mysie had been taken by surprise when Erin caught Mysie's arm mid-punch and flipped her, landing her in the dirt. As soon as the short woman got up, Erin swept Mysie's legs, knocking her prone again. Erin finished the bout with her fist frozen in a hammer strike an inch from Mysie's nose.

Uathach looked on with interest. She had been quick to criticize Erin but glacial to praise her. Uathach gestured to Daidh to take Mysie's place opposite Erin. Erin waited, sweating in the padding she was wearing. The armor was quilting over leather, and it felt like she was wearing her grandmother's comforter over her workout clothes.

Daidh took his position facing Erin, and they exchange bows. Erin had shared that martial arts tradition with her sparring partners, and they had enthusiastically adopted it. Following the bow, Daidh brought his hands up in an approximation of a boxer's stance. Erin went into a traditional tae kwon do starting position, then launched her attack.

She feigned a punch; Daidh's block came up as soon as her fist started moving. Instead of stepping into the punch, though, she sent a snap kick at his belly. His other hand moved to catch her foot but she turned and caught him in the ribs with a roundhouse. Her momentum carried her forward and she caught the side of his helmet with her elbow. The blow staggered Daidh back a step. Erin kept her body turning, launching a spin kick. Even pulling her strength, when her heel struck the same spot as her elbow had a moment earlier, Daidh was knocked to the ground.

"Oh shit!" Erin exclaimed. She had expected Daidh to block or duck her foot. Neither Mysie nor Daidh had seen modern martial arts, and they had no idea what she was capable of. "Are you okay? I didn't mean to hit you so hard."

Daidh held up a hand, then slowly got to his feet. He shook his head and adjusted the leather helmet. "I am not hurt; you just rang my bell. What was that?"

"Tae kwon do, mixed with a little kung-fu and karate," Erin replied, still feeling guilty—as much for clocking him as for the thrill of triumph she felt for a split second. "I'm really sorry; I didn't mean to kick you so hard."

Uathach was still observing quietly. Had she finally been impressed? "So, you've been playing us for fools?" she accused.

"What?" Erin was baffled.

"For the last few weeks, you've hidden this training, only to spring it on us to humiliate your practice opponents," Uathach stated coldly. "Has this been a game to you?"

"No!" Erin protested. Of course the red-headed bitch would find a way to turn this against Erin. "This is the first time we've done martial arts sparring. Up until now it has been all swords and staves."

"Wrong!" Uathach thundered, her pale face flushing red. "It has been fighting! When you fight, you use every weapon at your disposal! Do you think the Avram champion will hold back? Do you think he will fight you on your terms?"

"You know what? You've been on my ass since I've gotten here!" Erin said, feeling her blood grow warm. She'd had enough of this bitch riding her. "I've had a lot of teachers, and you're probably the worst. You've hardly taught me anything; we just drill and spar over and over!"

"You want a lesson?" Uathach marched over to the racks of practice weapon and pulled out two wooden swords. She tossed one into the dirt at Erin's feet. "Be glad I don't teach you with steel."

Erin snatched the practice weapon off the ground. She fought to keep the red from her vision, to hold her anger in check. Uathach wanted her to lose her temper so she could embarrass Erin and put Erin in her place. Uathach wasn't even human; she was some sort of demigoddess trained by her mother, Scathach, the paragon of the fighting arts. Uathach had centuries of practice; Erin had only been playing with wooden swords for a few weeks.

Uathach didn't bother to don practice armor before striding onto the practice field. "Just like your progenitor," Uathach scolded, going into the ready position. "So hot-headed and ready to rush in."

"Is that how he ended up in your bed?" Erin taunted. Two could play at this game. "He must have had something going for him for you to cheat on your boyfriend."

Uathach's somber facade cracked into a sneer. Her weapon blurred as Erin was forced to give ground, barely parrying the flurry of blows. Erin knew she couldn't leave the fight on Uathach's terms. Uathach was watching for her to kick, and Erin knew she'd get a whack on the knee or shin if she tried. Traditional tae kwon do wasn't good for close-in fighting, and neither were these wooden swords. Fortunately Erin had learned a lot more than the traditional style.

When Erin parried the next swing, instead of stepping back she surged forward, aiming a palm strike at Uathach's solar plexus. The redhead managed to turn aside so Erin's hand merely brushed her, but Erin jabbed her elbow into Uathach's ribs then swept the arm up to catch Uathach's wrists as the instructor brought her sword around to catch Erin's exposed flank.

Erin drove Uathach's hands up. With her weapon hand, Erin punched at the side of her opponents head. Uathach spun backwards and reversed her stroke, striking for Erin's sword arm. Erin tried to yank her limb clear, but the blow caught her on the arm guard. If not for the armor, her arm would have broken. As it was, Erin's sword tumbled to the dirt.

Erin's other hand grabbed Uathach's weapon and tugged. Uathach refused to release her grip and stood her ground. Erin brought up her knee as she was drawn toward her opponent, but Uathach twisted so the impact was on her hip, not her belly, and quickly stepped back before Erin could hook her heel and trip Uathach.

Still gripping the wooden blade, Erin thrust it forward, and the hilt jabbed Uathach just below the sternum, causing her to gasp for breath. Snarling, Uathach released one hand from the grip and punched Erin in the abdomen. Erin managed to catch most of the impact with her free arm, but it still stung.

Erin's eyes narrowed as her vision turned red. She wrenched the end of the wooden weapon up, toward Uathach's face, stepping into the push. As Uathach returned to a two-handed hold, Erin's free hand drove just below Uathach's armpit. Erin was rewarded with a yelp of pain as Uathach fought to keep her center of gravity. Two more rapid punches went into the same spot, forcing Erin's opponent to release the weapon with one hand to block.

Uathach caught the next punch, seizing Erin's wrist. Erin slammed her skull in Uathach's face. Even with the padding of Erin's leather helmet, the blow staggered Uathach.

The wooden sword was flung aside as Uathach lost her grip on both the weapon and Erin's wrist, falling back a step to widen the gap. Uathach noticed Erin's feral grin as the champion half-turned, then her foot pistoned across the space between them. The sidekick caught Uathach square in chest, and the impact launched her as though she had been kicked by a horse.

Erin seized the dropped weapon and charged toward Uathach, who rolled to her feet and into a defensive stance. There was no finesse to the sword's arc, just fury-driven speed. Uathach barely managed to get an arm up; there was a loud crack as both bone and wood snapped. Erin followed up with a punch to Uathach's jaw, snapping the redhead's skull back.

"Hold!" The imperious command penetrated even the rage-induced fog in Erin's mind. She froze, her fist drawn back for another punch. The gathered crowd parted, revealing Scathach, her expression furious.

"Just like Cu Chulainn, she has the frenzy," Uathach hissed through clenched teeth. "How can we put the hopes of the Exiled Folk in her hands?"

"Because it has been ordained," Scathach stated, stalking toward the two combatants.

"She's not one of us; she cannot champion us," Uathach said, clutching her broken arm. "She is mortal and of the Dunwold."

"Go have Ynidd tend to your arm," Scathach' said. There was no sympathy in her tone. She lowered her voice and said, "Do not think I am fooled. I know you took the practice field to goad the champion into losing her temper. I had hoped you would have put the past behind you; obviously, I was mistaken."

Uathach started to protest, only to be cut off by her mother.

"Go," Scathach commanded. Once Uathach departed, she turned to Erin. "You must get your temper under control. It can give you great strength, but if you let it run rampant, it will get you killed."

Erin nodded, trying to contain her shaking as the adrenaline rush wore off.

"I think we've had enough practice for today," Scathach announced. "I will see you here in the morning."

"You?" Erin asked, still quelling the after-effects of her berserker rage.

"Yes," Scathach replied. "I will oversee the rest of your training myself."

* * * * *

The following is an
Excerpt from Book One of The Balance of Kerr:

Burnt

Kevin Steverson & Tyler Ackerman

Available Now from New Mythology Press

eBook and Paperback

Excerpt from "Burnt:"

Tog shrugged. "I like chicken," he said as he pulled out his dagger. Standing nearly seven feet tall and weighing nearly three hundred and twenty pounds, a dagger for him was a short sword to most men. He cut a piece off. He didn't bother blowing on it and poked it into his mouth. There was instant regret on his face. He began breathing through his teeth with the piece of meat between them, the sharpness of his incisors giving away that he was half Orc, if his size didn't already reveal it. He grabbed his mug and drained it.

Kryder shook his head, cut another piece for himself, and blew on it. Before he took a bite, he said, "If I had a copper for every time I've seen you do that, I could exchange them for a piece of gold. I'm talking about a whole coin and not a quarter piece."

Tog wiped his mouth with the back of his hand, ignoring the remark, and said, "So when are we going to be contacted? Besides the cost of mugs, this place isn't cheap. It's not like we have coin to spare. We should think about an inn more in line with our coin purses."

"I don't know," Kryder answered. "The old man said someone would contact us here. If we go across town, whoever it is may not find us."

"Well I…" Tog started to say when he was interrupted by a loud voice two tables away.

"Look here, halfbreed," a man dressed similarly to them, in leather armor covered with a travel cloak and a sword on his hip, said loudly. One side of his face had a scar stretching from eyebrow to lips. He was speaking to them. "I don't eat with such as your kind."

The three men sitting with him laughed. One wearing a half-helmet with leather flaps hanging on each side added his own loud insult, "Since the rape didn't kill his mother, surely bearing an Orc bastard did the deed." The group laughed even louder.

Kryder reached down to his side and drew another smaller, more ornate dagger with his free hand. He laid them both on the table. He stood, turned around, and looked at the four men. Tog, on his feet nearly as quickly, reached over his shoulder and grabbed the axe strapped to his back with one hand. It was dual-headed and meant for two hands when used by a normal-sized man. He placed it on the table beside his own large dagger. A hand's length of the worn leather-covered handle hung over the edge.

The four men realized the object of their harassment and his companion didn't intend to leave. They meant to fight.

* * * * *

The following is an

Excerpt from Book One of Forge and Sword:

Keep of Glass

———————————

Steven G. Johnson

Available Now from New Mythology Press

eBook, Paperback, and (soon) Audio Book

Excerpt from "Keep of Glass:"

Trinadan peered at the spot Forge was examining. She thought she saw a bit of movement.

A second later, the wildlife burst into squawking, scrambling motion all around them. A family of rabbits rushed across the trail in a close grouping, making for the distance with great, stammering hops. Birds exploded from every tree and bush in the vicinity, fleeing upward like ashes from a drenched fire. She heard the bleat of red deer and saw a bluish-green lizard leap from tree to tree on fans of skin under its arms.

Forge was off his horse and on the ground in one step, as smoothly as if his horse were still. In another instant, he unslung and strung his bow, nocking an arrow as he knelt behind a blackberry tangle along the trailside. His gray eyes had not left the bend in the trail behind them.

"Forge, what—"

But then she heard it, the thunder of hoofbeats. Several horses, driven hard, had panicked the animals as they crashed toward the spot on the trail where Trinadan's little convoy stood idle. She barely had time to turn her charger around.

And they were upon her. Three horses, swathed in yellow and blue, rounded the bend at speed, weapons held high. They saw her and pointed, the leader in half-plate and a high bucket helm as he spurred into a full-tilt gallop, taking the lead from his two companions. She saw his lance drop to fighting trim, its head growing enormously as it arrowed toward her at the speed of a maddened horse. The head was not the basket-cup of a jousting lance, but real iron, forged and worked to a cruel point.

* * * * *

413

Get "Keep of Glass" now at:
https://www.amazon.com/dp/B08RMVLWXV.

Find out more about Steven G. Johnson and "Keep of Glass" at:
https://chriskennedypublishing.com

* * * *